# THERAPOSA

I0554464

## Jessica S J Brown

### In memory of Richie Brown

Travis carefully placed his finger on top of its spine, pulling it towards him and delicately drawing it from its sanctuary. Meticulously sliding it out of its plastic covering, his eyes lit up. She was gorgeous; a female of real beauty, and Travis' one true love. As he flicked through to his favourite part, his body tensed and his mouth began to water. Her legs were the longest he'd ever seen, dark and soft. He imagined her wrapping them around him sensually, like a velvet duvet gliding across his body, before she tightened her grip, disabling him, rendering him helpless.

As he turned the last page, Travis felt alone. He rewrapped the comic and returned it to the shelf. This was the problem with lusting after the imaginary. Theraposa couldn't exist in reality; she was too perfect. Travis had bought a similar specimen, but that had not ended well. He found that he could not control his disappointment that she did not fulfil his fantasy. Earnestly, in hope of unveiling something hidden, something more to her, he had killed and consumed her, such as Ornithoid was forced to do in *Theraposa's* final issue. But alas, the act had just left him more alone, now haunted by an overwhelming sense of guilt.

And a taste for flesh.

In an attempt to quench his loneliness, Travis decided to trawl the internet. Flicking through the usual pages, an icon flashed up for a dating website: 'Nerds and Birds'.

How vulgar, thought Travis, killing the page. He got up and walked to the fridge, where he remained, intermittently glugging orange juice from the carton. He stood for a while in a daydream. Unlike the average person, he hated time off from work. It was just more time for him to mull over his obsession, his paraphilia. On the other hand, it was time away from having to hide it from others. He never knew when they would appear to trigger it and, as soon as he saw one, there was nothing he could do to contain himself.

Travis walked back to the computer and started up a new tab. 'Nerds and Birds' popped up again.

Travis reluctantly found himself signing up to the website and began to scroll through the 'birds' section. 'Birds' weren't really what he was after, but they would have to do. He studied their names: Hot4Nerds, SpOcKsLuT, <Leia3, etcetera. The women all looked the same. So human, their vulnerability covered by thick masks of make-up. Then, as his cursor settled on TheraposaGirl, his heart missed a beat.

Her picture!

Her picture was near perfection. Her body was horizontal, face up to the sky, her arms reached back over her head, raising her body off the ground. Her legs went on forever, covered in smooth, dark skin, bent at the knee; the joints perfectly defined on each limb. Her presence surpassed the other specimens beyond recognition. If Travis was to find real love with a 'bird', it would be with her. And she liked *Theraposa*! The comic was somewhat of a niche market, and not a popular cult one at that.

She was online! Travis carefully typed 'H', slowly followed by an 'i' before replacing it with 'e.l.l.o.' Send. He anxiously sat and waited for a reply. Two minutes and six seconds later she answered…

After a while, she began to hint at meeting in person. Travis tried his best to avoid these situations, but he knew that eventually he would lose her should he not comply. He was worried. It was a gamble. He wasn't sure if their relationship could survive his affliction. What if it didn't? He could never live with himself. But he just couldn't lose her. Not now.

He would have to find a way to keep it from her. Chances were, it wouldn't even cross his mind.

Yes, I can do it, he thought.

So they arranged to meet at her local comic store. If she didn't turn up, there was nothing to lose. You couldn't be stood up when you were surrounded by comics. Colourful, courageous, lycra-clad, hero filled comics. Friday at twelve pm: so close, yet also so far away.

Boredom struck Travis once again. It was only Monday evening, which meant he had just over three days to kill. He had work, but that was never much of a distraction. He'd often finished his daily duties by lunchtime and couldn't understand how it took his co-workers an entire day to complete a couple of spread-sheets. They were just lazy, getting up every five minutes to make coffee and stuff their faces with cream cakes. Just get on with it. Efficiency was Travis' speciality.

However, in the next few days, Travis found his efficient nature was a greater curse to him than his paraphilia. His empty afternoons felt like years. What was this feeling of anxiety that constantly plagued him? He just could not seem to quell it. He didn't even feel like reading *Theraposa*. His normality both surprised and annoyed him. Perhaps he should abandon this whole idea?

But like all schoolboys with a crush, Travis did not do what was prob-

# Weirdbook

VOL. 2, NO. 17       ISSUE 47

## Features

## Short Stories

## Poetry

## Artwork

# FROM THE EDITOR'S TOWER

It's time for another *Weirdbook*!

Issue 47 is be our first one for 2024. Issue 48 will premiere in mid 2024.

This is our Halloween issue. To celebrate, we have a lovely Hallowen story from Taylor Grant. This is Taylor's first appearance in *Weirdbook*, and I hope that it won't be the last.

This issue is chock full of contributors regular and new. I guarantee there is something for everybody. We even have a brand new "Oron" novella from the amazing David C. Smith. And it's a humdinger that in itself is worth the price of admission.

We have tricks and treats from Cynthia Ward, John R. Fultz, Adrian Cole, Darrell Schweitzer, Franklyn Searight, Jessica Brown and many others. It's a great issue.

On a sad note, the *Weirdbook* family has lost another member. Frederick J. Mayer passed away this past April. This is a huge loss for the Weird community. Frederick was a teller of tales and poet extraordinaire. He was a good friend and mentor. He will be greatly missed.

I hope the upcoming months are good for all of you. Hang tough and be kind. No matter how much you might disagree on things. Life is short, and it wears down your soul to go around angry all the time.

I'm going to leave you with two quotes.

"If more of us valued food and cheer and song above hoarded gold, it would be a merrier world." —J.R.R. Tolkien

"I like living. I have sometimes been wildly, despairingly, acutely miserable, racked with sorrow; but through it all I still know quite certainly that just to be alive is a grand thing." —Agatha Christie

—Doug Draa, Editor

## Staff

**PUBLISHER & EXECUTIVE EDITOR**

*John Gregory Betancourt*

**EDITOR**

*Doug Draa*

**CONSULTING EDITOR**

*W. Paul Ganley*

**WILDSIDE PRESS SUBSCRIPTION SERVICES**

*Sam Hogan*

**PRODUCTION TEAM**

*Sam Hogan*
*Enid North*
*Karl Würf*

ably best for him.

* * * *

As Travis arrived outside a comics shop, three days later, he started to panic. Should he get out of his car? Or should he wait until she arrives? Or should he just casually browse around the store? It had started to rain, so staying put was perhaps the best option…but then a bigger problem arose: how was she going to recognise him? It had dawned on him abruptly that she might not even know what he looked like. He thought he might have sent her a picture a while ago, but he was not so sure now. Everything was always about her, and his interest in her. He had never stopped to worry about what she might think of him, physically. Well, either she wasn't at all concerned with looks (doubtful in Travis' mind), or the whole thing was a scam.

Travis thought over scenarios in his mind. He saw himself holding a placard with her name on, like business people do at airports. She'd enter the shop door, her figure silhouetted by the sun, before walking into the light, highlighting the contours of her perfect skin. She would look around earnestly for her suitor, before fixing her gaze on Travis, walking slowly towards him, and throwing her long, slim arms around his body.

No.

He didn't think so.

In fact, the whole idea made him feel ill and his face scrunched up in distaste of his thoughts. It was like one of those movies he loathed, the kind he would contemplate buying to have the satisfaction of burning it. Travis thought it his private mission to slowly rid society of its addiction to consumerist rom-coms. He would rather bear his curse than be brainwashed by that shit.

The rain was plummeting down now, a typical British monsoon. A car pulled up on the other side of the street. He noted the model: a Ford truck, like yokel serial killers drive in American horror films. Great, good timing. Kill me now, thought Travis.

Peering through the rain, he watched the driver get out. The figure was wearing a bright yellow raincoat. It turned in his direction, pulling down the hood.

It was Debbie.

The rain instantly drenched her, flattening her hair. This was not at all what Travis had expected. She was far too…human.

Ducking to avoid eye contact, and contradicting his previous concern that she may not recognise him, a wave of realisation passed through Travis. What had he been thinking? How could he have been so blind? How could he think that he may have found the 'perfect specimen' on a dating website? He should have known his desires could not be quenched by a 'normal' relationship.

As she walked into the store, Travis drove off feeling frustrated. He realised how much of the last month he had wasted talking and obsessing over Debbie. He didn't need her, he had Theraposa! He pushed his foot firmly onto the accelerator, his body tingled pleasurably at the thought. He needed to see her.

As he arrived home and prepared for his ritual, suddenly it did not seem enough.

He looked at the comic laying listlessly on his lap, and somehow the 2D illustrations that had once sufficed did not quite bring the same pleasure as before. Not now he had allowed himself to yearn after something real.

He needed a *real* fix. A real Theraposa. And this time, he would find her.

Travis did not know what had overcome him. For once, he didn't care about the consequences; the thought of giving in to his desire flooded him with a feeling that his fantasy of Theraposa could not sate. The ability to be himself, to unleash his dark side. It was irresistible. He needed a victim, but he couldn't find one here. He grabbed his coat. The rain was easing now, but had not subsided; it was unlikely there would be many outdoors.

KNOCK.

KNOCK.

Travis jumped guiltily, caught in the act of his disturbing thoughts. He froze, hoping his visitor would leave.

'Travis?' she called.

Oh god. Debbie.

He sighed in resignation. There was no denying his silhouette through the stained glass of his front door. But he really didn't want to speak with Debbie now. He had made his decision.

However, if she were to somehow invite him back to her house, it may be a good way to seek his fix...

But he knew her. He couldn't unleash that side of himself in front of people he knew, who were associated with him. As usual, his conscience and his devil were playing table tennis inside his mind, the ball bouncing guiltily between his two selves.

Travis reluctantly opened the door. Though it had stopped raining, she was still damp and lifeless.

'Did you forget?' She asked.

Travis didn't know what to say. He was not used to being confronted by women. He nodded clumsily.

"Silly. Come on, I know a good coffee place."

Despite his best wishes, Travis found himself being herded into her truck and ushered to the entrance of Maggie's Cake and Coffee Shop.

* * * *

While she was talking, Travis' thoughts returned to Theraposa. He imagined what it would be like if she were real, sat in front of him, in place of Debbie. He couldn't imagine her talking, nor did he really care what she would say. He would just stare at her, stroking her legs, one hand on top of the table, the other moving up her leg. He fantasised about how it would make her feel. How it would make him feel, the only time he ever felt true contentment. Truly like himself, whatever *himself* was. Allowing him to give into his urge, to devour what he desired, or at least the closest version he could find, might save him from his isolation. He knew the consequences, the pitted feeling of guilt, would haunt him for *days* after, but at this moment he was willing to accept the penalties in exchange for the chance to be sated for even a moment.

He imagined eating his victims. He was no Hannibal Lecter; he made no effort to transform their flesh into refined cuisine prior to consumption. More often than not, his ingestion of them was the cause of death. He rarely killed first. He liked them to still be moving, though his mind silenced their merciful pleas. He didn't do this because he wanted to, but because he had a dark compulsion to do so. It was a fruitless attempt to physically recreate the world he loved in *Theraposa*.

Travis awoke from his trancelike state. Debbie was staring at him expectantly. She wanted an answer. But what was the question?

Travis rooted through his brain, hoping that he had subconsciously absorbed something from her endless chatter. Eventually he blurted out his only thought.

'How did you know where I live?'

'You told me a while back in a message, remember?' she soothed, before flicking her long wet hair over her shoulder and resuming her stream of conversation. 'Anyway, I was just saying, I have something to show you, if you want to come back to mine?'

'Err…' Travis stuttered.

'You'll *love* it, I promise. It's just what you need,' Debbie winked knowingly. Travis could suddenly see a glimmer of what had attracted him to her profile picture. It seemed like so long ago that he had signed up to that website.

With an impulsive change of heart, Travis accepted Debbie's invitation.

He couldn't help but obsess over what Debbie could have to show him.

The possibilities queued up in his mind. It could be comic related? She could have another edition of Theraposa! There were some issues that he could not obtain, no matter how hard he looked, or how much he was willing to pay. A new copy may help to replete him, and quell his wandering thoughts. The idea made his heart skip a beat.

He was so occupied with guessing Debbie's surprise that Travis had lowered his guard, and forgotten about the fact his darker side might appear at any moment. With horrific consequences.

They arrived at a large thatched house in what seemed like the middle of nowhere. Travis' new obsession of trying to predict Debbie's secret had distracted him more than he'd like to admit. He was allured to Debbie's enigma, perhaps a dark secret of her own. He prayed that it was not something underwhelming, like a hoarded collection of stamps or My Little Ponies.

'Are you ready?' She asked. Travis looked deeply into her eyes in agreement. They were intensely dark, almost black. They were large and beady, the light reflecting in them in big, white, hollow circles. Over the course of their meeting, Travis had unwillingly found himself incredibly attracted to her. A scent had come through now that she'd dried off, something familiar, even sexy, but not something Travis could put his finger on. It wasn't perfume, as the scent of perfume equated with dog shit to Travis. It must have been some sort of pheromone.

As she walked, she emphasised every bend of her limbs, walking knee to heel, to the ball of her foot, before rocking off her toe, taking short, quick steps, scurrying along, yet still graceful. She opened the heavy oak door and dry warmth gushed out. She hurried Travis through the door, firmly pushing it closed behind them.

'Da Dah!' gestured Debbie. Travis looked around and gasped, the hot air sharply filling his lungs, making him cough. This new world seemed an age away from miserable England, which lay just seconds outside. He looked quizzically at Debbie for an explanation.

Now she had dried off and removed her Paddington Bear raincoat, she was just as majestic as Travis had imagined. She was tall, slim and athletic. The black slip dress she was wearing revealed her smooth dark skin. Reminding himself that it was rude to stare, he brought his gaze back up to her face. Her glassy stare lured him towards her.

As he stepped closer, he registered movement from the corner of his eye. This was it: the trigger. Travis panicked. Once it had a hold of him he couldn't control himself. It would take all his willpower to prevent it from happening. He needed to preserve Debbie. He actually liked her, he'd decided. And that was a very rare thing to happen.

He averted his glance in an effort to prolong his instinctive reaction.

But then suddenly, he caught the movement again. It was only for a second before it disappeared, but it was definitely in more than one place. Fuck. Trust this place to be trigger happy. Maybe it was because he was nervous. He was seeing what he wanted to avoid. Doing that thing you want to do least, just because you can't. Like needing to pee when you're stuck in the far corner of a cinema screen, with ten people between you and the aisle.

But this was much worse.

This was a matter of life or death.

Travis jumped as Debbie placed her hand on his shoulder. The scent caught his distraction again. It wasn't helping. He had such an urge to bite her. He wanted to evaluate the depth which that smell was saturated into her skin, how far it permeated her flesh and bones.

No. Not her.

He couldn't let himself do this to her. She had been good to him.

As he spun round to evade temptation, the bizarre nature of her habitat suddenly hit him. There were tanks, glass tanks, literally everywhere. The lighting was almost blinding, white-washing everything, sanitising it, like a psychiatric ward, or, God forbid, the afterlife. Then, movement; scuttling.

Something was scuttling in the tanks.

He slowly walked towards one and peered inside. It was like looking into a fraction of somewhere in North America. Its sand lining was stacked with rocks and an archaic looking broken pot. Travis had a sudden impulse to raise the pot, but refrained himself just in time. He could feel Debbie's gaze upon his back. He was pretty sure he knew what was hiding in there, and he knew his reaction would not impress her.

'You want a drink?' Debbie asked, uncomfortably close to Travis' ear. The pheromone concoction wafted into his nose, and his attention was once again drawn to her.

'Yes, please,' replied Travis, his muscles tightening. Something small jumped across two rocks in one of the tanks, making Travis flinch. 'I'll come with you,' he added.

'No, no,' said Debbie. 'You stay here and get yourself better...acquainted.' she winked her beady eyes.

He couldn't stay here, he had to leave. Travis gulped and went to follow Debbie. She had gone, but a door to his right still bore the vibrations of exit, so he darted towards it, trying not to look at the army of tanks around him.

He made it to the door and pushed through. The door was surprisingly heavy, like a fire door, but that was not his concern. Was he safe?

No. More fucking tanks. And this time, there was no escaping the movement. It was even more energetic in here.

Travis rapidly retraced his steps, returning to the lobby. He'll just leave. Run home. He was a long way from home, but that didn't matter. It didn't even matter that his home was practically in ashes. Anything was better than the situation he was in now.

But something stopped him from leaving: that familiar feeling that overtook all rationality and reason.

He returned to the tank with the archaic pot. He placed his hand into the container and lifted. Although what was underneath did not come as a surprise, Travis still gasped sharply, before exhaling slowly.

It was gorgeous, a female of real beauty. A true relation of Theraposa. She was pitch black and velvety. So sumptuous.

This was Debbie's secret, her thing to show him: spiders.

Spiders were her weird obsession.

Just like his.

But *definitely* not in the same way.

Travis snatched up the tarantula and stuffed it into his mouth. It was so large he could only get two legs in, biting down hard. What appeared to be soft and velvety, was spikey and dense on his tongue. He peered down his nose at the spider heavily protruding from his mouth. Its line of black, moist, beady eyes stared up at him seductively, and he realised why he had been so attracted to Debbie and that look she kept giving him. The creature strained against him, clawing at his face with her long legs, their barbs aggravating his skin. He crunched down harder. Travis remembered that tarantulas are seen as a delicacy in Cambodia, but he had forgotten one important fact to their consumption: they should be cooked, and also their irritant barbs were to be removed. She rose up impressively to attack, like a giant cracken. He felt like Perseus controlling his foe, his domination exciting him. He loved it when they fought back. But suddenly Travis felt an intense, sharp sting in his eyes. He staggered backwards, releasing his prey. Blinking through the pain, he reached for support, colliding with a large tank behind him and sending it crashing to the floor.

Travis hit the ground, hard, falling onto the giant shards of glass. After momentarily registering the pain of his wounds, Travis saw what he had unleashed. Through his hazy eyesight, he could depict hundreds of tiny, green and black spiders dispersing through the remains of their sanctuary. A sharp pain made Travis look down at his side. There was a large piece of glass protruding from just under his ribcage. Travis wrapped his hand around the glass, and pulled it out of its burrow, throwing it carelessly to the ground, before marching on with his mission, like a dazed Hulk wanting to smash.

Travis had lost all self-control and rationality. He started grabbing handfuls of the tiny spiders, packing them into his mouth, savouring the feeling of them scuttling around his tongue, teeth and gums, before darting down his throat, tickling his tonsils. As they hit his gag reflex, he was forced to open his mouth rapidly, allowing some of his victims to escape. Swallowing through his body's automated response, Travis continued to manically seize the spiders, gobbling them up, but taking care to chew them before swallowing, to halt their active legs. They were so small it was like crunching on small fish bones, like the kind you'd complain to Mum about when you found them in your battered cod on the beach. His tongue was turning a sickly grey colour, perhaps stained by the dye in the spiders, or perhaps a symptom of their rancid taste. Travis lay on his back, feeding himself the spiders like Caesar being fed grapes, deluding himself to the absurdity of his actions. He waited excitedly as the small creatures spiralled down towards him, their legs opening erotically, ready to succumb to Travis' desires.

After he had consumed the majority of the tiny spiders, and any that were left had fled the scene, Travis rose, pulling himself up on yet another tank. As he stood, his hand slipped through the lid, and plunged into its sandy carpet. His sight was obscured; everything appeared in a reddy-pink haze, like literally rose-tinted glasses, and metaphorically, too, as Travis was not at all distressed by the situation. He was like some junkie on a final limb; shooting himself up with coke, acid, Heroin, E, anything he could grab.

Foaming greyish froth at the mouth, he looked at what discovery his hand had made. He strained to focus, feeling even more delirious with the blood pouring out of his side from the glass shard. His hand was soaked red, shiny and tacky, like the lipstick smothered lips of those women he'd ridiculed online. His palm was flat, pressed against the bottom of the tank, sand invading his pores, clinging to his sticky hand.

Like a starfish, each finger pointed towards a giant spider. Travis lowered his head, exaggerating the movement in his drunken state, his front teeth colliding with the rim of the tank violently. Travis stood there, leaning on the tank, hanging by his incisors, gazing at the majestic creatures. The sudden movement had caused one of the spiders to move.

In place of his hand was now a huge, brown Huntsman spider. Travis lifted his hand, wondering how he had traded it for a far superior model, equipped with three more digits. The spider was flung off its new platform, and Travis realised that he was still lumbered with his regular hand, that he often thought was perhaps slightly too small for his frame. Can't have attached the new one well enough, he thought. Now it wasn't part of his body, Travis scooped it up, playfully tonging its leg before nibbling the end. The flesh covering the skeleton was oddly soft; it was like pulling liquorice off a wire cable. The spider was ferociously biting his hand back in retort, but Travis' delirium did not register its attack. Instead, he turned it upside down and sunk his lips and teeth into its abdomen. Its legs wrapped and flailed around his face, threatening to suffocate him. Travis just thought that it was writhing in pleasure, appreciative of his talented tongue, as he used it to search through the spider's internal organs. He started to suck the gooey entrails from its insides. The spider's frantic attempts to escape slowly ceased, as it eventually fell limp and obedient to Travis' maniacal slurping.

As though he had hit the bottom of a coke-glass, the straw loudly sucking up the combination of watered-down coke and air, Travis threw the empty carcass aside. He snatched up the four remaining Huntsman Spiders, wedging them under his armpits and lumbering forwards like a cave-troll in search of a new breed to taste.

Travis had completely forgotten about Debbie and her momentary absence, oblivious to the fact that at that moment she was returning with coffee and about to walk through the door. It was only the size of her abnormally large house, and the thickness of the oak doors, that had permitted Travis to trash the giant lobby so spectacularly unnoticed.

The door creaked open as Debbie leaned against it, back first, carefully balancing her carefully frothed filter coffees. Suddenly, registering Travis' destruction, she quickly released them and span around in shock.

'Travis! What the fuck are you doing?' She demanded shrilly. 'Oh my God, are you okay?' She flung her hand up to her mouth in horror as she noticed his blood-soaked t-shirt.

Travis had a mouthful of two more tarantulas and was starting to feel dizzy and nauseous. Hearing a loud, high pitched noise, he turned around slowly.

Debbie gasped as she saw the long black and yellow legs protruding from Travis' mouth. She remained frozen as Travis finally passed out, his hands, arms and face dappled by spider-bites and his clothes soaked crimson red on his right side from the waist down.

Travis woke up in darkness. As he came round, he felt weak, confused and was covered in a layer of cold sweat. A chill swept across him as he reached for his last memory. He couldn't remember much, like the morning after the time he drank most the bottle of his birthday gin. His only clue was the heavy weight of guilt pitted in the bottom of his stomach. What had he done? Or did he really want to remember? As he heard the sound of footsteps approaching the door of his prison, he realised that he probably had no choice. The time had come for his reprimand. He knew that one day this would happen.

Debbie turned on the light. Travis looked around deliriously at his surroundings, squinting through the light and his headache. Through his blurred vision he could make out a window. It had lacy curtains. As he tried to turn his head to look at Debbie, he noticed that he was resting on something soft: a pillow. He was lying on a bed. He wasn't being held captive after all! He winced as his head seared, and then winced again as he noticed the intense pain on his right side. Now he realised that his surroundings were no direct threat, he tried to focus his attention on himself and his wounds.

Although Travis could feel his body, which at this point he wished he couldn't, he noticed that he couldn't really move anything. He could turn his head from side to side, but as he attempted to use his hand to lift the covers and address his wound, he realised that his arm would not comply. It merely lay heavy like lead on the bed beside him. Next, he tried to move his legs. Nothing. The chills came back, laced with claustrophobia.

Debbie approached the bed and peered over Travis. Travis tried to focus his gaze, but struggled. His vision was pixelated, as though Debbie was a form of offensive imagery.

'Hello, Travis,' she said. 'How are you feeling?'

Travis groaned. His tongue did not seem to fit in his mouth. Everything was throbbing and swollen. Travis' eyes widened in a moment of realisation: the movement, Theraposa... He cringed at the images that were coming back to him in parts, like chapters of a flick-book.

'Yes, Travis. You should be ashamed', said Debbie, recognising Travis' sickened expression. 'You *ate* my *babies*!' She jumped onto the bed and straddled Travis, one hand either side of his shoulders, and lowered her face towards his.

She leant forwards, drawing out a knife from her back pocket. Travis breathed in her smell, bathing in its allure, and then coughed as blood clogged up his throat. Debbie smirked, resting the blade on her leg. As she sat her weight back onto her seat bones, Travis felt a wave of pleasure cut through the throbbing pain. She raised the knife towards his face in retaliation. Travis had not quite realised what the object was until the light glinted off the blade. However, the knife worried him less than it would the average hostage; every part of him felt as though it was bleeding anyway.

Whatever was coursing through his veins was causing his emotions to oscillate. One minute he was high as kite, and in the next he felt the pain rush back like being scalded with boiling water.

Debbie stood up purposefully, still straddling Travis, looming over him menacingly. Travis gazed up at her, transfixed by her expression, and still seduced by the uncanny power that she had over him.

As though a revelation had sprung to mind, she athletically leapt off the bed, landing lightly on the floor and in the same movement darting out the door.

Debbie had still not quite decided what she was going to do with him. He wasn't fatally wounded; he could still survive if she drove him to a hospital now, after all it wasn't her who had hurt him.

Yet.

No, he had to suffer. She couldn't let him *go*, the idea was absurd. She just needed to think of his punishment, her family's retribution for not only damaging her home, but for *eating* her children. She had never thought it would pan out like this. She knew that he obviously had some sort of spider fetish, anyone who was an avid fan of *Theraposa* usually did. He wasn't her usual type, but it was so rare to find someone who might, well, help her fulfil her sexual wishes.

She had left him in the hallway in hope that he would be ready for action when she returned. She wanted to play it innocent in case she had been wrong about him. And wrong she was, only not in the way she thought. Her plan had jeopardised her family's safety. She had been reckless and selfish: two traits a mother should never be.

But still, who the fuck does that? Who actually eats spiders? Why couldn't he just have made love to her whilst her children crawled over them like she wanted? Was that not enough? Was her family not enough?

After strong internal debate, Debbie reached a solution: she and her children deserved their revenge. And who was she to deny them that? Travis certainly wasn't in any position to deny her what she wanted.

She marched briskly into the next room. If a parent was allowed favourites, these girls would be hers. Their splendour and intelligence surpassed any species she'd ever seen, and the fact that they happened to be the deadliest in the world was merely the icing on the arachno-flavoured cake.

Debbie leant forwards, cooing softly. She lowered her hand gently into the tank, laying it palm-up, her fingers obediently pointed, and beckoned slowly with her forefinger. The only inhabitant of the tank appeared to be a stone skull, but as Debbie's cooing persisted, two small, black, shiny spiders scuttled out of their refuge and hopped onto their mother's outstretched hand.

Debbie raised her hand to her face, admiring her precious children. Their clean-cut legs looked like thin shards of black mirror, framing their curvaceous bodies with perfect symmetry. Their abdomens were perfect spheres, like black snooker balls, an assimilation which suited as they were about to end the game. On their backs was a red mark. Its shape was perfectly defined, as though an hour-glass stencil had been daubed with blood. An hour-glass to represent that Travis' time was up.

Debbie floated back into the bedroom. The girls were scurrying gracefully around her hand, gently tickling her skin, just the way she loved. She was going to enjoy this.

Travis looked up at her, coughing. He opened his mouth and gasped something.

'You're sorry? I'm sorry, we're all sorry, Travis,' Debbie retorted. 'But you've left me no choice. What sort of mother would I be if I did not seek justice for my family?'

Debbie set the two spiders onto Travis' chest. Travis' eyes widened. Despite his aching body he still couldn't help himself. He tried to raise his hand to grab the shiny black and red spider, but instead of obeying, his arm just hung like a dead weight. Travis was too busy wrestling with his paralysis to notice that Debbie had started to slip seductively out of her black dress.

Debbie stepped out of her clothes and walked towards the wardrobe in the corner of the room. She peeked through the crack in the double-doors, smiling girlishly, before proceeding to open them carefully, revealing hundreds of big, brown house-spiders, the kind that make you freeze as you see them darting out from underneath the sofa and across the carpet in the corner of your eye. They poured out of the wardrobe and swarmed up Debbie's body. They streamed over her skin, covering the contours of her body, dressing her in a brown crepe-like dress with kinetic stitches.

As Debbie resumed her position, looming over Travis with her big black eyes, he sacrificed his battle to move and aimed his focus at Debbie. His eyes lit up like a child who'd just been told he could open a Christmas present early. What had he done to deserve this? Did he care? Travis felt his trousers tighten as he stared at Debbie and her animated dress. Instead of threatening him at knifepoint, like she had before, Debbie smiled. He felt his pain wash away as she undid his zip, and Travis felt as though he'd finally found his fantasy in reality.

As Debbie reached her climax, the two Black Widows made their way towards his neck, moving symmetrically over his body, as though preforming a dance for their mother to watch. They reached his neck and stopped. Travis was in his element, this was better than anything he'd imagined, any time he'd had with Theraposa, and he wished it would never end.

Travis gasped as he felt the poison flood into his veins. His heart started to palpitate. However, to Travis, the sensation was not as unpleasant as it should have been. He felt like the romanticised, male Hollywood version of Cleopatra, with the deadly Asp replaced by two Black Widows. A Royal death. The two deadly creatures were now each sat on top of Travis' eyelids. They both bit down and sent their deadly elixir straight to Travis' brain.

Once Travis was still, Debbie walked to the wardrobe and watched as the spiders dispersed and hurried back into their home. Entering the next room, she ceremoniously returned the two girls to their tank, congratulating them on their clean kill. They obediently shot straight back into the stone skull.

Oddly, Debbie found that she felt satisfied. Although she wished for her children's revenge, she thought that killing someone, even if it was technically assisted murder or manslaughter, would leave her feeling dirty and plagued with guilt. However, the destruction of Travis had sated her entirely.

Even as she walked through the ruins of her lobby, she felt a sense of calm. She could deal with this. She would bury the parts of her children that were left, and she and her family would carry on.

But perhaps this is something that she would do again, she thought, as a smile widened across her face.

Besides, the girls did seem to enjoy themselves.

✗

# THE DRAGONS OF THE NIGHT
## Darrell Schweitzer

*We fight the dragons of the night in our despair.*

A madman.

The son overtook his father on a darkened plain amid some ancient stones. There was no moon. The boy could see the man moving against the brilliant stars, and he could see the stones. The boy wore old clothes and was barefoot and rode on a plough horse. The man was walking, and garbed for a journey, with heavy boots on his feet and a staff in his hand and a pack on his back, and there might have been a cooking pot on his head. It was hard to tell in the dark. But his old sword definitely hung at his side, clacking against his breastplate as he walked.

"Father, come home," the boy said.

"I can't. I have to go."

"Mother is weeping."

"She'll get over it. She understands. I have to go fight the dragons of the night."

"No, she doesn't."

"That's too bad then." The man rapped his knuckles against the piece of metal strapped to his chest. The boy recognized that thing now. It had been hung on the wall of their house for as long as he could remember, an almost shapeless slab of tarnished scrap. Sometimes his mother chopped vegetables on it, when his father was not around, as this were a substitute for the last words in some long-running argument.

The boy slid off his horse. For an instant he thought that there was someone else there, a third person, but, no, it was a trick of the darkness, of shadows. He took his father by the hand, but his father shook him off.

"Please," said the boy.

"Suppose a high-flying hawk drops down out of the sky for a time, to settle and make a nest, and raise nestlings in safety. That's how it is. Now I must return to the sky. To battles. To what I am sworn to."

"Father, this is crazy talk."

The boy, who had been leading his horse by the bridle, let go of it and ran in front of his father. But the man sat down among the ancient stones, in the dark, and said, "Maybe so, but you need to hear more of it."

The boy sat on a stone opposite, and then, he was certain for just an instant, a ghost in black armor, mounted on a ghostly steed came charging at them. The boy let out a cry and raised his hand to ward it off, but the man did not react, and it burst over them like a wave, only the boy felt nothing more than a puff of cold wind, and then the ghost was gone and a moment later he wasn't sure he had seen anything at all.

"Your mother heard the horns blowing, in the distance, late at night, as did I. For a long time she insisted it was a dream. 'Are we both dreaming the same dream?' says I. 'It must be,' says she. But it was not. Do not think, my son, that this does not hurt me, that my heart is not torn, that I do not love her still like a hero out of some wonderful old story . . . only the stories are less than entirely wonderful if you have to live them. Heroic strife is not all fun and games. There is a lot of pain. And now, I am summoned back to it all, and I must go."

Gradually it seemed to the boy that ghosts gathered all around them now, among the ancient stones, huddled thick as a herd of sheep, and sighing softly, though it could have been the wind, and the ghosts themselves could have been some illusion caused by a limitation of the eyes. If he looked at them directly, they weren't there. Out of the corners of his eyes, they seemed grotesque, with faces like dogs.

"But it's—"

"All just a story?" said his father.

"Something like that."

The boy looked down at his dirty feet, which he could not see in the dark, but that was better than gazing into his father's eyes, which even by starlight seemed filled with some frightening intensity.

"You will have to understand this as you get older," the father said. "Maybe your mother never will, but I think she already does. She just cannot bring herself to admit it."

"What? That you are running away?" the boy said angrily.

Now the father's voice became very calm, and somewhat terrible, and commanding. "Not <u>away.</u> No, never away. <u>Toward.</u> I am the hawk that fell out of the sky. Maybe for a while I fancied I could live among the chickens. Maybe I deluded myself. So, for a time I did, but the dreams came again, and I knew it was not so."

Then the boy himself heard, faint and far away, a horn blowing, though it could well have been herders in some distant field signaling one another, or a watchman in a town marking the hour of the night. But somehow he didn't think so. He was afraid it was not so. He felt fear and sorrow rising within him. He struggled to hold back tears.

"If you're a hawk," he said, "which am I? One more of the chickens to go in the soup at supper time?"

His father took hold of him and raised him up.

"What do you think?"

"I think you are a crazy old man with a pot on his head," said the boy.

"Is this a pot?" His father took off his helmet and gave it to him, and the boy realized, less with surprise than with dread, that it was not a pot at all, but a finely crafted war-helm, with cheek flaps and a kind of visor that lowered over the upper half of the face. He could tell by touch, though, that it was somewhat rusty. He toyed with one of the hinged flaps, which creaked.

His father took the helmet back and put it on.

They stood atop a fallen stone and looked to the east, where the sky was beginning to lighten. Something was moving on the plain before them, like a vast, silent army, or the wind stirring the tall grass like a sea.

"Here is what you need to know," said the man. "I am a paladin. I am one of the champions of the Sky King, whose brilliantly polished mask men call the sun. In the beginning of the world—before the beginning actually—darkness fought against light, but it's a battle that nobody can win, ever, because the gods themselves are fighting their own shadows, for they stood in the light and cast those shadows, and were afraid of what had come from themselves. They are fighting their own dreams, their nightmares, which, being the dreams and nightmares of gods, took on monstrous and solid shapes, and would have torn apart the world, and devoured all of creation—not just mankind, which was newly made then, but everything, the sky, the moon, the stars—and unless eternal champions battled these monsters, these dragons of the night, forever. The gods call to themselves champions, the greatest of men, or the maddest, who yearn for glory, who follow impossible dreams, and get swallowed up in them, even as you might be sucked up into a whirlwind if you don't have the good sense to get out of the way."

"These are stories, Father. I've heard them all my life."

"All quests and rescues and great deeds. Your mother never liked stories of that sort."

"No, she didn't."

"Your mother knew, and was afraid to tell anyone, that once upon a time one of the characters inexplicably fell out of the story, onto the earth, and he was in those days a mysterious and charming young man, who beguiled her, and she married him, and began to grow old with him, and she hoped that she could go on doing so, to the end of her days, and he hoped for it too, but then she, and he too, heard the horns of summoning, and they both knew it could not be so."

"This is crazy talk, Father."

"Absolute lunacy, I quite agree."

"Then come back home."

"I can't. Sorry."

Even as they spoke the run rose in the sky, and the boy's eyes were dazzled, and he could never account for what he saw. Maybe it was a kind of dream in which there fled before the brightening rays every sort of monster: great serpents, and giants, and, indeed, dragons breathing out white, cloudy vapor, beasts with clattering armor and gleaming spikes and claws and wings that stretched to cover the sky. These rushed over the man and the boy like a storm tide, and it may have been the wind of their passing, or just a sudden gust, that nearly knocked the two of them off the fallen stone they stood on.

And the horns blew, loudly now. Or it might have been thunder. Maybe a storm was coming up this morning, though for now the sun was very bright.

And the boy saw, in the brilliant light, that his father was not a seedy and slightly ridiculous old man with a pot on his head and a scrap of old metal strapped to his chest, but a knight, in full war-armor, with a spear in his hand, quite magnificent in his golden-trimmed war helmet. The visor was up, and his face was still visible, and it was still the same face, but somehow harder, firmer, less worn by time, though the eyes looked very old and the beard was as gray as it had ever been.

The horns blew like thunder, and the earth shook from a thousand times a thousand hoofbeats, and in the glare of the risen sun he saw the polished, burning mask of the Sky King, and he saw the King's champions all around him, buffeting him harder and harder as they leapt over and flowed around the standing stones like a fiery torrent; and the eyes of the Sky King opened behind the mask, and the voice was more terrible and more beautiful than any he had ever heard or could ever describe, but he couldn't make out what it said.

His eyes ran with tears. But somehow, dazzled and stunned and deafened though he was, he was still able to make out, as if he gazed into a raging furnace, moving shapes, and in an instant he saw his father snatched up and hauled onto a gleaming horse and vanish in the mass of golden warriors. At the same instant something sent the boy tumbling backwards into mud. But he got up on all fours and screamed for his father, and his father called back to him once, but it was just a cry and nothing more, not even a farewell or a command to go back home or anything.

That must have been the end right there. What seemed to happen next couldn't have happened, outside of delirium, or some kind of seizure. Nevertheless, with great effort, as if leaning against a hot, terrible wind, the boy got to his feet and groped his way back to his plough horse, which stamped nervously, not quite able to perceive what he thought he had, but still afraid out of dumb instinct.

He boy mounted. He kicked the horse's sides with his bare heels and got it to lurch forward in a lumbering gallop. He pursued. He rode into the light and somehow could see again. He rode with that incredible army with the Sky King at his side and the dragons of night retreating before him. All around the champions swarmed, and the gods themselves, some of them not at all human in their form, half-beasts, or living flames.

For a time he actually caught up with his father, and road beside him, and called out. His father raised his visor, and turned toward him, and the look on his face was hard to read, astonishment, then perhaps pride, perhaps sorrow.

The boy called out, "Father, I am a hawk and the son of a hawk!"

And his father replied, "Yes, you are."

"I want to come with you!"

"Then you are going to have to learn how to soar."

And the father seemed both proud and weeping.

"This is crazy talk," he said at last. "You heard it from an old man with a pot on his head."

They might have said between one another, but not much, because the boy's horse was a mortal horse and it soon fell behind. For a time he was merely blinded by the brilliant light, and when he could see again it was early evening, and he sat up stiffly, squishing in a muddy field. A storm had come up after all. The sky was dark and it was raining hard. His eyes were dazzled and it hurt to open them for more than a moment or two. He looked around and he saw his poor horse, dead beside him, its flesh steaming.

When he stumbled home, it was clear that something very strange had befallen him. His clothing was seared to tatters and he was sorely hurt. His eyesight was never very good after that, and sometimes he saw things that other people said weren't there. Sometimes glowing shapes floated before him in the darkness. Sometimes he spoke to them. People said he wasn't right in the head, that he'd been hit by lightning and it had addled him.

What had become of his father, no one could be sure. His mother finally said, in despair, just before she died, that he had been a mere tramp, a wandering madman, who had somehow beguiled her once upon a time, but then reverted to his old ways in the end and deserted her. He wept to hear her say that, for he knew she had lost the dream she and her husband had once shared.

But did he ever learn how to soar, that son of a hawk? Did he ever follow after? I know that he grew to become a man, because I am that man, but a man who doesn't see very well and talks to phantom lights and whose ears ring with sounds no one else can hear and wanders around with a pot on his head and carries he piece of metal which he insists is a breastplate but everybody else thinks is a piece of old junk isn't likely to learn to soar. More often than not, he will use that pot as a begging bowl. He may amuse people with his funny stories. Let them laugh. Let them be amused. Let them even pity him. It is all part of the greater story, a striving as heroic and as desperate as any battle fought against the dragons of the night by gods and armored knights, a means to an end, even as he might somehow in his loneliness comfort a woman who is herself lonely, yet destined, and he will treat her with love and kindness and tell her stories; even as the two of them have a son; and he will tell the son stories, and the son shall be the completion of his quest and his victory over despair.

For his father did reveal something more at the very end, something he could not tell just anyone because it was a thing of dreams, not expressible in words of the waking world. But he could tell his own son, when the time came. It was a name, not his own name but one by which a new champion would be able to announce himself among the heroes and the gods. A true name.

What he came to understand in his madness was that this name was not mine, but something to be passed on to another, a gift and a burden, and a weapon against the dragons of the night.

# IT STARTS NOW
## Lorenzo Crescentini

## Translated by Amanda Blee

Today the white doctor came to see me.

I pretended I wasn't crying but I think he noticed because he sat on the bed and patted my head.

He said I shouldn't be sad about what Bobo said. I told him I'm sorry about the red car, when's Bobo coming back?

Bobo is my friend. His mom works here at the centre and sometimes we play together.

The doctor said I don't know dear. I asked him if I'm really a monster, and he said you're not a monster, you're just special.

Because of the red car, I asked him, and he said yes.

He asked me if I was still writing with my mind and I said, yes, and showed him the sheets of paper on the table. He flicked through them and said good boy.

\* \* \* \*

Gus spoke to me today. He's the guy who cleans the floors, sometimes he talks to me through the glass. He's not like the white doctor. He doesn't smile when he talks, and he looks at me strangely, but he says things the white doctor doesn't say. He says it's wrong for me to play with Bobo because I'm different.

I also asked him if I'm a monster and he said a rose by any other name. I don't know what he meant.

\* \* \* \*

Bobo's mom came today. She was crying and asked how did you know. I didn't know what to do because I'd never seen a grownup cry before, so I said I don't know, I just saw it.

She told me you're a monster.

When she left the white doctor arrived. He told me Bobo died this morning because he got hit by a red car. He said I shouldn't be angry with Bobo's mom. She's sad and that's why she says bad things. I said I'm very sorry for Bobo and began to cry too and the white doctor said it's not your fault.

I asked him if I can go outside too one day and he patted my head again and left without saying anything.

* * * *

Today Gus told me that they'll never let me out and that I'll spend the rest of my life in this room. At first, I thought he was joking, then he told me they're studying me and want to use my powers.

It's because I'm special, I told him, and he laughed. Gus is a little scary when he laughs, because his teeth are yellow, and his eyes are cold. He pulled a bunch of keys out of his pocket and said, see, I can go anywhere, not like you.

* * * *

Today the white doctor brought me a cat. He said it was my new friend. The cat is tiny and soft and says mewww and rubs its head against my legs. He said give it a name and I called it Egg. Why Egg, the doctor asked, laughing, and I told him it's because it's as small as an egg. Then I asked when Bobo will be back.

He stopped laughing and asked if I'd seen other things. I said no.

I thought that if I stopped saying what I see, then maybe one day I can go outside too. The last time I did, Bobo got angry and told me you're a monster. So, I didn't tell the white doctor that there are other special people around, but that they pretend to be normal, like Gus, who cleans the floors and can go anywhere he likes. I've seen what the special people will do to the normal ones and it's bad, like the red car.

I didn't tell the doctor and he left quietly.

Gus arrived later. When does it start? I asked.

It starts now, he said, and unlocked the door.

# UNDERHEAD
## Charles Wilkinson

After Neil first became ill, the Company convinced him to work from home. Even as he was being rushed to hospital, they arranged for his laptop, which he'd left at his desk by the window in the sitting-room, to be delivered to his ward by motorcycle courier. Then for three weeks he had no communication with them, which wasn't a surprise. After all he was in a place where it was perfectly usual to be out of contact. Half awake, listening to a gentle hush of June rain above, the slow water seeping downwards, he became aware of disturbances in the ground above him: a spade slicing through the topsoil; the rattle of flung earth and gravel; an occasional clanging—steel edge on stone. Only after they started to lever off the coffin lid did he understand he was more than a pile of ash. He couldn't see anything but moonlight, to which he would never be fully restored. Indistinct faces peered over the grave; a new laptop was placed high on his chest, above his folded arms. Evidently death had not terminated his contract.

They were quick to remake his grave; before dawn, he heard the lifting back of the lid, the nails hammered in, the final celebratory slapping of a spade. He allowed himself another hour of subterranean repose before he logged on. Now that they had found him, the afterlife would be more than listening to the worm's slow passage through dirt; sensing a change in the soil's temperature; dreaming of the roll of weather and seasons; leaves glazing to dark gold in evening cemetery light; or the spindly grass under the evergreens susurrating in September wind.

The first email was from his line manager at the Company: "We gave you a month's holiday, including the minutes before the last when you were critical, the hours of the autopsy, as well as the week with the undertaker and the day of the funeral. Time management was never your strong point, but now you have eternity on your hands there will be no excuses for not meeting your targets, which you will find on the attachment. Head office will be in touch to discuss your widow's pension arrangements."

\* \* \* \*

As Matilda's husband is dead, she can stay in bed with her afternoon lover for as long as she likes. There's no need to fear the phone or a rattle in the lock; then the front door flung open, the clinking of the keys put down on the hall table, Neil's footsteps hurrying up the stairs.

Except for the June storm's thick grey streaks, worms of transparent wax, on the bedroom window panes, it's pleasant to lie next to her lover's warm body. In hour or so he'll leave and she will eat as she chooses, watch television by herself with no squabble over the remote and later a long hot bath with the door open: the well-earned luxuries of solitude.

'Did you see the executors?' asks Greg.

'Yes.'

'And so did he?

'Did who what?'

'The late and unlamented. Did he have life assurance?'

She levers herself up and looks down on Greg, so comfortable on a pale yellow pillow, his hand clasped under the nape of neck, his elbows the apexes of two tanned triangles. Recently returned for a holiday abroad, he seems every inch a beach idler, even though he's merely another lawyer. Is he thinking of moving in? Their affair had begun on the condition that he was not expected to leave his wife. His chest is thickly matted with black hair so that in places his flesh is not visible. Tufts sprout at the top of his shoulder blades. Lying there, he could still be, apart from the absence of dark glasses, stretched out on the beach: a man with a smell that alternated between sun-block and brine; his book lying spine upwards on the sand. At six o'clock, when he moved towards the bar, the towel's raised pattern would leave red welts on his back.

'There's some provision,' she remarks flatly, thinking of the life policies that will prove more than sufficient for her future needs.

'And the house? There's a child from his first marriage isn't there?'

Now providentially dead. She's glad she's managed to keep some of the details back.

'Indeed there is.'

'But there was some sort of previous settlement…am I right?'

Without answering, she slithers off the bed and makes for the shower cubicle. Once she's under the warm water, she pictures the June rain collecting in puddles on the lawn, puckering the surface of the green swimming-pool, spilling in thick gobbets from the guttering. It rained on the day she buried her husband. She thinks back to the cemetery: the Victorian gatehouse and iron railings; high cedars and yews on the periphery; the grounds bedraggled—tousled grass and weeds coming through on the gravel walks. The mourners were fewer than she'd expected. Perhaps Neil had not been all that popular at the office.

When she comes back into the bedroom, Greg is dressed but sitting on the bed. His silver hair has been cropped short and blow dried, which gives him an appearance that is both military and feminine. He looks at her, but she turns away. She will not answer questions that are intrusive and unintelligent. Of course, her husband left her the house.

* * * *

What does burial mean in a digital age? In Neil's case, extinction in the customary sense was clearly obsolete. Since the committal, he'd completed his work for the Company so quickly there was surplus time to weigh the advantages of being dead. He no longer had to travel to and from the office; not a moment was squandered attending to his bodily appetites or the whims of his wife. Although he was aware of the presence of his embalmed body, for practical purposes he considered himself incorporeal. Yet he had no propensity to ascend to another realm, if indeed that was possible. He remained an employee and earth bound. In some respects, he was more avid for information about the world than when he'd been alive. The circumstances of his departure continued to puzzle him. One moment he was at the peak of his professional career; then came dismissal, followed by a serious deterioration in his health; an illness that, as far he was aware, had remained undiagnosed. Once again, he reflected on the months before the interment, when he'd been struggling with a new job and gradually failing health.

For a time, he'd been able to conceal his dismissal from a firm of solicitors because the Company recruited him shortly afterwards. Yet he had to become more prudent with money. His new employers operated on a 'no win, no fee' basis, so there was a cut to his salary. The restaurants he took her to were more affordable; their holidays less frequent and no longer abroad.

His interview took place on a fine April day. The Company's headquarters was in the basement of a former factory on the south side, a place of abandoned warehouses and the rubble-traces of bulldozed residences in abandoned lots; nearby, a boarded-up, skeletal public house in dark red brick stood on the street corner. Opposite was a tract of land that had long awaited redevelopment, an empty space from which a terraced street and small shops had once sent streams of drinkers to the saloon and public bars. Only the ground floor and the basement of the old factory were still occupied. The Company had the use of a sparse furnished room below street level. No secretary was there to greet him, only a tall thin man behind a desk.

'We're a large outfit but with comparatively few overheads,' he said. The top of his bald head had a soft pale brown sheen. 'There's no need for a lot of office space as many of our operatives like to keep a low profile.'

'And so you're the only one here?'

'Yes, but it might not be a bad idea if you were to come in from time to time. At least to begin with.' The bald man glanced at him. 'I see you're surprised by our somewhat…austere…accommodation.'

'I had expected to see a few more people around. The list of directors on your prospectus is very long.'

'Most of them are sleeping partners.'

Later, when he looked at his contract, he found several unusual clauses, some of which he was only just starting to comprehend; for example, he'd once assumed that 'a willingness to work underground' meant he should be prepared to carry out covet inquiries if necessary. Now everything was plain, including the bald man's parting words:

'We're working towards the day when the dead can sue the living. Just think of the increase in the potential number of clients.'

Neil brushed the earth off his laptop and logged on. The machine was different to the one the Company had originally provided; there were new features he'd never come across before, ones specially created for those required to work in the dark. During the first weeks, as the grass grew over his grave, he'd resented being used as cheap labour. The Company wouldn't even have to pay his National Insurance. And where was the everlasting rest that interment traditionally came with? But as he explored his new machine's capabilities, he understood that there were compensations. His wife had made a mistake in disposing of the laptop that they'd shared at home. Now he had a good view of her on the webcam.

* * * *

Although it's morning, the afternoon lover is seated at her kitchen table. An unprecedented occurrence, for Monday is one of the three days of the week on which he still goes into the office. Greg is wearing a crisp white shirt, open at the neck, where the skin is loose; in contrast, his face is as wrinkle free as a young man's, even the crow's feet are only visible as thin silver lines when he raises his eyebrows, incredulous at the story he is telling her.

'I can't explain it. It's an informal arrangement that I've had with a man on the council for years. He's always been absolutely discreet and the whole business is embarrassing for him too.'

'So you're not on gardening leave. They've sacked you.'

'When I came in the other morning I was asked to clear my desk. I was being paid quite a lot for very doing little. I can't understand how our emails ended up in the senior partner's inbox.'

'Someone who doesn't like you very much has hacked into your computer and accessed your account.'

'Not according to the IT bloke I asked to take a look. There's no trace of spyware or any hint that my address has been used illegally. My files show I forwarded the whole conversation myself. What a disaster! I doubt I'll find anything really lucrative at my age.'

She put her hand on his arm. At least he'd the pluck to put her in the picture. What had shocked her was her husband's failure come clean about his dismissal. She'd heard it from Greg, who'd worked at the same firm.

'With your experience, I'm sure something will come up.'

'Something has. But it's not at all what I'm looking for. *Long* hours for *low* pay. It was rather odd how it came about. I found the letter on the door mat when I went home on the day I was sacked. Apparently it hadn't arrived with the usual post. As there was no stamp, I assumed it must have been delivered by a courier.'

For two weeks, she'd waited in vain for her husband to tell her why he was fired. Then, just as she was about to broach the subject, she decided there were advantages in being assumed ignorant. In any case, the state of affairs was not at first critical as it was evident he had money coming in from somewhere. It was only after he'd cancelled their holiday in the Caribbean that she told him she was returning to the pharmaceutical company, where she'd once held a research post. A temporary contract, she said.

'I've been told that the board won't pass on the evidence to the police. After all, I've been with them so long it would look bad for them too. But it worries me. What happened should be impossible. There's no telling when and where the emails might turn up.'

As the kettle chuckled to the boil, she searched for two mugs that Neil had never used and put the teabags in. In the days after her husband's death, she disposed of his clothes, books and record collection and everything else she associated with him; even the gifts she'd bought him over the years. Anything that might insinuate the memory of him into her new life. Yet somehow the reminders kept occurring: the names of mutual friends in his handwriting in the address book; a request to renew his subscription to a magazine; the plants he'd put into the border coming into bloom.

'Have you told your…wife?'

'No, not yet. I'm going for an interview with the firm I told you about. Some sort of 'no win, no fee' outfit. Not my style at all, but it may tide me over until something better comes up.'

Outside, the churning wind picked up, turning the smirr to wires strung crosswise along the window panes. There was an anonymous squelching in the gutters and something dripping heavily. Water collected in the seat of a deckchair Matilda had put out on the lawn to encourage the advent of true summer in place of a dishonest wet June, so rain riddled and with a tiny ration of sun.

\* \* \* \*

It took Neil a long time after his death to discover how she'd killed him. Matilda had always been reticent about her job with the pharmaceutical firm: 'I do the research; it's up to others to develop my findings.' When pressed she claimed that a first-class honours degree in Industrial Chemistry was the minimum prerequisite for an understanding of her work. It was only now, with the advantages of working sub terra for the Company, that he'd discovered that the pharmaceutical firm's principal contracts were with the Ministry of Defence.

Underground and immune from the easements of earthly light and space, the surrounding darkness concentrated his attention on the laptop's glow. He was oblivious to the infringements of worms, the water table's slow rising, fed by the June rains. He did not try to picture his headstone, the grey glimmer on the gravel walks, the rain dripping from the stricken pines. With no distractions, he completed his Company targets for the month quickly and accessed the pharmaceutical firm's files. It took him some time to find the employees' folders. Persistence being a quality that does not always come easily in the grave, he had to remind himself that to slip into the long reverie of death would be fatal to his plans. He had eternity at his disposal; his wife did not. He had to keep reminding himself of that, though betrayal helped to keep his rage raw.

The first occasion that had provoked his suspicions was when he went into Greg's office without warning. Matilda was seated on his colleague's desk, her legs slightly apart, the glimmer of an engagingly gauche seductress not yet faded from her features. Although Greg was at a distance—standing by the water cooler, pushing a plastic cup hard against the nozzle—his tie had slipped half way down his shirt, which was open at the neck, revealing ruffled chest hair, which someone might just have run eager fingers through.

Neil glanced from one to other. 'The affidavit,' he announced at last, in the tone of one with a warrant for the intrusion.

'Greg asked me drop in to give him a little advice on…pesticides,' Matilda said.

'Yes, a new case of mine. I'm acting for some sort of green group.'

'I didn't know that environmental law was a speciality of yours,' said Neil.

'It isn't…usually. This is just some pro bono work I've taken on for a friend of a friend.'

'I see. Well, when you've finished availing yourself of my wife's expertise, there are other matters we need to discuss.'

A month previously he'd seen a couple who might have been them walking into a restaurant in the City. He'd been on the upper deck of a bus, looking down at the throng on the pavements, the first leaves on the plane trees. As he hadn't glimpsed their faces, he dismissed the thought. There had been other indications: a phone put down hurriedly; more frequent visits to the hairdressers; changes to routine explained by her signing up for evening classes in Spanish. As he didn't speak the language, there'd been no way of testing her progress.

Shortly after his dismissal, he'd come home early one afternoon to find her in a state of disarray and the double doors that led onto the back lawn open, even though the day was far from hot. There was a faint disturbance in the woods that separated their property from a neighbour's. The grass had been cut too short to betray Greg's hurrying footprints heading towards the undergrowth.

His dismal from the legal practice, with illness and death in its wake, had followed shortly afterwards. The last remnant of digital chivalry dispersed once he had discovered her curriculum vitae on a file at the pharmaceutical firm. The subject of her doctorate was listed along with her current research interests. She was a toxicologist. With the new tools at his disposal, he accessed the hard drive on her laptop, but the real wealth of evidence was unearthed when he hacked into her email accounts. He'd never realised she had three. He forwarded the most incriminating conversations to Greg's wife.

* * * *

The weather changes without one temperate day by way of transition; the cold front's contours slithering off the map to be replaced by high pressure, immense spaces between the lariat isobars. Greg feels the wall of heat once he's slammed the door on his hatchback's cool air conditioning. As he walks down a street on the south side, he loosens the tie he's put on for the job interview; then slips the noose from his head. He takes off the jacket of his pin-striped suit and drapes it over his arm.

He's unfamiliar with this part of the city, which seems a strange place to open a law firm. The intense light defines the cracks on the crumbling red brick of derelict factories. The hoardings around the vacant lot awaiting development are covered with the curlicues of tags. There are vivid street paintings of aliens and women with snaky hair in psychotropic colours, the ideas purloined from forgotten counter-culture comics. A flat-roofed, more modern building has what must once have been a car showroom on the ground floor, a long white space, its eerie absence mourning the loss of sleek polished shapes, the potential for speed.

It's twenty minutes before he finds the steps leading down to the place. He's late. The early afternoon heat rebounds off the pavement and the grey stucco façade. As he fastens his tie, he feels the damp warmth of the collar. He's tempted to walk away, to take out his mobile and phone a few words of apology. Then he tells himself he must at least attend the interview. If the terms aren't right, he won't accept, or he can take it on for a month, until he finds something else.

He knocks on the door. An odd voice answers, strained and yet muffled, as though someone's shouting down to him from the floor above. Inside, the room's empty apart from a tall bald man behind a desk. There are no pictures on the walls. Greg wonders if the office has been rented specifically to carry out interviews.

'If you could just sign the contract…here,' says the bald man, after a few cursory preliminaries. 'At the bottom.'

'But you haven't asked me a single question.'

'Some candidates present themselves as employable at the very instant they arrive.'

'That's kind of you, but I'll need to read this.' Greg scans the documents. After the first week, he would be working round the clock. 'This ridiculous, I can't possibly accept these terms. And why the discrepancy between the perfectly reasonable remuneration in the first week and then what seems to be a complicated form of compensation in kind?'

'Well, during the first week you'll still be an 'overhead'. You'll need some funds. But once you're 'bedded in,' as it were, you'll find that your immediate needs will practically disappear.'

'I'm sorry,' says Greg, handing back the contract. 'This isn't an offer I'm interested in.'

The bald man smiles. 'In the long run,' he replies, 'it won't make any difference whether you sign or not. Of course, you won't have to come in while your time is still you own, but I'm afraid that there are some posts that one's appointed to…well, not for life…but regardless of one's condition.'

As soon as Greg steps back onto the pavement, he rips off his tie and stuffs it irritably into his jacket pocket. What a waste of time; the man was manifestly a lunatic. It is just past noon and the heat has colonised every inch of the street. There is hardly a sliver of shadow to slip into. When he takes off his jacket, the dark patches under his armpits have spread halfway down his shirt. It is far too early to go home. He decides to drive away from the centre of the city and to a park in the suburbs he has not visited since childhood. He remembers an ornamental lake, a band stand and a small green hut from which ice creams and soft drinks were sold. Although he drives around for several hours, he can't find it. He stops several times to question passers-by, but as he's unable to remember the park's name he's reduced to describing it as he'd seen it forty-five years ago. His enquiries are met with quick impatient nods or puzzlement. Perhaps it is in another part of the city.

It is dusk when he arrives home. The sky is a deep blue and tinted purple above the white facade of his mock Georgian home. As the car slinks, almost silent, along the freshly resurfaced drive, he's surprised to see that the steps leading up to the front door and the porch appear to be covered with black, blue and brown boulders. Only once he is in front of the entrance does he understand the explanation: old trunks, rucksacks, overnight cases, tote bags and bin liners have been piled up outside; not stacked but as if they'd been flung out of the front door and upstairs windows. There is luggage retrieved from the attic, suitcases he hasn't seen since his bachelor days. He unzips the nearest carrier bag: his trousers and shirts in turmoil.

* * * *

Neil knew how dry the gravel walks in the graveyard were; the trees ceased to drip; the June rains replaced by the sudden intensity of high summer. Chrysanthemums in glass pots next to the headstones of loved ones. Cabbage white butterflies flickering in the long grass. But beneath ground he was content with his laptop and its many applications; his files filled with statutes that show the jurisdiction the dead have over the living. As an underhead, a tenant of deep chambers, he was aware that his enemies, still walking in sunlight, were not above eternal law. He was in a place where verdicts cannot be overturned or codicils added. Haunting was one edict of electricity; a way the past punishes the present; every instant of lived experience was underwritten by incalculable laws: the decisions of the dead and the precepts immanent in hell and paradise.

A week ago he was in the CCT on the wall outside what was once his home. Greg arrived. It was enough to see the set of shoulders, his normally delicate features hardening, to understand his intentions. As he knocked on the front door, there was a view of the top of Greg's head, a bald spot that Neil had never noticed before. He heard the buzz and the release of the catch. Then he lost him for a minute on the staircase. The view from the webcam in his wife's bedroom distorted distance; the furthest walls curled, the planes slightly concave. Greg came into the room, his face more elongated than Neil recalled.

'Oh hi! I wasn't expecting you this morning.' A moment before his wife took in her lover's demeanour. 'What's wrong?'

'Don't pretend you don't know.'

'What? I'm tired tonight, dear. Please don't speak in riddles.'

'It was always your intention. To have me move in here.'

'It…most…certainly…was NOT! I mean you're lovely in small doses…'

'Oh you and doses!'

Greg killed her off camera. Even now, Neil was not quite sure whether he regretted this or not. Either way, the audio was excellent. Possibly hearing indignation choked in her throat was enough. What he hadn't worked through was her arrival in the newly enlarged grave. He heard her reproaches as he searched his laptop for a remedy. Her intention was to rebuke and upbraid him till the end of time. Somehow he must make the world understand how she killed him with a toxin that was still in development and quite undetectable by an ordinary autopsy. Until very recently he'd thought releasing the proof would be sufficient to have her exhumed. But there has been a change. Yesterday there was a new arrival in the cemetery. A murderer with a wrecked marriage of his own, one who would never have been buried in hallowed ground. Now they have cleared up their misunderstanding, Matilda has hired her own lawyer.

'Even when our attachments fade,' he thought, 'while the dry earth sidles through the coffin's cracks, and our friends and enemies no longer walk under the clear blue curve of sky, we will be slaves to an infinite technology, apart and together in a place where even the ghosts require regulations.'

✗

# BYE, BYE, CUBBY
## Franklyn Searight

Yanko Bozhidarov left his home shortly before dawn, grabbed the handles of his cart and pushed it to the edge of the forest and the winding trail leading to where he was working that day. He left behind him his wife, Mirela, who had also arisen early to take care of their baby daughter who was simpering in the crudely crafted crib adjoining their bedroom.

A forester, who lopped down trees to supply firewood for the town folk of Blagoevgrad, a nearby settlement, his day began early and ended late. In the cart were his hefty axe and toothy saw, essential tools of his trade, and the bow and arrows he might need to protect his life. The latter accessories were necessary because a wolf had been seen frequenting their area—reportedly, a werewolf, and responsible for the slaying of several town folk.

He was a superstitious man, as were most citizens in the year of sixteen thirty-two, a credulous bunch believing in witches and ghosts, vampires and werewolves and other specters prowling the night shadows. Legends were invariably created to explain those things they did not understand.

Most folk knew the power of pure silver while dueling with the supernatural, so Yanko, with no gun to defend himself, had contracted with the blacksmith to attach silver tips to the ends of three arrows, in exchange for three cartloads of wood. Every time he ventured into the forest since the werewolf scare he took his implements of archery along with him for protection. He was skilled with a bow and arrow and believed himself adept enough to kill any wolf, be it a normal or paranormal creature. It was an extreme measure to take, surely, but the potency of the pure metal was needed to subdue such an adversary and would be well worth the expense.

It was a good thing he had arranged for the protection when he did, for the following week he came upon a she-wolf, along with her whelp. He would have been content to let it continue on its way, but it must have been a hungry one—a ravenous one—and Yanko was a big man, large enough to provide the beast and her cub with a substantial dinner. Yanko fitted an arrow to the string and when it attacked from just a dozen feet away, he let it fly at the lunging animal, striking it in the chest.

The woodsman was surprised to discover it had no effect, other than to slow it down for a few seconds, and realized he must have used one of the untreated arrows. He had just enough time to fit a second projectile to the string, one tipped with silver, and then release it. Yanko had practiced for hours to prepare for such an event, and the wolf fell dead.

He watched as the animal turned into an old harridan—an extremely ugly and very hairy one—and then dissolve before his eyes, proving to the trembling man it was an actual werewolf. Moments later, the cub waddled over to the spot where its mother had lain, sniffing and whining at the silver-tipped arrow laying on the ground. Yanko felt sorry for it and decided to take the whelp home with him, believing the animal, when domesticated, would make an ideal companion for Rosie, his little girl. The two of them would grow up together, play together and be close friends and companions.

Unfortunately, this did not turn out as the woodcutter planned. The cub had streaks of wildness in it and Yanko found it impossible to tame and train. One morning, when Mirela went to her daughter's crib to awaken her, dress her and give her breakfast, she discovered Baby Rosie was not there. An examination of the small room revealed her in a corner, viciously ripped apart. Huge chunks had been chewed from her stomach and limbs and one side of her head was missing. Crimson gore was splashed everywhere: on the wall, the floor and what remained of her daughter.

The little cub was gone.

Yanko was unable to speak and barely able to function when called to the ghastly scene. The couple was certain a huge animal had made its way into their home during the night and was responsible for the slaughter of their child. He went outside to look for paw prints to identify the assailant and there he found the cub, playfully rolling in the dirt beside the porch, its fur clotted with dried blood and minute body fragments. Yanko killed the whelp, stabbing it in the throat with his knife. With his shovel, he dug a hole in the ground next to their garden and jammed the little butcher into it. For several hours, anger and grief and muddled uncertainty occupied their time before they attended to the burial of their little girl.

That night, Yanko was outside staring at the full moon and fearfully listening to the mournful howl of a canine. He was surprised the next morning to find the cub upon the porch, a few feet away from where it had been buried, waiting to get back into the house, his cute little face and jaw, once again, red with carnage. The fiend had sated itself upon another victim during the night. It was then they surmised the whelp must also be a werewolf with its mother's blood nurturing it when in its embryonic stage.

Furious, Yanko smashed in the little killer's skull with his shovel. Since the dead creature did not like the nice resting place first prepared for it, he took the body to the town dump and threw it in with the other garbage, its furry corpse adding to the mound of rubbish.

During the following night, Mirela trembled and her husband cursed when they again heard the howling of a wolf; neither was surprised to learn the next morning the little assassin was back. Not certain what to do, Yanko killed it again and disposed of the body on his way to work by throwing it into the swiftly moving current of a nearby river.

Once again, the next morning, it was found on their porch, wanting admittance, its fur soaked and matted with blood. It had rained during the night and its little paw prints could be seen leading out of the forest and up to the door. Yanko killed it and buried it once again and this time it stayed in its grave for three weeks, until the cycle of the full moon was once more upon them, and then returned again. They could not help but wonder if the influence of the moon reanimated the cub for a few days each month.

Finally, in great confusion, frustration and despair, Yanko retrieved his bow and arrows. With no hesitation, he shot an arrow tipped with silver into little animal's breast, killing it again, but in his attempt to remove the arrow, it broke off, leaving the tip embedded in the carcass. They placed the body in a corner of their home, as a memorial to their little girl, and the years passed with the animal never moving again.

To those who noticed it during the passing years, the whelp appeared to be a stuffed animal, like the cornhusk dolls children loved to cuddle; but those who knew better were aware what they saw was the corpse of the werewolf's offspring. Somehow, it remained undefiled, not subject to the deterioration of gaseous bloating and rotting. Perhaps there had been something in the bitch's blood, flowing through the prenatal veins of the fetus, preserving the body in its natural state.

As the years passed, more children were born to the couple, six males and five females, who were raised in their house, paying no attention to the wolf cub left in its allotted place. In later years, Mirela gave the ownership of the cub to her youngest daughter, encouraging her to forward it along to one of her own offspring.

And so, down through the generations, the little wolf cub, named Cubby, was passed from one generation to the next.

* * * *

Katherine sighed and shifted her frame on the couch as she finished reading the curious document. It gave her some background information about the stuffed animal sitting by her side, but was there any truth to it? It had been a strictly verbal account until written down in the mid-eighteen-hundreds, an incredible tale of spurious content. She set The manuscript down next to her and picked up the animal.

Cubby was a family heirloom she had seen many times while growing up, her experiences with the stuffed cub quite innocuous with no unpleasant associations, nor had she paid any special attention to it.

She studied it doubtfully. Children might have played with it at one time and its condition now was a bit shabby, its fur a little scruffy, concealing a small hole in its chest, but it was still in acceptable condition considering its age of more than three hundred years.

Cubby had recently been given to her by her mother with the assertion it was a family keepsake, an heirloom, an authentic antique for her to display and, in accord with family tradition, be passed along to her offspring just as it had been given to her, along with the document. To Katherine, it seemed nothing more than a worthless dust collector which should be consigned to the top of the closet, if not destined for the trash heap. But she did not want to dispose of it in haste—her mother might not approve—and she decided to give the matter more thought. Perhaps her seven-year-old daughter, Miley, who already possessed several stuffed creatures, might like to add this one to her collection.

As it turned out, Miley was delighted to have a new companion, inanimate though it was, and took to it rapidly. It sat near her at the table while she ate her meals, beside her on the couch while watching cartoons on television, and it lay across the foot of her bed when she went to sleep at night. Soon the two had bonded and were almost inseparable.

Weeks later, Miley was outside by the swing set, playing with her little friend Kimmy, enjoying the pleasant summer morning. Harold, her father, was cussing and jiggering with the obstinate controls of his lawn mower and Katherine was upstairs in her daughter's room, tidying up. There was little for her to do, as Miley was an orderly tot who usually did not leave her clothes or toys strewn about haphazardly. Cubby, the hairy wolf whelp, lay motionless at the foot of Miley's spread, as usual.

Katherine was sweeping beneath the bed, searching for possible dust bunnies setting up housekeeping, when the broom came in contact with what she thought was a toy. She brushed it out into the open.

"Very curious," she thought, bending to pick it up. She held it in her hand, wondering what it could be. It looked something like the broken end of a pencil, about an inch in length, its tip composed of some metal, a dull silver in color.

She shook her head in puzzlement and set it on the top of the bureau which she had just dusted. She would ask Miley about it later, thinking it might be a part to one of her toys, or something she had picked up in the yard.

* * * *

"But, Mommy! Really, it was *real!*"

"Nonsense," returned Mrs. Marlow, looking down upon the bed at her young daughter. This was the second consecutive night the little girl had screamed during the dark hours and then relaxed when her mother arrived to comfort her. She fell asleep again after a few minutes, her slumber uneasy and her twitching legs kicking off the covers from time to time. Katherine could not imagine what might be troubling her, unless it was the occasional baying of a coyote or dog singing to the moon and shattering the quietness of their neighborhood.

In the morning, Miley awakened at her usual hour, her face fretted with a frightful frown, her eyes red and puffy and blurry from a lack of adolescent sleep. The dreams of improbable doom, awakening her during the night with such frightening portent, were now but a vague memory.

"A dream is a fabricated mental image we make up while we're sleeping, dear and that's all it was. There was nothing real about it, at all."

"It didn't happen?"

"Of course, it didn't, Miley. A stuffed wolf can't bite you. Not really!"

"But wolves *can* bite. Daddy told me so."

"But he was talking about *real* wolves, Miley, not pretend animals stuffed with straw or horsehair, or whatever they used long ago when it was made."

Miley was not so sure. Cubby seemed to have changed over the last week, becoming no longer a favored toy to play with, only to look at. Touching it caused her fingers to uncomfortably prickle giving the impression this was longer just a cuddly wolf cub passed down to her through the generations.

Katherine had not told her daughter of the strange manuscript regarding Cubby, telling how it had passed down through the centuries and brought over to America when the family emigrated from Bulgaria in the mid-eighteen-sixties. Miley had been told Cubby was a family memento for which she was now responsible. She must not play too roughly with it, or leave it out in the rain, or shove food into its mouth and ruin it. She had not been informed it was rumored to be a real animal. The little girl had enough to worry about without that idiotic idea polluting her dreams.

"But look at my arm, Mommy," Miley persisted, holding it out for the older woman to examine.

"See?"

Katherine did see and grimaced. On the inside of the child's arm were the clear indentations of bite marks appearing to substantiate the little girl's claim she had been bitten. Three distinct depressions, deep enough to make visible impressions, but not hard enough to break the skin, could be seen.

Miley was persistent and not ready to concede to the more practical wisdom of her parent.

"See?" she said again, waving her arm about. "Cubby bit me here and here and here!"

Katherine shook her head, unable to come up with the words needed to convince the little girl how wrong she was and how right her mother was.

"You must have done it to yourself," she said, believing there was no other rational explanation.

"But the marks! And I can still feel the hurt!"

"Dear one, there can only be one reason for the marks. You bit yourself during the night when you were fast asleep, but you don't remember doing it."

"But I didn't, Mommy! Wouldn't I know if I bit myself?"

"Not if you were sleeping, you wouldn't."

Miley said nothing in reply.

"There," thought Katherine, "a clincher her daughter was unable to dispute with a reasonable explanation. She was totally certain her daughter's current aversion to Cubby was totally imaginary and Miley would eventually grow out of her fears. In time, it would be a subject of disagreement about which they would have a collective laugh.

"You know I'm right, dear. Now get dressed and down to breakfast before your food gets cold. Today is not a school day and you'll be able to spend all of your time outside, playing with your friends. Maybe, when Daddy comes home from work, we'll take you out for ice cream."

Katherine smiled as she stood before the stove preparing breakfast, thinking about Cubby. She cracked another egg into the frying pan's spattering grease and stood there watching it sizzle, cooking to a pale white encircling a golden sun. She had to admit the stuffed animal was a darling toy and had been reasonably well cared for during the different periods of its ownership. It was certainly old enough to be considered a primitive piece, an authentic antique. She had no idea of its value, or if it had any, other than sentimentally, as she had never taken it to a dealer for appraisal. It did not matter, however, if it had no worth at all; it was a family heirloom to be preserved and passed along to future generations.

She ladled hot grease onto the eggs until they were cooked. Miley liked having them prepared that way, and so did she.

It was later in the evening when Katherine confronted Harold, informing him what he said about biting and snarling wolves was causing some anxiety in their daughter. She patiently explained to him what his words were doing to her.

"It seems to be having a disturbing effect upon Miley. She used to like it quite a lot and enjoyed playing half the day with it, making up stories about it, and so on."

"Sort of like having an invisible friend?"

"I guess, but not quite—it's not at all invisible. She doesn't play with it as much as she used to, or enjoy having it around as much."

"It's illogical," he objected. "Aren't you as agitated as you claim Miley is? She's a perfectly normal child with both common sense and a healthy imagination, the same as other children her age. Of course, she imagines things, but it's no worse than other kids who create make-believe friends or pets, or whatever."

"It's not the same," Katherine objected. "Miley was obsessed with the wolf cub, but now she believes it's been biting her while she sleeps. She showed me her bitten arm as proof."

"Proof? Poo! Is her arm a bloody mess? Just how deep are the bite marks? I haven't seen them, but my guess is they resemble the teeth of a child. Can't you see Miley's been doing it to herself?"

"Oh, sure, you would think that, Harold; you've missed the point entirely. I know Cubby is just an old stuffed animal and there's nothing for Miley to fear, but…"

"She shouldn't believe such nonsense."

"Of course, she shouldn't—but she does!"

"Then it's up to us to convince her she's wrong."

"It's exactly what I've been trying to do, but without success. In the meantime, telling her wolves can bite just puts ideas into her head about her toy. Miley is a very sensitive youngster, with an overly-nurtured imagination we don't need to encourage. The next time you talk to her, pamper her sensitivities a bit; try to sooth her fears without making them worse."

"All right, dear. I'll be a more understanding parent."

"Thank you," said Kathrine, with just a touch of sarcasm in her voice, even knowing she had been victorious.

That night, Katherine had cause to reexamine her belief there was nothing paranormal about the brutish whelp. It was long past the midnight hour when she was again awakened from a deep sleep. The silvery orb, as seen through the unobstructed window in the second day of its fullness, was pursuing its normal path as it circled the drowsy earth.

There! The noise came again which had awakened her. The wild dog was back, sounding as though it was standing outside their bedroom window, robustly wailing to the moon. She reached over and gave Harold a sharp elbow to his side, harsh enough to interrupt his soft, rhythmic breathing, causing him to sit up and groggily rub his eyes.

"Wassat," he muttered, blinking.

"There's a wild canine out there," exclaimed Katherine.

Harold said nothing for a few seconds, listening.

"Maybe so. You want me to go out there and shoo it away?"

"Don't be silly. But can't we do something? It sounds like a zoo down there. If the brute keeps it up, it'll wake every cur in the neighborhood. I'm going to look in on Miley—see if it awakened her."

Katherine slid her legs off the bed and down to the floor, shoved her feet into comfy slippers and reached for her robe laying on a nearby chair.

"Now what?" Harold asked. "You gonna call 911?"

"Course, not. Told you, I'm going to see if Miley is alright. No telling how the yowling is effecting her nerves if she's awake."

"Now who's pampering her?" asked Harold.

"Go back to bed," she returned acerbically, moving to the door.

The trip to Miley's bedroom, next to their own, took only a few seconds, but was enough time for a series of frightening thoughts to parade through her mind. She entered her daughter's room, expecting to find the little girl fast asleep with Cubby at the foot of the bed.

A different scene greeted her, however. Moonlight streaked through the window, revealing Miley, still asleep, but obviously in a state of restlessness, her head moving from side to side. Soft whimpering sounds came from her, as though she was responding to something in her dream state. Her torso, covered by a Disney print bedspread, also rose and fell erratically. Animal motifs on the rainbow-patterned wallpaper seemed to smile down upon the little girl as she slept.

Cubby was not laying where he belonged. The whelp must have fallen off the coverlet and on to the floor, probably pushed there by Miley in her restiveness. The room appeared to be serene enough, but a tingle began to crawl along Katherine's spine as she sensed something was very wrong. A hasty examination revealed, to her dismay, Miley's bedtime companion had not been shoved onto the floor, nor was it anywhere else in the room.

The little girl must have moved her bedmate to another place, for some unknown reason and it was now reposing in one of the bureau drawers, or on one of the closet shelves. She resolved to ask Miley in the morning where she had placed the little runt.

Abruptly, the violent caterwauling stopped. Katherine stood there, unable to move, listening for it to be repeated. Hopefully, the mastiff had moved away, further down the block, to harangue her other neighbors. Satisfied, she walked into her own room where she found her husband fast asleep again. She placed her robe on the chair, removed her slippers and lay down on the bed.

She considered what all of this meant but was unable to reach any satisfactory conclusions. More than an hour passed before she was finally able to fall asleep again.

The incident of the howling mongrel would have been forgotten, but Katherine found Cubby the next morning in his usual place on Miley's bed. When she asked where it had been, the little child insisted Cubby had been there when she crawled between the sheets.

\* \* \* \*

Later that morning, while Katherine was at the local grocery store wheeling her cart nonchalantly along one of the aisles, she came upon Mildred What's-Her-Name, one of her neighbors who lived a few doors away. She did not know her very well, but stopped anyway to say hello.

"Hi, Katie," was Mildred's enthusiastic greeting. "Have you heard the newest gossip?" She put her purse in the holder, eager to impart the current news.

"No, I haven't. What's up?"

"Well," she said, leaning her arms against her cart, warming up, anxious to be the first to tell the latest. "George and I were visited by a wild dog last night…"

"Me, too," Katherine hastened to say.

"…it made an awful racket that went on and on."

"We heard it," Katherine offered.

"Didn't bother us for long, but there was plenty of trouble across the street."

"Really? What sort of trouble?"

"Well, I was outside picking up the morning paper when I saw Shirley Reynolds standing in the middle of her front yard, looking at a strange mound dumped there. At first, I thought it might be a big pile of dirt. I crossed the street to join her, wondering what it could be."

"And?"

"And, it was an enormous hound, half of its body eaten away, its intestines spilled out and laying on the grass and part of its head gnawed off!"

"My, gosh!"

"Yeah. Shirley just stood there, sort of stunned, eyeing it and not saying anything. She had a look of total horror on her face and her lips parted as though she wanted to scream!"

"My, gosh!" repeated Katherine. "What happened next?" she asked, stupidly.

"Shirley seemed to have trouble telling me," said Mildred. "Stood there like a rock for a minute before she could speak. And then she told me it must be the huge dog living in the house behind her. At first, she thought it must have been attacked by a lion, or something else with a set of fangs large enough to kill and maul such a large dog.

"I suggested it might be an alligator which had grabbed it, thinking it was something yummy to feed on. She asked me when I saw an alligator crawling around our neighborhood. The last time I saw a lion, I told her, trying to be funny.

"She told me she had been sitting on the porch swing last night with her husband, chattering away—maybe eleven o'clock or so—when they saw something slinking around the corner of the house and over to the next yard.

"I asked her what it was, real curious now.

"She told me they didn't know; they had gone back inside and off to bed a few minutes later. But she wondered if it might have been what had torn the poor doggie apart.

"I told Shirley I had heard something outside our house, too, barking and howling away and maybe the noise came from her yard.

"She thought it might have, and from now on their house would be locked up tighter than a prison after dark—at least until they were sure there was nothing in the neighborhood to worry about.

"I told her it was a wise idea and we'd do the same."

Howard was not impressed by what Katherine told him later on about the mangled dog found on Shirley's lawn.

"Nothing to worry about, dear," he advised her. "Roadkill, maybe, happens all the time. Probably killed by a car and someone dragged it onto Shirley's yard. Don't let it stretch your nickers out of shape."

"Why should I let the knowledge of a ferocious animal on the loose at night, roaming about our property, bother me?"

"Good! Glad to know it's not a huge thing with you, dear," Howard said, completely failing to note her sarcasm.

\* \* \* \*

Later that night, it seemed to Katherine as though the foreboding gates of Hades had opened wide, allowing anyone or anything to enter or leave, as they wished. The distraught mother was awakened around elevenish by screaming peals of torment made by her daughter who should have been sound asleep.

She rose from her bed, almost colliding with her husband, also awake—the man who boasted of his ability to sleep through the thundering falls of Niagara or the cheering NASCAR crowds. He confronted his wife, asking in agonizing bewilderment for an explanation to sooth the rawness of his nerves.

"It's Miley," Katherine shot back, her feet searching for her slippers next to the bed. "Probably another nightmare! I've heard her scream before, but never like this."

"Sounds as though she's been attacked by a mastodon."

"No, dear," she responded, now standing, her feet shod in pink, cushiony softness. "Maybe a werewolf, though."

A moment later she was on her way to the door without pausing to slip into her robe, her husband a step or two behind.

"Did you say *werewolf*?" he cried, following along in her wake.

"I did. Not a full grown one—a whelp."

"Nonsense, Kate!" he exclaimed, keeping up with her.

"Of course, it is, but…Look!"

The two were just in time to see a brownish blur streaking out of Miley's room and over to the staircase leading to the first floor below.

"What in God's name was *that?*" Howard demanded, with an even greater exclamation.

"Can't be sure," said Katherine, reaching the steps and looking down, "but I'm thinking it might be the damned wolf cub. You follow it and I'll see to it Miley's all right."

"Crazy talk," he said, reaching the steps and starting down.

"As crazy as looney talk can get," Katherine thought, but did not offer it as an answer. There was no logical reply to give. A moment later, she was at her daughter's room and dashing inside, thinking, "Maybe I should have told him it was Cubby, but he would have thought it was insane, rather than just crazy. He hasn't read the manuscript Mom gave me. When he does, he'll begin to see I'm not as demented as I must sound."

Miley was sitting up in bed, her back against the headboard, wide awake and trembling. Her screaming had stopped, although she was sobbing as strongly as she had when their little cat had been run over the previous year by a truck. Her hands covered her face; her eyes were opened wide, peeking through extended fingers as she reacted to the abysmal horror she had experienced.

"What is it, dear?" Katherine cried, sitting on the bed next to Miley, embracing her in an attempt to calm her down, assuring her the earth had returned to its proper orbit and all was well. Flustered alarm was in her voice, although she tried to avoid it.

Harold returned as his daughter's sobs decreased and he stood at the foot of the bed, consternation written on his face.

"Whatever it was," he stated, attempting to remain calm, "it got away. I was in time to see it scooting through the pet door Buster used to use.

"What was Miley yelling about, anyway?"

"We'll have to wait until she's settled down enough to tell us."

"Yeah?"

Harold made his way around the bed and stood looking down at his daughter, clutched in the arms of his wife. Impulsively, he drew back the cover and sheet, exposing the trembling legs and the gash in one of them through which the blood escaped and soaked into the sheets below.

"My God," he explained, an expression which he did not seem to tire of using, "something *bit* her!"

Katherine looked and saw for the first time the manner in which Miley had been mauled and did her best to remain composed.

"It might not be as bad as it looks," she considered. "We won't know until the blood's been cleaned off."

"But it'll be okay," she predicted in a calming voice. "We'll stop the bleeding and everything will be all right."

"But will it?" she wondered, during the following minutes.

Digital pressure was applied to stop the flow and the wound, which was not as deep as they had at first feared, was cleaned and bandaged. During the next hour, Katherine changed the tot into clean pajamas and put new, unsoiled sheets on the bed.

As they tended to Miley and cleaned her bedroom, Katherine made two observations she believed might be significant. The moon, as seen through the open window, struck her as being ugly and threatening, frowning down at them angrily. It seemed gigantic in its fullness and larger than she remembered ever seeing it before.

She also noted Cubby was nowhere in the room.

Inspecting drawers and closets and beneath the furniture, convinced her the cub was not where it belonged. Had her daughter taken it earlier in the evening and left it someplace in the house, or was there a different explanation explaining its absence? It occurred to her this was the last night of the full moon, which meant the horror might be absent until the next new moon arrived.

It was shortly after midnight before Miley's sobbing came to an end, her little body relaxed and she lay back, snuggled in her mother's arms to resume her sleep. When Katherine released her, one arm fitfully encircled the pillow upon which her head rested. Howard had returned to bed at some point, only to discover he was unable to enjoy a single moment of sleep, his mind jostled by unanswerable questions and unknown fears which had to be confronted and resolved.

When Katherine was able to rejoin him, she found her hubby sitting up, his legs swung over the bed, his face turned to watch the window casement and the frowning globe outside.

"I'm going down stairs to make some coffee," she announced. "And there's some chocolate cake left you can nibble on."

"Oh, sure. Another shot of caffeine to help us get back to sleep," he grumbled, sarcastically. "I've almost forgotten what sleep was like! Getting back to snooze-land may take a long time.

"Piece of cake sounds good, though," Harold decided, his voice softer. "And coffee is always welcome, although I don't need more of a stimulant than Miley's experience has already provided us. Besides, I need answers and, if I'm not mistaken, you can provide some of them. A midnight powwow is called for."

"I'll try my best to answer your concerns," Katherine agreed, following him down the steps, "but I can't answer all of them. I have plenty of them myself. But I'll tell you what I know and together maybe we can put some of the missing pieces together."

"Something like a jig-saw puzzle, eh?"

"Yes."

* * * *

Inconsequential table talk ensued as coffee percolated and little was said as Katherine finally doctored her cup with a touch of milk and some sweetener. She left and returned a few moments later with Harold's dessert, along with his coffee mug, steaming hot, which he gratefully accepted.

"Now," he began, after blowing his breath over the surface of the brew. "I want to know, first off, just what caused the wound in her leg. Please don't tell me it was a stigmata."

"Of course, it wasn't. But you might find the explanation even stranger. Miley told me it was Cubby who bit her—again."

"Nonsense."

"Is it? Listen to what I've learned about the brown cretin, even though it sounds like total lunacy. You remember the old manuscript I showed you coming along with Cubby when Mom first gave him to me? And the legend Cubby had been a real living wolf whelp?"

"Yes. I read parts of it. Sounded like a fairy tale—a Grimm one."

"Ha, ha. Finish your cake.

"I never paid much attention to the document," she continued. "Haven't not read it straight through until recently. Did I tell you it claimed Cubby— now don't laugh—was the offspring of a werewolf, no less? After Yanko killed the mother wolf with a silver tipped arrow, he brought the cub home as a pet for his daughter to play with."

Harold did not laugh, but he did smile at her, not outright expressing his feeling a gigantic hoax had been played.

"Then, what?" was all he could think of to ask.

"According to the text, in the days to come the cub killed the woodcutter's daughter and was slain by Yanko, using his knife, and burying it nearby in a shallow grave.

"The story does not end there. When the next full moon arrived, the cub returned to life again. This convinced Yanko it, too, was tainted with the loup-garou condition, contracted from its mother's milk. It was killed again and buried. During the next few days, none of the steps they took to dispose of the body were successful; each time, it returned to their little house after a night of carnage. Finally, Yanko shot one of his arrows, tipped with silver, into its chest—which broke off while being withdrawn. And, this time, with the silver lodged within, the body stayed lifeless."

Harold listened to the story with a curious smirk on his face, but said nothing until she was finished.

"But why did the family keep the corpse and pass it down from generation to generation?" he asked.

"Probably because of Yanko's cussedness. It had killed his daughter, eaten a large portion of her and he decided to keep it around as a trophy, sort of, to show people how he had taken his revenge against it."

"Do you realize how farfetched it sounds?"

"Of course, I do. The entire legend is unbelievable. I only mention it to you because everything happening now seems to support the old story and explain what's been going on in our neighborhood."

As Katherine spoke, a wretched howl came from outside, a few yapping and snapping sounds and then more sharp yelps of distress to disturb the quiet of the night.

"Listen, Harold. Cubby is out there now, baying at the moon, waiting for something to come along it can assault."

Harold smiled even more broadly, disbelievingly, but he continued to listen before he finally asked, "But, how can it be? Even if true, the cub has been dormant for centuries. How can it come back to life again after all this time?"

"I'm coming to that, dear. Last week, when I was cleaning Miley's room, I came upon something. Look!"

From a pocket in her robe, she withdrew the silver tip she had discovered under Miley's bed, attached to a splinter of wood and handed it to him.

Harold studied it, examining it carefully.

"So? What's this? Part of a pen?"

"Unless I'm very mistaken, dear, it's part of an arrow with a silver tip at the end."

Harold drew in a deep breath and let it out slowly. "So?"

"Don't you understand, dear? Cubby was killed by a silver-tipped arrow more than three hundred years ago. The power of the silver kept him in a state of oblivion all these years. I could be very wrong, but I suspect it recently worked its way out of Cubby and fell on the floor where I found it. Maybe it was dislodged from his body while Miley was playing with it.

"Don't you get it, yet? Without the silver inside Cubby, he's able to respond to the fullness of the moon, four or five times each month."

Harold's smile slowly faded as she told him of her suspicions. He examined the tip again, turning it over and over, admitting to himself it did make some kind of awful sense.

"So, you think—you actually believe," he said, summarizing her thoughts, "for a few days during the time of the full moon, Cubby is resuscitated and returns to life as a werewolf…err…werecub?"

"Exactly!

"And I also think Cubby seems to be growing larger from eating what it kills, little by little, although it might be just my imagination—I haven't kept any measurements.

"I also believe it's time for the adventurous cub to meet with a permanent death putting it out of its misery, forever."

"And how do we accomplish that?"

"W-e-e-l," she said, stringing out the word, making it sound much longer than it was, "it's always back here by the time morning comes. I propose we push the silver tip back into it, so it can't run away again, putting a temporary halt to its wild rampaging at night."

"But what if it works its way out again? Shouldn't it be destroyed permanently? If it can be regenerated once, it can return again. We don't want to come upon Miley someday, all torn apart, the same way it happened to Yanko's baby."

"I propose, Hubby of Mine, we cremate Cubby, burn him up until he's nothing but crispy, incinerated ashes and scatter them over the countryside."

"You know, dear," Howard conceded thoughtfully, "your idea might work."

The two talked for a while into the night, occasionally interrupted by the howling of a canine mournfully serenading the moon, as they considered what tactics they would use in the morning. They continued talking, willing to forego the comfort of their bed, until they were certain as to just what steps should be taken.

\* \* \* \*

They awoke early in the morning and, before considering coffee or breakfast, they left their bed to check on the conditions in Miley's room. The little girl was sleeping soundly, her lips pouting in an angelic pose of contentment. They were not surprised to find Cubby was back in the room, lying near the front of her bed, as though he had been there all night. While Katherine reinserted the silver tip into its furry chest to prevent it from getting away, Harold left to check the pet door, returning a few minutes later with the information he had found minute traces of fur adhering to the opening.

Outside, standing beside their barbecue pit, loaded with branches of wood, charcoal and chunks of anthracite, Harold placed the whelp on the makeshift bier. Katherine watched as he soaked it with kerosene and, stepping back, applied a match to the creature. The body's pelt caught on fire almost immediately. Katherine recited a strange incantation she remembered from a child's Halloween book and watched as the flames ascended skyward, blossoming in a crimson conflagration. At one point during the purification ceremony, Cubby struggled to his feet, raised front forepaws to the sky and released a soul-wrenching howl sending shivers down the spines of the couple, until the little wolf lay back upon its bier, covered with flames, with what might have been a serene smile of peacefulness tugging at its muzzle.

Slowly, the skin cracked and crinkled, turning into crispy cinders falling apart as the minutes passed and the burning corpse emanated a gaseous odor of foulness. After a while, the glowing embers disintegrated into particles of a dust-like residue Harold scraped into a box. Later, the charred remnants would be taken to the lake where they would rent a boat, row to the middle and scatter the particles in different directions.

On the way home, they would purchase a stuffed animal for Miley as a replacement for Cubby, perhaps a Teddy Bear, but definitely not another wolf.

"Bye, bye, Cubby," muttered Katherine, greatly relieved as Harold finished sweeping the incinerated residue into the box.

# DIMENSIONS OF SCALE
## John R. Fultz

In the towns and cities they sometimes called her "goddess," but this only made Scylla laugh. At other times they called her a demon and ran from her like death itself. Men pledged themselves to love her forever, and cast themselves from high crags when she denied them.

Women brought her burnt sacrifices and curious delicacies, but she never ate mortal food. She would drink with them sometimes, if someone impressed her, or in those rare times when she felt the need for company. She walked alone through field, fen, and forest, crossing strange kingdoms, following signs and portents, a single-minded will driving her toward the heart of creation.

Enemies came for her whenever she strayed far from civilized realms. In the wastelands and mountain passes, among the deep woodlands and trackless savannah, they came for her again and again. They flew on leathery wings, breathing fire or venom or clouds of black death. She cut them down with sword or spear, sometimes strangling them to death with her bare hands. At other times they came to her in the shapes of men scaled in bright armor, crusaders sworn to serve the dragon. They died in heaps like mindless things. Sometimes she gained clues from those she bested, but they were only small parts of a greater puzzle, one she was bound to solve.

Every Hoardworld was a riddle to be solved and thus ended.

Sometimes it took centuries to find the crux of a dragon's dream. She watched for certain patterns that remained consistent from world to world. She herself was one of those patterns, her essence composed of the same energy that gave birth to all realities. This power was also the lifeblood of the Celestial Wyrms, who dreamed infinite possibilities into existence. The hidden masters of reality lay asleep in a higher realm, while Scylla stalked through their dreams like a specter of death.

The patterns eventually led her to the crux of each Hoardworld. One of them waited for her now atop a frozen mountain. She climbed an ancient stairway of green ice, thrashed by treacherous winds. She felt the bitter cold beneath her cuirass of chain mail, but weather never did her any real harm.

Usually when she came this close to a crux they hurled distortions of time and space at her, but she had learned to sidestep such threats. The frozen stair wound itself like a corkscrew up the mountainside, and for days she came no closer to the grey clouds. Against all reason she climbed onward through biting storms, another week, then two more, and finally reached the peak. There she stood before the coral and bronze gates of a Wyrm Lord's palace. To greet her at the gates came the only true threat to her goal: the wyrm's champion.

Every crux created a champion to protect itself, so why should this one be any different? The champion this time was a scaled giant with the head of a slobbering boar. Its tusks were ivory, engraved with runes of poison and death. Its beady eyes gleamed bright as flames against the snow.

Scylla cast aside her cloak and drew her silver blade.

"Stand aside or die." She gave the usual warning. Only a formality.

The great boar-head snorted and grunted. Massive fists brandished a pair of iron maces large as ships' masts. "If you slay the Holy One who dwells within," the champion said, "you will end this world. So it seems that I must perish either way. I choose to die in battle."

Scylla understood. This was the way of champions.

The giant fell on her like a storm, maces smashing holes in the frozen earth. Avalanches slid down the faces of surrounding mountains. Scylla leaped through the air like a rising vapor, her blade singing as it flashed, carving slices from the giant's middle. When her attack was done, she stood at ease behind the beast. It swirled about with maces flying. The impact slammed her against a snowy bluff, then a wall of ice crashed down and buried her completely.

The boar-headed champion howled at the sky in triumph. It never glimpsed the streak of silver that flashed from beneath the icy rubble to slice clean through its wide neck. The tusked head rolled into bloody snow, and the headless body fell backwards, toppling over the edge of the peak into a deep crevasse. Scylla whipped her blade, slinging the red gore from its keen edges. A word of power from her lips turned the palace gates to dust, and the dragon chose that moment to charge forth like a striking cobra.

The wyrm's jaws enclosed her before she could escape, but she drove her blade upward, piercing its upper snout to the hilt. She held its mouth open with the power of her raised arm. Meanwhile, her booted feet pinned down the slimy tongue. The beast could not bite to crush her now, so it would spit fire, poison, or something worse from its gullet. Some cruxes tried to reason with her, bribe her, enchant her, but this one had attacked immediately. This must be the Wyrm Lord's last remaining crux, this realm the last of its Hoardworlds. If Scylla ended this final dream, the dreamer itself would wake and die. The desperate crux fought hard and with little strategy. Fear of annihilation made it reckless.

"Great Kathagulon," she called both the crux and its Wyrm Lord by name. Purple flames erupted from its throat and streamed across her flesh, but she did not burn. Scylla was made from a certain kind of fire herself, and fire cannot harm fire. So she held the beast's mouth open while it bathed her in a fiery cataract.

"I have slain more of your cruxes than I can remember," she said. "Are you the last?"

"You know that I am. This is the last of my dreams." The dragon's voice came not from its throat, but leaped from its mind into hers. "At least tell me the name of the wyrm-cousin whose champion is my slayer. Are you the Daughter of Skryolach?"

Scylla shook her head, shedding flames like drops of water.

She wrapped both fists about the grip of her transfixed blade.

"Know this then..." she said. "I am the Daughter of Thaxaullus." She drove the blade forward, ripping through the soft upper palate toward the wyrm's unprotected brain. From her stance between the dragon's jaws, it was easy enough to reach the target. The silver blade pierced long and deep. Kathagulon shuddered and shrieked. Scylla leaped from his maw as his massive body fell into death spasms, demolishing in an instant the towers of his dream palace.

For a single moment the world fell into stillness. The dust of the fallen palace rose to mingle with the falling snow. Scylla shivered. How many lifetimes had she spent tracking down this single Wyrm Lord? How many of his cruxes had she slain before this last and final one? Somewhere in the Waking World, she knew Kathagulon was waking from his long sleep to find his entire hoard of dreamworlds murdered and gone...hundreds of living dimensions reduced to nothing more than the sleep dust staining his eyes. Following that realization would come instant and irrevocable death. True death, not simply the demise of another dream-crux. No wyrm survived the death of its final crux, the theft of its last Hoardworld, the dissolution of its single remaining soul shard.

This is why they battled throughout eternity. Celestial Wyrms dreaming whole universes to life, each one seeking to destroy the others in order to define the parameters of reality. Eventually only a single Wyrm Lord would be left in all the cosmos, and that wyrm would dream forever, giving birth to untold realities. A hoard of worlds without end. Today Scylla had killed another of her master's enemies. Thaxaullus was one step closer to that ultimate victory.

The dead dragon's body faded away like a rising fog. The broken palace turned to mist, as did the dead giant. Scylla had known this kind of victory many times. She could not count the number of Hoardworlds she had slain, but she was used to what happened after the crux died. She felt the invisible ripple flowing from the emptiness where the crux's palace had stood. The colors of the sky and the world fell away, then all things turned to mist and were gone.

Reality dissolved, replaced by nothingness. Yet she persisted in the face of oblivion, a tiny flame lost in a void of roaring darkness. Stray planetoids and schools of flying comets swept about her, and she knew that a physical re-manifestation must follow soon. There would be another Hoardworld to infiltrate and eliminate for her master. Another dream-crux to hunt and slay. This was her iron purpose, the crux of her own existence, and it was all she knew. There was no end to it, until the day when Thaxaullus became the last of his kind. How many Wyrm Lords inhabited the Waking World she could not guess. But her master would never let her rest until they were all dead and gone.

Scylla waited in the void for her next transition. Yet this time her formlessness lasted much longer than expected. A comet of blazing energy collided with her naked essence, and something new happened. Understanding washed through the corridors of her mind as the dragon's fire had washed from its gullet. She created herself a new body from the raw dust of the void. Why wait for Thaxaullus to do it for her? The burning comet brought no pain, but sank deep into her cooling flesh. She burned with joy, drunk on the power of rushing epiphanies, a spear of enlightenment piercing her awareness as she had pierced Kathagulon's brain.

She remembered now the smallness of life before immortality. The days when she was a simple being, a young girl inhabiting one of the Hoardworlds. She recalled a field of yellow wheat, a warm hearth, baking bread, the feel of warm arms about her shoulders. The faces of her....

No, the Wyrm Lord Thaxaullus was her creator. She was an entity of cosmic energy and living sorcery. She was not a speck of dream who imagined itself truly alive inside a dragon's slumbering consciousness. And yet, she saw the faces of her parents. She heard their soft and tender voices as they stood over her crib.

"Scylla," they whispered to the tiny thing that was her. She stared up at them through infant's eyes. These were the ones who had named her. Not Thaxaullus.

Her parents.

Yet Thaxaullus had created her by the power of his own dreaming.

He had elevated her, transfigured her with his magic.

Now she understood—for the comet that burned her was composed of understanding—that she was once something else. A Hoardworld creature who had been raised from humble origins by the blessings of her creator. A tool forged to serve his cosmic designs.

The burning comprehension faded from her as she fell into a new world. She manifested on a field of high grass near a tangled forest where night had already taken root. She lay still, her skin steaming a bit, as the sun sank behind distant range of mountains. The sky was a hundred shades of red and gold. She raised newly formed hands to her eyes and found them wet with tears.

In the glow of a triple moon she rose up and began walking. She traveled in a straight line through the grass stalks, heading toward the shelter of the forest, but her mind zig-zagged with a chaos of revelations. Whose dream did she walk through now? Which of the Wyrm Lords created this world and this field and this forest? Did it even matter? If things happened the way they usually did, Thaxaullus would send a familiar to set the course of her new quest. Here was another world to wander, another lifetime of battles and chasing rumors and tracking down the crux who animated this dream dimension. Another mission of mystery and death. An endless cycle with minor variations.

Scylla remembered the familiar taste of loneliness.

As she walked, she wondered about things that she had never considered before the strange comet scalded her spirit. Why did the Celestial Wyrms hate one another so much? Why could they not exist in peace, each one lord of unnumbered Hoardworlds? Why this endless contest to inherit all of eternity when there was enough eternity for everyone to enjoy? The dreaming dragons waged war on one another exclusively through the medium of their dreams. Why did they not rise up to gnash and tear at one another in the Waking World? Were they too weak for such battles, or simply lazy? Perhaps they were forbidden to engage in physical warfare. Yet who or what could forbid such divine powers from doing anything?

Whenever she blinked, Scylla saw again the faces of her parents, warm and round in the soft firelight of her memory. She could almost remember their names. But there were other things…even more precious things…that she had lost. What were they? Who were they?

Thaxaullus would send a familiar to set the course of her new quest.

She walked like a ghost between the twisted trees, seeking the dark places where the moonlight couldn't reach. Better to weep in darkness. She did not truly understand her master or his serpentine kind. Such godly minds were beyond her.

Yet now she wondered about many things.

\* \* \* \*

The familiar came in the shape of a black python. It slithered up to her in the cold hour before dawn. She had found a neglected path to follow through the oaks, but now she halted as the reptile's head rose up to look her in the face. Its slit eyes were crimson, and its long body thicker than her waist. It called her name in the gloom, flicking a forked tongue.

She greeted it with silence.

"The master is pleased," said the python. "You have done well."

"How many has it been?" she asked. "How many wyrms have I killed in the Waking World?"

The serpent's head wavered sideways. "Don't you remember them all?" it asked. "Kathagulon was your seventy-first kill."

Scylla's head spun with fragments of memory. She remembered so many things now that she might as well have remembered nothing. It was all confusion. She focused on pulling a single image from the kaleidoscope of her consciousness. The smiling faces of her human parents. Yet every time they sank back into the melange of chaos.

"Are you injured?" asked the python. "You seem…changed."

She blinked at the serpent in the starlight.

"How long?" she asked.

"You're full of questions this time," said the serpent. It glided about her in a wide circle.

"How long have I served Thaxaullus?" she asked.

The serpent laughed. "Time has no meaning for beings like us."

"I was once a human—a mortal," she said. "I remember it now."

The python raised one of its eyes at her. "I have no knowledge of these things. Lord Thaxaullus created me to bring you his messages, to direct each of your quests. He gifts me with a new form each time I'm needed, and he allows me to roam this Hoardworld while he slumbers. I know nothing of your history except that you, too, are the master's creation. You must put all else aside as illusion."

"Illusion?" She leaned against the cool bark of an oak. "Or truth?"

The serpent wound itself about a branch above her head, then extended its diamond-shaped head toward her again. "Nevertheless… There are seventeen island-continents on this world," it said. "A crux of Lord Xallagarch dwells somewhere on one of them. At the heart of this forest you will find a monastery where a secret order of monks guards ancient wisdom. Including the spells you will need to locate Xallagarch's crux. Follow the flight of the great forest bats to this hidden monastery."

"No," Scylla said. "I want to see the master."

"Impossible," said the serpent. "You must attend your duties here."

She grabbed the python's head in her hands and stared into its blood-bright eyes. "Take me to—" She could not finish the sentence. Her act of rebellion had shaken loose another memory, like an acorn falling from a jostled branch. Another face. Another set of strong arms wrapped around her. The soaring of her heart, the quickening of her pulse. Eyes blue as a clear sky and a face that was rugged yet handsome. She could not name him, but she recognized him. The man she had loved when she was less than now. When she was human.

*Husband...*

The word unlocked a flood of memories. She wept as she wrestled with the black python. It coiled about her body and tried to crush her. She drove her sharp nails into its flesh, tearing black scales from its back. Blood dark as oil seeped from its wounds. She held its fangs away from her neck and met its eyes with her own. A war of wills began...

"Show me the way to the Waking World," she demanded.

"I cannot," said the python. "I know not the way."

"Yet you are a clue," she said. "A sign..."

She swept her silver blade from its sheathe as the python turned her loose.

"And I am a tracker."

As it rushed away, she ran along its back toward the departing head. A sweep of her blade separated head from body. She grabbed the tumbling snake-head with her free hand as the coils fell into spasms and eroded into a black fog. She mumbled a spell as the head began to fade as well, and she inhaled its substance like a foul smoke into her lungs. As the familiar of Thaxaullus it carried a portion of his magic, and now that mote of sorcery was inside her own body. It mingled and magnified the magic that was already there, the seeds of her creation and the fuel for her immortality.

She hacked, and coughed, and vomited, but refused to let go of what she had swallowed. The face of her dead husband swam before her, and she recalled the depth of her love for him. Yet still she could not recall his name. Another thing that had been stolen from her by the kiss of divinity. Finally, she fell into a patch of green moss and lay still in the pink glow of dawn.

As the sun came up, she remembered the faces that thrilled and pained her most of all.

The faces of her sweet children.

\* \* \* \*

Soon the sentinels of Xallagarch came for her. Nine black dragons rushed like storm clouds above the forest. She recognized them by their shadows, the sounds of their wings, and the familiar stink of dragonflesh. They had sensed her arrival and came to devour her. Any other time she would have fought and slain them all. They were the offspring of the hidden crux, the power that animated their world, yet they had no inkling of their true nature. They were simply agents of blind destruction and bottomless hunger. Scylla had no intention of fighting them this time. They were meaningless.

Drawing upon the sorcery she had stolen from the familiar, she sang an ancient spell and stepped between the worlds. The dawn forest faded, replaced by a howling wasteland where the bones of giants were piled into mountains. She followed the faint trail into an adjoining world, and another, and across a dozen wasted, empty domains. At least she found again the great void where stars and comets sang again about her head. Dimension after dimension folded about her, and at last her ultimate destination opened like a flaming blossom. She plunged through the flames like a meteor, and crashed into rocky earth with an impact that left her senseless.

As she lay between awareness and unconsciousness, she smelled the scents of the deep earth about her, and the odor of something ancient that stung her nostrils. She knew the smell, or a pale version of it. This was the true smell of dragonflesh, far more pungent than dream wyrms.

A low rumble rattled the bedrock beneath her, and the bones in her chest trembled.

She pushed herself upward and stood inside a vast, jeweled cavern. Stalactites pointed down at her from the darkness above, and a great heap of flesh and scales rose before her like a dark mountain. It exhaled a sulfurous stink from two great nostrils, and its blind eyes opened to gleam like giant lanterns.

Fear rose like a physical pain in Scylla's throat, but the faces she remembered burned in her mind's eye. Those images, those memories, gave her the strength to stand before the mighty Thaxaullus and not fall to her knees a blubbering mess.

The Wyrm Lord's lips pulled back from his yellow fangs, and his pale eyes blinked at her. Another rumbling came from his throat, and he shifted on his great belly in the darkness.

"You have succeeded in awakening me, Scylla," said Thaxaullus. His powerful voice shook the cavern. A shower of uncut jewels fell across the scaled hump of his back.

"Forgive me, Great Lord," Scylla said. She bowed to the monster. Fear reminded her that she was powerless here. Thaxaullus was the one wyrm in all existence that she could not harm or resist, and she had brought herself to stand before him like a petulant child.

Perhaps the memories had driven her mad.

"I am…" she said, "…sorely troubled, Lord."

"For that I am sorry," said the wyrm. "You have served me faithfully during my long sleep. You have my gratitude."

"Yet I have awakened you," she said, "putting an end to all of your Hoardworlds."

"Yes, but soon I will slumber again," Thaxaullus said. "Too many of my Hoardworlds had already been destroyed by the agents of my enemies.

When you awoke me just now, I had only a handful of cruxes left. But when I go back to sleep, I will dream into existence another continuum of realities, each one built about a freshly born crux. Therefore, you have done me a great service. A new long sleep will begin, and my world-hoard will be renewed."

"You wanted this," Scylla said. Comprehension swelled inside her now. She wanted to weep again for her children and her husband...for all she had lost so long ago. But now her eyes remained dry. Perhaps she was only capable of weeping inside the dragon's dreams.

"You sent that comet," she said. "You awakened my memories. You knew I would come here to confront you…"

"To awaken me," said the dragon. "As I said, you have served me well."

"Why do you not rise up from this dismal cavern and conquer the Waking World?" she asked. "Why not face your enemies in the flesh instead of only in dreams? Why play this endless game with me as a mindless pawn?"

The dragon shifted its bulk, snapped its tail somewhere in the deep cavern, and expelled more noxious air from its snout. Its blind orbs blinked at her. "The world outside this cavern died a long time ago," Thaxaullus said. "My cousins lie scattered across the end of time, where existence itself has run down and entropy reigns. Wyrms are the only life that remains in this burned-out universe. So we dream other universes into being, places where beings like you can exist...places where we can fly free in unspoiled skies and live the way our ancestors did. We battle inside these dreamworlds because they are the only worlds left that matter to us. Someday there be only one wyrm left to dream...one master of All That Is. I intend to be that wyrm."

"What about my parents?" Scylla asked. "My husband, my children? What happened to them? And why choose me to be your weapon?"

The dragon chuckled. "You are all my creations. They were mortals, and so they died. You would have shared their fate if not for my intervention. I spared you from death and gave you a purpose greater than you could ever imagine. And I gave you power to pursue that purpose."

"Everything I remember…" she said. "My life before you chose me… the ones I loved and lost. Can you bring it all back?"

The dragon huffed. "Somewhere in one of my new Hoardworlds, another Scylla will be born to a family exactly like yours. One day she will give birth to sweet children exactly like yours. In time, when her natural existence has run its course, she will be raised up to serve me as you have done. Does this comfort you?"

Scylla dropped the silver blade that she hadn't realized she was still holding.

"Yes," she said. She felt their tiny hands in hers again, remembered walking amid the golden fields. Laughter. A gentle rain. Peace.

A rumble from the wyrm's gut shook the cavern floor.

"I must feed before I sleep again," Thaxaullus said. "Therefore I call upon your loyalty one last time."

"Is that my final role?" she asked. "To provide fresh meat for your belly?"

"You always were a clever servant."

Scylla picked up the silver blade.

"I will not climb into your mouth," she said. "You made me a warrior."

"I wouldn't have it any other way," said the wyrm.

The scaly head shot forward as the blade flashed in her hand.

# A DEAD MAN'S TALE
## Adrian Cole

Dane sipped his third cup of coffee. He wasn't enjoying it, but it kept him awake and passed the time. It was close to 2 am. These days that was long past his usual bedtime. The cafe was part of a motorway service station, miles from anywhere, its lights a glare against the black wall of night beyond the high windows. From his inconspicuous seat in a corner, Dane could watch the entrance to the complex. Miller invariably came that way. He was half an hour late, but that was nothing new. He'd be out there, checking the car park, obsessed with the possibility of being tailed, although there weren't many cars, more trucks than anything, with drivers bedded down for the night.

Dane saw himself reflected in the window. Looking a little more haggard each time he sat here, slouched, world-weary. Soon be time to quit. Sixty was beckoning. He looked it, too. He kept relatively fit, but holding back the pounds got tougher by the year, hell, the month. This was a young man's game. Maybe this could be the last call out. If Miller didn't show, maybe that could be it. Drive away and into a private oblivion. He was never going to be rich, but he'd get by.

Obviously Miller did show. He entered the cafe and went to the counter, ordering a coffee. He looked around with apparent nonchalance, but Dane knew the former colonel was assessing every inch of the place, absorbing every detail. At 2 am there weren't many. A couple of travelers, a cleaner out in the corridor and a girl who looked like she was counting the day's takings further along the bar.

Miller brought his coffee to Dane's table and sat where he could also survey his surroundings. He sipped his coffee and grimaced. Anyone would have thought it was the first time he'd tasted the stuff.

"Thanks for coming," he said. It was a kind of code, the standard opening line. He sat stiffly, a military man to the end of his days, officially retired from service but too valuable to be wasted altogether. Dane had a good idea who Miller's bosses were, but he'd always known better than to ask.

"So it's urgent," said Dane.

Miller nodded slowly. "Ticking bomb. No one wants to get involved, but someone has to."

Dane smiled wryly. "Someone on the outside. And here I am."

"You can always say no. This time I mean it." Miller looked sincere. Worried, too, if only for a moment. His face rarely displayed emotion. This one apparently troubled him.

Dane waited. Miller would tell him what he wanted in his own time. Both men sipped their coffee, watching the shapeless night beyond. For a brief moment it was as if the night was watching them, darkness molded into faces.

"Last week a man was murdered in London. A fight in a night club. Stabbings. A couple of gangs carving each other up over drug turf."

Dane grunted. "It's the name of the game these days." It was becoming commonplace. A lot of this stuff didn't make the media any more.

"We had it played down. There were a few arrests, some small time crooks jailed. It'll become another statistic. What won't be known is that the fight was a cover. The man we're interested in had little, if anything, to do with the gangs. It was just made to look that way, to obscure the real reason for his death."

Dane waited. Miller reached into an inner pocket of his coat and pulled out an envelope. He produced a photo and handed it over. "You probably don't know him."

The man in the snapshot was gaunt, hair shaved tight, his expression deadpan, a cold challenge to the camera. Mid forties, eastern European maybe, possibly military, which figured.

"Mickey Karr," said Miller. "Worked in a number of roles for the Blake brothers."

Dane didn't need reminding who they were. The latest Kray clones, a terrifying presence in the capital. "Looks like a hit man."

Miller snorted. "No hiding it. The Blakes have several very hard men on their books, not that you could prove it easily."

Dane had never had cause to get anywhere near the dirty operations of the notorious brothers. They had a stranglehold on certain parts of the capital, and tentacles that stretched further afield, too. Including the continent these days. Black trading of every kind.

"You know who killed him?" Dane asked.

"We think it was the Blakes."

Dane shrugged. "Hit men have a limited life span. They know too much. One day the roles are reversed. You guys don't usually shed any tears. One less thug on the streets. I'd say the Blakes have done you a favor." He handed the photo back.

"Perhaps. But we think the Blakes killed him for another reason." Miller passed over more photos.

Pictures of a dead man, obviously Mickey Karr. His killers had made a real mess of him, or more specifically, his back. It was so badly cut it looked like the skin had been flayed from it, from shoulders down to the buttocks, a bloody rectangle. A professional butcher couldn't have done a better job.

"Nasty," said Dane.

"His real name was Oleg Kravyenko. He'd wormed his way into the Blake set-up, but his employers were the GRU, successors to the KGB. The best man they had. He killed three men for them, spies, all converted to our side, betrayers of their motherland. All within the last two years, here in England. We've never been able to prove it, mainly because the bodies have never been found."

"Now that he's dead, you never will find them, is that it?"

"In theory. We think we have a lead."

Dane again studied the photos, the bloody ruin of the man's back. "Is that where this comes in?"

Miller nodded. "Kravyenko—Mickey Karr—knew the Blakes would want to have him rubbed out eventually. He needed some kind of insurance to keep them at bay. Something that would incriminate them in whatever killings he'd done for them. A record, and with it a way to find where the bodies are buried. As long as Mickey Karr kept that information hidden, the Blakes couldn't risk killing him."

"Would this record have taken the form of a map? Etched on his own flesh." Dane tapped the photo showing the flaying. "A tattoo?"

"You always did catch on fast. Yes. A map, or diagram of some kind. We think he had a way of disposing of the bodies, and not just the people he killed for the Blakes. If the map was the record, it could contain the locations of the three dead spies, among others. We'd like to recover them."

"Not for sentimental reasons, though."

"We're not in this for sentiment. We don't want any political embarrassments. You read the papers. The Government is currently involved in some very sensitive issues with our Red friends. Last thing we want is a bundle of former Russian spies floating to the surface. As far as we know, Kravyenko may have left a way for the GRU to find them. A gun to our head if they did."

Dane handed the photos back. "You think whatever was cut from his back is still in existence, presumably with the Blakes?"

Miller shook his head. "I doubt it. They don't want the other bodies found and it's unlikely they know about the three spies. The skin map, or whatever, would have been carved up and fed to the dogs. Or otherwise disposed of."

"And how do you expect to find out what was on it?"

Miller studied the darkness beyond the window. It seemed to pulse forward, listening. "Somebody made that map. We want you to find them." He put the photos back in the envelope and pushed his coffee away. "You remember a woman called Anne Bell? She's one of my team, mid-twenties, dark hair, works in an estate agents."

Dane nodded. "I worked through her once. When I last spoke to her she'd built a web of contacts in the city."

"Some of them are part of the Blake brothers set-up. She knows a girl called Maria. You need to talk to her. She was Kravyenko's woman. And you're going to have to be careful." Miller was drumming his right hand fingers lightly on the tabletop. It was a rare sign of unease.

"If she's mixed up with the Blakes, I'd take that as read."

"She's given them the slip. It's likely they want her dead—well, she'd have seen that map. If she was Kravyenko's lover, we have to assume so."

"You know where she is?"

"Anne does. I'd start with her." He stood up and pulled his coat tighter. "Find me those dead men. Before the Reds send in a fresh man, maybe a team."

"What about the pay-off? It better be good."

"Find them and you can name your price. Shit, Dane, you could even retire."

Dane watched him walk away. And he'd never asked if he'd take the job on. But he'd left another envelope on the table.

\* \* \* \*

Dane didn't open the envelope until after the long drive back to London. In his flat he looked at the single sheet, an estate agent's advert for a house, with a note pinned to it. *Aunty A thinks this could be just what you're looking for.* Anne Bell, his contact, would be at the estate agents.

He slept for three hours, rose early and shaved, trying not to study his lined face more than necessary. Why was he doing this? For the money? It would be very good. Enough to get him a better place, maybe finish collecting those first editions he wanted. Or was it some ongoing loyalty to the old school, Miller and the others, serving Queen and country? Dane grinned at himself. If he quit now, he'd spiral down into premature old age and dullness. No, not too old yet, not quite finished. Vanity, then. What the hell. Get on with it.

\* \* \* \*

Anne Bell was expecting him. Miller's cover set-up for her was credible, Dane thought. Part time worker in the estate agents, out of the center, a few days a week. Not enough money to live off, so her evening job was as a hostess in a night club, as Annabella. One of a chain run by the Blakes.

Dane sat in her neat, pristine office, high street traffic behind him outside, churning through the day's light rain. She sat opposite, very smart, a perfect ad for the company, the wall behind her a chiaroscuro of house pics, geometrically arranged. Suitably convincing.

Dane pushed the house advert across the desk. "Miller sent me this."

She nodded, her smile as fixed as a model's. "This is about Mickey Karr." She leaned forward, as if enthusing about the house on offer. "We can talk in here." Meaning, no bugs.

"He had a lover," Dane said." You know her. Maria."

"Yes, a Romanian girl."

"Is she safe?"

"She's worried that the Blakes will ship her off to one of the Yorkshire sex chains. That or worse. I've got her out of their reach for now, but sooner or later they'll be looking for her."

"What's her part in this?"

"K never told her his little secret, and although they were lovers, or what passed for it, never let her see his back. One night she caught a glimpse of it in a mirror. She didn't tell him. He was a very hard man, nasty at times. She was afraid of him. Once or twice he hit her. It made her angry." She spoke coldly, indifferently, but Dane read her own suppressed anger in her eyes.

"That's when she let the secret slip. To the Blakes."

"Not directly. She was more terrified of them than K. One of their cronies picked up on Maria's slip of the tongue. It was enough. Once the Blakes knew about K's back, they acted."

"Killed him and destroyed the diagram. They did destroy it?"

"Yes. You want to meet Maria? She can't tell you any more. She won't trust you anyway."

"What does she want?"

"To be free of the Blakes."

"We'd all like that. There's only one way it's going to happen."

She gave him a weary smile. "They're too well protected. Miller would have told you that."

Dane shrugged. "I need to see Maria."

"She won't talk to Miller. K told her he's no better than the Blakes. She loved K, in spite of his nature. She feels responsible for his death."

"Does she know you work for Miller?"

"No."

\* \* \* \*

Dane rarely went anywhere in the city without checking out if he was being tailed. He'd warned Miller he wouldn't work if Miller had him followed. If anyone was keeping tabs on Dane, he knew it would likely be hostile. This time his back was clear. By the time he boarded his last tube connection he was confident of his anonymity.

Anne Bell had given him directions. A flat out in suburbia, as good a bet against prying eyes as she could find. She'd also devised his cover. He was a reliable friend who would arrange an even safer haven for Maria, where the Blakes were unlikely to find her.

The flat was at the rear of a chain of old stores, due for demolition to make way for an extension of the local housing estate. Dane rang the bell a few times. Eventually the girl opened the door, using it as a shield.

"Anne sent me," he said.

She let him in, locking the door before leading him up a staircase. The place was clean, sparsely furnished. Curtains partially blocked the windows.

Maria was blonde, and could have been an attractive young woman, but the strain of her existence had been cruel to her looks and her wasted body. Her hair straggled either side of a gaunt face and dull eyes looked on emptiness. Her clothes were cheap, but not shoddy. She'd made an effort with them, but not herself.

"You want some coffee?" she asked him, her eyes never meeting his.

"Sure." He sat and watched her in the kitchenette as she boiled the kettle and made instant coffee, though she didn't have one herself, moving methodically and mechanically.

"I was sorry to hear about Mickey," he said when she handed him the mug.

Her eyes flickered, briefly widening. "You knew him?"

"Met him a few times. I warned him when he started working for the Blakes he was taking a risk. They're a mad lot. Fucking mad."

She nodded.

"They killed him," he said, sipping the coffee and watching her reaction. "You know that?"

Again her eyes widened. "Yes. Bastards."

"No one's ever going to prove it, though. Not without evidence."

"No one cares," she murmured.

"Oh, I wouldn't say that, Maria. Men like the Blakes make a lot of enemies."

"You?"

"Yeah, but it's not something I advertise. I know a few. When I get you safe, you'll be under their protection."

"I can't pay. I've nothing. And I don't want to work like…like I have been." She had shed enough tears in her bruised life, though Dane could see them behind her eyes.

"You won't have to. But you can give a little something."

For a moment a spark of anger flared briefly. "Like what?"

"Just a bit of information. About Mickey."

"Even though we were lovers, I knew hardly anything about him."

"You knew about his tattoo. That's why you're in this mess."

"I never saw it properly. When they killed him, they cut it off him and burned it."

Dane nodded. "We know that. We also know that somebody must have worked on that tattoo. Mickey wouldn't have done it himself."

She frowned. "Yes, I suppose so."

"Think about it, Maria," he said gently. He put the mug down and sat back slowly.

"Did any of the others in the clubs have tattoos? They're a big thing these days."

She rolled up the right hand sleeve of her thin dress. She had a simple butterfly tattooed across her upper arm. "I remember," she said. "The other girls all had tattoos. I just had a small one. Some of them had lots. I don't like them. They are like—marks of possession."

"Who did yours?"

"It's a small place in the city. Cheap. *Scorch Marks*."

"Did Mickey have his done there?"

"I don't know."

"Did he know the place?"

"Oh yes," she said, pulling something from the shadowed memories she'd not wanted to examine. "Yes, he did. I told him the other girls had said I should get a tattoo, at that place. He said he knew it, but that was all. He said they were good and wouldn't hurt me." She gave him the address.

He changed the subject gently and made small talk for a while. Eventually he looked at his watch and stood up. "Okay, listen, the next time Anne arranges a contact, it won't be me, but it'll be friends of mine. Be ready to travel."

"I have nothing. I can go any time."

\* \* \* \*

The tattooist shop, *Scorch Marks*, was a colorful blaze, its woodwork painted black, writhing in examples of the art on offer, a bizarre combination of snakes, dragons, rockets, voluptuous women and guns. Dane recognized the place from years back, when it had been a book center, selling exotic fantasy, psychedelic posters and every type of scented candle imaginable. It had evidently moved with the times.

The place was squashed inside, where stacks of neglected books and magazines were still for sale. Behind the long counter and a spread of more examples of art, one of the salesmen—Dane took him to be the boss—was doodling on a pad. Dane could see a small workshop behind him, where machinery whizzed and whirred, busily satisfying a couple of seated customers.

The heavy-set man looked up. He was probably sixty, Dane thought, his long beard and wild hair gray. He wouldn't have been out of place astride a motor bike. His arms were an advert for the shop, covered from shoulder to fingertips in brilliantly vivid tattoos, their detail almost hypnotically intricate.

Further down the counter another man was working, head bowed, apparently lost in thought. Unlike the big guy fronting the place, he was little more than a bag of bones, his face white. If he wore tattoos, they were covered up, the man's clothes creased and grubby.

The big man nodded.

"You did some work for a friend of mine," Dane told him. "Sometime in the last two years."

"Name?"

"Mickey Karr."

The man's eyes flared briefly, though he hid his reaction well. Dane was too close to him to miss it. The man had recognized the name.

"Don't know him."

Dane described Karr, but it was already obvious he wasn't going to get anywhere. "How about your colleagues? Can you ask them?"

"Stubbs there barely knows his own name. Anyway, who wants to know?" The man leaned forward belligerently.

"I'm a friend. Mickey and I were very close."

The man stood up. "I don't want any trouble. Who do you work for?"

"How about you just check your records? You do keep records? For tax purposes and the like?" Dane made it sound like a veiled threat. He saw the barb go home. Any mention of tax normally had that effect.

The big man contemplated demurring, but grunted and shuffled off to somewhere in the back of the shop. Dane went slowly down to where the skinny guy was working.

"How about you?" he said quietly. "You know a client called Mickey Karr?"

The man shook his head and shriveled up even more. He was trembling like a puppy.

When the big man returned, his face looked set. "We don't have anything. Sorry, pal."

Dane left the shop in the late afternoon gloom and crossed the alley. There was a bookshop and Dane studied the gaudy display in its window, trying to think. The tattooist had known the Russian, he was sure of it.

Getting him to open up would be tough. Maybe he needed Miller to exert some of his pressure.

Dane walked down the alley, chewing over his next move. He was in a small maze of claustrophobic passages. Better to get away quickly. The big guy in the tattooists could be on the phone to someone by now, in all probability the Blake brothers, or one of their heavies.

Dane was being followed. It wasn't just his sixth sense that warned him. He attuned his hearing to a rhythm of steps on the cobbles. When he stopped walking, that rhythm stopped. Up ahead was a narrow doorway, set back in the brickwork, a shadowed place. He slid in and waited.

Several minutes later his tail passed the door, a bent, diminutive figure. Dane slipped out behind it. In the alleyway they were both partially masked in shadows, the buildings on either side practically creating a tunnel.

"Looking for me?" said Dane.

The figure jumped, turning around, stumbling. It was the pale-faced man, Stubbs, from the tattooists. He looked horrified, as if he would bolt.

"It's okay," said Dane. "I know you were following me. You want to talk?"

The man nodded. "Not here," he said, his voice little more than a rasp.

"You go ahead. I'll be behind you. But if this is a trap, I'll wring your neck."

"No. But it's not safe." The man moved off, more quickly, like a rodent scurrying through a drain. Dane followed, watching his back, checking every side alley. If Blake's mobsters snared him here, he'd be screwed.

Half a mile away, the small guy reached a row of dilapidated shops, most of them boarded up. He went up a side staircase, turning once to see if Dane was following. Dane weighed things up. It was times like this when he wished he'd brought a gun. It was rare that he carried one, but in this particular jungle it was a way of life.

He decided to follow the man up into the flat. He entered slowly, right hand in his coat pocket. The place hadn't been occupied for some time. The dust had piled up, the windows were thick with grime. Two of the wooden chairs had been up-ended. It looked as if someone might have conducted a rough search here and made no effort to cover the mess up.

"This was Ronnie's place," Stubbs said. "He looked after me."

"Who was he?"

"My mate in the shop. Snake, that big guy, he's the boss. Me and Ronnie were the two assistants. I heard you ask about Mickey Karr."

"Yes."

"You know he was murdered?"

Dane nodded slowly.

"I reckon the same people killed Ronnie. He knew too much."

"About what?"

"Ronnie did Karr. Special job. First time Karr came in was about two years ago. Then he used to come back to have bits added to his tattoo."

"On his back? What was it, exactly?"

"Sort of a map."

"Of what?"

"I never saw it. Karr wouldn't let anyone near. Only Ronnie."

"And now you think Ronnie's dead. You're sure?"

"Yeah." He shuddered. "I know it. He's spoken to me. Here, in this room." He said it as if he were talking about a phone call, but Dane knew what he was implying and masked his reaction. A ghost? Stubbs was quite serious.

"He's angry. Wants to get back at the Blake brothers. They did for him. Same as they did for Karr, right?"

Dane nodded.

"He'll show you the map. There's a copy."

Dane remained expressionless. A ghost was going to show him a copy of the map. Yeah, right. He waited.

Stubbs put his bony fingers to each side of his skull and closed his eyes. Dane watched him skeptically. This looked like it was going to be a load of bull, an attempt to throw him off the track.

Even so, the light dimmed slightly, as if the weather outside had closed in abruptly, prematurely. And the temperature dropped noticeably, to an unnatural, unnerving level. Stubbs's face was screwed up in concentration. It looked painful. When he next spoke, his breath came out in a white mist and his voice was an octave or two lower, hoarse and ragged. Clever trick, thought Dane.

"They searched this place, but they didn't look everywhere." Stubbs turned round, his motions stiff, jerky. He went to the window, an old sash cord type. Under it there was a ledge and below that some stained wooden paneling, tongued and grooved firmly into place.

"They never looked behind here," said Stubbs. He sagged down, apparently exhausted.

Dane looked for something to prize the panels apart, but there was nothing. Instead he kicked hard at the central panel and it cracked, splitting down its length. Dane kicked it again and was able to pull it away. After that it was easy to remove more of the panels. At one end of the run there was an old folder. Dane pulled it free.

He shook the dust from it and opened it. There was a batch of papers inside. Each sheet was a set of drawings, presumably roughs for tattoo designs.

Stubbs let out a deep sigh and sank back on his haunches, his head slumping. The coldness in the air subsided, ebbing like a tide.

Dane flicked through the papers. Each sheet had a name printed neatly along the top right hand edge. He found what he wanted. *Mickey Karr.* He removed it and took it to the window. The deep gloom had lifted a little.

Stubbs opened his eyes and stood up unsteadily, shivering. "Is it the map?"

Dane folded it carefully and slipped it inside his coat. He tidied up the other papers in their file and slid it back into the space behind the paneling. "Better put everything back. Make a good job of it, in case they come looking again."

Stubbs nodded, bending down and immediately fiddling with the panels. Dane left him to it. Outside it was bright again, a relief to get away from the clammy atmosphere of the flat and whatever dwelt there. He made sure no one was tailing him and slid into the human tide down to the Underground.

* * * *

He studied the map back at his flat. Under Karr's name, centralized, were three letters, O B R. There were no other words there, only rows of numbers, arranged in neat lines, some curving back on themselves, like paths. Others were arranged in rectangular groups, still more in triangles. Several of the numbers were ringed. Some kind of code and Dane was none the wiser for having it.

Washed out, he heated up an oven-ready meal. After he'd eaten it he pored over the map again, but could still make no sense of it. Maybe he should just get it to Miller and let him take it from there. He dozed off watching a documentary on TV, jerked awake and went to bed.

In the morning he rose early, showered and put on an extra layer of clothing. The flat was unduly cold, as if he'd left a window open all night. He was about to grab some breakfast, when he saw the books on his living area table. How the hell had they got there? He hadn't put them there. And no one could have broken in without him knowing. He swung round, half expecting someone to be standing behind him.

He shivered, thinking about the flat he had been in the previous day, and its unique coldness. Like this place now. He forced his mind to concentrate on the books. How were they on the table?

They were about London, and there was a large street map spread open. He had no recollection of having referred to it. Karr's enigmatic map sat beside it. O B R—the letters caught his eye. He went to close the street map, but the area at which it opened had a long road bisecting it from north west down to south east. The name printed along it leaped out at him. Old

Bromsditch Road. O B R. Coincidence?

He puzzled over it as he fed some bread slices into his toaster, put the kettle on, and flicked the TV on. The news channel usually kept him company before he left the flat. The words of the news reader were like a cold douche.

"The source of the fire is not yet known. Shops on either side have been damaged, but the fire was quickly contained, due to the swift reaction of the Fire Services. So far one body has been recovered, believed to be one of the employees, who apparently sometimes worked at night. It is unlikely there are any other victims."

Dane's mind blotted out the rest, but he knew instinctively which shop it was. The ironically named *Scorch Marks*. And the victim was Stubbs. He'd paid for the information he'd given Dane.

Dane looked again at the coded sheet of paper and then the street map. He ran a finger up and down the length of road, which was some way out in the suburbs of the city. As he did so, he realized what it was his attention had been pushed towards. The coded sheet suddenly made perfect sense.

He used his mobile phone and rang Anne Bell, using a private number.

"It's Dane. I have to go to a place called Old Bromsditch Road. Miller needs to know." He gave her some instructions, making her repeat them before ringing off.

Dane put on a heavy coat and this time slipped a gun into an internal pocket. If Stubbs had been a marked man, then he would be, too. It had to be the Blakes who had killed him. Snake, the big guy who'd run the tattoo shop, must have blabbed to them. They'd wasted no time taking action.

Outside it was another gray day, with a hint of drizzle. Dane used his car though he thought it likely he'd be followed. The Blakes must be on to him. In his mind's eye he saw again the street map and the extensive area to the north west of the road.

Where better to hide bodies than in an old cemetery?

* * * *

On his way, Dane's suspicions were realized and he knew he was being followed. He grinned sardonically—no surprise there. He drove through the open gates and eased the car along the straight central road of the cemetery to the distant crematorium. Gravestones crowded in on either side, along with tombs and monuments that went back into time's fog. These days there were few added, in spite of the vastness of the cemetery. Flower beds and ashes supplanted them.

As he drove, Dane looked left and right down endless avenues. The map he held gave him a few clues: he'd got a handle on how the key worked, the hidden messages left by Kravyenko. A lone figure caught his eye and he slowed, pulling over and tucking the car into a space beneath a tall fir tree, shadows partially clothing it.

He moved quickly down the narrow pathway between yet more graves to where the figure was bent over a small mound, tugging at weeds, tidying a lawn's edge. A gravedigger, or at least, someone involved in maintenance.

Dane waved at the man, who stopped and looked up at him indifferently. "Sorry to bother you, pal," said Dane. He gestured with the map. "I'm looking for a particular grave. I don't have a name, but I have a number."

The man rose. He was in his sixties, short and stocky, his bare arms muddy with the work he was doing. He frowned, as if the idea of numbered graves was unusual, but when he looked at the outstretched diagram, something in his eyes told Dane the opposite was true.

"Don't know anything about it," the man grumbled.

Dane leaned closer. "I think you do." He tapped his finger on one of the ringed numbers. "So don't screw me around."

"You with the other guy?" The man looked afraid.

"Just show me where it is. Then you can scram."

The man paused, but Dane's eyes were cold, hostile. There would be no arguing.

"Okay." He led Dane through the underbrush at the edge of the clearing, pushing aside clawing bracken and low hanging branches. Although there was no track here, the man knew his way around. Silence clamped down. Dane's fingers wrapped around his gun butt.

The ground fell gently away to a hollow, old graves and stones among thick grass. Sunlight slanted down to daub a small mound. Freshly heaped earth. A grave had been opened. Dane approached it cautiously and as he did so the man with him twisted away and bolted. Dane let him go.

He studied the map. There were several graves here, all clearly visible on the map. But the circled one was next to the open grave. He stood at its brink and looked down. There was an old coffin down there, its rotting lid partly exposed. But this was to be no exhumation.

A movement behind him made him turn, gun out. He didn't recognize the man who stepped into the clearing. He wore a thick winter coat, collar up, and had a woolen scarf wrapped around his upper body. Close-cropped, graying hair, Slavonic features. He, too, had a hand gun and the snout of its silencer was aimed directly at Dane.

"Mr Dane, I take it," said the man. The eyes, the granite expression, the complete coolness, said, Russian. It had to be Kravyenko's successor. "The map, please. Set it down, with the gun, and step back."

Dane knew if he tried to aim and fire, he'd be dead before he got a shot off. Slowly he bent down and put both the map and gun on some of the spilled earth. "It won't be a good idea to kill me," he said. "They're on to you."

The Russian waved him away from the gun, closer to the open grave. "They won't find you, Mr Dane. You'll lie buried there, anonymous and unseen, next to one of my countrymen, ironically. I can return at any time and have him and the others exhumed, now that I have the map. I don't need the old gravedigger."

He raised his gun. Dane felt every muscle tense, a cold flood of fear, imminent death.

The air hummed, as if a sudden gust of wind swirled around the clearing. Until now it had been airless. The unexpected movement distracted the Russian. He swatted at something like a kid trying to brush off a wasp. He backed up, cursing.

Dane dropped to the ground, snatched up his gun and rolled over in the grass. He heard the silencer of the Russian's weapon spit, several times. Bullets tore through the grass, hitting the ground, inches from Dane as he rolled again. He fired, the sound of his own gun magnified in the clearing, though he knew his bullet would be nowhere near its mark.

Another strong gust of wind, curiously centred in the glade, shifted overhead. Dane fetched up against a headstone and scrambled around it just as more bullets smacked into it. He raised his head but ducked as he saw the Russian striding towards him and firing. Again he returned the fire, but he was shooting blind. The Russian would be a crack shot. One clear view of Dane and this would be over.

Chipped granite flew from the headstone as Dane tried to get at least a partial view of the figure. Another gunshot sounded, the distinct crack coming from beyond the grove. Abruptly a silence fell over everything. The freakish gusting breeze was gone, the air so still it might have been frozen.

Dane rolled slowly away, gun aimed ahead of him. *Show yourself!* His mind cried. *One glimpse is all I want.* But the Russian was invisible, silent. Dane lifted his head, looking across to where the Russian had been standing. No sign. Dane rose higher, ready to dive into the deeper grass. As he did so, he saw his opponent.

The man had fallen and was slumped, face down. Dane inched closer. The Russian's gun was no longer in his hand, jerked loose by the fall. Dane saw the man's head. Blood ran down the side of the face. He was dead. Dane turned him slowly and recoiled in shock at the expression on the face. It was one of sheer horror, as though the eyes, frozen like glass, stared at something unspeakable.

As Dane stood up, a new figure stepped from the trees, a rifle in its hands.

"Mr Dane," said the man. "Not your day, my son."

Dane recognized him at once. Burn Blake, one of the notorious twins. His massive form loomed like the threat of murder, his stock in trade. His face was unduly white, scarred, his lips drawn back in a sneer. If cruelty had a face, this was it.

"You've been busy." Blake's voice was a barely controlled snarl. "Sticking yer nose in where it ain't wanted. Now yer can do me a favor. Chuck that gun away and drag that bastard over to the grave and shove him in." The gun was aimed directly at Dane's chest. Blake wasn't going to miss.

Dane found himself praying for the weird gust of wind that had saved him from the Russian. He felt a breeze stirring, but Blake was a rock, a callous, unmoving chunk of granite.

Dane tossed his gun aside. Slowly he bent down and put his hands under the fallen Russian's armpits.

"The dead can stay dead," said Blake, watching Dane's moves very carefully. "I don't give a toss who Mickey killed for the Russkies. The ones he did for us, well, it'd be embarrassing if they turned up."

Dane heaved the body to the lip of the open grave.

"Toss him in." Blake nodded as Dane complied. The Russian's corpse rolled down into the shadows, crumpled and suddenly diminutive.

"You want me to cover him up?" said Dane.

Blake laughed hoarsely. "Nah. I want yer to get in there with him, you git. Plenty of room. Two fer one. Very handy." He lifted the gun.

For the second time Dane felt the icy grip of imminent death. The air did stir and for a moment Blake scowled at it, but he stood his ground. He meant to go through with the execution.

In the distance a volley of shots disturbed the stillness. There were shouts, more shots.

Blake swore, momentarily turning towards the source of the disturbance.

Dane flung himself to the ground close to where his discarded gun had fallen. His fingers groped about in the grass, finding nothing for a moment. Then he had the gun and rolled with it. He fired instinctively but aimlessly.

Somewhere nearby Blake screamed, body twisted in unbearable agony. He fired into the grass. Dane felt the air close to his face stirred by the passage of the bullet. His shoulder bumped up against another tombstone and he wriggled around it. Blake was firing and swearing, himself taking cover.

The clearing fell silent for a moment. Dane could hear the rasp of his own breath.

"You ain't getting away, you bastard," came Blake's voice. It sounded stretched, working through layers of deep pain. "I've got a dozen of my boys out there, and brother Willy. If he gets you before I do, boy, he'll slice you up before we bury you." His voice choked off in another frightful scream.

Dane wriggled like a snake, making his tortuous way trough the tussocks of grass and another two headstones. There were more shouts, closer now, then gunshots and a shriek. Someone had been hit.

Blake stumbled forward like a boxer on his last legs, apparently determined to finish Dane, his gun firing randomly this way and that. Dane heard the bullets strike stone and earth. He rolled away again, and then risked lifting his head to see the maddened Blake coming at him from no more than a few yards away. Blood was pouring from his eyes and ears, as if something enormously powerful had *squeezed* his head. Dane took aim and fired.

Blake's body stiffened as if it had run into a solid mass—it toppled sideways. Dane was up and on him immediately. Blake was alive, sprawled on the grass, fingers groping for the fallen gun. Dane stamped down on its barrel, pinning it. He aimed his gun at Blake's head.

"Don't do it," said another man, coming into the clearing. It was Miller. The two men beside him had dogs on leashes, eager to be set free.

Dane put up his gun. "He's all yours." He stepped back, chest heaving, his body soaked with sweat.

Blake's face had gone gray. Those blood-filled eyes fixed on Miller, leaking hatred. He tried to speak but blood frothed at his mouth. Dane's bullet had hit him under the rib cage. Life was eking out of him fast.

"Willy will kill you for this." Blake's words choked off as he spat blood.

Miller shook his head. "Willy's finished. Same goes for the rest of your thugs back there in the trees." He turned to Dane. "Nice trap," he said. "I won't ask you how you nailed them."

Dane frowned. He decided not to correct Miller.

"You took a risk."

"I wasn't expecting the Russian," said Dane. He was pretty sure that Miller had been. It wasn't a comforting thought.

Several men, Miller's team, crowded in and Miller nodded to them. No one spoke. They simply dragged Blake to the edge of the grave. He was dead by the time they rolled him over and let him drop on top of Kravyenko. Someone got hold of a shovel and started re-filling the grave.

Dane found the discarded map and handed it over to Miller. "You'll want this."

Miller slipped it into a pocket.

Around them the air began to swirl, cuffing them lightly. Miller pulled his collar up, walking back towards the road.

Dane saw the faces in the trees, watching him, nodding like old friends. Stubbs and his mate, Ronnie, the tattooists, and there were others. Then the wind gusted, breaking them up and absorbing them. Their work was done.

Dane followed Miller. So was his.

# APOLOGIES TO A MANDRAKE

## Scott J. Couturier

*The mandrake shrieks, ripped from earth:*
*a violent & an abortive birth.*
*Child of loaming, cease your moaning—*
*your shrill suffering is not worth*
*more than my fearsome, foul charms.*
*A darkling spell I must enact,*
*hewing your excresence & diluting the essence*
*to fulfill a long-forged daemonic pact.*
*You will endure the bite of black-onyx blade,*
*& my enemy shall taste my wrath:*
*In a primordial tomb she wallows in gloom,*
*bones her meal & ichor her bath.*
*I shall craft a true-killing invultuation,*
*an effigy of clay & crimson hair:*
*Your brew will provide the fell poison descried*
*in auguries writ in innards of were.*
*So shriek not, infant thing, as I dice your flesh,*
*nor hold me in horrid contempt:*
*For my just end must condone each sordid bend*
*of sorcery my late self has up-dreamt.*
*The venom strained from your tumorous self*
*shall lave the effigy in toiling froth:*
*Though you perish, in this arcane butchering cherish*
*She knowing vicarious your death-pangs wroth.*

# Return to Sender: Armstrong-9
## Samson Stormcrow Hayes

When NASA first sent the deep space probe Armstrong-9 out of Earth's orbit, the only thing they expected it to return was data. But less than two years after it launched, hardly enough time to visit the asteroid belt, it did return. Of course, by then NASA had long since lost communication with the probe and though they still made daily attempts to regain its transmission, these were mere formalities to justify the multi-million dollar project.

Satellites first picked up the probe as it headed home, but then it again mysteriously disappeared. One moment it was hurtling toward Earth, the next it was gone. It hadn't burned up on reentry because it wasn't yet within our atmosphere.

Dick Mysyk, a man who lived up to his name, didn't keep up with science or news so he had no idea what the metallic object was sitting in his backyard nor how it got there.

It wasn't sitting in a charred crater, burned and damaged from reentry, but instead it sat upright, its dish pointing skyward and various antennae jutting out in different directions.

Mysyk looked around thinking this must be some sort of practical joke, but no one seemed to be hiding in the bushes snickering with laughter. He owned a lot of land and though he could see the distant lights of his neighbor's home, the field was too dark for anyone to see him. He thought about calling someone, but wondered what he would say. And who should he call? So he decided to investigate it himself.

He walked around the satellite a few times, using his phone's light to look for tracks. It had to get there somehow. It wasn't there that afternoon. But there were no tracks, not even a single footprint in the soft rain-soaked grass. The probe itself was completely silent. Not even the slightest whir of electronics could be heard.

After pacing around a little longer, he decided it was time to get a closer look. He noticed the NASA logo on the main cylinder so he approached and looked for any kind of panel or sticker telling him what to do. When he finally touched it, he felt a spark, like a burst of static electricity shooting through him. For a moment, his eyes glazed over. Then he recovered and tentatively touched it again. This time nothing happened. But by then it was too late.

He puzzled over it for a few more minutes, then went inside. Instead of calling anyone, he went upstairs and took a bath.

His wife, Debbie, arrived home two hours later. She called him several times before seeing their bedroom light on. She went in and noticed the bathroom door ajar. She pushed it open and looked disgusted.

The bathtub was filled to the rim with brown algae. Sticking out of the flat surface was a human torso dressed in one of Dick's shirts. She thought this some cruel practical joke. Then the torso moved. She screamed as it seemed to reach out to her. She fell backwards and then fell calm. She lay on the floor for some time before returning to the bathroom and entering the shower.

It was several days before their daughter called police for a welfare check. Two officers, Nunez and Madigan approached the house. They first noticed a strange smell, but it wasn't the smell of death, more like burnt coffee. They found the door unlocked and entered.

When they failed to check in, dispatch sent another car, but this time the officers didn't go inside. Fearing something had happened, they called for more officers who surrounded the house. Noticing the strange smell and the lack of response, they requested a Hazmat Team. When the Hazmat Team arrived, they immediately sealed off the house. They found the bodies of the police officers. One was sitting in the kitchen sink. The other had his arms in the open top washing machine. They took pictures, samples, documented everything, and then proceeded to bring in delicate instruments that failed to detect anything hazardous.

No one mentioned the giant probe in the backyard, because by then it had disappeared and reappeared in an open field in India where somewhat similar events followed. A day later, it was in South America. Then Japan. Once the water systems were infected the world over, most of the population simply died. Of course, there were a few remote holdouts with their own water supply, but inevitably they were either infected or eventually died off on their own as the air itself soon grew toxic.

It took less than fifty years to terraform the planet. The once bright blue green orb was now darker in hue than Mars. The oceans were covered in brown algae and slowly shrinking as they drank it up. The atmosphere had clouded over so almost no sunlight penetrated the atmosphere. Now that conditions were perfect, the first of Earth's new inhabitants appeared. Their forms emerged from the algae, grotesque bodies that resembled small shuffling mounds. When they first emerged from the algae, they were no larger than a teacup, but in a few years, they grew to the size of a small RV. Around the circumference of their bodies were large droopy receptors that acted as eyes, though they weren't eyes as we know them. They had three long trunks that could operate as a nose, mouth and hands.

But these were not Earth's new rulers, merely the custodians of what was to come. The true colonizers of the world arrived later. It had taken 54 million years, but now they had spread to hundreds of planets. Soon, they would rule the galaxy, letting nothing get in their way. Least of all a backward race of half-apes that sent out invitations to be invaded.

✗

# THE CHURCHYARD AT ERRIGAL TRUAGH
## Paul StJohn Mackintosh

*There stood a church in Monaghan*
*At Errigal Truagh*
*Whose graveyard spirit lured to death*
*None but the young and fair.*

*The last to leave a funeral*
*Would be called and delayed,*
*If a young girl, by a fine man,*
*And if a man, a maid.*

*Sweet consolation turned their head*
*From grief to wild bliss;*
*Their parting vow to soon return*
*Was sealed with a kiss.*

*Then clouded recollection cleared*
*Once past the churchyard gate*
*And they remembered the old tale*
*And realized their fate.*

*Once home, they took straight to their bed*
*And wasted fast away,*
*And the beguiled would lie dead*
*In one month to the day*

*When they were carried on their bier*
*To keep their promised tryst*
*And sleep for evermore beneath*
*The ground where they had kissed*

# BUTTERFLIES AND MOONBEAMS

## Kenneth Bykerk

### A Tale of the Bajazid

He eyed the waitress scurrying back and forth behind the counter with lazy intent. She was way past her last prime by at least twenty years but that didn't matter all that much to him. He was at least thirty years past his last best day. He wasn't getting no prime tail these days anyways, not even paying unless he went back to Nevada and dropped more money than he wanted but he liked his money more than he did vacant-eyed whores and the trumpery of brothels. He was more than fine with lot lizards behind dumpsters. He wasn't a wine and dine type of man, never was, and no one ever cared about lot lizards anyway. They were always around if he needed one and he wasn't going back to Nevada. No, he had other plans. He had been called.

"Here ya go, hon. Need more coffee?"

A plate with two eggs over easy, hash browned potatoes, sausage links, bacon and toast appeared before him. He nodded his assent for the coffee and stubbed his cigarette out. As she refilled his cup, he assessed her form openly. Not bad for a woman her age, he thought. Enough of a waist to grab but not enough to get in the way.

"Anything else?"

She knew she was being watched, he could tell. She stood not knowing whether to present herself for flattery not offered in ever so long or cover herself to avoid his openly sexual appraisal. He enjoyed this uncertainty he posed her and stretched it a few seconds more.

"This is fine. Thank you…" Never knowing when pretense could purchase advantage, he flashed a smile and took time to read her name badge. "Flo."

He dismissed her immediately, not even deigning to acknowledge some of the lines on her face must have once come from smiles. His eggs were hot and he really didn't care about her or the stories her wrinkles told. He played nice where it suited him, where it got him what he wanted and he might want her later. It would be nicer than the usual truck-stop whore in a men's room stall. She probably even had a place she could take him. He saw no ring on her finger which meant she most likely lived alone in a house stinking of too many cats. In the morning, he could ask her if she wanted to go for a ride.

The truck stop was on the outskirts of a little shithole junction called Ash Fork. It was a dying place, a town bypassed by progress. He'd been through Ash Fork many times over the decades, riding with the wind down Route 66, the world wide around him. Ash Fork was always a shithole, a little place for little people living little lives to live. When the I-40 went around the town in 1970, it became an even worse shithole and when a good portion of the town burned in '77, there wasn't much left of the hole to even shit in. Still, people persisted, like lice on a schoolboy's scalp, and the lights in town, fewer every year, still burned. With a modern, new truck-stop some miles safely out of sight of this place no one wanted to acknowledge, he doubted this diner, like himself, had that much time left. The inevitable could only be extended so far before empty shells were all that remained.

He was not a worn-out shell. He had more miles and more time on him than he ever thought he would, but he wasn't an empty husk just yet. He still had a little bit of life in him, enough to get where he wanted and do what he needed. When it was time to lay down and die, and he knew that he would know exactly when that was, then he would stop chasing at skirts. There was the problem though. He was older now, so much so that not even the middle-aged biker hags wanted anything to do with him unless it was lights out and money on the table. It was easier when he was younger. Then he didn't have to resort to so much guile or outright deceit. The time he rented a 4x4 pick-up with a camper shell still sat as a personal embarrassment with him but he had to do what he had to do and it had worked.

When he was younger, before he became a full outcast not just from his former brethren but from motorcycle gangs across the nation, it was easier finding another guy to ride with as well. Reputations develop and when one is unique, when there are identifying characteristics that separate from all others, those reputations do not vanish but form into legend. "If you ride with the Butterfly Man with ghosts in his eyes, you ride with the Devil". It amused him still when other old bikers would recognize the faded patterns on his jacket or his helmet and deflate in front of him. The week before, just prior to leaving Reno, his right to enter the bar of his choice was questioned by some leathered punk sporting colors and patches. He took off his sunglasses and the big, musclebound mountain stepped aside looking as if he'd seen a ghost. Even the toughest of the tough tend to turn timid when certain truths are revealed to them. Some versions of the legend even claimed the Butterfly Man was the Devil. While that always served to amuse him, it made it difficult to find someone to ride with.

Frank Stenoyer was not the Devil nor did he believe in the Devil. Such beliefs, he felt, were simply means to control the weak. What Frank Stenoyer believed in was something far worse than any devil spoken of in any book or from any pulpit and his belief was not based on simple, empty faith. It was his truth, his destiny and his duty. It was his promise, one which could only be broken at the greatest cost. Now here he was, eating greasy eggs in a diner outside of a shithole long past its prime trying to figure out how he was going to honor his commitment this time. He was getting tired and he was getting old and it was getting harder to fulfill his contract.

He had known this devil that was not the Devil his whole life. He was born to it just as he was born to his mother's faith. From his earliest instincts he had known it was there, just as he had known to suckle his mother's breast. This was the boogeyman that scratched at his window in the dark and the monster that hid under his bed. It was the pattern in the moonlight on his bedroom floor that spoke to him in his dreams. It was the bringer of terrors at night and the source of the anger that seethed beneath his surface. It was the voice that told him to push his brother and the one that whispered the excuse that he had slipped. He even had a name for it, one culled from childhood attempts at articulating the unpronounceable. He called it Guqon and unlike his mother's faith, this was something he could not shake off.

Frank Stenoyer was born to the poverty of a prospector in 1910 and raised in a back-water once called Jasper, hidden in a valley on the south-western slope of the Bradshaws. Jasper does not appear on any map nor do even aficionados of western ghost towns know the few ruins that remain once had a name of their own. On those maps that do detail this blind spot in the central Arizona mountains, references are made only to the Bajazid, the beck that carves the valley and rarely, a mention of the mining town east and upstream whose own ruins slip the attentions of the outside world. Baird's Holler grants its name by default to all the empty habitations that mark the valley. The small community of only about a dozen families was four miles and a couple hundred feet in elevation below the old town in a chaparral forest. His days free from the old Widow White's classroom were spent ruling over the other children in the valley as bully and tyrant until he had grown big enough for his father to give him a shovel and tell him where to dig. When the nation sank down on its knees after specula-tion proved fatal, Jasper withered in the collapse of fortunes and by 1936, there were less than a dozen people, all recluses, remaining among the collapsing shacks. The remnants of the Stenoyer family were not among that number though stones bearing that name were left to be forgot.

Leaving the Bajazid had not been easy. He had tried a couple of times since becoming a man and each time he returned within months at the latest. That the nation was in crisis and jobs were not to be had was the greatest reason. Neither Prescott, Wickenburg or Phoenix, the three cities that distantly triangulated Baird's Holler, held any prospect. At least at home on the creek he could do the hard work of his own prospecting and thus time and again he returned. When the Stenoyer family left the Bajazid in '35, there was not much family left and Frank's route out was different than that of his sister and his mother. He never did see his mother again and his father's stone was split.

In 1938, a Judge gave him a choice and that is how he ended up in the Philippines when war broke out with Imperial Japan. He was among those MacArthur left behind and his years in the islands were brutal and savage. When he was repatriated at the end of the war, he had survived two years playing fox and hound with the Japs, a game where he was the fox and every creature in the jungle hunted him. He had survived hunger and deprivation. He knew what it was to eat forbidden flesh and worms from the earth to survive. He knew dysentery and malaria and the sound one makes when their last breath is a surprise. He knew death in the night and he learned the power of terror. He knew capture and internment and torture and starvation and when he made it back to the States, he knew he didn't belong.

There was no life for him when he came home. He had no family, none who would acknowledge him. The skills he had picked up and honed his years mining along with those acquired during his service were for naught. At every turn were men with those very skills who lacked the volatile and volcanic personality that Frank possessed. In very short time he had gravitated to the roughest elements; disaffected veterans such as himself who had seen too much and done too much to countenance a return to general society. The skills he had learned in the islands, of how to forage and how to procure what he wanted through force and through guile served him where trade and craft failed. He became a man outside the law.

His post-war recovery and convalescence was in San Diego; he had returned from overseas a skeleton of a man. Six months in a government hospital and he was out on his own with a little back pay in his pocket which he used to purchase a '46 Harley Davidson Knucklehead new off the lot. He did not even make an attempt to re-integrate into a society he was never a part of. Having lived most his life without the comfort of electricity or plumbing followed by his years in hell, this new modern world and the freedom he found on the back of his bike was exhilarating. The one thing that held him back was lack of resources. When San Diego became too hot, he and another disaffected soul from his old unit saw the California coastline financed by a wave of burglaries, strong-arm robberies and narcotics distribution.

In the spring of '47, after a service station robbery outside of Bakersfield turned into a triple murder, Stenoyer and his friend headed south. After a quick stop in San Diego to coordinate distribution information, they took Route 90 along the southern border into Arizona with cocaine in their side-bags. Out of caution, they stayed on their best behavior from Yuma to Phoenix. This lasted the better part of two weeks. They sought out others of their select sub-culture, men who don't fit carving out their own world without concern for the plastic fantasy around them. One morning, bored and with nothing to do, Benzedrine and cocaine came to their rescue and they robbed fifteen service stations and neighborhood markets across the many towns that surrounded the small city of Phoenix. The end of their spree found them fleeing the tiny farming community of Surprise, heading up Route 89 fast as they could. At Frank's lead, they turned down a dirt road and then another until they were riding slow on old wagon trails and through dry washes. His partner was confounded by these turns and this trip into the desert wild as the sun sank low but Frank knew where he was going. He was going home.

"I'll tell them to kiss my grits! How you doin' hon? Can I get you some more coffee?"

Frank looked up. He had been ruminating in his hash browned potatoes. "Huh? Yeah, sure. Thanks."

"Here you go, sweetie." She had come to grips with his gaze. If there was to be such, she propped herself against the ice machine behind the counter and waited for its return. "You know, I always hated that show. As long as I can remember, people been telling me to kiss my grits. It don't help that I wear pink and people tell me I look somewhat like her."

Frank honestly didn't know what she was talking about. He just nodded and put a forkful of potatoes in his mouth.

"So you just passing through? Ha-ha! Of course you are. Ain't nobody passing to stay, least of all here. Where you heading off to?"

With a swallow, Frank, realizing now might be time to stake his claim, mumbled, "Baird's Holler."

"What's that? Bears Hollow?"

"Baird's Holler."

"Baird's Holler. Never heard of it. Where is it? In Arizona?"

"Yeah, it's a little town south of here. Ghost town."

"Why are you going to a ghost town?"

"It's where I'm from."

"Oh, you're from a ghost town? Wow! That must have been exciting."

"It really wasn't, unless you don't like flush toilets and electricity."

"Why are you going back? Got family still there? Do people still live in ghost towns?"

"Some do, not here though and yes, I do got people there."

"Oh."

"I'm going to place flowers on my parent's grave. I do it whenever I'm in Arizona." This was a lie. He had no idea where his mother was buried. He did know where his father was but he had never in all those years placed a single flower on that broken stone. The most he ever left there was urine, but Flo didn't need to know that. She only needed to think he was a sentimental old man.

"Well, that is really sweet! How far is this Baird's Holler?"

"South of Prescott some miles. North of the desert. You know where Crown King is?"

"I've passed the turnoff on the Black Canyon."

"Baird's Holler is on the other side of those mountains. It's really beautiful back there. Would you like to come? I could have you back in three, four days, your choice. I wouldn't mind someone riding with me again, if even for a little trip. It would be nice."

Oh, he had her hooked and he could tell. There was a look in her eyes, a pause that she couldn't transcend. Her hand was raised, frozen as her mind fought between reason and excuse. She was saved by a cup waved from down the counter. With a quick pat to his hand and an "I'll be back", she hurried to refill her customers and assess his offer.

A soft wave of relief washed over Frank Stenoyer. He had been starting to worry. It was two days ago in Reno that the butterfly landed on his hand. That was the sign, the call of Guqon that he knew he must heed. He left immediately, his hotel room still paid for the month. If he returned, he returned. He just needed to go forthright and he did. That he had no one with him and none he knew to take, he had been getting worried. It had been four years since last the butterflies came and time had isolated him. That Flo paused, that she thought about it so quick on such short notice heartened him. He might not have to kidnap someone after all. That was hard to do on a bike and jacking a car left his chopper untended for the duration. It also left a trail with which to be caught. A willing yet unwitting sacrifice was always easiest.

Jimmy had been willing. He rode there of his own accord. Yes, he followed Frank but they rode together and they were seeking sanctuary. After their spree hopped on jets and their flight through the desert, they began rising higher and higher until they came upon an old road widened to accommodate commercial trucks but years unused. Frank explained that higher up the mountain was an old mine that closed down in '29 and that is who made the road. The old road, or what remained, was but a decrepit wagon trail. That was proven true as they turned from the mine road to follow such a trail downstream a short way until they came at last to the memory of Jasper. When Frank stressed to Jimmy that there was no way any authority was coming up here, that this forgotten place was theirs where they could disappear at any time to let things cool off, Jimmy pulled a bottle of whiskey he'd taken in the last robbery from his bag in approval.

The moon was up full and early that night, cresting the mountain in the east as the sun sank to the depths of the west in the hour after their arrival. The butterfly landed on the bottle as Frank raised it in the moonlight. It was an unusual occurrence, a butterfly at night, and together they marveled in drunken wonder at it. It was the size of a monarch with large, broad wings patterned in black and white. At full spread, the display took on the aspect of a ghostly scream. The impulses of the deranged are never to be questioned when amphetamines madden the mix. At a joke on not bringing food along, Frank popped the butterfly whole into his mouth and declared through fluttering teeth that the problem was solved.

It was a spectacle singular and exhilarating. Jimmy had laughed and claimed now there was none for him but Frank deferred. He felt it. He felt that old, familiar presence he had known since he suckled at his mother's breast. It filled him and thrilled him and his voice was laced with cold certainty and hunger. At the invocation of more, the air filled with the silent wings of thousands of such butterflies as they swirled and fluttered in the dappled moonbeams that pierced the oaks above. Jimmy was rightly startled, first with awe and wonder at the rise from Frank's command, but as the butterflies began to land on him in increasing numbers, worry and fear took hold. As Jimmy screamed in desperation, the butterflies gathered thicker and thicker about him.

When Frank woke the next morning, he felt stronger and healthier than he had since his days chasing snitches and cowards through these hills as a kid. He felt fantastic. He started to call out for Jimmy but caught his voice. There was no need. He remembered the feast the night before, the beautiful glory of what had transpired. He had danced in the moonlight as the butterflies swarmed and fed, his friend's transition taking several agonizing hours. With each bite the butterflies took, Frank had experienced a short, miniscule burst of pleasure. When Jimmy's soul surrendered at last, Frank collapsed in ecstatic release. He felt no loss at his friend's consumption, no low emotion at all. With dispassionate mien, he picked through his friend's clothes for drugs or cash he could use. Of the body, there were only bones picked clean to be tossed aside.

"Hey there, how serious were you about that offer of yours?" With hands adept at the maneuver, Flo made the empty plates disappear from in front of Frank.

"Dead serious. I miss having a woman behind me."

"I'll tell you what, you tell me your name and I'll go talk to Lemuel over there, he's my boss, about getting someone to cover my shifts and you're on."

"Frank, Frank Stenoyer."

"Pleased to meet you, Frank. Flo Lipinski. I'll be back in a bit." With a quick refresh of coffee, she was off.

With a half-hearted snort of amusement, Frank wondered if his charm was back or if she was just so desperate living in this shithole that she'd run off with any old geezer on a Harley who gave her the time of day. It mattered not. He had his prize. That she wanted to go was all that was needed. She would find a way, of that he was certain. Then all he would need to do is pretend for a day or two as they made their way to Baird's Holler that he gave a damn for what she said. As soon as they made it to Jasper, she was Guqon's and Guqon would reward him as it always did. He needed that. Ever since Jimmy, that singular sensation produced was his own desperation. He was surprised, as he sat there at that counter hunched over his coffee with a cigarette between his fingers that he had, at his age, an unannounced erection.

Jimmy was the first. That moment was revelatory. It opened Frank to that voice he had always hid from, that temptation in the darkness that called to him through his fear. In the depths of his soul, he heard that call and understood. He was free to leave, free to travel the world and live to his carnal extent as long as he returned when summoned. This place was his haven, protected but in return, offerings must be made. Frank accepted eagerly and made good always on his promise. After the third visit in the six months following Jimmy and with the pleasure promised so great, he tried to crowd his reward and brought up unbidden a man he tricked into following him. The butterflies did not come and Frank was forced to smash the man's head in on his own. There was no pleasure beyond what he took with the brick in hand, no release fed to him in little bites that pinched off equal parts flesh and soul. Guqon admonished his greed.

For forty years, Frank Stenoyer, the Butterfly Man, roamed the highways and then interstates of the United States. As time passed, he took on an affect uniquely singular amongst the growing culture of outlaw bikers. Upon his black motorcycle and his black jacket and the helmet he wore, white marks, stripes and patterns, had been painted. The work was crude at first, then touched up professionally at cost to resemble the patterns on a curious butterfly he produced for the artist to follow. Centered on the back of his jacket amidst those swirls and stripes was an abstraction that reminded of a ghostly howl. That spectral visage, after years, repeated itself elsewhere as well. The irises of his eyes faded slowly from the deep dark brown they were to a cold, midnight black and over them, like a glaucoma patina, milky white spectral faces appeared over those chill orbs.

Over the years, stories grew of the Butterfly Man with the ghosts in his eyes, told and retold at truck-stops and clubhouses across the nation. He was a hard man, without loyalty to any. He was a freelancer amongst the different outlaw motorcycle clubs, travelling between them at will regardless alliances and animosities. He was seen as both a blessing and a curse to ride with. His viciousness in brawling was sought after and feared, depending on who he was riding with. Money followed him, as did bodies or the absence thereof for some stories told were darker, fairytales for outlaw bikers. People disappeared around him and rumors of a Devil's pact followed. Then came tales stranger such as the eight who went up a mountain and the one who came back down with maddened eyes and stories of demon butterflies. Soon other such tales appeared, stories too strange to be countenanced by anyone of rational mind. Still, even those who did not add foolish credence to such tales avoided the Butterfly Man. The unembellished tales were bad enough.

The stories were true and more so than any telling. When called, when a butterfly would find him somewhere in the land, he would return to Arizona, return to that dilapidated cabin that was his childhood home. When called, he always brought someone with him. Sometimes other bikers, sometimes a woman who thought she had her man and sometimes they were bound and brought in the trunks of their own cars. They all disappeared to the kiss of countless butterflies but those few who escaped with their souls flensed, their minds scathed and stories beyond belief. When the butterflies could not reach him, when they were barred access, they fluttered at the windows and let their shadows dance in the moonbeams that fell on his floor as he suffered their absence, his failure to respond. His illness was not a manifestation of his psychological repressions or any of that other bullshit the shrink at Folsom tried to feed him. It was Guqon but this he could not confess. His release was unexpected with considerations to his collapsing physical health and unusual errors discovered in his initial arrest. The ossuary beneath his father's cabin expanded and the butterflies gave him back his health.

"Here's your ticket. I'm off at ten. All I need to do is go home really quick, change and tear open a big bag of food for my kitties and I'll be ready to go. Or, or you can stay at my place tonight and we can get going bright and early and refreshed, if you know what I mean. Lem…that's Lemuel, we call him Lem for short 'cause it doesn't sound right screaming Lemuel across a kitchen. Lem is being an asshole. I told him…here, let me fill that for you… I told him I have not taken a day off in three years, not even vacation owed me. He called me a lying bitch and I called him a fucking jackass, pardon my French, and that's where we are now. He thinks he can stop me and I think he can go to hell. What do you think."

"Thanks for the coffee. As for Lem, fuck him. Do what you want to do. Looks like he owes you."

"Damn right! I cover for everyone who calls in, always! I'll be right back. I'm going to go remind him of that right now. Lem! Lem!"

She disappeared into the indistinct noise of the kitchen, her voice adding to the din. Frank shook his head. She was a talkative one. At least it will be satisfying to see her go. Oh, the things he had to suffer for Guqon.

As the name crossed his mind, he looked up and out the window behind him. There was his bike, visible from his seat at the counter, the black and white stripes children would mistake for a zebra unique in the lot. Above his bike, a small flight of fluttering shadows gathered in the haze of the incandescent-neon war. They bore a missive, one he had long awaited. He had always known he would know when it was his time to go. He had always known. It was time to stop chasing skirts.

He took out his wallet to pay his ticket. The thought of just riding off crossed his mind but he didn't need highway patrol looking for an old man on a bike, not this night. A ten-dollar bill would cover his tab with a generous tip included. He separated a lone sawbuck from the thick stack in his wallet and put it on the counter. Then, without care of his public setting, took out a small sniffer and did a shot up each nostril. He had a long ride ahead of him.

As that familiar drip started down the back of his throat, he acted on an impulse he could not account the origin of. He opened his wallet and counted out five twenties, more than what he would need for gas, a room in Prescott for the night and a good breakfast in the morning. The rest he didn't need. It was just paper now, its value meaningless. The truth of his debt, the only truth that mattered, was one immune to such meaningless paper. He tried to think of any reason at all against his impulse and several came, all instinctive or learned but when applied to that with no value, they all failed. With another shot up his nose, he got up and walked out of the diner, that pile of meaningless paper on the counter. He had a long ride ahead of him, enough time to shrive the shame of his generosity.

✗

# HEX ON THE BEACH
## Bryce Beattie

I let the enormous bronze knocker fall and clang against the door, sending an echo bouncing around the mansion. While I waited for an answer, I checked my pockets for any brass knuckles, knives, or other weapons I forgot to leave in my motorcycle's saddle bags.

I found none, which was good. I was clean. You never know how a new client is going to react to that sort of thing. Or how well the rich ones are going to check.

A minute or two later, the immense hardwood door opened, revealing a giant of a man staring down at me with a look of total boredom. He must have been just shy of seven feet tall and wore an immaculate black suit.

I craned my neck to look him in the eye. "Yes, I'm here to see Mr. Oppenvelt."

He raised an eyebrow. "And you are?"

"Joshua Goodstone."

The eyebrow stayed up. "Do you have an appointment?"

"No, but-"

"Just a moment." The guard or butler or whatever he was slammed the door in my face.

I wondered what the proper amount of time would be before etiquette allowed me to start kicking the door in a furious rage.

Just as I reached for the bronze ring again, the door swung open.

The tall man said nothing and made no welcoming move. He kept his right hand on the door, with the other held behind his back, just out of my view.

We stood there in painfully uncomfortable silence. Him, just staring at me with his towering stillness and me looking from him to the open doorway and back.

I wasn't sure exactly what he expected me to do and he looked like he might actually have the patience to stand there all day long, so I stepped in.

The giant slipped whatever he had been hiding in his left hand into his pocket. "Very good. Step this way, please, Mr. Goodstone."

He led me into a waiting room, instructed me to stay put, then disappeared.

I sat on a couch upholstered with alligator hide and looked around.

Every conceivable fixture appeared to be made of or at least plated with silver. I had never lived in a house as big as that one room. The whole place vomited opulence to the point a Saudi Prince would judge it over the top.

After far too long of a wait the giant returned, now pushing a withered old man in a wheelchair.

The old man had a woven blanket on his lap, but it was clear he was missing most of one leg. From what could be seen, the remaining leg was twisted and shriveled. The deepest of his visible scars cut from his right ear almost to his nose.

He tilted his head back and squinted. "So who are you?"

"My name is Joshua Goodstone. You probably won't have heard of me. I was sent by the man I know as Gray."

"Goodstone?" The man wrinkled his brow and looked me up and down. "Were you involved in the collapse of the New York chantry about a year ago?"

"I was there, yes, but it wasn't my fault." I gave a meek shrug. "How would you even know about that, anyway?"

"I think it must have been written up in the Caster's Advocate."

"The what?"

"It's a…" He held out his hand. "Never mind. I'll explain another time. I'm Claudius Oppenvelt. I'm pleased to meet you."

I stood, took his hand, and gave it a vigorous shake. "How many tests are you going to make me pass?"

"Excuse me?"

"Your man here-"

"Reginald."

"Your man, Reginald, here, didn't invite me in. He was verifying that I'm not a vampire or other beast that can't cross a threshold without invitation."

Claudius cracked a smile.

"You asked for verifiable information and then shook my hand. You want to make sure I'm bodied and not Fae. They never give a straight answer."

Claudius cocked his head and nodded.

I straightened my back. "And then there's the hidden camera in here. You've been watching me these past ten or fifteen minutes, waiting to see if I pocket some silvery knickknack. You want to know if I can be trusted." It was a gamble, because I hadn't actually seen anything. But, powers of observation always seem most impressive if the observations themselves come in threes. And it seemed like the kind of thing an eccentric millionaire might do.

It paid off, because Claudius laughed. "Fair enough. And why are you here?"

"A man I know as Gray told me you might be in need of help with a…" I tick-tocked my head. "…supernatural problem."

"And who is Gray?"

"He's a…" I clicked my tongue and winked. "Never mind. I'll explain another time. But he occasionally lets me know where my help is needed."

"And how much do you charge?"

"Oh, I never charge, Mr. Oppenvelt. But if you feel compelled to give me a gift when I'm done, or a pillow to rest my head on for a few days, I won't refuse."

"And how do you survive, not charging?"

"People are generous, and my overheads are low." The truth was, most of my daily-use possessions were either with me, on my motorcycle, or in the backpack I left back at the rundown motel.

Claudius nodded and said nothing for almost a minute, then turned and looked up. "Reginald, you are excused, but send in Devia. I'm sure she's close by."

Reginald nodded. "Very good." He turned.

Before the giant had even reached the door, a young woman breezed into the room. She was fit and wore a strange knitted vest with a wispy tail that hung almost to the floor. Her hair was the sickly pale green that sometimes occurs when a blonde dyes her hair black then tries to go back.

"Yes, grandfather?"

"This young man here says he's here to help with our supernatural problem."

Her frown deepened. "Yeah, I heard."

Claudius dropped his voice to what I assume was his you're-in-trouble tone. "Why don't you tell him what our supernatural problem is."

She looked me up and down. "One of Grandfather's books was stolen."

Claudius tapped his fingers on his lap. "What kind of book?"

She clenched her jaw. "Some old grimoire spellbook thing."

The old man narrowed his gaze. "And how did it get stolen?"

Devia threw up her hands. "You know, I'm madder than you are about it. But not just because of the book."

Claudius stared back at her with equal intensity and raised his voice. "How did it get stolen, Devia?"

She whirled on her heels and practically shouted at me. "I was hanging out with that bitch Bridget, only I found out that she was just using me to get close to Grandfather and his stupid collection of magics and she convinced me to let her see the Grimoire of Tossed Souls then she knocked me out and took off with it and now Grandfather doesn't care how I'm feeling about all of this he only cares about the stupid spellbook and-"

"That's enough!" The old man's nostrils flared.

"What? You wanted me to tell him about it." She made a show of folding her arms.

I shuffled two steps back.

"Go to your room."

Her eyebrows peaked into jagged knives. "Excuse me? I am an adult. You can't send me to my room, you old coward."

He stabbed a finger toward the door. "Just get out!"

She spun and stomped away, mumbling obscenities as she went.

"I apologize for her behavior. She is more than a little dramatic." It took Claudius a couple of deep breaths to settle down.

I was unsure if I should say anything about the little family eruption. After a couple of moments' refection, I decided it best to pretend the shouting match didn't happen. I didn't know these people well enough to take a side. "So what can you tell me that might help?"

"The thief's name is Bridget Deshayes. She is a legitimate witch that lives in the area. I've heard she has some skill in…assault magic. I'm afraid I don't know much more than that." He looked toward the empty doorway. "Despite her fury, I'm confident Devia is still holding something back, protecting that thief. Until this, they have been quite close for the last couple of months. You may need to go through her things. And Reginald can get you the code to track her cell phone."

I was not about to do any of that unless I absolutely had to. "Do you have a photo or drawing of the book? And if you don't mind my asking, what exactly does it do?"

"It has an octagonal driftwood carving, called the seal, embedded in the cover. I'll sketch it for you."

\* \* \* \*

A half hour later, I saw myself out. Devia sat on the steps to the driveway near my bike.

She sheepishly stood as I approached. "Look, Joshua is it? I'm sorry about before. My grandfather knows how to push my buttons. And I do want him to get his book back."

"You sure? Your grandfather seems pretty confident you're still helping out this witch."

She shook her head. "He's an idiot. He does not now, nor has he ever understood what I'm feeling or what I want."

"I don't doubt that at all. Is there something you can do to help me track her down?"

"No tracking necessary. I can drop you a pin on your phone. The GPS will take you straight there."

"If you know where she is, why don't you go?"

She took out her phone. "I can't take her. I'm certainly mad enough, but she's a stronger caster than I'll ever be. What's your number?"

I told her, then thanked her for her time. This might not be such a hard job after all.

Her lip quivered and she nodded. She was doing a good job hiding it, but I could tell this was eating her up inside. She turned away and started up the steps.

Just before I started my motorcycle, she looked back over her shoulder. "Oh, and Joshua?"

"Yeah?"

"When you find Bridget…" She took a deep breath. "Kill her."

\* \* \* \*

Bridget's getaway place was an hour and change south of the Oppenvelt's manor house. It was a perfect motorcycle ride: winding, empty roads, long stretches overlooking undeveloped beaches, warm sun overhead, and a cool breeze coming off the ocean.

While driving along one section of highway that led a couple of miles inland, I followed the GPS instructions and pulled onto a dirt road that pointed back toward the ocean. The dirt road ended in a gravel parking lot surrounded by a clump of scruffy trees. Distant patches of ocean were visible through the brush.

I took the only visible path, which led through the trees.

A ramshackle cottage leaned among a nest of boulders. Beyond that a ways was a sharp drop-off, possibly a cliff. After all, the water still looked far away.

Between the cottage and the trees there was a lot of open space. It would be no use trying to sneak up. If the witch was home, then she'd already seen me.

"Hello?" I called out as I climbed around the messy ring of boulders.

The cottage creaked and shifted. The main base was made of thick, roughly squared off logs, probably six or eight inches thick. From where I stood, it appeared to be hovering two feet off the ground.

I hopped down from my rock, squatted, and peered under the hut. The whole thing was supported by two enormous chicken legs the thickness of tree trunks. I almost laughed.

"Hello?" I called again through the open door and peered in.

Most of the front room was visible through the opening. Dried herbs and animal parts hung on strings from a rack on the far wall. Cluttered shelves overflowed with grimy bottles and dusty books. There was no sign of anyone being home. I pulled out the drawing Oppenvelt had made for me of the book's cover. A trident set in an octagon surrounded by a dozen or so cryptic symbols.

All I had to do was go in and find the matching cover. And again, the door was just left open, clearly an invitation. I practically wouldn't even be trespassing.

As soon as I raised my foot and tapped the floor, the hut's legs straightened and house sprang upward.

My eyes widened and I stumbled backward, tripping over a smaller stone. I crashed to my back, somehow managing to not crack my head open.

The hut raised one of its giant, taloned feet and brought it down at me.

Blood pumping, I rolled against a boulder, narrowly dodging the strike.

The hideous leg raised again, intent on killing me.

A pit opened up in my stomach. I scrambled on hands and knees for dear life.

The giant chicken foot crashed down again, sending a spray of dirt and rock through the air.

I managed to get my feet enough under me to leap frog a boulder and landed outside the rocks. If I could make the trees, maybe I could get away clean. That would be a feat indeed, as the hut had much longer legs than I.

I ran a few steps but didn't hear any stomping behind me, so I spared a glance back.

The witch's hut lifted a leg and took two more lazy swipes in my direction, then the whole thing shook and settled back down in the center of the nest.

I bent over and caught my breath. Perhaps this wasn't going to be all that easy, after all. What would it do if I was able to jump through the doorway altogether and land inside?

As if to answer my thought, the hut's door slammed itself closed.

If the witch were home, she certainly would have made herself known by now. Maybe I could come back to the hut later. It would still be there when I wanted to try again.

I dusted myself off and headed toward the cliff edge and the ocean. Down a ways to my right was the top of a haphazard staircase. Directly in front of me were two anchors bolted into the rock and connected by a chain. It was the kind of setup rock climbers use when top roping.

I stepped up and peered over the edge. The view was absolutely breathtaking. The lazy ocean lapped against rocky shores, stretching undeveloped to the horizon in both directions. A cool breeze came off the water and up the cliff. The ocean smelled fresh and inviting, even clear up where I stood. My perch on the cliff had to be almost one hundred feet above the beach.

In a patch of unbroken, rockless sand almost directly below was a circle made around a collection of strange symbols drawn into the sand. A woman stood in the center of the circle with her arms waving in giant swooping motions. And it was hard to tell from this height, but it looked like a book lay on the ground in front of her.

I smiled. That had to be my witch.

From the cliff top, I could see where the incline of the rock face mellowed and curved out toward the sea. The staircase descended along this section, cutting back about halfway down and ending almost exactly below where it began. And really only the top little bit of the staircase looked dangerously steep.

* * * *

The hike down took longer than I imagined. And I did not look forward to the return trip.

I paused as I reached the last few steps.

She hadn't noticed me yet. Or if she had, she didn't let it show. Instead, she sat cross-legged on the sand, her raven hair bouncing and swirling as the ocean wind ran across the sand and up against the cliff. She flipped back and forth now between two pages of a book while cursing up a storm. Something about how the stupid thing didn't work.

Washed up seaweed strung around her made up her casting circle. A big pile of the stuff lay among the rocks beyond.

I was surprised I had made it this far without being detected. Maybe she was just too wrapped up in her angry study.

Many rock tips jutted out of the sand between her circle and me. Some of them were large enough to hide behind, but there was no way I could sneak all the way up on her. That meant I'd have to be more direct and just hope she didn't know any fighting spells or kung-foo or anything. Not knowing exactly what to expect is the worst part.

The instant I set foot on the beach, a ripple shot across the sand. It must have been some kind of magical alarm.

The witch popped up to her feet, allowing the book to flop onto the beach. "Who the hell are you? What are you doing on my beach?"

I raised my open hands about shoulder height and walked a couple of steps. "My name is Joshua. Are you Bridget?"

Her eyes narrowed like she was trying to start me on fire with her glare. "Did old man Oppenvelt send you? I swear, I thought Devia would try to hide her shame for at least a week before running to-" Her face scrunched up. "-Grandpa."

I pointed in front of her. "Is that the grimoire?"

"What makes you think I'm going to give it to you?"

"Hope?" I shrugged. "Maybe your guilty conscience?"

She raised a sharp eyebrow. "Stealing from that hoarder? If Devia hadn't told him it had been taken, that negligent, dried up, wasted shell of a powerless loser wouldn't even have noticed."

"So you're admitting that you stole the book and you attacked Devia?"

Her nostrils flared. "You can't steal something if it doesn't even belong to the victim."

"Are you saying Mr. Oppenvelt acquired it illegally?"

"No—it doesn't matter how he got it." Color flooded her cheeks. "He didn't deserve to keep it."

I shuffled forward. "That's a funny way of looking at things."

"He doesn't deserve it. He hasn't practiced for years. He doesn't even care about true magic anymore. He's a disgrace to the craft and that book was just going to sit, gathering dust on a shelf in a vault until worms crawled their way in and ate it. And I will kill you where you stand if you take another step."

"That's funny, because the last thing Devia said to me was that I should kill you."

"What? That bitchy little drama queen. One little bump on the head and she's out for murder?"

"Well, on the drama queen front isn't that-" I fought the urge to smirk. "-and I have waited my whole life to tell this to a witch—isn't that the cat calling the cauldron black?"

Deep down, she wanted to smile. I know she did. Everybody loves jokes like that. To mask her true feelings, she flipped me the bird. "Ha, ha. I'm done, smartass. Get off my beach."

I was not about to comply, but I still didn't know what she was capable of. I didn't want to run the risk of being lightning-bolted to death while mad dashing for the book.

"I'm leaving without the book. You know, the one you stole?"

"I got news for you, cowboy. You may not be leaving this beach at all, except in tiny shreds in the beaks of scavengers."

She extended arm behind her and snapped her fingers. A length of seaweed flew from the pile to her right hand. She smashed it into a ball then held it out toward me.

I looked toward the waves then back at her. "That was neat, but am I supposed to be frightened by a lump of kelp?"

She made a strange motion with her free hand and the ball was engulfed in a blue-green flame.

"Ok, that's-"

She dropped her right hand, but the flaming plant didn't fall. It hovered for half a second before shooting across the beach and slamming into my chest.

I landed flat on my back with a whomph and slapped wildly at the tiny inferno on the front of my jacket. The flaming ball fell off and continued burning in a pile on the sand.

Her attack was fast, but not that fast, maybe I could rush her between fireballs. I rolled to my knees and looked up.

Just in time to see another flaming ball of seaweed leave her hand.

I flung my body flat against the sand and flopped behind a large rock.

"I don't practice myself, but you're doing the summoning wrong. You're supposed to stand outside the circle so that whatever you summon is bound within."

"Shows what you know. The Grimoire of Tossed Souls has the power to summon Trinor, a greater sea god. And he's so big, he won't fit in the circle. So it's a barrier to keep him out."

"No offense, but it doesn't even look like you exactly need a barrier to keep him away."

"And are you willing to die for a book that might not work? I've been trying to summon with it all day, and do you see any gods here? I'll tell you what." Her voice calmed. "If you walk away now, I'll let you go. Just get up slowly and go."

I peeked over the edge of my temporary stone shield.

Another fireball shot straight for me.

I ducked my head so fast that I hit it on the rock.

The flaming seaweed sizzled in the shallow water behind me.

"Ow!" I rubbed my forehead. "What was that?"

"Oh, I was just kidding. I am going to kill you. And then once I figure out this summoning, I'm going to take my sea god to the Oppenvelt's giant disgusting manor and have him wreck it, just because they sent you."

"You know what? You are totally lame." I swung my weight back into a crouch. "Plus, you have the most clichéd witch hut ever, Baba Yolo."

"Nobody still says yolo, you idiot. And you're lucky you didn't go inside my little cottage, or it would have shaken you out, chased you down, and killed you."

If I was going to rush her, it needed to be soon. She had a lot of seaweed, and I was not going to be able to dodge forever.

Here's the thing. When you are fighting a supernatural beast, there is almost always a shortcut for beating it. A special knife, a particular type of wood, the color blue, saying "please" in German, that kind of stuff.

A witch is just a human, though, so she has the same weaknesses as any other human: money, lust, gluttony, and getting punched in the stomach really hard, that kind of stuff. And no matter how many balls of flaming seaweed they summon and hurtle at me, I still find it difficult to bring myself to hit a woman.

Another fireball crashed into the sand next to me.

But for some reason I suddenly had no qualms with picking up a handful of wet sand and chucking it at her head. So I grabbed the sand and stood.

She was ready with another ball of fiery pain.

I did my best John Woo action movie dive and flung the wet sand.

My conjuring assailant caught a mouthful of grainy beach goodness. Some probably got up her nose, too.

"Boom. Take that, Ursula."

I scrambled up and made a break for her, jumping the seaweed circle. I dove to my knees, ducking below a wild swing, and grabbed the book from the sand.

She took another swipe at me, this time gauging claw marks into the back of my neck. I was only saved from foot-long gashes by my motorcycle jacket. I pushed back to my feet, kicking up a spray of sand behind me.

Sputtering and spitting, she chased after me. "What did you call me?"

The moment she crossed the seaweed circle, a warm gust and a deafening noise erupted from the ocean.

We both stopped in our tracks.

The stiff breeze carried with it the stench of rotting fish. Fifty yards out into the surf, a jet of water shot into the air.

An SUV-sized nightmare rose up from depths and stood upon the water.

Its body appeared to be slopped together from a collection of bizarre sea life parts strapped to a misshapen coral skeleton draped in rotten seaweed. One hand was a huge crab claw and its face was the front half of a colossal anglerfish.

Its hideous mouth stretched wide, brandishing a wealth of sword-like teeth. Its voice shook the sand. "I am Trinor, claimer of sea-tossed souls. I have come for my book."

The shaking intensified and a sandbar rose from the depths, pushing apart the water, extending from the shore to where the monstrosity stood upon the waves.

My eyes widened, and my heart pounded with renewed vigor. I couldn't even stop myself from smiling. This was turning out to be a much better gig than I had thought. I hadn't felt this alive in a long time.

The witch faced her summoned sea god and pointed to me. "I knew it would work! Kill him!"

Trinor gurgled up a disgusting laugh. Its jaw moved, but the chest-rumbling voice seemed to come from all directions. "I am not your slave, little witch. You have no power over me."

I turned and ran for the stairs. I relished the idea of doing battle, but I'd need a solid plan and probably a better weapon than the switchblade in my pocket. And hopefully that thing's powers wouldn't work as well further inland.

"Kill him! He has your grimoire!"

The beast walked toward shore. "I will kill whom I wish. So start running."

She turned tail and raced after me.

I pushed my legs as hard as they could go. Stairs flew by as I booked it for the cliff top.

Bridget was close on my heels in no time. The sea god continued its methodical gait toward the beach.

I hoped that Trinor's girth would make it clumsy for him to take the stairs behind us. I would need every possible second to figure out what to do about the summoned deity. By the time I hit the switchback on the stairs, my legs burned like crazy.

Another couple of steps and two hands pushed on my back. "Move it!"

I sprawled forward, flinging the book as I tried to catch myself. It was no use. I crashed against the rocky stairs. Pain exploded in my knee and chest.

The witch stepped on my legs and back as she climbed over my prostrate body in her furious flight.

It was both painful and painfully embarrassing. I hate it when people walk all over me. I groped out, trying to catch her ankle, but only grabbed a cloud of dust. To add insult to injury, I saw her snatch the dropped book.

There was no time to sulk, though, so I sprang back into ever-so-slightly-limping action and started back up the stairs. I tried to think of something witty to shout at Bridget if I caught her.

As we neared the top, a rumbling crack-whump shook the cliff side. The sea god had jumped and begun to climb, pounding claw and hand-holds into the rock as he went. Its massive form dripped water.

Either my legs stopped complaining, or I figured out how to ignore them. I didn't have time for them to give out. After all, I'd lose the book for good and get all murdered by a monster unless they kept moving.

Bridget added a little distance to her lead. The jerk was probably used to these stairs by now.

I gasped and wheezed on the last, steep section, but cleared the cliff top.

Up ahead, the witch did her best to keep running. She wasn't moving very fast any more, though, and she clutched her side with her free arm.

The cliff-side pounding grew louder. The sea god had to be close to the summit.

Bridget ran for her shack with ever decreasing speed.

I chased her just as fast as I could, which was also not very fast, but step by step I gained on her. Every few yards, I looked back to see if Trinor had finished the climb.

We hadn't made it to the nest of boulders when the sea god pulled itself up over the edge and roared again. The wind picked up, bringing with it hot, moist, and putrid air.

The rotten and moldy fish smell was so bad, it was all I could do to keep from gagging.

I looked back in time to see Trinor tear a small boulder from the ground and hurl it at us.

"Bridget, move!" I reached out and pushed her to the side, then lunged the other way.

She stumbled to her left, and the stone to passed through the space her head would have been. The giant rock bounced on the ground and then broke against a stone from the nest.

The witch finally turned around. Her eyes widened.

Trinor laughed, louder this time. "There is nowhere to run. Give me the book and I will allow you to die quickly."

The fetid sea god took slow, careful steps, like it was savoring the experience.

Bridget opened the book and flipped several pages. "C'mon, where is it…" More pages.

I pointed to the book. "Keep moving. You're not going to have time to work whatever you're looking for in there."

She shot me the stink eye, then returned to her book.

I took two steps away from the slow-stalking deity and motioned for Bridget. "I'm serious, that thing is going to kill us. Come on."

She shook her head. "Screw it." She tossed the book aside and performed a rapid succession of positions with her fingers, then held one hand out.

Three seconds later, a patch of seaweed flew up over the edge. It zipped through the air to her open hands. She magically ignited it and flung it back at the sea god.

The flaming ball of seaweed slammed into Trinor's chest, where it stuck and continued to burn. The behemoth stopped, looked down at the tiny flame for a moment, then continued.

I stepped back twice more. "That's not a good sign."

Her eyes stayed fixed on Trinor. "And what are you doing to stop that thing?"

"Use your shack!"

The witch extended her hand again and twiddled her fingers as if playing a piano. As she worked her magic, a blue mist surrounded her hand.

The hut jumped up and shook, ruffling its thatched roof into a mohawk. Then it bolted for the ocean monstrosity.

Trinor's gait accelerated, the occasional thump-thump of heavy footfalls being replaced by a roar of approaching thunder.

God and cottage charged each other. Papers and cookware crashed round inside the hut, with the occasional piece of something flying out the window.

I watched, enraptured by the impending clash, but kept backing up, in case I still had to make a break for my motorcycle.

The witch's cottage leapt into the air and brought both legs up, bearing the enormous talons at the end of its leathery toes. The hut's midair slashing tore long gashes into the sea god, nearly separating claw arm from torso.

Bridget whooped a little victory shout.

I wasn't quite so confident.

Pieces of draped seaweed reached out for each other and wove the shoulder and chest back together.

Trinor staggered for a moment. "Your deaths will now be painful."

The two clashed again, but with far less momentum. The sea god grabbed and clutched the cottage, shaking it back and forth in the most bizarre sumo match ever.

The behemoth sea beast arched its back. The shack jumped again, taking god and itself into the air. The flight was an unstable and extremely short half flip. The god slammed onto its back and the cottage crashed down on its roof. Wood splintered and broke, spilling books and potion making equipment. The destroyed hut continued to roll until it was back on its feet. Unfortunately, the only part still attached to the legs was the supporting floor. Roof and all but a stick or two of walls had broken off.

A light blue smoke wafted up from the wreckage as enchantment bled from the cottage.

Bridget stood in place, feet frozen to the ground, and body shaking.

Trinor stood and the coral chunks that made up its core shifted around. A deformed and half-decomposed starfish slid out of the god's neck then attached itself to the shoulder.

It occurred to me I should head for the parking lot. I had put a few yards between me and the witch and that might be head start enough. The surrounding trees would give protective cover, and I could easily outrun the sea god once I hopped on my bike.

The witch had stolen the book and attempted to raise a god, thinking somehow that such a summoning ever works out for the summoner. Not to mention the fact that she had attempted to kill me. She was about to get smacked with a giant load of what-goes-around-comes-around.

And right now, I had nothing on the ocean monster. I was slow, weak and squishable. There was absolutely no way I could win the fight. If I could just make it to my bike, I might stand a chance.

It was a long way to the clump of trees and parking lot. I might not even make it that far. I certainly wouldn't make it if I stood around, thinking, like an idiot.

But, if I did run for the parking lot, Bridget would die.

Choices.

Trinor was now right in front of the witch. It raised its arm across its horrid body, preparing to backhand Bridget from this earthly existence.

I sprinted for her.

The sea god swung his arm.

I dove for the tackle.

The deadly claw passed inches above us as we fell to the ground.

I rolled off Bridget's prone body and grabbed the book.

"Fool!" Trinor raised its claw again.

I paused for a heartbeat, then just kept on rolling.

The massive claw pounded a foot into the dirt and rock where I had just been.

Before Trinor could raise its claw for another strike, I was on hand and knees and ready to sprint again.

I clutched the book to my chest and took off directly under the sea god's arm.

Trinor gave an awkward, unprepared kick, but missed.

Bridget screamed something, but the blood pounded in my ears and I couldn't make it out.

My first target was the still-dying demolished shack. A wave pure exhilaration washed over me as I pushed my body to the limit.

The rumble of profoundly heavy footsteps began behind me, slow again at first, but I knew when it got up to speed, the sea god would catch me without problem. Within a few massive steps, it was right behind me. I could even imagine the terrible claw being raised to pound me into the ground.

I hopped over some debris and up onto what was left of the witch's hut.

The floor platform wobbled and made a feeble attempt to throw me off, but it was too weak and too slow. It only raised up after I had jumped off.

Which was fortunate, because that was the moment Trinor tried to step on it. The raised floor was just high enough to impede the monster's step. The cottage didn't provide much in the way of push back, but it was the correct awkwardness, height, and leverage to trip the god outright.

Trinor's hulking frame came crashing down atop the platform, splintering it in two. The ground shook, and I'm pretty sure I heard the sea god's voice, still coming from all directions, curse in the style of a drunken sailor. Trinor wasted no time posturing or intimidating when it stood this time. The colossal beast simply rolled over and was back on its feet.

It had bought me a few precious seconds, and I would make use of every last one.

The chase was furious but destined to be short. Apparently a god can move pretty fast when motivated.

I didn't slow as I approached the cliff edge. I just hoped I remembered the right spot.

The massive footfalls seemed to increase in power as we ran toward the ocean.

My heart pounded and my legs screamed.

Trinor roared its eyeball-shaking roar. Its pungent breath nearly knocked me over.

A few steps from the cliff, I saw gleam of metal. I had aimed my insane retreat correctly. I threw myself down and slid baseball style. Just before my legs went over the edge, I flung the book and grabbed for the climbing anchor chain I had seen before.

Somehow, I was able to catch hold with both hands as my body left the cliff top.

Just above me, Trinor, the claimer of tossed souls, horrendous sea god, and putrid sack of rot, jumped into open space, hand and claw grasping wildly for the book. A stream of putrescent filth-water dripped on me from its disgusting form as it passed overhead.

Book and god fell.

Trinor shattered upon the shore's rocks, releasing a wave of bitter energy and sticky, acrid air.

It burned at my eyes. My stomach dry heaved. It was all I could do to hold on.

The nauseous gust passed, leaving the only one thing between me and a pleasant evening: a hundred foot drop to my death. And maybe a witch, too. I didn't know where she was going to land.

My fingers ached and threatened to let go without my permission. I tried to do a pull-up, but my arms were having none of that. I kicked and slid my feet around until I found a spot where my right toe could dig in.

Bridget's head appeared over the edge of the cliff. "Need a hand?"

I couldn't even grunt a response. I pushed with my shaky leg and pulled with my quivering arms.

Bridget got a hold of my hair, then my jacket, then my armpit, and together somehow we got me back over the edge to safety.

I coughed and gasped and when I could finally speak, I looked her in the eye. "Well, it just suddenly hit me, you know? Stampede."

"What?"

"Don't you watch classic movies?"

"Yes, but again I say, what?"

"Tremors, you know at the end?"

"I'm not certain 'Tremors' is really a classic."

I feebled up a shrug and attempted to stand. "Not every joke lands." Things started to go black and my left knee screamed out in pain.

Bridget touched my arm. "We work pretty well together. And you're pretty cute. In fact, I could really fall for a strong, smart, sexy man like you who isn't afraid to take action or to do what's right in the face of danger and maybe we should just make love right now."

I actually didn't hear any of that last part. I was too busy passing out from exertion and pain. But I'm pretty sure it's what she said.

When I came to, The last sliver of sunlight was sinking into the horizon. I had been dragged further away from the edge and I was covered in a blanket. I groaned and sat up.

Bridget sat behind me on the ground, cross-legged and reading a book. "Oh, good, you're awake. I was afraid I'd have to go get somebody." She closed the book. "I guess killing a god takes it out of you."

My mouth felt gummy as I spoke. "I'm not sure it was the god himself. I think it was just a puppet avatar or something." I really needed a drink.

"Why do you say that?"

"I'm pretty sure a chicken hut can't scratch a real god. Plus, gods are too proud to stink like that."

Bridget chuckled. "So what's the plan now? Are you going to try to kill me again?"

"Try to kill you again?" I frowned. "That would require a first time, wouldn't it?"

"But you said Devia-"

I raised a hand and nodded. "I said she told me to kill you. But, she's not the boss of me, and I'm not a hitman. Besides, you're too..." I shook my head and shrugged.

"Fair enough." She smiled. "I won't kill you either. And as a peace offering, you can have the book."

I twisted and looked over where she pointed. The spellbook had been retrieved and lay a couple of feet away. A crack split the fancy wooden seal in the cover.

"What? Is broken or something?"

"That asshole Trinor tried to kill me, so I'm done with it. It's too dangerous for me." She gave me a witchy wink. "Plus, the fact that it doesn't work anymore does make it easier to give up. And I did try."

My body creaked as I stood. "How did you get here anyway? Do you have a car somewhere?"

"Naw, I hitchhiked."

"Of course you did." I pointed a thumb over my shoulder. "Well, can you drive a motorcycle? I think I broke a couple of fingers on that chain and I'm not sure I can work the clutch."

* * * *

The next morning, Devia pulled open the massive front door before I could even knock. "Did you kill her?"

I rolled my eyes. "I've never really done the whole murder thing, kid."

She furrowed her brow and slugged my arm. "I told you to kill her."

"Well, her little beach cottage is splinters now. Does that count for something?"

Devia rocked her head side to side. "I guess. Come on in. Looks like you got the book back."

The Oppenvelt mansion seemed even bigger the second time around. And it showcased more art than any museum I had ever been to. Devia led me into the same sitting room I had used before.

"I'll tell grandfather you're here."

A few minutes later Reginald wheeled in the aged collector.

I stood, looked at Claudius, and nodded. "Mr. Oppenvelt." Then I looked up at the giant of a man pushing the wheelchair. "What's up, Lurch?"

Reginald grunted.

Oppenvelt smiled. "How did it go? Devia isn't really talking to me, but she looked pretty excited."

I handed the broken book to him, and waited for the certain scolding.

He stared at the cover, rubbed his fingers over it, then stared at it some more. "How did you break this?"

I looked around, but there was no one for me to heap the blame upon. I'd just have to take my licks. "It may have been dropped once or twice-"

"That can't be it." The old man stabbed a crooked finger at the cover. "I've tried to destroy this a dozen times, in a dozen ways, with nothing so much a scratch."

"Okay, I may have thrown it off a cliff. And then the avatar of the sea god Trinor fell on it. I'm actually surprised there's any of it left at all to bring back."

Claudius chuckled. "You don't do things half way, do you?"

"Where would be the fun in that?"

✗

# THE SPECTRAL KNIGHT
## K.A. Opperman

He stood upon a rotting bridge
All vague with ghostly fog,
Where never hummed the swarming midge,
And never sang the frog.

Just where this was I do not know—
But through the woodland wide
I'd wandered long through autumn's woe,
With silence at my side.

The spectral knight said none shall pass—
He spoke with rasping breath
That I should go and love my lass
Instead of courting death.

But I was mad with black despair,
And swiftly drew my sword
To slay the knight that waited there
The somber bridge to ward.

I stepped upon the haunted planks—
But oh, the icy chill
That rose from off the riverbanks,
And seemed my heart to still!

My limbs grew numb and slumberous,
And barely would obey;
My weapon seemed so ponderous
Amid the dreadful fray.

And soon I knelt in sore defeat,
A sword-point to my heart—
And yet the knight did not complete
The victor's wonted part.

He bid me go and love my lass,
And savor living breath,
For soon, too soon, he'd let me pass
Into the land of death.

# FERAL

## Joe Arcara

His back hurt. Hurt to distraction. He shifted against the couch, trying for relief from the burning and itching. He tried concentrating on the television monitor. It filled the wall, but his mind returned to the scratches that hadn't yet scabbed over. Deep wounds newly placed on a back covered with scars.

Lisa cuddled next to him, stroking his arm, touching his face, concern for him plain in those emerald eyes. "Does it hurt bad, Sam?"

He shifted his shoulders, grimaced. "No more than usual, I suppose."

"Oh, baby, I'm so sorry. I'll put more lotion on your back later. It seems to help, right?"

Sam frowned. "It helps some, yes, but it hurts like hell. Do me a favor, Lisa, and get the cognac I left on the bar. I can't get up right now."

"Sure, Sam, I'll get it. You rest." She gazed at him, those amazing eyes finding his. "You know I love you completely, don't you, Sam?"

He sighed, nodded. "Yeah, I know."

She smiled, relieved, and stood. She had the body of an athlete, sinewy muscle over soft curves. She turned, facing the bar, crouched, her muscles bunching, and leaped across the room, grabbed the snifter quicker than he could see, and leapt back, all in the space of a heartbeat. She was genetically enhanced.

She gave the glass to him, stroked his cheek. Kissed it. "Would you like to lie down and rest, or shall we watch the evening news, depressing though it may be." She smiled, leaned over him and gently licked his ear. He braced himself, forced himself not to cringe away from her touch.

"I'm not tired, just uncomfortable. Let's watch the news." He turned away from her. "Morty, turn on Action News."

"Turning on Action News" a robotic voice confirmed. The wall filled with a silver haired man, resplendent in a tailored suit sitting behind an oval mahogany desk.

"Curt Calloway here. Now, the news. Feral packs roaming the streets are instilling panic in residents. Enhanced miners are striking in West Virginia, and in Somalia, a Lion brigade, led by Tiger special forces, are encountering heavy resistance. Martha Collins is in the downtown area where feral packs are still marauding. Martha?" A golden-haired reporter dominated the screen. Lisa waved a hand, and the sound went mute.

"I hate hearing about the ferals. It scares me, Sam." She leaned into him, causing his cuts to burn. He allowed her touch.

"If it weren't for you, that might be me. On the streets, homeless, hungry. Angry. Running with a pride. I'm so lucky to have you, Sam."

He closed his eyes, choosing his words. Lisa had been his live in for two years, and until six months ago, life had been perfect. Soon, she had began to change. More aggressive. More assertive. Their lovemaking had gone from tender to violent. During sex she clawed and bit, screamed like the wild thing he feared she was becoming. More cat than human. He was becoming afraid of her. "You know I love you, Lisa." She smiled, moved closer to him. "But sweetie, I'm only human. You must be more careful with me in the bedroom. You're hurting me."

She peered up at him, tears streaming down her cheeks. "Oh, Sam, I'm so very sorry. I don't know what comes over me. I love you so much, and when we're together, I get so excited! I can't seem to control myself! Sam, I'm so sorry. I would never hurt you on purpose. Please believe me."

He sighed, put his arm around her shoulder, grunting from the effort, and squeezed her to him. "I know, Lisa, but this can't go on. You must be more gentle, okay?"

She stared up at him, nodding, miserable. "I swear, Sam. From now on, I'll be better. I'll be perfect."

He smiled at her, but she had made the same promise many times. He kept his hand resting on his thigh, tried to look relaxed. He wasn't. He feared for his safety. "Okay, Honey, I believe you." He waved his hand, and the volume resumed on the television.

"Thank you, Martha, for that startling report." The newscaster's voice quavered, genuinely concerned. "Now, a word from our sponsor and benefactor, Geo Splice."

* * * *

The commercial began with classical music. A variety of working men and women came on screen. Soldiers, policemen, actors, miners, beautiful men and women. All appeared human. All were enhanced with the genes of animals. Bulls, lions, tigers, bears, dogs and cats were used to increase strength, stamina, even sexual libido. A voice over began. A famous actor, fatherly, respected, enhanced, spoke along with the pictures.

"Geo Splice. Making the impossible possible for forty years. Making humans better, stronger, faster, all for the betterment of mankind. From embryo to birth, Geo Splice is there for all of us." A crescendo of music, followed a fade out.

She whispered, almost to herself, "Mankind's slaves." He pretended he did not hear her, but his heart beat faster, a pounding fear against his chest.

"I really am puked out, Lisa. I think I'll turn in." Her green eyes stared at him. She inhaled sharply, testing the air, like she smelled his lie. Finally, she smiled. "Sure, Baby. You go rest. I'll be right in to rub your back with the lotion." She caressed his cheek. Kissed it, her lips soft and gentle.

He awoke six hours later. Her side of the bed was empty. His hand searched. The sheets were cool. He searched the apartment. Checked the balcony. It rose one story from the street. Lisa was gone.

Sam sat on the couch, closed his eyes, relieved. The pain in his back had lessened, and he considered his options.

Lisa had worked as a receptionist when they had met. She was everything he ever wanted in a woman. The gene splicing, so common now, didn't really matter to him. Ten percent of the human population was enhanced, and natural borns like himself had stopped caring much. Enhancers were human. Just, well, different. What to do about Lisa? She was stronger than him. Faster. Much more athletic. She could kill him if she chose, and if her aggression continued, she might.

The only option was to make her leave. He really didn't want that. He still loved the girl he'd first met. His eyes grew heavy. Where the hell was she? He slept.

He awoke to the balcony door sliding open. Lisa stood by it, early morning light a backdrop for her ripped clothing, disheveled hair, and smell. She stank. She stared at him. Her appearance did not seem to bother her. "What's it like, Sam, to have parents? To be human?"

"Lisa, you are human."

She waved a hand at him. "No, not like you. Humans created me. Born in a test tube. Raised like cattle in a laboratory. Not human. No, not quite."

Sam leaned back into the couch. Her state of mind frightened him. "Lisa, what's wrong, Honey. Tell me what's wrong."

She shook her head, sniffed the air. Lifted an arm and sniffed herself. "I stink. I need to shower. But first…" With a speed not human, she ran to where he sat, crouched over him, her eyes bright and cool. "I went out last night, Sam, but you knew, didn't you? I met people. People just like me. And Sam, I had a real good time." She leaned down and bit his shoulder, drawing blood.

He gasped, from the pain and from her stink. She released him. Her lips dripped red. His blood. She smiled at him. Her eyes did not soften. "Things will change, Sam. You're not in charge, anymore. I'm better than you. We're better than all of you. I'm going out again tonight. When I come back, be ready." She grabbed his crotch and squeezed. He cried out, the pain all consuming. The world dimmed. He almost fainted from agony. She released him. "Tomorrow, I'll do whatever I want to you." She smiled again, turned, went into the bathroom.

He reached over, his stomach cramping, the pain lessening, but still so bad he staggered to the kitchen sink and vomited. He stayed bent over, his breathing ragged, tears welling in his eyes, listening to the shower running.

The bathroom door opened, and she entered the bedroom and shut the door. She was singing softly to herself.

Sam would not go near the bedroom though his clothes were there. He was trapped in his own home with someone who once loved him. He cleaned the sink, splashed his face with running water. He stared at his hands. They were shaking. He limped into the living room, removed a blanket from the ottoman, and lay on the couch, trembling. He fell into frightened sleep.

He slept through the day into dusk. He awoke stiff, achy and hungry. The bedroom door was open. Lisa was gone again. Sam reached for his phone. If he didn't get help, he did not think he would survive the night.

The Police could not help. Packs of ferals were rampaging through the city. They would try to send someone but did not know when. The streets weren't safe. Was there some place in the building he could barricade himself? No. Hiding wouldn't work. She would smell him.

He went to the balcony door and peered down at the street below. A group of men and women ran past, so fast they were almost a blur. Ferals. He wondered if Lisa was out there with a pack or pride. He decided she must be.

It was almost sunrise when she returned. Again, she leapt from the street below onto the balcony. The door slid open. She entered slowly, sniffing the air. Like last night she was dirty and stank. This time, there was blood on her hands and mouth. She licked her lips and smiled. "Sam! Get out here! And what's that stench? What are you up to?" Her voice was loud, confident, self-satisfied.

Sam entered the living room. He had never been so afraid of anyone. He forced himself to make eye contact with her. "This is my home, Lisa. I don't want you here. I want you to leave. Now."

She laughed, her look disbelieving, but amused. "I told you, Sam, things are different now. I decided to not hurt you too much. I was just going to fuck you senseless and let you heal until the next time. Now, I'm angry. Take off your clothes and get in the bedroom, Sam. We'll see how well you can beg for forgiveness. And hell, what's that horrid smell? It's disgusting!"

"I suppose, that would be me." A young woman stepped from the kitchen. Tall, broad shouldered, her stomach flat, her gait calm and sure.

"A dog?" Lisa screamed. "You brought a fucking dog into my house?"

"Not your house, Lisa. My house. Meet Roberta, from the Pinkerton detective agency."

Roberta smiled at Lisa, who stood stunned, her mouth open. "I'll bet she told you she had pedigree genes, didn't she?"

"Yes. Persian."

"Persian, Siamese, Maine Coon, they're all good. She's not any of those. She's a Tabby, and the reason she turned. Geo Splice won't use tabby anymore. They turn feral. All those packs running amok on the streets are ferals."

"Fuck you, bitch! I'll rip your heart out!"

Roberta's smile broadened. Given the circumstances, Sam found it odd how his heart beat faster at how attractive Roberta was. "I'm sure you would try, but my genes are pit bull, and I am trained in all lethal and non-lethal forms of combat. If you attack me, I will kill you. Now, the owner of this home has asked you to leave. Please do so."

Lisa appeared stricken. "Sam, please, I…."

"I want you to leave, Lisa. Don't come back."

Lisa crouched, snarled. Roberta ran towards her, a blur of motion. Lisa screeched, turned and ran onto the balcony, leaping off it and onto the street. She stared up at them, snarled, and ran down the street, towards a group of ferals.

Roberta turned to Sam and smiled. "Tomorrow we'll have a crew come in to make your home cat proof. We'll make sure you're well protected."

Sam shook his head, still frightened at what almost befell him. "But, what about tonight? Once you leave, she might come back!"

"Well, I suppose I may have to just stay with you until morning." She grasped his hand and smiled, her eyes large, soft brown and welcoming.

"Yes, it would be nice if you stayed."

"Well,' she said, moving closer to him. "You know what they say."

He shook his head, puzzled. "No, what do they say?"

Her smile broadened. "Man's best friend."

# SIGYN HANTA AND BRONWYN DULCEA SPERANZA

## Patrick S. Baker

"Cause of death?" Detective Sigyn Hanta asked the coroner, Guzman, as they looked down at the young man's body. The corpse lay on the sidewalk of a quiet street, sightlessly eyes gazing skyward. A three-inch wide, circular hole in the chest the only obvious trauma.

"Gaping chest wound is my prelim finding. Once the autopsy is done, I'll know more." Guzman responded flatly.

"Like the others?"

"Yes, as far as I can tell. If this is the same weapon, than my answer is the same; a round, silver blade with a spiral pattern. Can I take him away now?"

"Sure," Sigyn said.

"Avi?" the detective turned to Goldman, the uniformed sergeant in charge of the scene.

"Yep, Robert Holder, 26 years-old, about forty-two in cash, cards and ID still on the body." The sergeant went on to describe how his officers had secured, and searched the scene and what they found.

"Hoof-prints?" the detective asked.

"Yep. Just like the other scenes," Goldman said. "A cowboy vigilante?"

"If he used a Colt Peacemaker, maybe. But he stabs them."

"Literally a white knight?"

"Hopefully someone would notice that," Sigyn said.

"At least we have a witness this time," Goldman pointed to the young woman sitting on the curb, a watchful female officer hovering near the teenager.

"I'll talk to her. Run our victim."

Goldman nodded.

Sigyn strode over to the witness. The detective was aware her size; six-foot-one and 170 pounds, mostly muscle and that she tended to intimidate people. Of course Sigyn used her towering stature to good advantage with suspects and perpetrators when a little intimidation was a good thing. But her size was a bit of a drawback with friendly witnesses. So she sat on the curb to make the younger woman as comfortable as possible.

"I'm Detective Sigyn Hanta," she introduced herself. "Do you mind if I ask you some questions? While Officer Caldwell sits with us?" Sigyn indicted the uniformed officer.

"No, I guess you kinda have to. I'm Virginia Lee Logan, my friends call me Ginny."

"Can you tell me what happened, Ginny?"

"I was on a date with Rob. I'm only seventeen, I'm not supposed to see guys as old as him . . ." the teen started to tremble.

Sigyn put her hand on her shoulder, "Go on".

"We had a pretty good time. The restaurant was nice, the Cellar Bistro, it's just across the park. I even had some wine. I felt so grown-up. Anyway, it was getting late and wanted to get home, so I wouldn't get in trouble with my folks. So we cut through the park. My house is two blocks that way." The girl pointed. "About halfway through the park he kissed me, and I let him, than he started to grab me tight and to get rough. He grabbed my wrists when I tried to pull away."

Ginny showed Sigyn her wrists. They were bruised.

"I kicked him hard right in the junk and broke free and ran. He chased me. I got across the street and he caught me from behind. He fell on top of me. I shut my eyes. Then he wasn't on top of me anymore. I rolled over and saw . . . " the teenager's voice trailed off.

"Saw what, Ginny?" Sigyn asked.

"You won't believe me."

"I will."

Ginny took a deep breath. "It was a white horse. I'd been crying, so I couldn't see too good. But I saw white horse legs. Then they galloped away. I yelled for help and I guess someone called nine-one-one, because it wasn't too long before the police showed up."

"Did you see who was riding the horse?"

"No. I didn't."

"Did you see the rider's feet or legs, maybe their shoes?" Sigyn pressed gently.

"No," Ginny responded. "I mean I didn't see anyone riding the horse. I didn't even see legs or feet."

"I'm going to have Officer Caldwell take you home now. Unless you want to go to the hospital to get checked out. We have your address if we need to talk more," Sigyn said.

"Take me home, please," Ginny said. "What am I going to tell my mom and dad? I'm a good girl."

"Tell them the truth. You went out on a date, you thought he was a good guy, but he wasn't. He tried to hurt you, but you fought him off and then the police showed up when you shouted for help."

"That's the truth," Ginny said and started to weep. "He was a nice guy, but then he got mean. I was so afraid. I've never been with a guy. I want the first time to be special, not . . ."

Ginny leaned into Sigyn and she waited for the girl's sobs to fade. Sigyn turned the girl over to Caldwell so the officer could drive her home.

"Our victim had a record," Goldman told Sigyn. "Two arrests for statutory rape, both times the charges were dropped."

"That is three," Sigyn said. "The other two victims had been convicted of sexual assault."

"So a horse-riding vigilante that targets sexual offenders," Goldman went on. "Hard to care much about victims."

Sigyn looked hard at Goldman, who dropped his eyes.

"We don't judge the victims," the detective said. "The first two were plain murder. This one might be justifiable defense of another, but the vigilante should have stuck around."

"Sergeant Goldman, Detective Hanta, we've got something," a uniform officer named Hosten called from up the street.

The two joined Hosten and he pointed at the ground.

"See, the horse came off the street here and went through the grass into the woods," Hosten said. "I followed the tracks to the tree line. Odd thing is the horse is riderless. It's about 1200 pounds and about 16 hands high and not in a hurry. It was traveling at the cantor, not a gallop."

Sigyn and Goldman looked at Hosten.

"My grandfather was a guide in Arizona," the uniformed officer said by way of explanation as he smiled and shrugged. "I grew up around horses and learned how to do some tracking. I never thought that skill would come in handy on this job."

Sigyn got out her phone and pulled up a map of the area.

"Okay. These woods run to the interstate. Goldman, get some units on the highway to block that. The rest of us will form a skirmish line and sweep the woods."

"Maybe we should wait for back-up?" Goldman suggested.

"No, he might get away," Sigyn said and waved the police forward into the trees.

She moved quickly. On her right was Hosten, no one was on her left. She went ten feet into the woods and she drew her .40 caliber P226 Nitron service pistol and flipped on the tactical LED light.

A will-o-wisp shimmered, waved and danced. Slowly it solidified into a white horse with red-roan forelock and a single silver horn. Sigyn blinked hard and shook her head. She turned to ask Hosten if he saw the unicorn. The male office was not just still but totally motionless.

The unicorn gambled up to Sigyn, head down, non-threatening, and nuzzled the detectives extended weapon hand.

"This is taking place in a moment between moments," the unicorn announced, in a soft, genderless voice to Sigyn's unasked question.

The detective holstered her weapon and thought: *Either I'm hallucinating. Or this is real and very strange.* In any case, she had to handle the situation like it was real. If it was a hallucination, then no harm done. If it was reality than it had to be dealt with it like it was reality.

"Please stand still and let me read you your rights . . ." Sigyn recited the Miranda rights from memory to the mythical beast. This routine action calmed and focused the detective's mind on the situation.

"Did you kill three men?" Sigyn asked.

"Indeed, my maiden protectress," the unicorn answered. "They were evil; rapists, attackers of women. I could do nothing else and nothing less. The last was going to defile a maiden, I could not let that happen."

"How did you escape detection until now?"

"Only women who have never known a man may see me. That is how I know you're still a maid."

"What am I going to do with you?" Sigyn sighed. "I can't take you into custody, I can just see this in court! But I also can't let you keep killing people, even if they are 'defilers'."

"Not to worry, my warrior damsel," the unicorn said and somehow smiled. "Now that we have met, I know my *cinniuint*, my destiny, is to be with you."

"Wait!" Sigyn started.

The beautiful horse form shifted and danced; shrinking, changing. In a blink of the eye, the unicorn was gone and now a woman stood.

The woman was breathtaking in her sheer loveliness. Long auburn hair with a single silver streak, startling green eyes, flawless skin, full lips. She was Sigyn's height and weight, with softer curves. Just the kind of woman Sigyn liked.

"I am Bronwyn Dulcea Speranza," the former unicorn said. "It means fair-breasted, sweet, hopeful one."

"Holy crap!"

\* \* \* \*

Unable to close the vigilante slayings, Detective Hanta-Speranza requested a transfer to the Special Victims Unit. She had a special affinity for the work, closing 90% of her cases. Her spouse, Bronwyn Speranza-Hanta, worked at a riding academy; where she had a special affinity for horses.

# EGO URN
## Eddie D. Moore

Jerry stared blankly out the window as the AI drove him home. He was still lost in his thoughts as the 2086 Ford Taurus crawled to a stop in the driveway. A soft chime and the AI's proper English caused him to blink and focus on his surroundings.

"Welcome home, Jerry. Do you wish to choose a new destination?"

"No thanks, Vera. I just didn't realize that we were here already." A smile spread across Jerry's face when he noticed the light flashing on top of his dronebox. "I must have missed the delivery notice from the drone service."

The top of the dronebox slowly opened as the AI commented. "The drop was made at 2:52 this afternoon."

Jerry stepped out of the car and said as he went to retrieve his package, "Vera, put the car on charge for the night, and I skipped lunch today, so you can start dinner now."

The front door unlocked with a soft click when Jerry glanced at the sensor pad mounted near the top of the door. He sat on the sofa and opened the package. The tall blue cylinder he placed on the coffee table was sleek and had three black buttons on top: Vol +, Vol - & On/Off. He quickly read the familiar packing slip:

Mr. Vancroft,

The memory and personality scan during the last week of your father's life was completed with an accuracy of 99.87%. The enclosed Ego Urn has been loaded with all the data collected during the scan.

Any new memories stored in the Ego Urn will be uploaded each night for safekeeping should you require a new unit due to failure or damage. It is our pleasure to help keep families together, and we are thankful that you chose Egoite to fulfill your family's post life needs.

The unmistakable smell of chicken Alfredo coming from the kitchen told Jerry that dinner was nearly ready, and he could hear the soft whine of robotic arms preparing his meal. He pressed and held the On/Off button until a soft blue light began to slowly pulse near the base of the Ego Urn, and a tiny green indicator flickered to life beside a small camera near the top.

"Dad, are you there."

The blue light quickened as a familiar voice answered, "It's good to hear your voice, son." The green light stopped flickering. "Ah, I can see you now."

"How do you feel?"

His father deadpanned. "Umm. I'm dead, son. I don't feel anything anymore."

Jerry smiled. "I'm glad to hear that even death can't rob you of your sense of humor."

"Seriously, even breathing was painful near the end… Well, I guess that's one less thing to worry about."

"What's it like in there?"

"The virtual environment they created for me is beautiful. I have a cabin by the lake, and as long as the urn is connected to the WIFI, I can watch video, listen to music, play games or communicate with the outside world. The list of things I don't have to do is just as important: I don't have to pee every twenty minutes, I don't have to swallow those horse pills the doctor gave me. I don't have to mow the grass. This is practically heaven. I should have kicked the bucket a long time ago."

Jerry placed the ego urn on the mantel beside an urn with a pink light at its base. "I'm glad to hear you are enjoying yourself. I've got a surprise for you."

"I'm not sure how it can get any better than this… Am I finally getting grandchildren? You would wait until I'm dead to carry on the family name."

The light on the other urn flickered as a feminine voice said, "Herald, is that you?"

A moment of surprised shock passed before the blue light flickered again. "Mary? What are you doing here?"

"We were married for forty-two years. Aren't you glad to see me? It's been what three months? I heard that they moved you to intensive care right after I passed."

Vera announced softly, "Dinner is ready."

Jerry grinned and went to the kitchen to get his plate. When he returned to the living room, the conversation between his parents had grown much more animated. He took his first bite and nearly spit it out as he tried to hold in his laughter.

"Mary? How did you get into my cabin? This is my virtual environment."

"As long as we share the same WIFI network, we can visit each other's living space."

"Oh for Criminey's sake. We shared a living space for four decades. You do know the vows were until death do us part, right?"

"Our bodies may be dead but I think we are both very much alive. Just think of it, Herald, we truly do have forever in our future."

An exasperated sigh came from Herald's urn, and Jerry could see the roll of his father's eyes in his mind. "Jerry, shouldn't your mother be help-ing your sister at her house?"

✗

# SHADOW BAY
## Ashley Dioses

*The ropes around my wrists were tied*
*So tightly they were stained*
*With scarlet drops from just inside*
*My skin so pale and drained.*

*My ankles they were bound the same;*
*Before them I did stand.*
*They called me Witch and tarred my name—*
*"Confess!" they did demand.*

*My herbs and remedies could heal*
*So well they sought me out.*
*They faulted me so they could steal*
*Great cures they then could tout.*

*would not lie to save my skin,*
*So they discussed my death*
*By fire or water for my sin—*
*The Bay would take my breath.*

*The Shadow Bay lay still and black,*
*Its floor all lined with bones*
*And skulls of witches—stack on stack—*
*Each tossed like they were stones.*


*They gagged my mouth and weighed me down,*
*A ball of iron strapped*
*To both my ankles so to drown*
*And ever keep me trapped.*

*I prayed to God, but He did not*
*Appear to me below*
*The icy waters where I'd rot—*
*But someone else did show….*

*On wings as black as night he came,*
*My prince of fallen realms.*
*In darkness he was my own flame,*
*With eyes the hue of elms.*

*From out my mouth he took the gag,*
*And neared his lips to mine.*

# SWEET HONEY IN THE BONES
## Matt Thompson

The boy on the gallows bore the startled expression of one who wasn't sure whether or not he was the subject of some elaborate practical joke. The market square was only around half-full for his demise. A desultory air hung over the scene. Spatters of rain fell onto the cobbles, swilling into the gutters in a rank foam. The stench of burnt goat meat wafted across the crowd from a stall set out in front of the semi-derelict church. No-one seemed to be buying.

The wooden platform creaked and swayed beneath the feet of Babak and Khattab, the executioners. Their victim was one of the apprentices to the city bee-keeper. Supposedly he had stolen a loaf of bread from a city council-approved bakery. His guilt or innocence, naturally, was irrelevant; it was of no real concern to the governors. Execution fodder they required, and execution fodder they received, one a month come rain or shine.

The boy scanned the crowd as if to locate the trickster who had put him here. There was no joker; only the sullen, solemn faces of those townsfolk who had braved the cold of early springtime in order to see justice done—although whose justice it was would have been hard to discern.

Hidden towards the rear of the gathering, the physician Ibrahim observed proceedings with no little sense of trepidation. He felt nothing other than sympathy for the poor boy. His overriding concern, though, was for the preservation of the body. The last one he had been sent was in no fit state for dissection; the soldiers had taken it upon themselves to inflict the agonies of the flame to the poor fellow, leaving both his skin and internal organs unusable. He had let the imam know his feelings. That man, however, had done little more than mumble pieties before shuffling back to his papers, leaving Ibrahim in the constant state of uncertainty he had, unfortunately, become used to.

Stood beside him was the stall-keeper Lubaba, Ibrahim's neighbour in the run-down district of the city he rented his workshop in. She leaned in and muttered behind her hand: "It's as well it was him. Could have been any of us."

Ibrahim pursed his lips in disapproval. "But did he take the bread?" he whispered back. Lubaba merely shrugged, and turned her attention back to the spectacle on the gallows. The executioners had donned their masks.

Black, ragged, the cloth stained with grease and spittle, the coverings made Babak and Khattab resemble demons from the underworld of myth, manifested on the Earth to exact primal justice on the sins of mankind. That, Ibrahim supposed, was the idea anyway.

The boy's eyes went wide; understanding finally forming in them, he let out a series of chittering yelps, writhing on the platform in an attempt to squirm free of the rope braids hanging loose around his neck.

It was no use. Babak raised a gnarled hand. The crowd fell silent. Even the boy ceased his contortions, standing acquiescent now, resigned to his fate.

Ibrahim tensed himself for escape. As soon as the trap-door was opened and the boy's life was extinguished he planned to retreat to the safety of his workshop, there to wait for the corpse to be delivered by order of the governors themselves. He was in no doubt they wished to discover whether the anatomy of an Arab was in any way different to that of an African. Even though he had told them it would be exactly the same they had been insistent. He sighed; the boy on the gallows would die for no more reason than that, and he would never know it.

A cry rang out. Babak's arm swept downwards. His accomplice wrenched the lever towards him. The trap opened, and the boy plummeted silently through the aperture. An audible *crack* sounded, echoing from the stone walls of the church and back across the square. The boy swung on the end of the rope, his legs kicking out in reflex concord with his nervous system as it dwindled and died.

Soon he was still, and the onlookers drifted away, back to their lives in the city of Yaqut, the jewel of the Western Plains and home now to one less citizen.

\* \* \* \*

Ibrahim regarded the body on the mortuary slab with a practised eye. On a shelf nearby his cat, Jarad, eyed the corpse with disinterest. The boy's head sat at an unnatural angle on his neck. An angry welt ran across his throat where the rope had burned the skin, but otherwise he seemed unblemished. Fortunately his eyes were closed. Ibrahim hated to see suffering.

The body had been delivered to him an hour beforehand by Salah, the captain of the City Guard, a man who regarded Ibrahim with little more than dripping contempt. As he directed his men to lay the corpse out he had jabbed a scarred thumb at it. "What would be your plans with it, master Ibrahim?" His voice was a growling, splintered thing that gave Ibrahim the impression it was trying to choke the man to death every time he spoke.

"Anatomy," Ibrahim had said, "is an inexact science, Captain Salah. Leave me to my ministrations and I will leave you to yours."

The look of fury on Salah's face told him he had overstepped an invisible boundary. It would be a wise move to act in a more deferential manner from now on. At least the man hadn't returned. Negotiating the tangle of competing interests that ruled over Yaqut—be they spiritual, military or bureaucratic—was a fool's errand. But one could make things more difficult for oneself than necessary, and he chided himself for having edged so stupidly into a dangerous situation.

Putting the Captain out of his thoughts as best he could, Ibrahim picked up his blade and set to work. As he sliced the boy's abdomen open a smell wafted out from within, one he couldn't remember encountering before. It reminded him of honey, or lavender. Jarad's ears pricked up. Mewing in sudden concern, he jumped to the floor and padded silently away into the shadows. Frowning, Ibrahim pulled back a lip of yellow fat, wiping away the blood that seeped onto the tabletop.

A tiny shape nestled next to the boy's liver, curled up as if asleep. Not six inches in length, it looked almost human.

Ibrahim froze. What was the thing doing there? He had dissected many cadavers before today—human, canine, ovine and others. This, though, was the first time he had seen anything like this. Did the boy have a unique anatomy? It went against everything he had ever learned, every piece of evidence he had so carefully notated.

He reached into the open chest cavity and gave the creature, if that was what it was, an exploratory poke. As his finger touched it the thing shuddered. Ibrahim leaned in to look at it closer.

It was, indeed, human-shaped. Pale and veined, it resembled the unborn foetuses he had seen when pregnant women came to him with excruciating abdominal pains or already-miscarried babies. But the creature before him was most definitely alive—it clung to the liver, lips puckering as it sucked at the flesh, drawing out, Ibrahim guessed, what nourishment it could.

He thought quickly. Clearly it wouldn't survive for long like this. He shuffled across to his specimen shelves and emptied one of the jars of its contents, a mould-ridden appendix. He filled the vessel with water from the bucket and gingerly extracted the creature from its nestling place, trying to ignore the miniscule bleats of panic it gave out. Once it was safely ensconced in the fluid it seemed to calm down.

Only for a moment, though. Soon enough it began to gasp and spasm. Its face, blank and almost—but not quite—human, winced in agony. Ibrahim wondered if it would survive the ordeal. Did it need a different kind of sustenance? It had been suckling at the boy's organs, after all...

As quickly as he could he scooped a measure of the boy's blood into a vial and poured it into the jar. The creature sucked at the pink fluid surrounding it with greedy abandon, clenching and unclenching its barely-formed fists until the water churned and frothed.

Ibrahim spent the next hour siphoning what plasma he could from the boy's veins and organs, decanting the thick fluid into a number of bottles for safekeeping. He wondered what he could gain from this unexpected turn of events. Notoriety, he hoped; but only of the right sort.

As he extinguished the lamps later that night he fancied the creature turned its head toward him in the dark. Moonlight from the high windows glinted from its skin. He shivered, despite himself, and pulled the door quietly shut behind him.

* * * *

The next morning he found it gasping for breath, seemingly at the point of expiration. The fluid level in its jar had dwindled alarmingly overnight. After he had topped it up again Jarad rubbed against his legs, purring. Ibrahim reached down to pet him for a minute or two. When he straightened back up he realised with a start that the jar was almost empty again.

"And what's that all about, hmm?" he muttered to the cat. Jarad watched with wide eyes as he eased the stopper from the nearest bottle of blood and tipped it into the jar. The creature immediately set to suckling. The level began to decrease even as Ibrahim watched.

As he was refilling the jar yet again he made an inventory of the plasma he had left. One, two, three…it wasn't enough. Would the thing die without the sustenance it had always known? By the time he had mulled it over it was writhing in panic inside the almost-empty jar. His stocks, obviously, would diminish to naught before the morning was out.

Jarad jumped up onto the dissecting table. Beside the animal lay the sharpened knife Ibrahim always used for slicing flesh open quickly and easily. Sighing, Ibrahim made his calculations swiftly and without sentiment. After all, there were many stray cats roaming the city streets. That was where he had found Jarad in the first place—would it really make so much of a difference if there were one less?

He undertook his task in as expeditious a manner as he could manage. The cat's blood was plentiful enough to replenish most of the bottles. Surprisingly, they lasted well into the afternoon before he had to go in search of another feline incumbent of the back alleys. That one, a female, scratched his hand so badly he threw caution to the wind and squeezed a little of his own blood into the mix too.

* * * *

By the end of the day it had become obvious the creature was grow-ing. Not only that—it was beginning to pay attention to its surroundings. Ibrahim had thought he was imagining it at first. As he pottered about his tasks it felt as if he were being watched. He put it down to nerves.

Not for long, though. He caught the creature at it when he mishandled the executed boy's liver, turning suddenly to catch it before it landed on the floor. Its eyes, wide open now, gazed on him unblinking from within its jar. The blood-infused water made it glow in the candlelight, reminding him of the religious icons in the city's little-used Christian church. They, though, were likenesses of saints and martyrs. The creature looked to him more and more like a human; or, at least, the potential form of one.

He tried to ignore it and continued with his note-taking. Numerous vials of cat's blood lined the shelves. Poor Jarad had been joined by two more of his kind already. It might pay to look further afield. Fortunately none of the citizens that had come to him that afternoon for tinctures or potions noticed anything untoward. But how long would that state of af-fairs continue?

Just as he was preparing to leave for the night an insistent knock came at the door. He stiffened. Was it Captain Salah? A delegation from the gov-ernors? The imam? He realised he had no idea what he might tell any of them, should they discover his secret.

He opened it to find his neighbour Lubaba. As she mumbled her greet-ings he smelled alcohol on her breath, a dangerous pastime in Yaqut. "What did you report back to the Council then?" she slurred. He ushered her inside, fearful of the consequences if he were to be seen with her in this state.

"I will tell them," he sniffed, "that the organs of an African are no dif-ferent to ours."

Lubaba gave him a suspicious glance and cast her eye along the shelves. "That Captain," she spat, "has his eye on the likes of us. There are forces in this city you little understand, physician. You spend your time in this hovel with your books and your ghosts, and all the while the Guards are plotting, plotting."

"I...I rather think that unlikely," Ibrahim stammered. "The thirst for knowledge is stronger than any superstition."

"Is it?" She poked his chest, causing him to step backward in alarm. "Physician, be careful. There is talk that you are summoning the spirits of the dead in here." She tapped the very jar the creature had been placed into. Fortunately it had sunk to the bottom, curled up as if asleep. "Don't be so sure that it won't be you on that gallows soon."

Finally Ibrahim managed to get rid of her. As he was preparing to leave he caught the creature staring at him, its eyes shining in the gloom.

Not for the first time he wondered why he was taking such a risk in keeping it secret. Was it truly knowledge he sought? Or was it a metaphysical dread he felt, despite his protestations of scientific curiosity?

"I should give you a name, shouldn't I?" he murmured. The creature gazed back, silent. "Lemma," he said. "Lemma shall be your name." That, apparently, had been the name of the boy he had found the creature inside. It seemed fitting somehow.

Outside, the crisp air of evening entered his lungs with sweet cleanliness, a rush of goodness to wash away both the evil of what he was doing and, lurking in the back of his mind, his own moral idleness.

* * * *

By the following day Lemma had outgrown its jar. Around noon-time Ibrahim carefully lifted it out and deposited it into a larger container, already filled to the brim with the blood he had let from a number of his patients that morning—an elegant solution, for the time being, but not one he could continue with indefinitely. At first the creature took to its new home with evident glee, sucking and slurping at the fluid until it dropped into a deep sleep. When it awoke Ibrahim could feel its eyes on him, following with interest his dissections and note-taking.

In this way they continued for several days. By then, though, it was clear that Lemma was ailing. The fluid had turned cloudy, flecked with black trails of a mucoid substance. On the morning of the seventh day since the discovery Ibrahim lowered his finger inside and tickled the creature on the crown of its head. Now it had grown to some three times its initial size. It resembled more and more a human baby, albeit an infant with no distinguishing facial features whatsoever. Everything was there— mouth, nose, eyes, ears and all the rest. But there was nothing about it that Ibrahim could have said indicated individuality or personality. And in that, Lemma was more unique than any other form of life he had ever seen.

The creature shied away from his touch, at first. Then, with infinite shyness, it reached out a stubby fist and clutched at his finger, drawing it towards its own mouth. Ibrahim let it. He had a strange feeling—as if a question that had been lurking in the back of his mind was about to be answered.

Lemma opened its mouth and bit down. Ibrahim felt a sharp pain. When had the thing grown teeth? He hadn't noticed. Its bite was strong. Red swirled out into the water. It suckled at his digit with intense concentration, the same single-mindedness Ibrahim had seen in nursing babies. As he withdrew his hand Lemma cried out, the sound muffled by the liquid. He inspected his finger. Rows of tooth marks extended along its length, the skin torn and punctured.

Lemma stared at him in fierce challenge, unblinking eyes shining through the murk within its jar. Ibrahim, after only a moment's hesitation, knew that the inevitable course of action he had been mulling over would, at last, have to be put into effect.

* * * *

The thin sliver of the moon barely illuminated the gloom of the street. The lights of the brothel burned with a dim flame. Ibrahim, hidden away in the shadows opposite, shifted his feet. He hadn't yet seen what he was looking for. The few patrons who had exited were young and sober. No— he was after a different type of customer.

The cobbles beneath his feet made it hard to find a comfortable standing position. The buildings around him lay shrouded in darkness. Workshops, mostly—shodders, saddle-makers, barley-grinders, a number of whom were, he didn't doubt, enjoying themselves inside the looming bulk of the brothel right now. While he, unfortunately, was out here in the cold night, waiting for the chance to do something that would, were he caught, lead him to the gallows as surely as if he had slapped one of the Council members in the face.

As he was brooding on the possibility of doing just that some day the door opened and a figure stumbled out. Hidden beneath a shapeless hood, he looked far stronger and taller than most Ibrahim had spied that evening. He shuffled off in the direction of the barracks, pausing only to expectorate into the gutter.

Ibrahim moved into step behind the man. His fingers curled around the length of iron piping in his pocket. His thoughts had gone blank; considerations of right or wrong seemed far away, irrelevant. All he knew was the here and now, the details of his pursuit: the uneven gait of his quarry, the slap of the man's sandals on the roadway and his hoarse breathing, louder and louder the nearer Ibrahim came, the feel of cold metal in his hand as he raised the pipe above his head...

And the crack as it connected with the skull, a wet, muffled squelch of blood hitting the paving stones, and then the man lying dead at his feet.

His mind empty, Ibrahim managed to hoist the body onto his shoulder. He staggered into the nearest alley. A covert route to his workshop would be best. Trying in vain to ignore the wetness spreading down his back as his victim's life-blood drained away he made it back before the moon rose to zenith, the warning voice in his head a faraway thing he could safely ignore.

* * * *

Head in hands, he sat before the mortuary slab. The man's hood was still down—he hadn't dared remove it yet for fear he would be forever haunted by the face of the one he had murdered. Lemma battered at the glass of its container in a frenzy. It must be able to smell the blood, Ibrahim realised. Let's hope it's the only one.

He took a deep breath. "It is done," he said out loud. Lemma quieted. "It is done, and there's no going back. So let's get the rest done too." He took a deep breath and pulled the hood back, hoping against hope it wouldn't be someone he knew.

In a way it wasn't. Could he say he had ever really known Captain Salah? His lips parted, one eye socket crushed, the Captain's face looked as peaceful as Ibrahim had ever seen it. The visages of Babak and Khattab swam before him. When he closed his eyes he could see Lubaba and the townspeople gazing up at him, the noose casting a shadow over his sight, the distant hills outside Yaqut as far away as the stars.

He picked up his scalpel and sliced Captain Salah's robe open. Soon the body was naked on the table before him. In this state it looked no different to any other he had dissected. He made a deep incision in the chest. Blood spilled out, still warm to the touch. He collected it up as best he could. Lemma was hooting and chirping and flapping like a caged bird. Ibrahim hurried across to the shelf. As he was pouring the precious liquid into the jar he considered his options.

One: say nothing.

Two: admit everything.

That seemed to be it. If he said nothing the body would have to be disposed of, somehow. And if he admitted the truth?

Then—torture, castration, burning, skinning: and the final ignominy of a public execution, left dangling on the end of a rope as Babak and Khattab played to the crowd by spinning the remnants of his body in circles and spitting in his face.

He shuffled back to the mortuary slab. Already he could hear Lemma slurping the last of the blood into its gullet. It was growing again, he was sure of it. He would need a new jar soon, assuming he could find one big enough.

He spooned steaming gouts of viscera into the bucket once more. Sighing, his mind made up, he began to think of where he might dispose of Captain Salah's remains.

\* \* \* \*

By the time two days had passed the body was buried in the woodland outside the city, and Lemma had grown so large Ibrahim was forced to move the creature to the small cellar beneath his workshop. The previous occupant, a butcher, had dug a shallow trough in the dirt floor. Ibrahim filled it with water and lowered Lemma in, doing his best not to scratch its fragile skin. It must have doubled in size since he had fed it Captain Salah's remains. It mewled and grasped at the hem of his robe.

"Oh no," Ibrahim said. "If you take all my blood too then where will we be?"

Alarmingly, he had begun to hear rumours sweeping the city. "They say the Captain has gone missing," he overheard a woman say in the market the next morning. "The Guards are demanding to know where the Council are keeping him, I heard."

"Oh yes?" the stall-holder replied. "Well, they may be in for a surprise."

And he tapped his nose, as if to say: the secret will out. Ibrahim turned away before anyone could see the guilt he knew was written all over his face. He scampered back to his workshop as fast as he could. So wrapped up in his troubles was he that he didn't take in the fact his door was ajar until he was already through it.

"Physician," Babak said as he stumbled inside. He stood nearer to the trapdoor than Ibrahim felt comfortable with. "Come in, do."

The leering, malodorous figure of Khattab held the door open for him, bowing as Ibrahim tiptoed past. Babak looked around in interest. "Quite a collection you have," he rasped. "No need for you to buy meat, I suppose?"

Ibrahim saw with horror that one of his specimen jars lay shattered on the floor, the organ that had been inside it nowhere to be seen. The front of Babak's tunic was stained with an indeterminate liquid. The executioner grinned; there seemed to a portion of gristle stuck between his teeth.

"They're running around like ants up there in the Council chambers," Khattab said. Ibrahim fancied he could smell something emanating from the floorboards beneath their feet; blood, and honey. He tried not to cast his eyes downward, difficult though it was to concentrate.

"The Council can't believe their luck. The Guards are looking for a scapegoat. And us..." Babak laughed. "Us, we've been thinking. Because sometimes people have to do things they don't want to. Isn't that right?" He took Ibrahim's chin in his hand and swivelled it around to face him. "Sometimes events get away from you. Things get out from under your control. And then..." He jerked Ibrahim's head from side to side. "Then, physician, there might have to be actions taken. Changes made. A painful process, sometimes."

Khattab sniffed the air, frowning. "Blood," he said.

"Look around you, executioner," Babak murmured. "This place is a slaughterhouse. And there are some who look unkindly on such matters." Ibrahim widened his eyes. "That's right," Babak continued, smiling. "The more spiritual factions of the Council chambers have been expressing disquiet about your role, or so I heard. The sanctity of the soul, was it?"

"I...I don't...I mean..." Ibrahim's stuttering deteriorated into nonsense. He clamped his mouth shut before he blurted out something incriminating.

"Maybe the good Captain is up there now," Babak said. He pointed ceiling-wards. "Heaven. The fruits of goodness. He lived a good life, he did."

"That's right," Khattab said. "They found some bones, I heard. Outside the walls. I can arrange to have them brought to you, if you'd like?" Ibrahim, mute with terror, shook his head. "No? Well, doesn't matter, physician." He opened the door, Babak grinning beside him. "Whoever did it, they're long gone now. So keep your eyes peeled."

Babak looked him up and down and laughed. "There may be some," he said over his shoulder as he left, "who have less regard for your welfare than we do."

As he was closing the door behind him a muffled cry came from beneath Ibrahim's feet. Khattab stuck his head back into the room.

"I know a good rat-catcher if you need one," he smirked. "He might even work for food." He indicated the row of organs on the shelves flanking the doorway, sneered, and slammed the door behind him.

* * * *

That night Ibrahim went in search of felines. They seemed to have sensed imminent danger, though. The only cat he encountered hissed at him from its perch on a high wall and vanished. He gave up on the idea and turned for his workshop, thinking once more of the travails he would have to endure if Babak and Khattab were requisitioned to do their worst. He had seen the aftermath of their ministrations too many times on his slab to think they might show him mercy.

As he rounded a corner, lost in thought, someone reached out of the darkness and clutched at his sleeve. His cry of surprise came out as a terrified bleat. A foul-smelling hand covered his mouth. The stench of rotten fruit filled his nostrils. He squirmed free, only to see the sweating figure of Lubaba stood before him, panic in her eyes.

"Listen," she hissed. "I just saw some Guards hanging around your place. They're after you, they're after me. I'm leaving tonight, physician. If they come for you, you tell them you never spoke to me. Got that?"

Ibrahim did his best to collect himself. "But...why?"

"Who cares why? Don't matter! One side rises, the other falls. If you don't want to get caught in the vice then run, man. Run! And hope they don't get wind of where you've gone."

With that she scurried away into the gloom. The night, and the city, seemed very, very dark all of a sudden. Buildings loomed on all sides—hiding what, and whom? Ibrahim's journey back to the workshop was undertaken in panic, a crawl through shadows that hid nothing.

Fortunately whoever had been there had departed without attempting to force entry. He collected his notes from their hiding places and stuffed them into a satchel. He thought about Lemma, sequestered in the cellar beneath him. A day ago he had left the creature the last of Captain Salah's blood to sustain it. How horrible, he thought, to waste such a specimen. How painful, to leave without saying goodbye.

The clock hands rested on twelve. He had time—probably. He eased open the trapdoor and kindled a lantern. As he descended the steps he wondered where he could escape to. Somewhere far, far away, he thought, might be best.

A smell came to him: honey, thick and viscous in his nostrils, mixed with blood and something new—was it…milk? As he approached the pit he could see a shape lying within it, dark and fleshy. But surely it wasn't Lemma? It was far too large, almost the same size as a…

As a man. The creature stared up at him. It had legs now, and arms. A fully formed torso—although no reproductive organs were visible—and a face. A very familiar face.

He couldn't have guessed how it might have happened. But the creature, the foetus he had nurtured from the moment he set eyes on it, was now the exact double of himself. Indistinguishable, he supposed, apart from the fact that its gaze was one of blank incomprehension and idiocy, and his own expression was surely one of shock, bewilderment and religious terror.

He reached out a hand. Lemma reached its own hand out in return. Their fingers intertwined. A shiver passed through Ibrahim, an ice-cold absence of humanity, a stench of the grave. He hauled the creature to its feet. Somehow it balanced there without falling over. As he led it to the steps he found it was able to walk, with a gait not unlike that of a human. Up the stairs, past the shelves, over to the slab…

Ibrahim dug into his pack and extracted the spare robe he had been planning to take with him. He heard cries from outside, somewhere nearby, and the clash of swords. Hurrying now, he slipped the covering over Lemma's head, manoeuvring its arms into the sleeves. He stood back and admired his handiwork. He didn't think, on a cursory glance, anyone would be able to tell the difference. When they came to castrate him there would be confusion, no doubt.

But it would be nothing that couldn't be explained away; a secret the strange physician had kept to himself. Had anyone ever seen him in the brothel? Well, then.

With a last, lingering look he left Lemma to its fate and slipped through the door, taking care to lock it behind him. Who would he be, now? Not Ibrahim the physician. That man would be dead, taken apart piece by piece by the horrified figures of Babak and Khattab, and left to die on the end of a rope as the sullen citizens of Yaqut looked on.

He made his way to a little-used gate at the southern tip of the city. Once he had eased it open and slipped through the smell of the woods at night came to him—herbs, pine... Smoke, too, drifting out over the city walls. He hurried away into the darkness. Whoever he would be from now on was immaterial. At least he would be alive.

The scent of honey drifted down to him from the hives that dotted the trees above. He thought of his face, innocent as a newly-born child on the figure of Lemma. It seemed a fair exchange, he considered. A life for a life, a soul for a soul.

And the thought cheered him as he fled into the darkness and the open countryside beyond, a dead man reborn, free to remake himself as whatever his heart desired.

# NIGHT SHIFT
## Cynthia Ward

After the scowling RN had moved out of earshot, Dr. Burke turned to his colleague and asked, "Are the nurses on the night shift *all* dogs?"

Dr. Thakur raised his eyebrows.

The anger flared, eating Burke's stomach the same way it had during the investigation.

"Dipak," he said, "you know the accusations were false. Some nurses wanted attention, and made me a scapegoat because I expect a little promptness when I give an order."

Thakur glanced up and down the hallway. The nurse had disappeared through the door at the end of the service corridor. The men were alone.

"Richard," Thakur said quietly, "you need to be careful what you say right now."

Burke's eyes narrowed, and he opened his mouth for a reply.

He was interrupted by a shrill sound. It was a loud whine, accompanied by a thunderous rhythmic thump. It sounded like a piece of machinery, but not one Burke recognized.

"What's that?" he said.

Thakur moved down the service corridor. Burke hurried to catch up.

The noise escalated to a roar.

"Heavy metal," Burke muttered. "They don't run a very tight ship on the night shift."

The guitar shriek echoed in the service corridor. All the doors lining the corridor were closed except one. Burke imagined the noise bursting it open.

Thakur looked through the opening. "Conchita," he shouted, "turn down the music. This is a hospital."

The volume didn't change, but after a few moments, a girl stepped through the open doorway. She was short and had black hair that fell past her shoulders. She wore scrubs, the loose top patterned with Hello Kitty figures. She looked barely twenty.

Pretty, for a fence-climber, Burke thought. Face like an angel, if angels had dark skin. His gaze moved lower. Skinny, and trying to look skinnier in that baggy top. But she can't hide a rack that big.

Burke expected the girl to be cowed by his build. Most people looked a little daunted when they first laid eyes on him. He was six feet six and, despite his schedule, lifted weights daily.

The girl barely glanced his way before returning her attention to Thakur, her face smooth.

"Thakur, don't yell." Burke heard her soft voice clearly despite the music. He was surprised she didn't have an accent. "This is a hospital."

She turned her back to Thakur and walked away. She never looked at Burke, though he'd positioned himself so her hip bumped his thigh as she went back into the Records Room.

What a bitch, Burke thought. Nice ass, though.

"See that you keep the noise down in future," Thakur called after Conchita.

She didn't reply.

As the doctors moved down the corridor, Burke remarked, "I've never seen that girl before."

"Conchita's a new clerical hire," Thakur said. "She keeps to herself. I suppose she's a stereotypical night-shifter—"

His face went blank as he remembered Burke was moved to the night shift as a disciplinary action.

Burke said, "Her music's as loud as ever."

Thakur's eyelid twitched. "That woman is—"

"Code Blue," said a disembodied woman's voice over the intercom. "Room 2021."

"Excuse me, Richard," Thakur said.

"Don't worry," Burke called after the cardiologist. "I'll lay down the law."

\* \* \* \*

The cavernous Records Archive was partitioned into narrow aisles by ceiling-high metal racks. Every rack was filled with file-storage boxes, attesting to the hospital's recent switch to an electronic records system. The air tasted of dust. The music bounced off the boxes and racks and walls to strike Burke's eardrums with almost physical force.

Burke closed the door, turned the lock quietly, and let the screaming guitars lead him to Conchita.

The clerk was halfway down the last aisle, crouching to slip manila folders in a box on the lowest shelf. The music came from a tablet leaning against the rack. The girl's back was to Burke. Her squatting position pulled the blue scrub pants tight across the rounded cheeks of her ass.

Burke reached out, smiling in anticipation of Conchita's scream. Even if she tried to pull free, he wasn't concerned. He had experience dealing with resistant women, and there was nobody around. If anyone did take a shortcut through the service corridor, the stupid bitch was playing her music so loud, it would hide any sounds.

When his hands closed on her shoulders, Conchita didn't move or make a sound. He'd never gotten a reaction like that before. It would be a nice switch, dealing with a bitch shocked motionless.

Tightening his grip on the petite girl's shoulders, he tried to twist her around to meet his stare.

It was like trying to turn one of those flesh-and-steel Terminator robots from the movies.

What the hell? Burke thought. The bitch is barely five feet tall and skinny as a willow switch, except for those melons up front. She can't be that strong—

The clerk turned her head and regarded Burke with eyes that glittered like chips of black ice.

Burke showed his teeth. "Didn't Dr. Thakur tell you to turn that noise down, Conchita?"

She faced the file box, pulling her shoulders out of his grip as if his fingers were made of tissue paper.

"Who cares if the music is loud?" Crouched on her toes, she reached for the top folder of the small pile on the floor. "This is the storage area. Nobody's here but me. *Doctor.*"

The last word dripped with contempt.

What a bitch. Wasn't that always the way with the pretty girls, no matter what their color? Ice queens, every one. No time for anybody.

"You have a very bad attitude, young woman."

Conchita didn't glance at him. She slipped the folder in the box and said, "I don't just have an attitude problem, doc. I have a problem with my temper."

"So do I."

Burke seized her shoulders and jerked.

The clerk toppled backwards.

As Burke controlled her fall, guiding her to the floor, he said, "You have a lot of problems, bitch. But I'll overlook them, if we can work out an accommodation—"

The girl howled.

Wordless, her voice rose above the machine-gun blast of the music and struck Burke motionless.

Conchita braced her palms on the floor and pulled her shoulders from the doctor's grip and stood to face him.

Her face had disappeared beneath a dark pelt, and her mouth was *stretching.*

Burke screamed.

Conchita's laugh was more harsh than the music.

"In the Records Archive," she said, "no one can hear you scream."

She closed suddenly hairy fingers on Burke's shoulders and threw him against a storage rack. Fastened at floor and ceiling, it shook as if resonating in a powerful earthquake. Some boxes tumbled. One opened, spilling a blizzard of paper.

Burke sprawled on the floor and a full box landed on his back with the solidity of a cement block.

The woman thrust a muzzle full of sharp teeth in Burke's face. He tried to scramble away from her. He was pinned in place by the box, and the claws sunk in his shoulders.

He whimpered.

Releasing his shoulders, Conchita one-handed the box off Burke's back and tossed it aside like an empty styrofoam cooler.

Then she sank the claws of both hands deep in Burke's biceps and triceps brachii. He screamed. The pain worsened as she raised him in the air.

"I've heard how you treated the clerks and nurses on the day shift." Conchita spoke softly, her voice undistorted by her muzzle. "Those women told the truth about you, but your male colleagues wouldn't believe them."

She flung him up the aisle and laughed, saliva dripping from her fangs.

"Go tell the truth about the wolfwoman, Richard Burke." She laughed again, her face human, her expression angelic. "Find out what it's like when no one believes you."

# THE HORROR FROM THE STARS

## Steve Dilks

### 1.

The little oasis city of Ibn-Shahk sweltered in the morning heat. The cattle herders had left at dawn and now the narrowed streets echoed to the chatter of house wives and the cries of shop traders.

Along a narrow lane, the shadow of a big man fell across the stones. He paused, looking around him, one hand resting on the hilt of a big scimitar at his side. He wore the white robes and headdress of a desert tribesman, but even a quick glance showed this was no true son of the wastes. He was a giant compared to the slight inhabitants of Ibn-Shahk; ebon skinned with eyes as dark and hard as flint. Beneath his robes could be glimpsed the blue gleam of a mail shirt.

Bohun of Damzullah had only arrived in the city the evening before. He had important business with the sultan and he was in no mood for distraction, especially one as now confronted him.

The children crouched over the man cringing in the dust of the alley looked up sharply at his approach. A tall boy held a stick with which he was using to antagonize their victim. The other children laughed as the man attempted feebly to ward them away.

"What do you do there?" the stranger growled, his voice reverberating off the sun baked walls.

Seeing the size of the man that confronted them, the big youth cast down his stick and ran. The others followed, their brown feet scampering in the dust, insults drifting back over their shoulders. Shaking his head, Bohun let his hand fall from his hilt. "Thank you, stranger," croaked the old man. The big Damzullahan spared him barely a glance as he strode past.

"If you seek the sultan, beware…evil is abroad in Ibn-Shahk."

Bohun stopped and turned slowly on his heel. "And what would you know of my intentions, old man?"

The pile of rags sitting in the shade of the wall looked up and grinned through broken teeth. "Bahti knows many things. He was not always a wretch fit only for the cruelty of children. Once I was a ferry man on the River Zallam—until the river sickness took me. With the sickness came the visions. Sometimes a madness grips me." He held out a small wooden bowl and rattled a copper piece inside. Frowning, Bohun reached into his robes and drew out a coin. He flipped it into the bowl. "A good trick. Buy yourself some food and lodgings for the night." The old man snatched the coin and, gumming its thick edge, looked up. "You have broken chains with your bare hands and sailed the seas to be here…in search of a woman."

Bohun stood frozen for a moment, his hand resting lightly on the hilt of his sword. Despite the blazing heat, he felt a chill roll down the back of his spine.

"A skilled trick indeed," he murmured. "What else can you tell me?"

Blinking through rheumy eyes, the beggar creased his face as if deep in thought. "You come from the savannahs of the south but they are barred to you. In your homeland you were a champion—*to a king!* But betrayal has since made you an outcast." He shook his head. "The visions were strong just then. Now they are gone. Sometimes the fates dare not reveal too much. Sometimes they are afraid."

Bohun stood contemplating the old man's words. He made a clicking sound with his tongue and shook his head. "It is true," he muttered. "I come here to barter for my wife who is kept in the harem of your sultan. I made a trade with the eastern tribes of the Gharubah. They gave me a message entreating your ruler for her release in exchange for gold."

The old man squinted up at him. "Ahh…so! And if our blessed sultan does not honour the bargain?"

Bohun glared, his hand tightening on his sword hilt. "Either she comes with me or I fall here. It is of little consequence."

The old beggar nodded. "You are a strong man with a good heart. I have nothing to give you save words. So listen;

"Not for nothing did I say that evil lurks in Ibn-Shahk. Some months ago, caravan masters came in from the desert telling stories of a star they had seen falling from the sky. Word of it reached Akim Harrad, our sultan. He has always been vain. Seeing it as a sign from the gods, he ordered expeditions to find it. Eventually they found *something.* Since then, things have changed. People began disappearing. First it was just common folk and beggars, like myself. Now none is safe. Daughters of merchants fear to walk the streets. Some say Akim Harrad is behind it all. Whatever awaits you in the palace, my friend, be on your guard. A word of caution for your kindness."

Bohun nodded. "I will heed your words, old man." With that, he turned on his heel and moved on down the alley. Coming to an intersection, he glanced back but the old man had gone.

# 2.

All along the main thoroughfare, carts rumbled by with their oxen and hawkers cried the delights of their wares. Bohun barely heeded as he shrugged through the teeming throngs. Between the palms and minarets, his eyes were fixed on a big structure standing in the distance. Surrounded by four onion domed towers, it was a flat roofed edifice—the palace of Akim Harrad, the sultan of Ibn-Shahk. No expression crossed his face as he came to stand before it. Yet in his eyes smouldered a deep light. The long days spent in the saddle under a burning sun, weathering sandstorms and fighting hyenas, were forgotten now. Even the old man's warning was a fast fading echo in his mind. The fears and superstitions of these people meant little to him. His only thoughts were of the woman he loved held captive within those walls.

He moved across the street and came up the steps. Two guards standing at the entrance eyed his approach warily. They held long bladed pikes and gold embossed shields. Over their mail were long sashes of red silk.

"That's far enough, stranger," one growled. "What do you on the steps of the palace of his most glorious magnificence, Akim Harrad? Speak! Or be cut down where you stand."

Halting below them, Bohun spread his hands away from his weapons. "I have a letter for the sultan, sealed with his mark from the sheikh of the eastern Gharubah tribes."

"Eh?" sneered the other guard. Snapping his fingers, he jerked his helmeted head. "Let us see."

Reaching into his robes, Bohun drew out a wooden tube, pulling out the scroll just far enough so they could see the seal. One of the guards gave a surprized grunt. They muttered to each other then called inside the palace. Presently, an extravagantly dressed plump man appeared. He wore a long beard and had dark beady eyes. Those eyes rested on the Damzullahan as the guards related to him what they had seen. He nodded slowly and smiled at Bohun. "May I see this document?"

Bohun hesitated. "Who are you?"

"I am Vizek, the sultan's chief treasurer."

Bohun shook his head. "The message is for the eyes of the sultan." He had not come so far to be parted from his only hope now. If need be, he would defend the parchment with his life.

"Very well," said Vizek, salaaming. "If you will follow me."

Passing the guards, the Damzullahan stepped into the shadowed interior of the palace. His eyes had only just adjusted when they came out into a magnificent hall. The chief treasurer walked ahead of him, his robes swishing out over the inlaid floor. As Bohun made to follow, two guards standing at the hall entrance crossed their polearms in front of him. The

Damzullahan stepped back with a snarl, his hand reaching instinctively for his sword hilt.

"Be not alarmed," said Vizek, turning. "I see you are unused to palace etiquette. It is customary to relinquish weapons before being admitted into the presence of the sultan."

Inwardly, Bohun cursed his own eagerness. Moving his hand slowly down to his sword belt, he unbuckled it before reluctantly allowing it to be taken by one of the guards.

Seldom had Bohun seen such opulence. From somewhere music played a dream like refrain on a stringed instrument. A peacock in full plumage walked past, pecking at grain that had been strewn on the white marbled floor. Beyond columned archways, the sound of distant fountains could be heard. Incense filled the air. At the far end of it all sat the sultan himself.

Akim Harrad was a fat, tired looking old man with eyes that shone with dulled mirth from years of extravagant living. Beneath his turban, a grey waving beard reached down to his chest. His robes were of sequined jewels, a rioting clash of colour whenever he moved an arm to pick a sweet meat from the trays which surrounded him. Nubile slave girls lay all around his high seat, lolling on cushions, tempting him with these delightful dishes. Behind the chair, a slim exotic looking naked girl stood fanning him with slow sweeps of a many feathered fan. Bohun noted that she was an ebon skinned beauty from the far lands of Khamsu. She eyed the Damzullahan boldly before averting her gaze back to the top of the sultan's head. Stood to the other side of the chair was a gigantic black bodyguard stripped to the waist. He wore wide silk pantaloons and gold slippers. His head was cleanly shaven and from one ear dangled a gold hooped earring. His thick arms were folded across his breast and in one hand he held a mighty curved scimitar, much wider and longer than Bohun's own. He flashed Bohun a look of unfeigned hatred before regaining his composure and staring solemnly into space. He was of the Mungawii and no love was lost between his people and the nation of Damzullah.

They came up to the dais now and Vizek went to his knees, touching his forehead to the ground. "Your magnificence, a foreigner desires audience. He comes bearing a parchment with your seal from the eastern tribes of the Gharubah."

Bohun stood with legs braced and arms folded. Akim Harrad swept him over with a cool gaze, chewing distractedly on a sweet meat. One hand pushed aside a proffered gold dish and he waved a ringed hand.

"Does he have a name?"

"I am Bohun of Damzullah. Forgive my travel stained appearance. I have ridden hard these past weeks to bring you this." Reaching into his robes he drew out the scroll. The giant bodyguard stepped down and took it, handing it to the sultan. Akim Harrad broke the seal and, unscrolling the papyrus, sat for some moments reading. Nodding, he rolled it up again and handed it to Vizek.

"Aatami."

The giant bodyguard salaamed.

"In my seraglio there is a young woman from Damzullah. I have just learned that her name is Dana. Bring her to me."

The bodyguard jerked his head over to two mailed soldiers standing between the columns. They departed with a jingle of mail. Bohun's heart hammered in his ribs. Did he think to see a calculating look in the sultan's gaze? He could not be sure.

Presently, a red curtain at the side of the hall was thrust open and the two soldiers emerged again.

He saw her then—for the first time in many months. From the alcove, across the marbled floor she came, walking between the two guards. As they came up she lowered her head in weary resignation. No longer was she the proud, full bodied woman he had once loved. Nay; the woman that stood cowering before him now was naked and thin, her hair cropped close to her skull, her back crisscrossed with welts from the kiss of the lash. In her eyes was the downcast look of shame and defeat.

*"Dana!"* Her name was torn from his lips. Stumbling across, he knelt on the floor before her and swept her up into his arms. He felt her body stiffen at his touch. His hands felt the welts on her back, the bruises that swelled her limbs, and he bit back a sobbing curse. He knew that months in slavery could change even the hardiest of men. But for women it was infinitely worse. In his burning obsession to find her, he had not prepared himself for the reality.

"B-Bohun?"

"I told you I would come."

"Bohun...you must be away," she whispered. "Evil walks here. I have stared into the dark heart of Chaka. It is too late for me...too late. But you must go." She whispered the words as her head bent down to his. He knelt on the floor before her, his arms encircling her waist, his face pressed into her belly. He lifted his head and stared up into her eyes. He saw fear there. Fear and pain. A dark mist descended over his vision and a red rage fired his brain. His hands yearned for a length of steel to lay waste this palace and drench its marbled walls in blood.

"It seems that the sheikh of the eastern tribes holds you in high esteem. It is known that Akim Harrad is a just and merciful man. But I am afraid, the girl cannot be allowed to leave these walls," said the sultan. "But you are weary. Be our guest and let us feed and bathe you...I insist." He smiled languidly and snapped his fingers. As if at some pre-arranged signal, the guardsman at the hall entrance way drew the doors shut with a hollow boom.

Bohun rose stiffly to his feet. He turned to face the sultan, his hands clenching in murderous rage. He looked into his eyes and saw only cold-ness there. He noted the ready positions of the guards, the look of sly malice on the face of Vizek, the chief treasurer.

It seemed to Bohun that the end of the trail had come. He had found his love. Now he was prepared to sell their lives as dearly as he could. He did not intend that either of them should survive. This time there would be no taking of captives, no bartering for life over freedom. This time there would only be death.

He laughed. A wild laugh that was the guttural cry of some savage beast.

The guards fell back at the sound and in that moment Bohun struck. He whirled, grasping for the sabre sheathed at the nearest soldier's side. Ripping it from the scabbard he thrust forward, ramming the point through the mailed breast, driving the blade in deep, his shoulder slamming into the man as he bent over, a yard of steel dripping crimson from his back. Wrenching the blade free again, he leaped back as the corpse fell to the floor. The second guard gave a fearful shout even as he drove in with his glaive. It struck Bohun's side, piercing the robes and glancing from the mail shirt beneath. Grunting, the giant black grasped the haft and, dragging the weapon toward him, butted the guard in the face. The man staggered away, his nose a bloody ruin, and the sabre flashed down in a crimson arc, splitting his skull to the teeth. Soldiers came in yelling from the shadows. Dana fell to the floor. Grasping at her husband's thigh, she lowered her head in acceptance of what was to come. With one hand, Bohun ripped the desert robes over his head and hurled them with a laugh into the faces of the approaching guardsmen.

"Now, dogs, you will see how Damzullahans die! Your children's children will remember this day."

He looked across, seeing Akim Harrad staring in disbelief. He saw the giant bodyguard with his scimitar upraised. In that moment he calculated the distance between himself, the sultan, and the soldiers sweeping toward him. He could cut the sultan down and be back to end Dana's life before he himself was overwhelmed. With thought came action. Like a charging lion, Bohun leaped to the dais, steel swinging in his hand. Akim Harrad pressed himself into his chair, eyes wide with terror. Too late, Bohun saw the bodyguard move across and tug at a brocaded rope that hung from the ceiling. Then the ground gave way beneath him and he was sent plunging into darkness below!

# 3.

There was a moment of sickening vertigo and then he hit the ground, landing with a cat-like agility into a crouch. He had not fallen far but, as the trap door swung shut above him, he was plunged into darkness. He stood frozen until his eyes became accustomed to the gloom. As his vision slowly adjusted, he noted the glow from a torch bracketed on a wall behind him. From it he could make out a rough estimation of his surroundings. Directly in front was a wall and behind him a long stone corridor that stretched off into darkness. Raising his sword, he could touch the ceiling with its edge but no amount of thrusting could budge the trap. He did not waste time in trying. Nor did he waste time in useless self recrimination. Instead, he turned and loped down the corridor on noiseless feet, his eyes flickering into the shadows cast by the guttering torch. That its flame moved so erratically told him that somewhere up ahead was a way out. Suddenly, to his right, he heard a rustle and clink of chain. He froze, his sword raised defensively before him as he twisted into a crouch.

"Who goes there? Show yourself, demon!" a haggard voice cried out.

Bohun's eyes narrowed to slits. He saw an iron grilled cell. Two brown hands clasped at the bars and beyond them he found himself staring into two sunken eyes, mad with terror.

"I am no demon. I am Bohun. Trapped down here as you are."

At the sound of his voice, the wild eyed prisoner jerked his head. His hair was dirty and unkempt. "Gods! Take your sword, man. Thrust it deep. Strike true. Let not the feeder get me. I beg of you!"

As if for emphasis, he thrust his bony chest up against the bars, his eyes pleading. Bohun shivered then turned away and slunk back into the shadows. A desperate wail followed him as he groped his way out of the torchlight, one hand feeling shakily along the rough hewn wall. Presently, he sensed rather than saw a lessening of the darkness ahead. A draught of clammy air clung about his face. Dimly, he made out a faint grey light. Moving cautiously toward it, he came to a small flight of steps that led up to a solid wooden door. There was a square grille at head height in that door and it was beyond this that the murky light came. He padded up the stair and peered through. As he did, a figure moved in front of the grille and stood facing him. Vizek! Instinctively, he drew back but was too late. The treasurer clasped a thin pipe to his lips and blew. A yellowish dust shrouded Bohun's face and his curse ended in a hacking cough. He reeled away and it was as if his legs had suddenly turned to water. He was unconscious before he hit the floor at the bottom of the stair.

* * * *

He came to slowly, groping through the mire of his sluggish dreams.

Opening his eyes a crack, he found himself staring into a white marbled chamber. Across from him a gold barred window let in a cool rippling breeze. It played upon his bare torso, rousing him from his stupor. Outside, he could see the cold glittering stars as they blurred slowly into focus. He grunted and sought to rise, realizing that his arms were bound tightly behind him. He sat up on a marble divan and swung his legs loosely over the side. Although he had been stripped of his mail, he still wore his breech-clout and high strapped sandals. Above him, a gold censer hung from the ceiling. From it drifted the dark misted scent of myrrh and cinnamon. But it was not these sights that stirred the Damzullahan into straining his muscles against his bonds. It was the sight of the figure before him, his face turned casually away as he gazed out into the night beyond the bars of this opulent prison.

"Given time, I know you could break free from the cords that bind you," sighed Akim Harrad. As he spoke he did not turn but stood gazing out into the night, his hands clasped behind his back. Bohun said nothing. They were alone in the chamber. He spied only one entrance and exit. Strangely, that door was barred—*from within.*

Bending his head, he flexed his arms and shoulders until the muscles stood out in great iron bands.

"Did you ever see such a sight?" continued the sultan, his voice barely above a whisper. "The stars…so aloof in the heavens. What worlds beyond them, we wonder? What battles fought out there in the unreachable vastness? What glories to be had? The gods…yes, the gods alone know."

He turned to face the Damzullahan.

"I have touched those glories," Akim Harrad continued, his voice low and intense and his eyes held a fanatical gleam. "I have gazed upon the faces of gods and seen things that would blast your very reason… I have touched both divinity and blasphemy."

"Dog! Where is Dana?"

The sultan spread his hands and stared at Bohun as if seeing him properly for the first time. "We need her. Savage as she is, she is of nobility. She is strong and her blood line pure."

"Need her for what?" growled Bohun.

Lifting a ringed hand, the sultan stroked his beard. The Damzullahan's blood ran cold when he saw the thin smile that touched his lips.

"It is beyond your understanding, but know this—you too, shall witness glory before you die!"

He moved forward then, staring dispassionately. His eyes held a strange light and his lips writhed into a twisted grin. Then, slowly, to Bohun's horror, his eyes began to roll back. His mouth opened into the semblance of a silent scream. He sank to his knees and threw his head forward. Bohun stared transfixed, the sweat frozen on his naked ebon skin. Akim Harrad's jaws began to widen, elongating impossibly downward. His eyeballs had rolled all the way back into blank white orbs. Something began to bulge in his throat before forcing its way out of his mouth. Long feelers began lashing frantically at the air. Then behind them came something indescribable. A corpse pale body, slimy and gelatinous, like some monstrous insect. It forced itself out of his mouth, oozing down and flopping out onto the marble. Akim Harrad collapsed to the floor. The creature flexed its pale armoured shell and came erect, elongating on spider like legs. It stood about knee height. Madly lashing feelers whipped in front of it as it began to scuttle ominously in Bohun's direction. Under the shell were row upon row of sharp curving teeth. The whole body was as one gigantic mouth and those teeth opened and closed as if already feasting on human flesh. In that moment, Bohun knew madness. He screamed and broke his bonds with a mighty surge of strength. The cords snapped and he came to his feet just as the thing hurled itself upon him. He caught at the flexing body with both hands and held it away at arms length though every muscle screamed in violent protest. Twisting his head to one side, he grimaced as feelers whipped wildly at his face and coiled about his torso. More by instinct than design, he swung round, seeking to break the armoured shell of the thing against the marbled dais. He raised its heavy weight above him then brought it slamming down. There was an audible *crack!* but it seemed to clamp on harder, the appendages coiling around his thick thewed arms and neck. Again he sought to break the shell but this time he could not lift the creature high enough to inflict much damage. The feelers had coiled around him with supernatural strength, limiting his range and pulling him ever closer to the gnashing teeth of its mouth.

Straightening, he turned and rammed it hard against the wall. This time the creature made a sound as its shell connected forcefully with the unyielding marble. It gave a loud and urgent high pitched scream. Gritting his teeth, he drove in again and again. Then he tore back, releasing the grip of one hand and ripping the appendages from around his throat and arm. He struggled free and staggered back into the centre of the chamber.

The thing writhed itself into lashing knots on the floor and, as he stared aghast, he felt something grope at his ankle. It was Akim Harrad. The sultan sought to rise, his hand clutching feebly at Bohun's sandal. His eyes were glazed and a thick white drool dribbled from his lips. "It must feed…let it feed."

Bohun fell back to the wall behind him, horror and loathing knotting a fist deep inside his stomach. The thing had righted itself now and was sending its feelers out along the floor in slithering, undulating waves. It rose up grotesquely and began to walk on spindly stork like legs. The *clack, clack* was magnified horribly in the room as it advanced slowly into the chamber. Eyes wide with dread, Bohun was barely aware that he had nowhere else to go—that he gripped the wall behind him with outstretched hands. Then realization dawned upon him and he glanced wildly around. To his right, bracketed high up on the wall, was a torch. Instantly, he ripped it down and leaning forward, waved the flaming object before him in one hand.

The thing paused then scuttled toward him with preternatural speed. Legs coiled under him, Bohun pushed himself out from the wall and rammed the flaming torch straight into the oncoming mouth. The creature recoiled screaming. It rolled back into a ball along the floor.

"No!" screamed Akim Harrad. He rose feebly and staggered toward the thing. Stepping into his path, Bohun pushed him away with his forearm. The sultan reeled back, looking up dazedly at the big Damzullahan looming over him.

"Damn you!" snarled the big warrior and swinging up the torch, caved in his head with a single bludgeoning blow. Then Bohun took a hesitant step forward and, licking dry lips, drove the torch down into the creature. It recoiled, spitting and flaming. Then he had leaped up and stamped down viciously again and again until the thing was a broken, jelly like mush on the floor. Tendrils twitched spasmodically then were still.

Panting, Bohun drew a shaking wrist over his brow. He barely noticed when he let the torch drop to the floor. He stood for a moment shaking with horror then brought his head up sharply. Beyond the chamber, he heard a voice raised in alarm followed by running feet and the clink of arms. Fists began banging on the door and he remembered that it was barred from inside. Glancing around, he saw nothing that he could use for a weapon. Knotting his fists, he drew his lips into a thin tight line and prepared to die.

## 4.

The door crashed in and men spilled into the room with sabres bared and shields raised. Those first over the threshold fell back from the sight that greeted them. At the centre of the chamber stood Bohun; a half naked ebon giant, head lowered and fists hung low at his sides. They saw the corpse of their sultan and the stiffened remains of something unwholesome smeared into the floor.

"Your sultan is dead," boomed the ebon colossus, flexing his hands, "and many more will be joining him before this night is through." As the words left his lips, he tensed to spring among them.

Vizek pushed his way through the mailed throng. "Unbeliever! Your death will be slow and painful."

The men hesitated, looking at each other. Then one of the guards, lowering his shield, let his sword drop to the floor. Another stepped forward and did the same, the steel ringing hollowly on the marble.

"What is the meaning of this? Your sultan lies dead!" hissed Vizek.

"He was a man accursed," said the first soldier.

*"Li'ana al mubarak hu shihadati!"* proclaimed the second. "He cavorted with demons."

Others murmured their agreement. "And you were part of his evil," accused yet another. "Abducting citizens for that vile *thing* controlling him."

An angry buzz rippled throughout the room and soldiers gripped their weapons, staring intently at the treasurer as he sought to back away. He found his path blocked by a wall of interlocking shields. He turned, his face pale as they closed in all around him. "No! He made me do it—don't you see?" His pleas went unheeded as the armoured men closed in menacingly. Then, as one, they seemed to crash together and Vizek was buried under a wave of slamming shields and deadly flickering blades. There was a high pitched scream then the shields parted again and a barely recognizable figure slipped wetly to the floor.

"So ends the lives of all traitors!" spat a soldier. The others slammed the hilts of their swords against their shields with a wild shout—*"Hai!"*

As the echo of that proclamation died out, Bohun stood motionless.

"Well?" he growled.

The soldiers stared back at him, their hook nosed faces resolute. Then a guard stepped forward. Retrieving his fallen sword, he rose with it in his hand and, holding it by the blade, offered the pommel to the half naked Damzullahan. Bohun stared hard into the man's eyes. Like most soldiers of that little oasis city, these men came from a long line of desert warriors. Quick to call down vengeance on their enemies, they were quick to bond in a brotherhood of blood.

"You killed two of our men," he said tranquilly. "The blessed god demands that we extract vengeance for that. But it was in self defence against the directions of a madman. By riding us of him, you have redeemed yourself. Evil dwells in the tunnels under the palace. Many of us have lost loved ones to it. We did nothing to save them and for that we are damned. We must flee and return to burn this place to the ground. I see in your eyes that you have no such plans. Take this sword, then, and do what you will. May it serve you better than it has served me."

Bohun took the hilt and nodded grimly. The guard stepped away. His head was lowered, whether in shame or in reverence, the Damzullahan neither knew nor cared. The soldiers parted from before the door and, walking through them, Bohun, stalked silently from the chamber.

A flight of stairs wound downward and, gritting his teeth, he quickened his pace, coming down them at a run. He was inside one of the four onion domed towers of the palace. Though he did not know the layout, his sandaled feet were set on a course more resolute than if he had been guided by the brightest desert star. At last his feet hit the marbled floor and he came across an ante chamber decorated with friezes and murals. A rug covered the centre of the room. Opening the door at the far end, he found himself gazing down the shadowed length of the hall where he had first been received. The high chair stood ghostly silent now. He pulled the door closed again and stepped back with a frown into the antechamber. He turned his attention to the rug and, moving over to it, flung it aside. He was not surprized to see a big brass ring set in the floor beneath. Smiling grimly, he gripped the ring with one hand and tugged. A section came up easily in his hand, revealing a set of stone steps leading into darkness. He came down that stair silently, the crescent steel clenched in his fist. This was undoubtedly the way Vizek had come when he had blown the dust into his face after he had fallen through the floor trap. Down here was where the evil lived. Thoughts of Dana and their liberty were pushed to the corners of his mind now. Here, in these tunnelled depths, was an abomination not of this earth. Every fibre of his being cried out and would not rest until it had been wiped from existence.

A torch was bracketed on the wall to his left and he took it down. To his right was the thick door with the grille through which Vizek had blown the sleep dust. To one side of it, he saw a rusted set of keys hanging from a nail on the wall. He thought of the prisoner in his cell beyond that door and took them down. Fumbling, he finally turned the right one in the lock. Coming swiftly down the small steps he moved across the corridor, waving the torch to and fro until he made out the iron bars of his cell.

"Man! Do you yet live?" he hissed out into the darkness. A stirring of chains told him all he needed to know. He padded up to the bars. "I am setting you free."

The man, blinked up at him stupidly. "The sultan?"

"Dead. Are there any more down here?"

The man shuddered and huddled into himself. He shook his head. "Gone...all gone beyond the door through which you came. I heard their screams, though. The feeder...how did you survive it? Is it dead?"

Bohun was silent as he groped with the keys. Finally, he pulled the rusted door open. Unchaining the man, he lifted him to his feet. "Come," he growled and half dragged him out into the corridor. He held the torch high in one fist, his head craned forward to scan the lapping shadows. Then they had made it up through the doorway and out onto the foot of the stair. The man squinted painfully in the glare of the light from above. Bohun gripped him hard by the shoulder and stared into his face. "By Chaka—go man! Go and don't look back." With that, he propelled him onto the steps. Giving him one last look, the man turned and began clambering shakily up the stair. Raising his sword, Bohun turned and loped back into the darkness. He passed the door on his right and followed the left hand wall as it curved round to the left.

He did not have far to go. A blue light began to bathe the corridor and he felt the breath of a clammy draught on his naked limbs. At last, he came to a square cut chamber. As he neared, he slowed, looking dazedly at the sight before him. Here the blue glow was at its strongest—pulsating from a great rock that stood on a waist high pedestal in the centre of the room. From it were spun glistening silvery strands, stretching outward in all directions from floor to wall and ceiling like a monstrous web. As he gazed on it, he felt the pulsing of the blue veined stone like an insidious heartbeat. It shuddered through him, throbbed inside his skull and deep inside his own heart as if it seeking to coerce every living part of him. It was as if, somehow, those vibrations could take control of his very actions. He thought of Akim Harrad and the grotesque thing that had lived within him and shook with revulsion. Remembering the sword in his hand, he bared his teeth and stepped forward. Even as he did, he was bombarded with a powerful wave of energy that thrust knife like into his brain. Fool to think that the thing did not have ways of defending itself! He staggered and would have fallen but for the determination inside him. He cried out and, though his brain felt as if it were being ripped apart, he still stood. He was frozen, unable to move—unable to form a coherent thought. The gigantic web began to vibrate now, rippling in seductive, silvery waves. A strand parted from the ceiling and came drifting down, almost ethereal in its lightness. Delicately, it swam out, reaching sinuously toward the invader in its domain. It curled effortlessly around his shoulders, the tip wavering inquisitively before his eyes. Touching his forehead with a light caress, a thrill of static energy washed through him. It slithered round and, questing, entered his left nostril. Slowly, it began to thread its way upward. He was held in a rigid paroxysm of ecstasy, his sword hanging in one hand, the torch burning forgotten in the other. He felt something touch his thoughts and it was as if the universe opened up before his eyes.

The thing was communicating with him.

## 5.

Words and images formed inside his mind in a language he did not know. A language that he yet, somehow, understood.

He saw a black emptiness pin pricked with tiny glittering stars. Through that emptiness came a blue veined rock, spinning silently through the void... Impersonally, Bohun's mind's eye took in all that he saw.

Through the uncharted chasms of space and the raging infernos of the deepest nebulae it continued its eon spanning journey. Untold millennia drifted by as, deep inside that rock, life lay dormant, awaiting the right moment to awaken.

Then came a yellow sun and a vast object that rose up in the form of a blue green world. Through the atmosphere of that world it fell, ice and fragments burning as it screamed through the sky to land in the hot, desert night. There it lay; smouldering in a bubbling crater, as life, at last, began to stir.

The men that found the stone brought it to their city, proclaiming in triumph that the gods had blessed them. Their ruler guarded it jealously, marvelling at its radiance—an aura that was truly of the heavens. Afraid that it would become prey to thieves, he housed it in a secret chamber in the tunnels beneath his palace. At night he would come and sit before the pedestal upon which it was placed. There, gazing on it, he sought to learn wisdom from the gods. In the mornings his eyes would have a far, haunted look and he would speak strangely to his advisors. They became worried for him and sought to curb these nocturnal visits. One night, they followed him down, seeking to dissuade him from his obsession. With the dawn, only the sultan came up from the tunnels. The advisors were never seen or heard from again.

Now the scene shifted and he saw the chamber within which he stood. He saw the life force of the strange stone grow from pale to a deep throbbing blue. He saw its tendrils spreading out before Akim Harrad as he sat in a trance like state. He saw them reach out to the walls and the floor and the ceiling, weaving an impossible web before him. Then, finally, it whispered to him its most guarded secrets. A tendril entered, even as it had Bohun, through his nostril and began to attach itself to his mind...then, as the power grew, another and yet another tendril would come, entering through his mouth and ears. At last the star stone was strong enough. At last it had found its perfect host and could plant its alien seed. Inside something began to grow...and the thing within needed to feed.

Only one man was aware of Akim Harrad's terrible secret. That man was Vizek, who, with designs of his own, arranged for strangers and women to be snatched from the streets. There, before the pulsating blue stone from the stars, he watched as captives were fed to the unwholesome life form that lived within his ruler. He watched from the shadows, knowing revulsion yet also a perverse pleasure. He revelled in the screams from its victims—the young girls and women that he brought to be devoured alive.

But it was not enough.

The feeder needed to reproduce. It needed to spread out among this new world. A slave-girl was brought into the chamber. A young woman whose skin glistened like polished ebony. As she was led before the stone, the web began to vibrate and hum a strange harp like melody. Stood before the pedestal, Akim Harrad regarded her with lust in his eyes. He lay with her then, copulating with her in the dust as cries of anguish were torn from the woman's lips…the seed had again been sewn. This time in the womb.

Bohun's mind's eye viewed these scenes dispassionately. He was not aware of his own existence. But suddenly, sensation began to stir within him. He felt pain…searing, jagged pain. Slowly, then with growing realization, Bohun began to waken. Sight and sound hit him simultaneously and he reeled back, eyes flying wide. The torch in his hand had burned down and was starting to scorch the flesh of his thigh. It was this pain that had brought him out of his trance. As he staggered back, the mind link was broken and the tendril whipped out of his nostril. At that moment, Bohun looked around, seeing many tendrils weaving sinuously before him. He felt the steel in his hand and, with a wild shout, struck out, severing those that came nearest him. They parted like cobwebs before his flashing sword. The blue veined rock on the pedestal filled his vision now. With each throbbing pulse his head pounded with pain and he struck out again, moving forward with only one thought in his mind—to destroy. He brought up the torch in his left hand and flung it at the collapsing web. There was a flare and a whoosh as it struck. Blue flame rippled as it caught in the glittering strands.

Deep inside his mind, he felt a scream of mental anguish. It came from the stone, he knew. It threatened to split open his skull but he staggered on. Then the blue flames had raced along the collapsing web and devoured it. With supernatural quickness the rock became enveloped. That flame was cold, colder than the space between the stars and Bohun backed away in fear. The scream grew to an unbearable pitch then suddenly the rock pitched forward. It crashed headlong to the floor, splintering into two separate halves. From it a green mist evaporated and then the scream was silenced. Impossibly, the blue fire raged on, devouring the rock and the remnants of the collapsing web. Finally, it died out altogether and all that was left were stiffened strands of web and the two frosted halves of the stone lying broken on the floor. Frost gleamed everywhere in the chamber.

Cautiously, Bohun stepped toward the pedestal, particles of ice crunching under his sandals. He stared at the sundered halves of the rock for an instant then brought his sword down—once, twice, in quick succession. They shivered to bits under the fury of his strokes and those pieces he ground to dust beneath his heel. Shivering, he stepped back out of the chamber.

He stood as if in a daze, trying to comprehend all that had happened. Then he lifted his head as fear clutched his heart anew.

*Dana!* He wheeled and raced back down the corridor. He barely saw the stairs that he bounded up to emerge out into the ante chamber. His thoughts were a riot of confusion and fear. Images and words came back to him in disjointed flashes. He remembered the visions in his head…the thing's need to reproduce… Akim Harrad copulating with his wife before the blue stone. Then he remembered his wife's words to him in the sultan's throne room—*"Evil walks here. I have stared into the dark heart of Chaka. It is too late for me…too late…"* The memory of those words hit him with the impact of a thunderbolt. He came out of the ante chamber, pelting full tilt down the length of the hall. He had no idea where he was going, only a blind sense of reasoning to trace steps where he had already been. He was dimly aware of people shouting in panic all around him, fleeing like shadows through the archways of the palace as they sought to escape. A mailed soldier passed him, giving him a wide berth, seeing the crazed look in his eyes. Then he had ploughed headlong into a slim white shape. He reached out, gripping a pale arm in his hand. He swung the woman round and the bangles on her limbs clashed startlingly. She fell to her knees, painted eyes wide with fright.

"Dana! Where is she?" he snarled. The girl looked up dazedly. He shook her roughly. "Where?"

She cried out and looked back quickly over her shoulder. "In the harem—she—please…let me go!" She twisted in his grasp and he released her. She sped away but he was already moving, coming to the red silk hanging at the far end of the hall. He ripped the gauze aside with one hand and flung it to the floor. He came down a carpeted hallway, emerging out into a spacious marble chamber. In contrast to the rest of the palace, all here was still and calm.

A single copper oil lamp burned from its bracket on the wall. Cushions and rugs were strewn on the floor between couches strategically positioned for the art of seduction. Beyond them were hangings of red and yellow gauze. He moved in silently and, as he did, he saw the shadowed outline of a woman lying on a couch behind a silk curtain. His heart in his mouth, he approached slowly and, with one hand, reached up and thrust the hanging aside.

Bathed in the light of the glow from the single lamp, Dana lay; her sleek ebon skin slick with sweat, her breast rising and falling in slow rhythm. She lay naked on a divan strewn with leopard skins. Her eyelids fluttered now and her head turned slightly as Bohun knelt down beside her. One hand reached out and a smile curved her lips. The slender arm seemed to lose its strength and then collapse, her fingers tracing a soft caress down his chiselled face. At the side of the divan lay an over turned goblet, its fragrant nectar forming a small puddle on the floor.

"Poison," he breathed. Gripping her hand, he pressed it to his lips and squeezed his eyes shut tightly.

"Dana…" the word came as a tortured gasp.

"I could not live with it inside me, Bohun," she rasped. "It is the only way. Mourn for me and weep, my love. But then live. Do not bury me in the dust of this land. Bury me deep in the earth by the water and sing the songs of my ancestors. In T'agulla's domain I will await you. He will guard and keep my spirit…safe…" Her breath ended in a sigh and she stiffened. A trickle of blood crept from her mouth and she was dead.

### 6.

Mist crawled along the reeds and drifted out over the river as the sun began to break against the sky. As it did, fishermen on the banks of the river Zallam paused from casting their nets to witness a strange sight that greeted them in the light of the early dawn. A raft came moving almost solemnly down the waters, poled by a tall, well built black man. He was wide shouldered, wearing the robes and headdress of a desert tribesman. His face was chiselled as if from iron and he stared grimly ahead, looking to neither left nor right. His eyes were dark and hard as flint. Belted at his waist was a curved scimitar and at his feet lay a long object wrapped in a linen shroud. He stood brace legged over this object and the lithe men along the riverbank knew him for a man in mourning. Then the mists had curled over him and the raft was gone, leaving the fishermen to draw up their nets and wonder if they had really seen him at all.

That afternoon the raft came to a fertile pasture and the big warrior carried his burden through the long grass into a glade. There, under bowed trees, a grave was dug and the man, who had once been the champion of Damzullah, laid his wife finally to rest. He sung the dirge of his people and the songs of her ancestors. The sky was dark and the sun an extinguishing red flame when all was done.

A day later he arrived at a small trading outpost. Tents flapped in the wind where dark eyed men squatted together in the sand. They eyed the stranger suspiciously as dogs yapped and fought for scraps in the heat. After long talks, a caravan master, ready to leave for the coast, offered him a job as guardsman.

\* \* \* \*

In the long weeks that followed, turmoil swept over the city state of Ibn-Shahk. The palace was burned to the ground. Those faithful to her dead ruler, Akim Harrad, were seized and stoned to death. His bodyguard, Aatami, was caught trying to escape. Refusing to be taken alive, he killed most of his pursuers before being brought down by an angry mob.

Eventually, soldiers were sent from the outlying provinces to deal with the unrest. They came marching up through the gates to find a city deep in the throes of violence. Order had broken down as rival gangs fought openly in the streets. Bitter enmities flared up and the little oasis city found itself a battle ground for a short but fierce civil war. At the end of it, Ibn-Shahk was a smoking wasteland, its citizens scattered. Merchants told stories of a gigantic black warrior who had brought doom upon the city, slaying its sultan. One old man, who claimed to have been held prisoner beneath the palace, told another tale. He told of a despot ruler that worshipped strange and terrible gods who preyed upon his own people. He spoke of a swordsman from the hot savannahs of the south who helped rid the land of its curse. Though a search was made for this man along the outlying provinces, no evidence of him was found and the story passed into folklore.

* * * *

The noise and dust of the small coastal outpost stifled in the afternoon heat. No breeze blew in from the ocean and the sea was like a mirror lying flat under the blazing sun.

Bohun stared out from the shack that served as a tavern at the great war-ships lying off shore. Everywhere armoured men moved, their breast plates flashing like burnished gold.

"Out of the way!" roared a big soldier, barging up and brushing aside scrawny natives that held out their begging bowls to him. He kicked them into the dust and, swaggering into the tavern, doffed his crested helmet. Sweeping back his red cloak, he crashed into a rickety chair and rested his iron grieved boots up on the table. "Wine, damn you!" he shouted at a black native woman who scurried away to do his bidding. He swivelled his head, seeing Bohun leaning against the open window, regarding him.

"Ho, a big lad, this one! You're not from these parts. Whence you hail?"

"Damzullah."

"Never heard of it. Shit hole, is it? That why you left?" He laughed uproariously at his own jest, drawing appreciative titters from the soldiers sat either gambling or drinking in the cool shaded den.

Pushing his way out from the window frame, Bohun kicked up a stall and sat opposite him. He jerked his head. "That fleet. Where is it headed?"

The big soldier blinked at him, noticing the easy grace with which he moved, the hilt of the big curved scimitar at his side. "Where have you been? There's a war on, lad. We're the royal fleet of Valentia. Sent out by the emperor's decree. We're on our way to Dionyssa to crush the oily bastards and send their fleet to hades."

"I would join you."

The big soldier made to laugh then stopped, running a hand over his jaw and reaching for the wine cask instead. He took a swig and wiped a bronze wrist guard over his lips. "Well, it's true we are short of men. I can't promise a standard uniform—not until we reach Dionyssa, but if you can keep steady pace with an oar—well, we'll need you. That sword will have to go though." He pointed at the two handed hilt jutting from Bohun's waist. "Only standard spatha for infantry, whether you're a general or recruit." He slapped a hand on the metal scabbard at his own side.

Bohun nodded. The big soldier laughed and, thumping his fist down on the rough hewn boards, pushed the wine cask over to him. "Then welcome to the army, lad! Onward to Dionyssa!"

Swinging up the wine cask, the Damzullahan gave a mocking salute before taking a long swig and slamming it back down on the table.

"On to Dionyssa," he said.

# BELLICO AND THE HUSKS OF THE "HEAVENSENT"

## Richard Toogood

There is no joy in being old.

And no prizes for getting that way either.

I was still a gormless youth when I was first told this and so I dismissed it as a morbid and cynical sentiment. [A redacted number of] decades later and I can testify to its axiomatic wisdom. For as I sit here in this draughty garret, with its leaking roof and its unreliable plumbing, so it increasingly takes on in my mind the projection of my own decrepit body. My eyes are clouded by cataracts now and my fingers contorted with arthritis. While the indignities inflicted daily by treacherous bowels and a failing bladder are best kept between me and my cronies in the post office queue.

But at least I can console myself with the knowledge that my wits as yet remain my own, and that I am not lost in a fog of confusion and spouting gibberish as so many of my contemporaries seem to. That at least remains my belief for I presume that were I to be so afflicted then I would have no means of knowing otherwise.

Even my correspondence these days seems mostly given over to mutual commiseration upon the miseries of infirmity. Indeed I received a letter only the other day from one of my muckers in far off Proctokopolis in which he compared his own tribulations to "a living death".

The expression caught me completely unawares I must say, and had the effect of catapulting my thoughts back across the chasm of years to those aforementioned days of my callowness and to the recollection of a dreadful experience calculated to put my friend's glib phrase into its proper perspective.

At that time I was being retained to record the reflections and ruminations of the barbarian adventurer Bellico the Bastard. He was an ageing figure by that stage, grizzled inside as well as out, and had become much troubled by the question of posterity. He had seen so many remarkable things in the course of his long and turbulent career, had fought so many terrible battles, both suffered egregiously and conquered triumphantly, that it perturbed him to think that it would count for nothing if there was no means of commemorating it all. He had no statues to record his accomplishments; there was no kin to testify to his fame. And so he had employed me to compile a memoir of his adventures for the edification of future generations.

It would be an exaggeration to describe this undertaking as a biography. Bellico liked to recount his escapades in haphazard fashion, supplying only the vaguest inferences to enable me to link one to another. It did not escape my notice either that certain events seemed to crop up repeatedly under drastically different circumstances which lead me to suspect that facts were being confused and muddied in his memory. But they were still memorable and eventful days trailing in his wake as he travelled from place to place seeking either the rainbow's end or the vagabond's grave which, so far as he saw it, amounted to much the same thing.

The particular day to which my friend's chance remark returned me in such abrupt a fashion was one which began inauspiciously with a profanity of ear blistering virulence. Bellico and I were stood upon a bleak rocky shore that fringed an uncharted island situated somewhere in the vast southern ocean. And we were staring forlornly after the departing ship that had just stranded us there at arrow point. To make matters worse there was a wintery edge to the wind and what looked to me like the beginnings of a storm beginning to agitate the turbid clouds atop the mountain peaks. It was small wonder then that Bellico felt compelled to repeat his potent oath. I wanted to echo it myself.

I took a despondent inventory of our meagre resources. Foremost amongst them, in my estimation at least, was the row-boat into which we had been forced on the business side of bent bow staves; the captain had been reluctant to further endanger his depleted crew by ferrying us ashore. There was also three days worth of rations and one rundlet of drinking water to share between us. All told it was not a manifest guaranteed to inspire much confidence in our chances.

And there was Morguemonger, of course; the terrible mace which was at once both primitive fetish and primary weapon to Bellico. I will ration my expenditure of ink concerning Morguemonger at this point in deference to those critics who have accused me of a morbid profluence on the subject over the years. I will simply restate the fact of its extraterrestrial origin and reiterate the grim and malign character which, by some ineffable means, I was always convinced the thing possessed and leave it at that. Potent implement though it was I did not foresee it being of much benefit to us in that dead and remote place.

Having exorcised his wrath by colouring the air a resplendent shade of blue, Bellico suddenly appeared almost cheerful by his standards. I looked on as he hauled the row-boat out of the surf and dragged it high up the beach to a sheltered and secluded spot.

"Unlikely we'll have any further use for it. But better to know it is there than sacrifice it unnecessarily to the tide."

It was not until much later on in our association that I appreciated his efforts to educate me in practicalities by means of these gruff commentaries of his. My own upbringing had been conducted in the insulated surrounds of academia, which might have left me well versed in all manner of quaint and redundant disciplines but utterly clueless when it came to the business of survival in the wild. By contrast Bellico had been born in a blizzard, or so he claimed anyway, and had hunted his own game for as long as he could remember. I had cultivated an image of him hurling spears from his cradle which I maintain is not the exaggeration that it may appear. There is no denying that life was brutal in the mountainous tribal lands that he came from but it clearly instilled an appetite for the hunter-gatherer regimen which he always relished any opportunity to pursue.

But all I could think of at the time was the quiet snug cabin I had slept in the night before. As was so often the case in those days my comfort had rested gingerly on the shallow foundation of Bellico's volatile temperament. In the end it had taken nothing more provocative than an ill-judged jest and in the wink of an eye the middle deck was a battleground with bloodied mariners being hurled this way and that. I retain a memory of Bellico planted with his back to the mast and with his mallet-like fists swinging in all directions. He had succeeded in putting half the crew in the infirmary before they finally brought him down, burying him under a weight of bodies whilst raining cleats and kevels down upon his head. For all the fact that we were paying passengers the captain had swiftly reached the conclusion that Bellico was as welcome on his vessel as an unstable and explosive cargo. His parting comment had been something to the effect that we could count ourselves fortunate that he hadn't arranged a summary burial at sea for us both. History damn him for a sentimental softy but that's just the way he was. And we could ask anyone.

Looking around I did not think it likely that we would be in any position to either confirm or dispute the captain's temperament for a considerable length of time. If indeed we ever would be. The terrain was entirely slate grey in complexion, metamorphic in texture and utterly cheerless in character. I presume my expression must have betrayed the deepening despondency I felt for it prompted a gruff attempt at morale boosting from Bellico;

"Wearing a face like a slapped arse isn't going to get us anywhere scrivener" he said, hefting the water butt onto his shoulder and shoving the haversack of rations into my arms. "We will follow the shoreline as far as we can. That is where any habitation is most likely to be found. If the way becomes impassable then we will head inland."

I nodded dumbly; flabbergasted by his blunt refusal to be disheartened by circumstances no matter how bleak they might appear to the untutored eye.

"Your problem scrivener is that you see every challenge as an insurmountable obstacle. Any general who took to the field nursing an attitude of that sort would have beaten himself before giving the enemy an opportunity of doing it. Life itself is one incessant hardship. It is in the manner that we contest adversity that truly makes us what we are."

I felt like an alien interloper as we trudged through that silent sterile landscape. The only movement was supplied by the windy quiver of grass tufts which sprouted from crevices; the only sound came from the sizzle of the surf as it fermented upon the shingle. We saw no signs of human intrusion or of animal activity. Life itself there appeared to adopt the furtive status of an unwelcome intruder. The scree littered slopes and the ponderous outcroppings wore an expression of disdain as we plodded dolefully past them.

This pronounced sense of extrinsicness however did not extend itself to my companion. On the contrary, Bellico had begun to exude that aura of rugged contentment which was natural to him but which he seemed to lose whenever we made one of our infrequent visits to cities or found ourselves travelling through tamed and cultivated terrains. Bellico detested city life. In marked contrast to most barbarians I have known the amenities and luxuries of civilised living had never held any allure for him. He scorned them as decadences calculated to make a man soft. It was really no wonder then that he acclimatised so easily to the challenges of that place. With his squat rough hewn body and crudely weathered head he carried the look of a man similarly formed by geological forces rather than biological processes.

How long we trudged along that dismal shore I do not know. My attention was entirely focused on keeping a constant watch upon the horizon, straining to detect any sign of a sail of deliverance but nothing rewarded my efforts. The seas are vast and empty in those latitudes, and we possessed no means of alerting anyone to our presence even had a vessel chosen that moment to cruise fortuitously past us. My feeling of despondency deepened into despair.

Eventually we found our path blocked by a jutting headland around which the waves gnawed and foamed rabidly. We turned our feet inland and so began a series of exacting crawls over rubble strewn escarpments, hair-raising sidles around precipitous bluffs and desperate scrambles along jagged ridges. Before very long my fingers were scraped raw for hands trained to the use of the stylus make poor equipment for rock climbing with. But in the end our efforts brought us to the head of an elevated plateau. And that is where we made a discovery that brought us both to a halt and even succeeded in wrenching a startled grunt from the normally imperturbable Bellico. For lying there before us, strewn over a wide area, was the rusting wreckage of an airship.

At that time no airship had ploughed the clouds of Vitracolee for more than half a century. As I recalled from my historical studies they had been a short-lived experiment in alternative travel. Audacious in concept and calamitous in operation; their alarming habit for ending their voyages in uncontrolled and terminal fashion had seen them dubbed "catastroferries" which put paid to the whole idea of them in very short order. Although this was the stuff of recent history insofar as Bellico and I were concerned it still came as an almighty surprise to us both to find the remains of one so unaccountably littered there upon that remote and isolated territory.

We picked our way solemnly through a scattered debris of splintered spars and corroded ironmongery, past the rusted ribs of its iron skeleton as we moved in the direction of the crumpled gondola.

It was a marvel to me to discover that this had not disintegrated entirely upon impact, having clearly plunged from a considerable height. It was nonetheless twisted and concertinaed into a grotesque abstract shape, with peeling ribbons of paint stirring feebly in the wind like palsied fingers. The atmosphere was colder and dryer there and the surrounding rocks had protected the wreckage from the worst effects of the scouring wind. We could still discern the original cadmium orange hue of the hull. And as I circled around to the far side I found I was able to trace the faded and flaking black characters of the vessel's name:

H.E.A.V.E.N.S.E.N.T

I heard Bellico's grunt of recognition as I exclaimed the name. The disappearance of the astroschooner (*AS*) *Heavensent* was in those days a famous aeronautical mystery. The ship had been the trophy project of a demented entrepreneur by the name of Protillo Levak. And if it comes as a surprise to my regular readers to find me conversant with such facts, when precedent has shown me usually woefully ignorant in the matter of journalistic trivia of this sort, there is a perfectly reasonable explanation for it. Levak had once been a generous patron to the academies which I attended and so the story of his deranged exploits was the stuff of college folklore.

As I remembered it the *Heavensent* had originally been conceived by him as a means to search for life forms which he had convinced himself could be found living in the clouds. After a series of promising test flights the *Heavensent* and its crew of six had departed in earnest pursuit of Levak's objective with the genial maverick himself at the helm. And that was the last that was ever heard of either of them. The story had persisted for more than fifty years that Levak had flown so high that he had escaped the atmosphere altogether and had ended his days upon the moon of Clindrovane. When I reported this fanciful notion to Bellico he received it with the expected sneer of derision.

"Clearly not that far then. But they obviously travelled much further than anyone would have believed possible at the time."

Bellico merely shrugged, seemingly ambivalent about the entire subject. He was stood in his habitual pose with Morguemonger balanced across his shoulder, the spiked head positioned, as I persisted in thinking of it, in poisonous proximity to his ever amenable ear.

It was at that moment that the possibility occurred to me that the ship's log might conceivably have survived the vicissitudes of the years and could yield some insight into whatever calamity had befallen the vessel. With that thought in mind I ducked into the gloomy interior. And scant seconds later spurted back out again, flailing and floundering in panic, my eyes bulging, my mouth yammering soundlessly, and sporting a pallor which Bellico was later to admit made him think I had been siphoned by a famished vampire.

I lay on my back, gesturing like an imbecile, and breathing in a hyperventilated gasp.

I heard Bellico bark a derisive laugh;

"The squeamishness of you civilised folk never fails to amuse me, scrivener. But I think this is a lot of fuss to be making over a few old bones."

I could only shake my head wordlessly.

"Freeze dried corpses then. Not all that surprising given the conditions here. I suppose that would give a milksop like you a start."

There was something desiccated in the look of the things certainly, but as they lurched menacingly out into the light in pursuit of me I found it hard to accept that they qualified as corpses. There were six of them in total and the shreds of distinctive livery that still clung to their wasted figures left little room for doubt about whom they had once been. Following some strange compulsion they mustarded as a group before us, much as they must once have done while posing for the painting that hung in the refectory of my old college. But as intimate with the details of that work as I was I found nothing to recognise in the ghastly sunken faces of those blanched beings now confronting us. For their teeth had been methodically filed into fangs and their stringy hair fluttered in the wind like cobwebs. A chorus of incoherent voices washed dolefully across their withered tongues.

But it was the sight of their eyes, first seen glowing in the darkness of the gondola, which now threatened to purge my bowels in sheer terror. Buried within the excavated pits of their sockets there glimmered a cold green light that was not remotely human in character. It was as if some alien parasite had hollowed out their skulls from the inside and now squatted within peering venomously out. An inspired conjecture on my part as things transpired but not one I take much pride in.

I heard Bellico bark a startled oath and lunge forward swinging Morguemonger in a destructive arc. The nearest of the beings crumpled in an implosion of splintered bones leaving a plume of powdered grey flesh roiling in the air where the thing had stood. But as this dissipated and dispersed in the freshening wind so Bellico and I found ourselves confronted by a cloud of queer green smoke which seemed to flicker with a sporadic radiance like the lightning that grumbles in the belly of a pregnant thunderhead.

A moment only this strange tableau lasted before the cloud funnelled itself forward at astonishing speed enveloping Bellico's entire head in a suffocating sphere of vapour. I saw his lips part, although whether this was in an instinctive gasp for air or in order to bellow a profanity there was no way of knowing. For even as his jaws gnashed so the cloud was siphoned into his mouth.

The effect of this occurrence was as instantaneous as it was ghastly to witness. His face suddenly drained of all character and expression. Nothing now animated it except for the malevolent flicker of an alien intelligence which glimmered greenly in the shadow of his heavy brows. With terrible and unmistakable purpose his head swivelled menacingly in my direction.

If my heart could have abandoned me at that instant by plunging down through my bowels then I have no doubt that it would have done so and with little remorse either. Not only had I been deprived of my patron and protector but in the same fell swoop he had been recruited to the malign forces confronting me.

I think I can be excused for admitting that my first panic-stricken impulse was to run. But where could I possibly flee to? I was marooned on an uninhabited island. And to make matters worse Bellico remained in possession of the only available source of drinking water. The row-boat remained an option. However the thought of perishing thirst-crazed in the limitless ocean held no greater allure for me than being devoured wholemeal by the advancing horrors.

For one fleeting second my hand did stray to the hilt of the feeble little knife I kept in my belt but the idea of putting up a fight against such overwhelming odds struck me as laughably absurd. I could write well enough of the desperate battle madness of the cornered barbarian warrior but emulating it in practice was out of the question.

Deprived of the alternatives of both flight and fight this seemed to be an ideal opportunity for a triumphant flash of creative thinking on my part. The timely recollection of some snippet of arcane knowledge perhaps, which might come to my rescue and by so doing vindicate a closeted upbringing. But wrack my brains though I did no viable course of action sprang to mind. If I was correct in my assumption that the crew of the *Heavensent* were possessed by the very stratospheric life forms they had gone seeking then what could I do to oppose them with nothing more useful at my disposal than the wreckage of their own airship which, I had no doubt, they had deliberately scuttled there to spare others from the hideous fate that had overtaken them?

There was nothing I could do. Which is why I stood there fatalistically watching those ghastly figures shuffling inexorably towards me. I took no consolation from the fact that Bellico himself lurked to the rear of the group, his face suddenly strangely contorted as if some tumultuous battle was being waged within his brain. My attention was wholly captivated by the awful death which was about to claim me with clenching freeze-dried fingers and masticating jaws.

And it would have done if Bellico had not then come to a complete halt with Morguemonger extended strangely before him like a drum major's baton. Barely registered by my fear swamped mind he was wrenching the haft of the weapon in a series of complicated counter-rotational twists. This was something I had never seen him do before and the glazed expression he wore seemed to suggest that it was an action being undertaken without conscious thought on his part. I was aware of a scarcely audible click and suddenly the mace head was rotating and beginning to emit a weird high pitched whine. One final twist of the pommel and the entire mace was suddenly ablaze with a coruscation of violent blue/white light.

In the same instant Bellico himself became entirely sheathed in a shimmering nimbus. The sparse grey fuzz of his hair blazed about his head like a corona. His eyes rolled back in his head and an expression of orgasmic glee contorted his features. Waves of sizzling energy rippled around his body and the air began to char with the smell of ozone.

Shielding my eyes as best I could I saw the weird green vapour jet violently out of his ears and nostrils. Bellico then lunged forward. And even as I stared with appalled fascination at the skeletal hand grasping for my eyes so its owner was abruptly yanked backwards, hoisted into the air and then dashed to osseous rubble upon the ground at my feet. As the four remaining abominations pivoted around so Bellico's shimmering fist drove through one gaping face, the entire head collapsing into a sinkhole of disintegrating bone. Then Morguemonger crunched down on the rest. And even as the possessed husks of the *Heavensent*'s crew crumpled into shattered fossils so they flared and combusted at the blazing mace's purging touch.

This was not the end of the matter of course. We were now left with the problem of six evicted alien parasites pulsing furiously in the air above us. And I found myself profoundly conscious of the fact that I was now the sole vessel available to host them. But clearly conscious of the pitiful threat my possessed form could pose to the vengeful Bellico the strange alien creatures ignored me and merged instead into one enormous bank of swirling green fog. To my stressed and suggestible mind this seemed to take on a vaguely demonic configuration with flailing tails and multiple gnashing jaws which loomed hugely and menacingly over the two of us.

True to form I felt myself quailing awestruck but Bellico remained undaunted and stood his ground, pounding Morguemonger repeatedly against the hovering monstrosity's nebulous form which, in defiance of all logic, quaked with vast convulsive shudders to the impact of the blazing mace. Time and again it lunged at him, striving to breach the protective carapace of blue energy that cocooned him and each time it was rebuffed. And as it recoiled so Morguemonger punched deep smoking craters into its form. When it attempted to flee it found that Bellico had twisted one of its swishing tendrils of a tail around his leg, anchoring it to the ground. And even as it strained against this like a leashed cur at its stake Morguemonger beat out its doom in inexorable metronomic fashion.

BOOM! BOOM! BOOM!

It ended as abruptly as it had begun. There was the fall of a sudden silence and with it the sight of wisps of inert green gas dissipating on the strengthening wind. All at once I found myself alone with a heap of half cremated corpses and a prostrate Bellico who now lay flat on his back and snoring stentoriously.

As I shuffled a stupefied path towards him so my eyes strayed warily towards Morguemonger which remained resolutely clenched in his fists. The mace was once again an inert hunk of brutal black iron with nothing to indicate that it was capable of being anything else. Had the stress of the situation caused me to imagine the weapon's weird transformation, I wondered? There was little chance of clinging to that delusion with the acrid stench of charred flesh lingering in the air. Nor was I able to invest much hope in the idea that Bellico had been conscious of what he had done. Therefore the impetus for what I had witnessed could only have come from one source. This concession sat rather queasily in my stomach to say the least.

"Morguemonger was not forged in any mortal furnace, you fool. It was hammered out upon the anvil of the stars. There is no force in nature impervious to its power."

How often had I heard those very words or a thousand variations upon them? Spat with toxic vitriol usually whilst Bellico was busy beating some writhing preternatural horror into oblivion. There had been no triumphant roars on this occasion but the result had been no different. Not for the first time I found myself speculating whether Morguemonger was an implement or an entity or some strange fusion of the two? No answer was forthcoming then and I am not altogether certain that one ever did come. But as I drew near so my eye was caught by a crescent of reflected light which curved about the spiked head like a smug and conspiratorial smirk.

A short while afterwards a revived Bellico clambered to his feet. He conceded no memory of what had occurred but blithely dismissed this as the natural consequence of the battle madness which he told me sometimes possessed him in these situations.

"Another one for your book, eh scrivener" he said having cast a satisfied eye over the pitiful remains of what was left of the *Heavensent*'s crew.

"I have my doubts sometimes that you believe even half the stories I tell you. But you can't dispute the evidence of your own eyes eh. Take a look at that little lot and try to deny what the old man's still capable of."

I found that I could only nod mutely.

As we made our way wearily off of the plateau so we found ourselves rewarded by the sight of a bellying sail heading straight towards the island. The captain had proved to be every bit as soft-hearted as he claimed to be and had repented his decision to maroon us.

While we waited for the ship to arrive I passed the time jotting down the notes which have provided the basis for this account. But I did not reflect too deeply upon what I had experienced, being too immature at that time to do so to any profit. It is only now in these last dwindling days of my life, when I have had the experience of seeing friends lost to the tragedy of senility and witnessed frightened strangers peer suspiciously out at me from familiar faces, that I can properly appreciate what the *Heavensent*'s stricken crew must have endured. While I do not relish what I so nearly suffered at their hands, I bear them no malice.

I did wonder though why I had not told Bellico the truth about what had happened. Perhaps I feared that he would not have believed me. Or maybe the fear owed more to what might happen if he did. In any event, I am glad now that I chose to leave him with his delusions. For if I have learned anything over the course of a long and vicarious life, it is that equally we are all victims of such. Each and every one of us. In one form or another.

✗

# DON'T OPEN YOUR EYES
## Taylor Grant

Willow House, as it was called by those who knew its grim history, seemed to shun the light, even in the brightest part of day. The last house on the dead-end street of Willow Lane, it stood like a lone sentry; long forgotten, yet unwilling to abandon its post.

Inside its shadowy recesses, Jessica Lewis trudged up a flight of circular stairs to the second floor. Ahead of her, a young real estate agent tugged anxiously at his ill-fitting coat for what she guessed was the hundredth time.

The topic of missing persons had yet to come up and the tour was nearly over.

The young man, whose name tag read 'Brandon', gestured for her to enter the master bedroom. Jessica empathized with his situation, of course. Espousing the virtues of mountain views and pegged hardwood flooring was one thing. Acknowledging that every previous owner of the house had gone missing on Halloween was quite another.

Brandon glanced around the room uneasily as he pulled back the curtains of the tall window to showcase the view. Jessica gave him another once-over and decided he couldn't be more than 23 years old. He looked like he was wearing his dad's suit in the hopes of appearing more professional.

She almost felt sorry for the kid; he would be easy to bulldoze.

The room smelled of emptiness, of things long forgotten, of people long gone. Jessica thought of the previous owners who had lived, laughed, made love, and perhaps died in this very room.

Brandon cleared his throat then, startling Jessica from her reverie. She was about to ask him about noise from nearby roads or neighbors. but he was already gesturing for her to follow him.

He spun on his heels and strode out of the room, as if attempting to inject a purposeful confidence to his movements.

\* \* \* \*

Jessica had an arsenal of negotiation tactics she'd honed over the years, and the young agent had fallen for each of them.

As they stood in the home's reception hall, she talked him through a litany of repairs needed and overestimated costs on all of them. She noted that in his oversized suit, Brandon looked like a turtle withdrawing into its shell.

It seemed as if he wanted to escape the house, his eyes continually searching for…

What exactly? she thought. The ghosts of the missing owners?

Jessica stood in front of the door, blocking him. It was time to call out the elephant in the room.

She asked about the history of Willow House.

Brandon visibly reacted, glanced away, and then slowly returned her gaze.

In some states, real estate agents were required by law to disclose prior deaths in the house or anything significant that might devalue the property. This was not one of those states.

"Ms. Lewis…" Brandon said, clearing his throat. "Other than some of the minor repairs discussed, the seller hasn't mentioned any material defects, so I—"

Jessica cut him off with a dismissive wave. I already did my research, *Brandon.* "I know all about the previous owners. I just wanted to make sure you know that *I know.* So, you'll understand the reasoning behind my final offer."

Jessica leaned in, self-assured, and gave him a low-ball number. Flustered, the young man mumbled something about discussing it with his client and rushed out the front door.

Jessica knew they would take it. The house was unsellable.

She would change that, of course.

That was her whole hustle.

\* \* \* \*

Four months later, Jessica was living in the unsellable house on Willow Lane.

Ten years prior, she had figured out a great niche business: buy stigmatized properties at cut-rate prices and resell them to unsuspecting buyers for a huge profit.

She jokingly coined the phrase 'Haunted Flips' to a few close friends to explain her business model. She'd move into allegedly haunted houses and renovate them to create forced equity. There were certainly financial advantages to buying as a homeowner rather than an investor, but it also gave her the ability to refurbish at her leisure. Plus, she rarely had to hire contractors because she'd learned to do many of the repairs herself over the years, further maximizing profit.

"Buy the worst house in the best neighborhood," her mentor had said early in her career, and while not always true, it had worked for her most of the time. "A great neighborhood is like a rising tide," he often repeated. "It will lift the price of all the homes around it."

Finding a buyer, though? That was the tricky part.

Jessica had spent years developing ways to lure in the trusting, the clueless, and the technology-challenged (if you couldn't use a search engine well, you couldn't investigate a house very well). She'd had particularly good luck transforming alleged haunted houses into vacation homes and selling them to international investors with poor English-speaking skills.

Now, it had been three days since moving into the house and Jessica hadn't seen anything creepier than a long-abandoned spider's web.

*Typical,* she thought while inspecting one of the guest rooms. This was her thirteenth time living in a haunted house and she'd yet to experience anything remotely supernatural. It had reached the point where she wanted to see or hear something out of the ordinary. If only to keep things interesting.

As she surveyed the room, it was clear it would be easy to renovate; it just needed new paint and a light refinish on the hardwood floor. She jotted down some notes and kneeled to take a closer look for any buckling in the hardwood. There was none, but what caught her eye were clumps of jet-black hair in several places, particularly against the baseboards.

She grimaced. The room hadn't had a thorough cleaning.

The hair was quite long; the kind usually reserved for the young. Was it the hair of one of the missing children?

She shook away the awful thought and went back to her notes, recalculating her budget. The bedrooms were going to cost even less than she'd planned.

Deal of the century, she thought.

* * * *

Willow House was a two-story, brick Colonial-Revival style home with a gabled roof, a porch with wooden bench swing, and an arched portico with classical columns. It had the simple symmetry and structure of the 1920s colonial style with a taste of Victorian-era architecture.

There had been some obvious renovation over the years, but the lack of regular upkeep was in stark contrast to the other well-maintained homes and manicured lawns along the affluent, willow tree-lined street.

The front yard was a jungle of overgrown shrubs, knee-deep grass, and weeds flourishing in the flowerbeds.

Inside were high ceilings and tall windows, along with intricate detailing and moldings. The second floor consisted of three bedrooms and a bathroom at the end of the hall, while the traditional first floor layout included a reception hall, kitchen, living room and dining room.

The sparse furnishings around the house were the most basic Jessica could procure, and what she referred to as her 'renovation starter kit'. There was no sense in moving in more than the essentials since she would have to move it out again in a relatively short amount of time.

Now, as she sat on her favorite 'traveling couch', calculating flooring costs, an aggressive *knock knock knock* shattered the silence of the living room.

Jessica grumbled under her breath and went to answer the front door.

\* \* \* \*

Claire Vass had flawless skin, bright blue eyes, and came bearing cookies, gossip, and a barrage of questions. Jessica guessed she was in her 50s but easily looked ten years younger.

As the self-described '*cul-de-sac* welcoming committee', Claire never seemed to run out of words or the energy to use them. In the hour since her arrival, she'd managed to deluge Jessica with dirt on every single person living on the short street.

Mr. Kane, for example, was apparently a pervert who watched animated porn on his big screen TV with the shades open. Old Lady Livingstone was to be avoided at all costs, unless one fancied a 3-hour rant about nothing. And perhaps, most important of all, she was advised to never step on Mr. Yarwood's lawn or touch any of his prized azaleas, or she would not live to regret it.

The conversation, which began at the front door, eventually moved to the wooden swing on the porch, which Jessica had wiped off as best she could with a rag.

"You're very attractive, you know," Claire said, examining her closely. Perhaps too closely. "Planning to get married? Kids?"

Jessica forced a smile; she had never accepted compliments well.

I'm not the settle-down type, lady, she wanted to say. Plus, I'd rather gouge my eyes out than stay on this dead-end street any longer than I have to.

Instead, she said, "You never know. But I love having my independence."

That was her shorthand for I don't need to get married to be fulfilled, Claire. I love my career, love to travel, and I don't like wasting time on dating apps.

Claire watched her for an uncomfortably long moment. Finally, she said, "Well…I think you're incredibly brave for buying this place. A single woman in a house with that kind of history? I admire you."

Jessica forced the umpteenth smile of the conversation. "No, I'd be brave if I *believed* in ghouls and ghosties, but I don't. It's just a fixer upper to me."

Claire's phone buzzed and she quickly read a text.

"Oh, that's my husband, Bill, wanting lunch." She shook her head in mock disappointment. He can tell you how to fix a bad fuel injector, but still can't fix a ham sandwich without my help."

She reached over and gave Jessica an unwelcome hug. "I should get going. It was a delight getting to know you a bit better."

Then, as if remembering something, she reached for the plate of cookies she'd brought with her, now sitting on a nearby wicker chair. She folded back the aluminum foil to reveal home-made cookies in the shapes of pumpkins, black cats, and ghosts.

She handed them to Jessica as if they were spun from gold. "These are home-made, by the way; aren't they adorable?"

Jessica gave the woman her best *yes, they're adorable* grin and accepted the plate. "Really kind of you to bring these, thank you. Looks like you really like Halloween." *I mean, Christ, it's still September, lady.*

Claire smiled, but there was no warmth there. "Oh, we take Halloween *very* seriously around here."

She started down the porch steps and gave an odd little wave.

Jessica didn't wave back.

* * * *

A week later, after a three-day trip to visit her mother, Jessica came home to something out of a blood-soaked nightmare. As she turned onto Willow Lane, she gasped. Everywhere she looked there were relentless scenes of terror, torture, and mayhem.

Sure, she had seen neighborhoods that went all-out with Halloween decorations, but this looked like something borne out of Hell, a disturbing fusion of nihilism, rage, and carnage.

Realistic female mannequins were nailed to upside down crosses and drenched in blood. Male and female figures were impaled on spikes and frozen in silent screams. A life size child was half in and half out of a metal meat grinder, his lower half reduced to sludge in a red-stained bucket. Several lampshades appeared to be made from skin, stitched together from human faces.

A family of four hung by their necks from the same thick branch, eyes bulging, duct tape stretched over their mouths. Some poor souls were sawed in half, while shredded limbs, glistening intestines, and gore-covered heads—some stuffed into large mason jars—were scattered about.

There were classic Halloween tropes as well, but not the silly decorations you picked up at the local drug store. These skeletons, skulls and animal skins looked alarmingly real. Several black cats seemed to be authentic corpses stuffed by a second-rate taxidermist. Pumpkins and turnips were lit up by candles, and oddly, plates of food were everywhere.

But what stood out most were the army of 7-foot-tall demons.

Normally, Halloween figures didn't bother Jessica, as they were not to be taken too seriously. Who hadn't seen a store-bought mummy, vampire, or Frankenstein's monster at some point?

But there was something terribly *off* about these figures.

Positioned at strategic points amidst the contiguous yard displays, it was clear they were meant to be seen as the perpetrators of the blood-drenched chaos.

Jessica didn't recognize any of the grotesque things. She didn't know the names of such archaic European demons as a *Bánánach* or a *Fear Gorta*; she didn't know how to differentiate a bogeyman from an imp. But what she did know was that the realism in which they were portrayed was deeply unsettling.

They were murdering people. Shredding people. *Eating* people.

This isn't a celebration of Halloween, Jessica decided. It's a celebration of depravity.

As she finally reached the end of the cul-de-sac, she decided that the worst aspect of the whole sordid affair was the kids.

There were young children, smiling and posing amidst the offensive displays, parents laughing as they snapped photos with their phones.

What in the actual fuck—

Jessica slammed her car into the driveway and parked, hitting the brakes harder than she'd intended. She stormed towards her home, thought better of it, and turned again to see the *Grand Guignol* that had become Willow Lane.

Every house—except hers—had partaken in the madness.

She spotted Mr. Kane, facing her as he stood on his horror-themed lawn. He was an older man with wispy white hair and dressed smartly in black slacks and a maroon-colored shirt.

Wait—, she thought after a closer look. That isn't maroon—it's soaked with blood.

He was drinking what looked like an iced tea in one hand and offered her a friendly wave with the other, as if it was just another day in suburban paradise.

Jessica didn't wave back.

It's October 1st, you twisted fuck. October 1st.

* * * *

"We can't do anything about that, ma'am," the female police operator said on speaker phone. "Halloween decorations are protected by freedom of speech. We get calls about Willow Lane every year."

Jessica's breath caught in her throat, and she held back a torrent of expletives. "I find it very hard to believe the police are OK with these displays. They're disgusting, violent and horrifying. No child should be exposed to these kinds of things."

The operator didn't sound impressed. "Ma'am, it would have to be something way more graphic, something with profanity or nudity. If there was something written that was extremely offensive, or a written threat, a real person's name for example—then maybe we could do something."

"Great. You've been an incredible fucking help," Jessica said before hanging up.

She threw her phone onto the couch in exasperation. "It's October 1st for fuck's sake! I have a whole month of this shit?"

As Jessica paced the living room, she suddenly recalled a bizarre moment with Brandon, that little dweeb of a real estate agent, during her initial call about Willow House. One of the first questions he'd asked was if she celebrated Halloween.

She'd found that odd, of course, and after an awkward silence, told him it wasn't something she cared about either way. When she asked him why he wanted to know, he'd mentioned something about the neighborhood taking the celebration seriously. Jessica hadn't understood the context at the time and had quickly changed the subject.

She plopped onto the couch and rubbed her face, exasperated at the situation, which was as ludicrous as it was annoying. She thought about moving into a hotel for a few weeks, or maybe staying with her mother up north until November.

But that meant that she'd lose a full month of renovation and that would throw her whole two-year schedule off. She was already looking into another "haunted" place near the coast that she wanted to buy as her next project. It had a large back yard, a tremendous view overlooking the coast, and frankly, was a bloody steal.

Jessica sighed. No, they're not ruining my plans. I'll just keep my head down and stay busy renovating through most of October.

However, that didn't mean she had to embrace her neighbors' Halloween madness.

Was madness even the right word?

Or was it a kind of…mass hypnosis?

She'd only had brief interactions with several of them. Mr. Yarwood talked endlessly about his azaleas, Mr. Kane tried—and failed epically— to flirt with her, and there had been one tortuously long conversation with

Old Lady Livingstone that, as Claire put it, was about nothing.

They were annoying at most.

And yet, while Jessica didn't believe in the supernatural, she understood humanity's capacity for evil. The fact that all previous owners had gone missing on or around Halloween was not lost on her.

While she bristled at the idea of anyone thinking her superstitious, she was also no one's fool. Sometimes discretion was the better part of valor. It was at that point, she decided she wasn't going to stick around for Halloween after all. From experience, she knew there was a lot she could accomplish in the next three weeks, if she stayed focused.

Then, perhaps a few nights before October 31st, she'd slip out under the cover of night. Her mom would be thrilled at a surprise visit, and she could safely ride out Halloween far from the demented Willow Lane clan.

After today, she decided, she would no longer interact with them. Lately, she'd gotten too loose with her personal code: never get close to neighbors during renovations. She'd learned the hard way that there were too many questions, and some people didn't take well to her mercenary view on house flipping.

She was there to turn a quick profit, not join a community.

With that decision firmly in place, she grabbed her tool belt with a look of grim determination and headed upstairs to get some renovation done. She hoped it would take her mind off the sick and twisted displays on Willow Lane.

\* \* \* \*

Jessica evaded all communications with her neighbors over the next two weeks. Claire Vass dropped by unannounced *twice* and Jessica hadn't answered the door either time. She also didn't eat the Halloween-themed cookies Claire kept leaving on the porch.

She stopped returning friendly waves from nearby residents as she drove past the hellscape that was their lawns. She had food delivered often to reduce her trips to the grocery store; anything to avoid looking at those repulsive front yard displays or interactions with her neighbors.

However, the constant reminders of Halloween lurking in the background had piqued her interest in the subject matter. And after a few late-night web searches, she learned more about its history than she'd ever cared to.

Jessica was Welsh from her father's side, and she'd heard a little about Halloween's medieval origins in Europe when she was a child; but that was the extent of her knowledge.

Digging deeper, she learned that Halloween was a descendant of *Samhain*, a 2,000-year-old pagan religious festival celebrated by the Celts, halfway between the autumn equinox and the winter solstice. Several sources claimed that ancient Celts believed the veil between the living and the spirit realm grew thinnest at this time, and all manner of supernatural beings could pass through as they pleased for one hallowed night.

Spirits, demons, and other beings from the Otherworld would cross over to cause mischief. So, the Celts placed offerings outside to satisfy them, in the hopes they wouldn't harm their livestock or storage of food.

In addition, they would light bonfires; carve frightening faces into root vegetables; and wear eerie masks and costumes made from animal skins, all in the name of warding off real demons and ghosts.

Conversely, she also read articles from historians and renowned Halloween authorities who dismissed all these ideas as erroneous, exaggerated or frankly, bullshit. Some experts claimed that supernatural elements of Samhain's history were simply hyperbolized over generations to add mystique to Halloween's origins and sell more Halloween entertainment and merchandise.

Jessica much preferred that kind of logic, and yet as her web search deepened; she discovered illustrations depicting all manner of creatures from Celtic demonology. She was stunned that a few were strikingly like the demons displayed on Willow Lane. She recalled that many of the decorations looked archaic; right down to the candle-lit turnips.

She again thought of the experts' opinions and laughed out loud at the thought of upwardly mobile suburbanites warding off demons. Yet the idea lingered long after she'd shut down her computer. Had Willow House's haunted reputation caused a sort of mass paranoia on this street? Sure, maybe the supernatural aspect was bullshit, but was it possible her neighbors were simply delusional? Was it possible they were actually trying to drive away spirits and demons, as in some accounts of ancient *Samhain* tradition?

Jessica found it difficult to sleep, gazing up at the coffered ceiling for hours, contemplating the mysteries of the house.

When she'd discovered it earlier that year, all that mattered at the time was that it was a stigmatized property and had sat on the market for nearly twenty-five years, unheard of in such an otherwise great neighborhood.

The profit potential was what excited her, not digging for information on missing people that were presumed dead.

As a real estate agent, she had plenty of tools at her disposal to investigate the history of a property, but she had never been one to seek out juicy details on grisly news items. She didn't watch true crime stories or slow down to stare at car crashes, and she certainly didn't delight in the tragedies or sufferings of others.

All she cared about was the unsavory reputation of the house and how much it devalued the property. The individual stories and details of its former owners were for ghost hunters, armchair sleuths, and lovers of the macabre.

However, even as a nonbeliever, Jessica had to admit there were some strange coincidences at Willow House. Perhaps most significant was that it remained unoccupied in twenty five-year cycles, like clockwork. For another, no one had lived in the house longer than a year before they went missing. And most mystifying of all, the disappearances always occurred on or near Halloween. She noted that a couple of exact dates remained unconfirmed because two previous owners hadn't been listed as missing right away.

Definitely fucking creepy, she thought.

Now wide awake, Jessica found herself drawn to her laptop again. After booting it up, she began searching for news stories on the previous occupants of Willow House, of which there were plenty. All the disappearances remained unsolved. For this reason, most of the stories repeated the same information, offering nothing more than rumors and conjecture.

The most recent missing owners, Drew and Grace Campbell, an entrepreneur and travel nurse respectively, had been responsible for much of the modern renovations to Willow House. Constant world travelers, they were last seen on October 31st, 1997, the same day they returned after a three-month trip across Europe.

There had been no signs of a robbery or a struggle. All their belongings were intact. It was as if they had simply vanished from the face of the earth. If they had left willingly, which was doubtful, they had taken nothing with them, including their cars.

The owners prior to that, back in 1972, were Stephen and Annie Valentine, and their children Christine and Jane. According to one story in a local paper, the Valentines were a conservative Christian family that didn't celebrate Halloween.

A diligent journalist had uncovered quite a bit of drama around the Valentines' offense at the neighborhood's elaborate Halloween decorations, which they said, quote, "celebrated demons and Satanism." Official complaints with the police had been filed and threats were exchanged.

The same article revealed that several neighbors had been questioned regarding the disappearance of the Valentine family in the days following Halloween. And while the term 'Persons of Interest' was not yet in fashion, it was implied from the news story.

No arrests were ever made.

Jessica shook her head at the implications. Apparently, Willow Lane's overblown Halloween celebration went all the way back to the 70s. And it seemed she wasn't the only neighbor to take offense.

Now, fully down the internet rabbit hole, she learned that the owners prior to that moved into Willow House in 1947, the year the Cold War began between the U.S., the Soviet Union, and their allies. Floyd and Becca Probert, a dentist and a school administrator respectively, mysteriously vanished. No signs of a struggle, nothing stolen, and their car left behind.

They had been seen the night of October 31st taking in a movie at the local theater. That was the last time they were heard from again.

Hours later, when Jessica had gone far back enough to research Finlay Henderson, the original owner of Willow House in 1922, information was scarce.

The few details available were that Finlay was a Scottish immigrant who had done well for himself in the newspaper business. Some articles praised the fact that a Scottish immigrant from such humble beginnings had accomplished so much in his ten years in America. Others called out the peculiarity of a single man buying a two-story, three-bedroom home for himself in 1922.

He was last seen on October 31st.

There was one interesting detail about Henderson that stood out amongst all the others. According to several sources, police had discovered "strange, inexplicable symbols carved into the walls of the master bedroom," with one witness describing them as "magic sigils of some kind, possibly of European origin."

No one had been able to decipher their meanings.

Of course, this single detail was tremendous fodder for countless internet sleuths and ghost hunting fanboys. Some posited that Henderson had carved the sigils into the walls to summon ancient demons for wealth and power. While others believed he had tried and failed to carve sigils to protect himself from something *inside* the house.

The fact that everyone had disappeared on Halloween led some to speculate that the house served as a portal when the veil between the living and the spirit world was at its thinnest, as ancient Celts believed during *Samhain*.

It was at that point Jessica emitted a scornful laugh.

Stick to the Halloween experts, Jess, she thought, snapping her laptop closed for the night. Forget the supernatural. This house ain't no fucking portal.

As she reached across the bed to turn out the light, she glanced at the walls where Finlay Henderson had once carved the mysterious sigils. They were long gone, now; the walls had either been replaced entirely or the carvings had been concealed with cladding and layers of wallpaper a hundred years old.

Jessica sighed heavily, turned out the light and eventually fell into a fitful sleep.

She dreamt of unspeakable horrors lurking inside the walls.

* * * *

October 31st was in four days and Jessica was so sick of the glorification of Halloween, she swore she'd never celebrate it again, even on the relatively mundane level she had in the past. For a while, she'd considered putting up the cheesiest, most absurd decorations she could find, just to ridicule her neighbors. But then she thought, *no, it's better to ignore the celebration entirely. That will let them know what I think of it.*

In the late afternoon, she realized a quick trip to the hardware store was needed in order to finish some minor touchups to the master bedroom. She'd already packed her suitcase and hidden it under blankets in the back-seat of her car, eager to skip town after dark. As usual, she hoped to avoid any neighbors who tried to catch her eye.

Five minutes later, seven of them did.

They stood in the middle of the road having a heated discussion, and as a result, were blocking her car. She recognized some of them: Mr. Kane, Old Lady Livingstone, Mr. Yarwood, and right in the middle was Claire Vass talking up a storm, waving her arms excitedly.

They seemed to purposely ignore Jessica. Finally, she gave a light *honk* to get their attention.

In unison, everyone spun toward her, glaring at her intensely. Jessica felt a surge of fear rise in her chest.

Claire gestured to the group as if she were calming down a mob, said something which made them chuckle, then sauntered up to Jessica's driver side window with a smile from ear to ear.

"Well, hey stranger!" Claire gushed. "Y'know, I've stopped by twice to catch up with you. You must be a busy bee, hon. Buzz buzz."

Jessica gritted her teeth and forced a smile. "Yes, a busy bee indeed. In fact, I need to get to the hardware store before they close. So, if you wouldn't mind…?

She gestured to the glowering group standing in the middle of the road.

Claire leaned in, causing Jessica to lean back. "Y'know hon, some of these folks are starting to think maybe you don't like our Halloween decorations. Tell me that's not true."

Jessica used every last ounce of self-restraint. "Look, if this is about me not decorating my home—"

Claire laughed. "No, no…you don't need to decorate *Willow House*. That's the scariest one on the block!" And then she laughed even harder.

Jessica steeled herself. "Claire…the hardware store closes in less than an hour.'"

"Oh right, sure…" Claire said, and withdrew from the window. But then she leaned right back in, glancing around the interior of the car. "But you're planning to celebrate with us on Halloween, right? We're counting on everyone this year for the biggest turn out yet."

"Oh, definitely…" Jessica lied, offering the last smile she had left. *As in definitely getting the fuck out of Dodge tonight.*

"Wonderful," Claire said, clapping her hands lightly. Then she turned to the group in the road and shooed them away like a farmer scattering chickens.

Jessica drove past them, then looked back in her rear-view mirror as she reached the end of the street.

All seven neighbors stood silent and motionless, watching her drive away.

* * * *

Jessica sighed with relief when she returned home, and no neighbors were in sight. There were, however, a few random spectators taking photos with their kids amidst the Halloween grotesquerie.

Jessica stopped to let an obese family of three cross the street in front of her. As she sat in her idling car, she did her best to avert her eyes from the depraved street decor.

A name on a nearby mailbox caught her eye.

Scurlock. Where do I know that…?

She glanced at the nearest mailbox on the other side of the street, which read: *Livingstone.* The next one after that read: *Tallon.*

Jessica had a crazy thought, and when the pedestrians had cleared, she raced the rest of the way home. She wanted to get to her computer quickly and confirm those names.

Once she was inside and settled, Jessica crouched on the living room floor with her laptop, a half-eaten chocolate bar and a nice *Pinot Noir.* She ordered a pizza with extra cheese and looked up articles she'd bookmarked from previous web searches.

It didn't take long to find what she was looking for.

In one of the more comprehensive articles about Willow House, she spotted the names Scurlock, Livingstone, and Tallon. The names on the mailboxes were the same as the neighbors mentioned in connection with the disappearance of the Valentine family back in '72.

They had been questioned extensively, but none were ever arrested.

Was it possible her neighbors were relatives of the same families mentioned, the sons and daughters of that previous generation?

What about Old Lady Livingstone? If she'd been born and raised here, she was old enough to have been alive for all the previous owner disappearances except for Finlay Henderson back in 1922.

And what about the names themselves? Jessica was annoyed with herself that she hadn't noticed it before. She quickly did a web search to verify what she suspected.

She raised her glass to herself in a mock toast. "Fucking Sherlock Holmes over here, thank you…"

Scurlock, Livingstone, Tallon and all the previous Willow House owners had either Irish, Scottish, or Welsh surnames.

She finished off the wine in her glass and thought about the neighbors she knew. Mr. Kane, the pervert, had an Irish last name. Old Lady Livingstone had a Scottish last name, while Mr. Yarwood, protector of the neighborhood azaleas, was Welsh. Nosy neighbor Claire Vass had a Scottish surname, and of course, Jessica's own last name was Welsh.

That can't be a coincidence. And if it wasn't, what did it mean?

Then came a chilling thought. The Celts were an ancient group of people who lived more than 2,000 years ago in what is now Ireland, Wales, Scotland, and much of Europe.

Those same Celts who celebrated *Samhain*.

Jessica poured her third glass of wine. Are you really following this line of thought, Jessica? Seriously.

Suddenly, a loud *bang bang bang* at the front door. Jessica nearly spilled her wine.

She got up with a grunt and said, "That better not be fucking Claire."

It wasn't. She had forgotten she'd ordered pizza.

A teenaged pizza delivery boy with blue-dyed hair and hands that shook, stood in the cool night air. He was clearly nervous, his eyes darting to avoid Jessica's gaze.

"Sorry, I have to go grab my wallet," she said. "You want to come in out of the cold?"

"No ma'am—I'm okay right here."

Jessica couldn't blame the kid. The house's reputation obviously preceded it, even with the local pizza joint. She gave him a nice fat tip for his bravery and quickly settled back into her investigation. The more she read, the more she was convinced she was making the right decision to leave town that night.

She would drive up north as a lovely surprise to her mother and stay for a full week or more. Her mother would be delighted. Most importantly, she would miss several days before and after Halloween.

Jessica still didn't believe in curses, ghosts, or the supernatural, but when it came to being an owner of Willow House, the law of averages was undeniable. There was a big difference between superstitious and cautious.

But her escape plan was not to be.

An hour later she barely made it to the toilet as a torrent of foul-smelling vomit erupted from her. The retching seemed endless, as if every ounce of fluid inside her was desperate to purge from her body. She'd experienced food poisoning before, but this was far worse than any she'd known.

Her vision began to blur as darkness closed in around her.

Weak at the knees and quickly losing her equilibrium, her first thought was to call her mother. She rushed toward the master bedroom to grab her phone, but her legs gave halfway.

The last thing she remembered was the coppery taste of blood in her mouth.

* * * *

Spinning blackness. Muted voices. Waves of nausea.

Jessica floated in and out of consciousness on an ocean of pain. She felt her limp body being lifted by several hands at one point. Later, she recognized the comfort of a bed, followed by more rolling darkness.

Daytime came and went…twice, three times, four…as if spirited away.

She dreamt of sigils, demons and pumpkins filled with blood.

For a moment, she floated back up to the surface, drawn to a familiar voice.

Was that Claire?

Jessica's eyes fluttered open, but her eyelids wouldn't cooperate. She caught a glimpse of several dark figures standing around the bed, watching her.

Claire's voice: "You gave her too much, you idiot."

A young male voice: "I'm sorry…"

"You could've killed her."

Jessica struggled to stay conscious, but the unrelenting blackness crashed down and dragged her back into its depths.

* * * *

It was nighttime again when Jessica became fully conscious; memories stirred in her like dead leaves.

She suspected four full days had passed, which made it Halloween night.

But that was the least of her troubles.

Someone had first drugged and then shackled her to the bed in the master bedroom. Archaic-looking iron clasps held her wrists and ankles, both her arms and legs pulled taut. She spent the first hour trying every conceivable angle to yank herself free, but this only resulted in torn and bleeding skin. The next hour was spent screaming for help.

No one came.

She remembered hearing Claire's familiar, grating voice. You gave her too much, you idiot. You could've killed her.

Who had she been talking to?

The pizza delivery boy. He drugged me.

It was at that moment Jessica confirmed there had never been anything supernatural about the house. The only thing to fear on Willow Lane were the neighbors.

How many generations did this madness go back? All the way to 1922? And to what end?

She started thinking about the disappearances of the other previous owners. Little details started to snap together like pieces of a mental puzzle.

She remembered that the Valentines hadn't decorated for Halloween due to their religious beliefs. And the Proberts were seen taking in a movie the night of the October 31st, so perhaps they didn't celebrate either.

The Campbells had come back from a three-month trip to Europe, returning on Halloween day. It seemed unlikely they had decorated three-months before they'd left. And it wasn't hard to imagine they wouldn't rush out to get decorations on the same day they returned.

There weren't many details about Henderson in 1922, but Halloween didn't pick up steam until the 1930s in America, so it was likely he hadn't decorated either.

While every owner had an Irish, Scottish, or Welsh surname, which was strange but not improbable, perhaps the most important common denominator was that none of them celebrated Halloween.

Were the denizens of Willow Lane that fucking insane? Had they killed the previous owners for not honoring the tradition of their ancestors?

But then Jessica had a far more disturbing thought. There was another possible connection with all the owners, including her. In the ancient celebration of *Samhain*, there were animal skin costumes, frightening faces carved into candle-lit root vegetables, demon, and spirit masks, and more.

Together, they all had one singular purpose: protection.

So, what happened to those who didn't protect themselves? Was that an open invitation to entities from the Otherworld? Was there *something* on Willow Lane they needed protection from?

That was when Jessica noticed the sigils.

All along the walls and ceiling, they began to appear. Subtle outlines at first, as if drawn on tracing paper.

She tried to sit up to get a better look, but to no avail. *No, that's fucking impossible...*

Moments later, they were deep red like a branding iron, as if being heated in a forge.

Jessica shook her head and blinked her eyes. I'm hallucinating. I must be. It's...an after effect of the drug.

A *thud* from somewhere in the house.

Jessica's head spun toward the bedroom door. From her vantage point, she had a good view of the hallway and the top of the circular staircase.

A *dark figure* was slowly crawling up the stairs. She heard a *creak.*

It didn't appear human.

Her eyes snapped shut as a subconscious reflex. She pretended to sleep; a child-like reaction to a situation in which she was trapped and vulnerable.

Just be still, she thought. Please God...

Another *creak.*

Then...she felt a presence in the room.

Something was watching her.

All her senses seemed heightened. *What is that smell?* It reminded her of the musky feral scent of her mother's cat.

A moment later, there was movement, if only slight.

It seemed to move along the wall...then the ceiling.

*What is it?* Her mind screamed, her heart hammering so hard she was sure it was audible to the thing in her room.

Thump!

It sounded as if it had dropped from the ceiling back down to the floor at the edge of her bed. A scream rose in Jessica's throat as if she were being roasted alive, but she held it back.

A moment later she felt the mattress of her bed sink; the box springs groaned under the weight as something crawled in bed with her.

Jessica's shallow breathing became even more rapid, and tears streamed down her face. She'd managed to keep her eyes closed, but there was no disguising her fear now. The *thing* positioned itself so that she could feel its breath, which smelled like rotted meat, hot on her face.

Long, coarse hair brushed her cheek as it lowered its face toward hers, perhaps an inch away from her nose.

God...help me please! Her mind shrieked.

A familiar sound then. At first it seemed to be smacking its lips. But that wasn't quite right. In her imagination she could see its wide lips stretching across a set of massive, glistening teeth.

The sound of a hideous smile.

Time moved as if it were a predator on a silent stalk; several terror-filled minutes passed but neither Jessica nor the thing gave an inch.

The experts had been the ones full of shit, after all.

Rain began to tap the window like an unwelcome guest, and Jessica heard it thrum and clatter on some broken roof tiles.

*As long as I keep my eyes closed—I'm safe,* she thought, as if trying to convince herself.

Somehow you know that too, don't you?

So, I'll just lie here.

And I'll never open my eyes.

Never.

Never....

\* \* \* \*

Outside the house, a slanted sheet of rain swept like a scythe across the backyard, where everyone who lived on Willow Lane gathered to stare up at her window.

Each was cloaked in animal skins, dressed as various demons from the Otherworld.

Claire Vass stood front and center beside her husband Bill. She had been fortunate to spot Jessica's suitcase peeking out from underneath a blanket in her backseat. She gave a silent prayer of gratitude.

As they continued to congregate, Mr. Kane held the arm of Old Lady Livingstone to make sure she didn't slip in the rain. Behind them were Mr. Yarwood and his blue-haired son Dylan, who had paid off a pizza delivery person and laced Jessica's food.

Claire spoke in an ancient Celt language as she traced ancient sigils in the air with one finger.

The others began to do the same in a synchronized fashion for several minutes, until the ritual was complete.

Brandon, the real estate agent, looked satisfied as he stepped up toward his father. He whispered, "Thought she was *so* smart. Thought she'd hustled us."

Mr. Kane offered a pleased smile, knowing everyone could expect twenty-five more years of prosperity. Proudly, he placed his hand on the young man's shoulder. "You did well, son. She was a perfect sacrifice."

As the rain grew in intensity, the denizens of Willow Lane continued to stare up at Jessica's window, waiting.

✗

# THE IRON LAW
## David C. Smith

Who can distinguish darkness from the soul?

> *William Butler Yeats*
> "A Dialogue of Self and Soul"

## 1.

By midday, sweating, he came to the gates of Ilrukad, a small town, little more than a village held within walls of brick, and entered the first public house he came to. He took a table so that his back was to a wall. He was tall, a few years short of thirty summers, dark-haired and dark-eyed, with a full beard and with blood fresh on his cuirass—a warning to the other patrons to be wary of him, just that.

He was otherwise in a short woolen tunic and worn leather pants, worn leather boots, and had a heavy sword byside and knives in his belt. No other armor or weapons; either he had given them up or abandoned them. The blood on his leather and bronze-embossed corselet was not his own, guessed those regarding him in safety from where they were, and they noticed bruises on the left side of his face and a cut on his right arm. It wept blood. Whatever he had been involved in, chances were that he had managed the best of it and left anyone else around him wounded or worse, back on the road.

The mistress of this tavern came by him with a plate of warm beef cut into strips and brown bread and vegetables, as well as a most welcome jug of beer and a gourd to pour it into. This the warrior did immediately and drained the gourd fast before pouring himself another. He wiped his mouth with a blood-stained hand.

At a look from her husband, a fit man of middle years behind the counter, the graying wife said to her guest, "Come far?" She spoke Ormosan, born to it.

His own was rough as he shrugged and told her, "A league and more."

"Shall I fetch an expert to look at them cuts?"

Having asked it, she worried what he might do in response because one never knew how some persons might react, especially fighters, but it was her way to look after her visitors, even the ones as rough as her own grown sons, so she had come out with it.

The stranger judged her as he chewed his beef, then lightly shook his head. "Thank you, no. I've suffered worse and managed till now."

"Let me know when you need more to drink or eat." She returned to stand behind the board with her husband.

The fighter regarded the room as he took his fill. The others in that generous space were largely no more dangerous than the woman or her husband, simply travelers or residents of the town. The one he settled his gaze on, however, held his look in her own.

Of twenty-and-some summers. Young. Tall. Nearly as dark-haired as he. Slender and well-dressed, her unblemished light skin softly tanned, not burnt by the sun, so she was no peasant or worker. Her dress was long and neatly embroidered, and with a vest just as well made, as were her boots, which might have been fashioned this morning, so clean was the soft leather. Unusual, however, was the long glove she wore on her right hand, the sleeve of it reaching to her elbow. It was of heavy leather and done around with mail, hard protection.

She stood now, waited a moment to let him have the full look of her, then crossed the floor to sit at his table across from him. "If I may."

He nodded and pushed the plate of food toward her.

"Thank you, no. May I introduce myself?"

A second nod.

"I am Irté. I know who you are."

He dropped his right hand to his side, letting the fingers rest on his round sword pommel. With his left hand, he took up the gourd to drink— or to splash the beer in her face if need be.

"You have no need to fear me, Oron."

He cleared his throat. "I sensed someone following me on the road ever since I killed the brigands. You?"

"Yes."

"How then did you pass me and reach this place before I did?"

"I was not on the road. I was here all morning. I sent my sight to find you."

"You're a witch." He brought his right hand back to the tabletop, bringing with it as he did one of his knives.

And used it to cut the meat.

Irté noticed the size and heft of that knife and again assured him, "I mean only to speak with you and hire your sword. Your name is not unknown here."

"In Neria? Which is where we are if your border posts told true."

"You're in Neria. But we speak three languages here. Everyone along the border does."

"So you've been using your witch's sight to follow me. I know of such things."

"And I know you've fought ghosts and werewolves, shapeshifters and sorcerers, and no doubt other monsters besides, although no one has taken your sword. You are the Wolf and you still walk the earth. Some say you're either cursed by demons or protected by the gods to be here yet."

"Cursed, more like it," Oron told her. "And gods are demons in finer robes, no better than that."

"Still, I think you know things that I do not. I wish to buy such knowledge if you'll assist my brother and me. Or hire your arm."

"I'm a fighter. Any knowledge I have pertains to that. The sorcery and demons—those I leave by as they have learned to leave me alone. You have wars here in Neria, and I'm a killing man. I mean to hire out my sword or join a mercenary band. Show me where one is. It's why I'm here."

"Then let me hire your arm before you go east to join the mercenaries."

"Tell me first how you know about me. I'm unknown here."

"Unknown to those in *this* hole," Irté said, nodding to take in the room. "But I see around me with this." From inside the sleeve of her glove, she removed a square of metal on a chain with a sign made on it. Oron had seen such sigils and markings.

"As I told you," he said. "You're a witch."

"My brother created this sign. He's the one who opened this path for himself to engage with the powers around us. He has resurrected an ancient god."

"Some demon."

"Older than that and stronger, he surmises. He and I mean to save the people of our home place against a man who intruded months ago and has imprisoned the people there."

"Who is he?"

"Kest."

Oron shook his head, finished his gourd, and pushed it and the plate away. "I don't know the name."

"He claims to have come from Semkorra in Argalon, northeast of us."

"I've heard of it. Many of their people are learned."

"This one is learned in the darkest of ways. He came to our community offering to help us prosper. Increase our crops, strengthen the soil. It was his way of insinuating himself among us."

"And after he'd done it, he betrayed you. An old maneuver."

"Yes. But don't judge us, please. We were desperate. My brother and I inherited the village. Our forebears founded it. We love the people in our charge. But we were in despair after two bad summers and a harsh winter."

"He saw this himself by one of those signs, and so he came to you."

"We believe now that Kest himself inverted the seasons to harm us so that he could appear to us as a savior," Irté told Oron. "We opened our gate freely to him, and when he created the illusion that our crops had returned, we offered him gold. That was when he overpowered us. He brought in his company of followers. Brutes, criminals, free swords to protect him, and he made his place in the temple of our goddess, Ethed. With his sorcery, he weakened and betrayed even our protector. Her temple is his home now. And my people are dying as this sorcerer steals the life from them."

Oron asked her, "How many in his company?"

"At least sixty. Most live now outside the walls, encamped there. Inside, he works in secret in Ethed's temple, and our old and children wither while She can no longer answer their pleas."

Oron asked, thinking aloud, "What does he want? Power? Gold?" But immediately the warrior made a snuffing noise and answered his own question. "He thinks he is now a god himself."

"Yes," Irté told him. "He intends to endure forever. He claims to have lived already a hundred years, and he looks no older than you or I."

"Then he's left other dead villages behind him."

"We investigated, my brother and I, and the fifty of our people who escaped before he circled our village with his fighters. We sent riders into Ormos, thinking we might find the road he followed. We learned of one village that had been destroyed by a wanderer from the east. Our rider told us that what remained were graves and corpses, some few still alive, but their land poisoned. Who else could have done it?"

Oron said, "Whatever he has become, sorcerers die on an edge of steel like anything else in this world."

"Which is our hope if you will support us. You see this sign my brother made. To fight Kest, Edron is seeking to raise another ancient god and control its power."

"He could fail as easily as succeed." Oron winced, and his hands atop the table curled into fists, the display of a man aware of the danger presented by other men who have bargained with shadows and abandoned the use of their own strong arms and fists for more sinister weapons.

Irté said, "He knows that such powers can darken his soul and that he could be lost to us, but, Nevgan, we're determined to help our people. What else can we do? Not fight back and become like other villages he's ruined?"

"No," Oron agreed.

Irté asked him, "What can I do to convince you come with me and help us?"

They looked each other fully in the eyes.

She told him plainly, "I could offer you myself, but I can't provide you more than any common woman could. Gold we have, but it's contained inside the village. But you walked to this city, Oron. You lost your horse when those men killed it."

"They did."

"I'll buy you a horse of your choosing. Come with me to my village to see for yourself the harm Kest has done us. While my brother learns sorcery, the fighters with us are practicing their skills. These are men and women who will follow your word. Our home is a day's ride away. Let me buy you a horse and begin our bargain that way. When my village is free, you may take as much of our gold as you wish."

Oron considered the offer. "I *am* in need of a horse."

"Then let me do that for you."

"One thing more," he said to her. "I believe you. One of those bandits I killed, as he died—he spoke of a sorcerer not far from here."

"But how did he know of him?" Irté said. "And why would he know that?"

Oron shrugged. "He was a free sword and a hard man. Word of a chance at gold spreads quickly among such castoffs. Perhaps he wished to join Kest's company once he'd finished with me. Taken my weapons."

Irté agreed. "What one thing more do you wish?"

"Tell me why your arm is in that sleeve. From Kest?"

Irté leaned forward on the table and pulled free the glove. She revealed a limb less than useless, burned to the elbow, red and black and scarred, the fingers nearly gone. It resembled a broken, burnt tree limb more than it did anything human.

She said, "Kest did this to me as I ran to escape from him and his guards. He touched my hand, gripped me—and left the arm as you see. Another moment, and all of me would have been burned alive." As she struggled to pull the long glove back up her forearm, she said, "I swear to you, my brother will succeed in killing this sorcerer, come death or Hell."

She was brave and determined. Oron took his knife from the tabletop, returned it to his side, then reached inside his waist belt, past the knife handles there, and removed two coppers.

As he dropped them onto the tabletop, he told Irté, "Show me who sells good horses in this town."

## 2.

She bought the Nevgan the finest horse to be had in Ilrukad, an excellent stallion that responded well to the fighter's words and strong hand. Before leaving the town, Oron washed himself and his armor in a public fountain, making sure to cleanse the deep wound on his arm. Irté then did something unfamiliar to him: she rubbed the silver bracelet she wore on her left arm strictly along his wound, finally rinsing blood off it at the fountain.

"Why?" Oron asked her.

"My grandfather taught it to us. We don't understand why, but silver—not gold—helps the wound to heal cleanly."

They bought bread and cheese wrapped in old cloth and bladders of water to carry with them. They took the western road, Irté directing her horse along the untamed way that was little more than a wagon path. Thrice that afternoon they passed other riders heading toward the town; all nodded in greeting; none made threatening gestures. Oron anticipated that further bandits would attempt to waylay them, but they were in open field lands and farmland, not among secluded woods of birch and elm, which had been his path this morning.

Birds sang—jays calling and sparrows chipping, Oron decided—and a gentle breeze coming down from the north cooled them and brought the good scents of the earth, welcome after the clogged odors of Ilrukad. In the early afternoon, they saw on either side of them the huts and homesteads of farmers, with cattle and sheep at their grazing, but as they went on, the land became rugged, unlikely to be tilled anytime soon, and then again made up of woodland that grew into true forest, heavy with oak and maple, flush with streams of fresh water.

As they went, Irté spoke of what had befallen her home, Weslen, the village and the land around it having come to be called by her grandfather's name. The events caused by the sorcerer were sufficiently clear to Oron, who was reminded of other men in his experience who had enslaved towns and territories with their appetites to improve and exalt themselves. As he spoke, things he said corroborated what Irté had heard of this warrior. More so than she had anticipated, she felt that she and her brother had been correct in seeking out this leader and killer, as dangerous a man as the sorcerer they meant to confront. Of Edron, she told Oron that she expected her brother to have learned much by this time, dedicated as he was to developing his abilities in practices that would empower him.

"We will pass by him tomorrow," Irté told the Nevgan. "He has placed himself in ruins that are part of a hillside not far from Weslen."

"You had such a place so close to your home?"

"We didn't know of it until Kest imprisoned us. My brother discovered it. We suspect that even Kest is not aware of it. My brother's opinion is that the glamor that anciently protected the place was sufficient unless someone deliberately sought it out. Kest did not. My brother did."

"How did your brother learn of it?"

"He looked at scrolls in our grandfather's library. This was history our grandfather forbade us to read. Now we know why. Every knot of land in this world contains a secret past reaching back to when the demons created Attluma. Its antiquity may be hidden, but the scars remain. The authors of the scrolls did not know precisely of this place's location, but instructions they contained dared my brother to begin practicing the arts that could open opportunities for us. He placed himself in a drugged state and dreamed that the hills half a day's ride from us hid this old secret. He explored the outcroppings there. One offered a small tunnel, which he entered and where he found a wonder: deep in the earth, an ancient idol and engravings in the rock wall surrounding it."

Oron grunted; considering this caused him discomfort. He was reminded of the serpent mound in which he had recently died and then been returned to life by an ancientess who herself was only partly human. That old tunnel has been burrowed out by demigods, and the scratchings on the walls had fogged Oron's senses with ghostly impressions—the shadows and whispers of beings no longer embodied on the earth. Still, their shadows and voices, caught within the rock deep underearth and held within those scratchings, were, as Irté said, scars, remnants of an inconceivable past. As old as humanity was, human beings were but a recent intrusion in this world born so long ago of such shadows and voices. Demons and gods buried deep or held under by spells ages old yet remaining alive and aware, breathing, watching, waiting....

"All during the spring," Irté said, "and now this far into the summer, Edron has spent his life in the company of the ghosts and spirits of that temple. It *is* a temple, Oron, but one so old and foreign, we can hardly comprehend it or even the souls that created it. Still, they must have been human, or partly so. And they communicated with inhuman things, the powers that first created the world. Edron has followed them down that path. He deciphered their marks on the rock walls. He drew the necessary symbols and called upon the thing, the spirit, the god that had its home in that cave. The thing came back to life; it came out of the walls and up from the earth, climbing toward him like an old ghost; it answered my brother; and he has been given its strength. I fear for him, but we must do what we can."

\* \* \* \*

They rested late in the afternoon to take in the shade of an old oak's great arms. After dismounting, Oron let his water loose nearby; Irté, used to privacy, took herself behind a stand of elms. They nourished themselves on the bread and cheese. Then Oron, walking and stretching, noticed fish in the water of a nearby stream and told Irté that if they were to follow that stream, they would have food before nightfall.

Follow the stream they did, leaving the road but continuing west. At dusk, Oron fashioned a spear from a tree branch and soon enough caught a bass and two perch, which he quickly prepared with a knife while Irté, under his direction, made a cooking circle of rocks and gathered wood and tinder to begin a fire.

"You grew up knowing such things," she said to the Wolf as they ate. "To catch fish and hunt game."

"I did."

"Many of our people are good fishers and hunters."

"But you have never done these things yourself?"

She had not, she admitted, and reminded him of the chores that had filled her and her brother's days, overseeing the village with administrative duties, constantly making many decisions.

Nevertheless, Oron told her, "Knowing how to fish and hunt and make a bed for yourself under the sky are necessary."

Irté replied, "I'm learning already," and for the first time that day, she smiled.

Night came down. The air was warm, not uncomfortable. They let the horses feed on what they found and lay back and looked at the stars overhead, for there were few clouds. The star patterns, Irté told Oron, were as she knew them to be and not distorted by whatever gloom Kest had raised within Weslen. Staring at those stars, she said she was reminded of her girlhood, when watching the living night above her, the scattered stars and the moon steering its path overhead, made her so happy and complete that she had wanted to leave the earth, be that free.

"You will be that free again," Oron promised her.

Irté believed him.

* * * *

The next morning, as they sat eating further of the bread and cheese, Irté said to Oron, "Thank you for not forcing me last night."

"I don't do that," he told her, and then, with half a smile: "You might have burned me with that sign and done me quite some harm."

She laughed lightly. "True. My brother gave me this soon after he began his spirit quest. He was pleased to learn how successful it is."

"Will it kill Kest?"

"We don't know. Likely not. But it might save my life if it comes to that." Irté asked him then, "Oron, are you helping me because your own village was taken by a sorcerer?"

He stopped chewing. "You know that?"

"I heard it. Stories about you travel, but how true any of them are... who knows?"

"That one is true."

"And your people are gone?"

"Yes."

"And you killed your own father?"

He stood now and told her, "He brought it on himself, just as any of my enemies have. Your sorcerer will join them."

Irté, cautioned by his tone, put away her food. Time to continue their ride.

Oron asked her, "How far to your brother?"

"Only until noon high. We'll see Weslen along the way."

* * * *

Their morning was as pleasant as the previous day had been, relaxed. They spoke little, but Irté's anxiousness—because of the sorcerer, for her brother—was evident. Oron, however, took each moment as it came. The sun rose behind the trees surrounding them and came into sight against an egg-blue sky. They entered an area of scrub and outgrowth, grasses that settled in the visiting breezes, and then an uphill climb where the way was stony. As they reached the level height of this rising, Irté led the way past a thin stall of pines and pointed down. Oron paused his horse beside hers and looked at the village in the low plain beneath them.

Weslen.

It was as he had surmised, a home of many tens of buildings, several of stone some two stories tall, and otherwise houses of timber, all enclosed within heavy stone walls two man-lengths high. He judged it able to contain a thousand and a half persons within those walls, perhaps a bit more, sufficient to have built a rude, heavy temple of stone in the center of the village, a structure with the idol of a seated goddess atop it, a robed woman holding a serpent in one hand and a pine cone in the other—ancient symbols of wisdom. There were many paths between the buildings, many wells built of brick, and dogs and chickens, pigs, goats. But few people. Oron saw perhaps twenty-five or thirty drawing water or flushing flapping chickens toward some coop or enclosure. But there were no cattle outside the village walls—the cattle and sheep would all be gone by now, killed and eaten by the rough fighters who sat encamped in the shade near the village walls. Outside the temple, several of these rude mercenaries pestered a young woman who came by them.

"So few of your people remain?" the Wolf asked Irté.

"Many hide indoors now. Their strength is leaving them. Kest draws the life from them daily. See how unclear the air is?"

The Nevgan grunted. It was as though a wall of shivering haze contained the buildings and people with the imperfection of the waving film of heat above a strong fire.

Now two of the women near a well spotted Irté and Oron on the height and lifted hands to salute them, although they did not call out. Irté lifted her own sleeved right arm in a similar gesture, a greeting, and Oron heard her make a sound then, and he looked at her.

She had choked from holding in powerful emotion.

She lowered her head and told him, "I cannot help myself."

Some of the ruffians lolling outside the walls stood and also saluted Irté, mocking her. One turned around and showed her his hindside.

Irté said, "You see what we confront in those arrogant men."

Oron told her, "I have known such men all my life."

She reined her horse away. "My brother is not far."

* * * *

Irté made a sign with her left hand as they approached her brother's place and muttered syllables unknown to Oron. Doing so was necessary, she explained, because Edron had placed a protective veil about the area to guard against any intrusion by Kest or his hirelings. Oron felt no sense of it as he rode forward beside her, and so trusted that she had cleared their path.

The outcropping was large, heaved up among the birch and pines surrounding it, a thing of sandstone and chert and dolomite, the ragged, gray, and dour face of a recessed earth god. Oron saw that the entrance to the cave wherein was the temple Edron had found was not sufficient to let anyone pass without ducking or crouching. The way to that opening was a steep climb that followed no path, simply was a scattering of dead branches, old leaves, the bones of small animals, and other forest detritus.

Edron was not within the cave. He stood at the base of the climb in a worn and plain woolen cloak, the hood thrown back. He was not quite as tall as Oron, slender, with his beard grown out. His hair was dark but already showed streaks of white and gray, evidence of his having communed with the dead or other spirits, which had taken some of the life from him. But his eyes were as bright as polished onyx, dark beneath dark brows, and onyx was the proper description, for here was a man who had faced down his fears in his effort to rise above the human.

But Edron did not move. He stayed within a wide circle he had drawn around him on the ground, the circle apparently keeping him apart from the two men who now faced Irté and Oron as they dismounted to rest their horses.

One was taller than the other and older by several years. Both were ragged and unkempt but clearly were fighters, men of the road or out to be hired, weaponed many times over with steel in their belts and byside in wooden sheaths.

Oron suspected that he recognized the shorter and younger of the two.

He said to him, "You attacked me yesterday, you and the others."

That one smiled, proud of himself. "I did. And then rode to join this man's company and work for the devil himself, Lord Kest."

The taller man frowned and faced the other. "You attacked this man?"

"I did. Here is one of his knives. I took it from his boot." The shorter one removed a blade from his belt and displayed it.

"Do you know who this man is?"

"What does it matter?"

Oron and Irté regarded each other and watched the two with wariness.

The older man said with anger on his tongue, "This man is Oron! *Oron*! The Wolf of the North! He is a king among fighters! I was with him when he fought Lord Ogrum and his werewolf!"

Oron kept still.

The older man fairly screamed, "You're not fit to *lick Oron's boots*!" and drew his sword.

The other had no time to defend himself. That quickly, the longsword was through his bowels and then across his neck. The head went free to the ground while the arms trembled, the legs gave way, and blood jetted from the shoulders, spraying the nearby leaves with color.

"Dog!" The killer wiped his blade on his woolen cape and faced Oron as the body struck the ground.

Oron asked, "You were with my company then?"

"I was, brother. I was one of the many who fought with you. You won't remember me because we were all the same, but my name is Ferent."

"And now you're with Kest."

Ferent laughed easily. "Wolf, I loved fighting in your company, but your concern was never to take gold and treasure. You dealt with what came. Many of us left you because we wished for money and women. You did not."

Oron said to him, "It starts small, like a seedling, doesn't it?"

"What does?"

"The hunger. One taste, and you want a meal, then a feast."

"True, Wolf. And see how it has elevated me. You're a leader born, and still you mock the ambitious."

"Fate found me out, Ferent. It was not my seeking."

"I know that. You're said to be a man of destiny. Splendid—the fighter of destiny who refuses to drink from the cup Destiny offers him."

"And your destiny is with Kest."

"It is, brother. I must guard this magician or kill *him* if need be." He nodded to Edron, behind him. "And now you've kindly brought me his whore of a sister!" He laughed. "I'll kill them both."

Oron told him, "I am no longer your brother."

"I know that," said Ferent. "Oh, that I know." He lifted his blade. "You trained me, Wolf, and I have lived and prospered since those days. I know your tricks."

Oron drew his own sword. Irté made a sound; without looking at her, Oron nodded his head, indicating that she stay away. He glanced at Edron within his ring; the man simply watched as things occurred, apart from them, not speaking.

Oron moved forward, taking a low middle guard, as the smiling Ferent came ahead, teasing Oron with feints, trying to draw him in. Oron kept his distance, circling, and knew it when Ferent finally came at him with a high move, the same he had used on the fallen man.

Oron easily backed away and brought his blade up to deflect Ferent's. Steel scraped steel, an unnatural sound in the somber quiet of that space. Oron came in and turned to one side as he brought his blade close to Ferent, intending to disembowel him, a move he knew the other man would recall. Ferent jumped away, understanding, and lifted his blade as he stepped to one side and brought it down.

Oron came forward, letting Ferent's weapon pass beside him, and pushed his sword into the man's belly through his side. Ferent's expression was one of surprise; he hadn't expected the Wolf to move in so swiftly and to slide in so easily. This was a new Wolf.

Ferent sank to his knees, letting go of his weapon and holding his stomach. He smiled, now in pain, and felt the blood at his waist and his insides beginning to push free with each failing breath. He said nothing, shook his head, and watched the ground as though some sudden, profound meaning were there, then fell forward.

Oron wiped the sweat from his forehead and said to the dead man, "Brother…there are no tricks.

### 3.

Not yet cleaning the blood from his weapon, Oron looked toward Edron. The young sorcerer made a sign with both hands, a magical gesture, then stepped free of the circle inscribed among the leaves and stones.

As he approached Oron, he nodded and said, "Thank you for coming, *dessek*." It was an ancient word for a leader; Oron had heard it only once before, spoken by a sage as old as the word itself in a marketplace at some crossroads whose name he had forgotten. Edron looked at his sister. "You have brought him, as promised."

"Yes." But Irté hesitated as she approached her brother, watching him carefully as though concerned with any alteration to himself caused during his deep studies and practice.

Edron smiled at her. "Don't be afraid, sister. I haven't changed so much!"

"But you have."

Oron watched her, still holding his naked sword in his right hand.

Irté reached inside her protective sleeve and removed the silver sign she carried, the metal sigil that protected her. She asked her brother, "Edron, do you remember when you made this device for me?"

The sorcerer regarded her uncertainly. "Of course. Why ask? Irté, let us sit together and have a meal and plan our attack on Kest." He looked warily at Oron.

She ignored his suggestion. "Was it during the sinking of the quarter moon or the rising of the new moon? I have confused myself."

Edron smiled. "It makes no difference, sister! The sign is the sign as I made it."

"Enough," Irté said, and looked at Oron. "This is not my brother!"

Edron cried out a word, then a string of syllables Oron had never heard before, as he ripped his robe from himself and transformed. The air shimmered about him, and darkness came from him, mist from his pores and nostrils. His face twisted, he leaned forward, and his naked body became misshapen, the joints humping out like those of an animal.

The thing crouched. Oron came at it, sword forward and up and down in a perfect line, cutting through the monster's right shoulder, freeing the arm. Further smoke came.

Irté cried out again.

The thing moved from side to side, looking for some way to approach Oron, and hissed.

Oron jumped. He came in so closely that he stood within the dark mist of the thing as he brought his sword across cleanly, opening the monster's chest to let more smoke flow.

The thing moved away. Oron returned with his sword and beheaded it, or nearly did.

The shining bald head with yellow smoking eyes dropped to the left and hung there by a stretching rope of muscle, the jaws snapping, before the legs gave way and it dropped.

Oron waved away the smoke that remained in the air.

"Don't breathe it in!" Irté told him as she came close.

"Too late!" He shrugged, feeling no effect of it. It was nothing more than he had ever known in fighting sorcerously encouraged spirits or ancient ghosts; it might have been the creature's blood he was breathing in, not its spirit or magic, dying and powerless as it was.

"One of Kest's demons," Irté said. "I should have anticipated this. But he stayed within that ring. His glamor held secret what it was."

Oron grunted again as he walked toward Ferrent's corpse to clean his sword on that corpse's cape. As he knelt, he asked Irté, "What of your brother? Dead?"

"I sense not."

She passed him, her fine boots becoming soiled by the blood on the ground, and just entered the opening in the hillside, pausing and lowering her head. She called, "Edron!"

Oron joined her as a man's weak voice came from within. "Here! The spell has passed!"

And in a moment, the young sorcerer himself appeared, naked but for animal skins wrapped around his waist. He put his hands out to his sister; Irté took them, then drew him near.

"You're wounded?" she asked.

"No." He shook his head and looked at Oron as he continued. "Kest caught me as I slept. I guarded myself, but his spell slipped in. He meant for those men to kill you both if I could not protect you. Thank you, *dessek*. You have protected my sister well."

"As she did me," Oron replied, looking at the witch. "But this thing—" he nodded to the monster on the forest floor, already disassembling itself, revealing murky bones and tendons "—is not of Kest."

"I'm ashamed to admit my trickery," Edron said. "I created it from parts of dead animals."

Irté was upset. "But why?"

He faced her. "I know this man is a hero, and you've done well to bring him here, but—" he looked at Oron "—what if you were a trick of Kest's? You might have been a creature of *his*, not the true Oron. How would Irté know? How would I? It would take time and effort to untangle. He is clever."

Oron said, "Another reason why the smoke was not poisonous."

"Yes. I had no desire to endanger you if you were truly who you say you are. But if your reaction had given me any hint that you were less than human, I'd hoped to kill you, false thing that you were."

Oron told him plainly, "But you were too weak by then to fight me if I had been a demon."

"You're correct," Edron admitted. "I did what I could to make that monster. Yet it has cost me."

\* \* \* \*

Oron dragged Ferrent's body, and Edron the bandit's corpse, away to a deep slant in the forest, where the ground gave way in a sharp decline to rocks and crowded overgrowth. Crows appeared, and fast animals in the brush hurried down the decline to feast.

As evening came down, the three gathered around a fire Oron built.

Fish roasted on spits above the flames. The three spoke little, allowing the tension between Oron and Edron to fade with the daylight, that annoying deception Edron had created. The horses grazed nearby. Nightbirds called.

Oron finished what he had eaten, threw the bones into the fire, and asked Edron, "No spies from Kest come here at night?"

"I have a spell around this place so that I would know if just such a thing happens."

Oron said, "Irté explained this."

"Some nights ago," Edron told them, "I heard someone cry out, no doubt one of the sorcerer's men. I have not been disturbed since." He looked at his sister. "If that man tried to cross my barrier, he was well burnt for his trouble."

Irté nodded.

Oron said to Edron, "I must know what you've prepared. Your sorcery, and who among your people will be fighting the sorcerer's men. Where are they now?"

"Not far from here. We've stayed apart so that Kest's men could not attack all of us at once. They are training themselves as well as they can."

"Tell me more of Kest. I've killed many devils," Oron said, "and each of them had some deceit to them. The fewer surprises, the better."

The facts were quickly shared; they were as Irté had explained to Oron in the tavern. His sight told Edron that Kest was aware that the younger man was learning sorcery to fight him—indeed, had given himself over entirely to the forgotten earth god of this lost place. There was power in what Edron had learned, and Kest had been wasting some of his own strength in sending lines of power toward Edron, trying to interfere with the young man's deepening wisdom and growing ability. Edron felt certain that he could defeat Kest or at the least wound him gravely, and thus allow Oron to kill him.

The young man declared, "I have studied as deeply and as quickly as I have been able. The carvings in this cave opened and came apart when I said the perfect words I have learned. It was as though I were reading from starlit scrolls that floated on shifting clouds above the ocean of Time, all illuminated. In my sight, even the constellations spoke to me as they did to the earliest seekers and wisdomites. I have gained quite some power. Look here. The oldest sorcery is as old as fire."

He put his hand into the flames.

Irté gasped.

His hand was unhurt, and the flames turned a deep shade of green. As Edron waved his hand through the fire, images appeared. Oron recognized Weslen, its walls, its houses and stone buildings, the temple built to its goddess, and the armed men camped outside.

With a further wave of his hand, Edron revealed Kest himself within that temple. The sorcerer appeared to be as Irté had told Oron, a young man, not at all a bent creature a hundred years old. He was dressed as plainly as Edron, in the ragged tribon of a philosopher, and seated on a wooden bench, apparently engrossed by the scroll he was holding open before him on a low table. Around him burned flames in tripods, and vapors rose from bowls—incenses to relax the mind and keep one open to suggestions and intrusions from kingdoms outside this world's heavy common reality. Kest leaned backward, resting his hands on the open scroll. He murmured silently, closed his eyes, and breathed in the fumy air.

Oron noticed three silvery shapes near the sorcerer, no more than tall, white cloaks without faces or hands, and six servants, human, dressed as he was, as scholars.

Edron explained. "The white ones are further guardians, *dessek*. Slaves he has made of spirits or other dead things. Once they were human, age upon age ago. He has conducted many trials in his desire to know everything and rule all. I know that he has placed the spirits of dead religionists within the ghosts of animals, combining the two to see what effect he can gain, wisdom or deviltry or both. He is not above having his own jokes on the world. Imagine the soul of some priest of Cae or Sorkendum shrieking in pain from inside the ghost of a baboon or dog." He smiled as though ill. "The people with him are followers who hope to become like him one day. They prepare his meals and bathe him, dress him, and keep his scrolls in repair. Enough."

He waved his hand again, dispersing the images, and shook the hand as he removed it from the fire. Small flames briefly danced on his fingertips, then flitted away, and no part of the hand was singed or burnt.

He said, "This is the creature we confront. He was dying when he resurrected his old god to bring him back to life. God and man, or demon and man—now they are one. Kest feeds the demon as he feeds himself from whatever living things are nearby and will do so to the ends of the earth. In this way, he wishes to become immortal. He weakened even our goddess, Ethed, the All-Mother, though she still works to guard our home from where he has consigned her."

"So Irté explained to me," Oron said. "And your own wild god empowers you."

"Yes. I am its servant. This is the respect I show to the earliest gods of the world."

"What is this god?"

"It is nameless, as are the sky and the air. But I call it the Setet. It is an old word for 'Great Presence.' "

"And Kest's demon?"

"Its name matters only if I were to invoke it in spells to fight it," Edron replied. "Tython, it is called." He said it, then spat into the fire as though poison had formed in his mouth.

Oron asked, "How long before you intend to attack?"

"As soon as possible. I am strong, but keeping the Setet alive in me costs me. And the longer we wait, the more of our people die."

He looked at his sister, who nodded in agreement.

Oron was thoughtful. "I'll train your people as well as they are able to learn. Here is my thought. We are at war with a sorcerer and his demon and his hired fighters. Companions at war empower themselves by seeking allies. I ask you: do gods and demons speak to each other and come to terms?"

Both Edron and Irté understood immediately what he meant. Edron said, "The Setet and Ethed together can fight Kest and Tython."

"Yes."

"This is a good thought. The Setet guards us as we attack from without, while Ethed becomes stronger within our walls and her temple."

"Yes," Oron told him.

Edron said. "Let us attempt it."

Irté offered, "Let me say the prayers to Ethed even now and speak to her from my soul. I have sworn an oath to her. I will ask her to be prepared to be empowered by the Setet."

Edron nodded. "This we can do." He turned to Oron. "You have prepared a plan for the battle when we confront his fighters?"

"Yes." The Nevgan cleared a space on the ground to one side of him and with a stick drew a circle, the walls of the village. "Here is Weslen. Here is its gate, on the east. Expect the sorcerer's hired fighters to guard the gate, as we have seen them sitting outside. They haven't protected themselves with barricades or trenches, so they assume they have little to fear from us. We will use that. Do you have just one gate for the village?"

Irté told him, "There is a tunnel hidden in the temple of our goddess. It leads into the forest to the west. But it's not a wide tunnel."

"Still, your people can use it if they need to."

"Yes."

Oron dragged the stick back and forth on the ground, in front of the east gate, then farther away and to the sides.

He said, "Kest's fighters all are mounted and know how to fight that way. This is to their advantage. As soon as they see us, they will ride at us." He asked Edron, "How many horses do you have?"

The brother looked to his sister to confirm what he said. "Twenty. We have twenty horses."

"Kest has three times that. Do your people know how to ride well?"

"You mean, to fight on horseback? No. It could be attempted, but it would no doubt mean the death of those riders."

"Then you must create some distraction to counter Kest's fighters while protecting your own."

Edron told Oron and Irté, "The scrolls speak of a time when the followers of the Setet confronted an armed host meant to slay them. The worshippers of the Setet defeated the invaders when the god called up a wind and a mist to betray the movements of his people. Some of the winds carried men to their deaths. Further, their priest fashioned stones into ghosts that moved among the enemy host to kill them at a touch."

Oron grunted. "The earth is filled with the dead in every direction. Their bodies are just below us. We who walk the earth will forever slay each other and leave ourselves buried and forgotten. Even now we may be sitting atop your god's ghost army."

Irté said, "Ethed speaks of such things in her songs. She went down into the land of the dead and returned not only with wisdom, but also with a flaming sword and shield."

"The gods are as many as the trees in the forest," said Edron, and made a sign before himself.

Oron said to him, "If you can create such a mist and these ghosts from stones, then our work is half done. Will your people not be afraid?"

"They understand that I am calling upon old shadows and ghosts for their benefit. They will abide by my decision."

"So, then," Oron said, returning to draw the point of his stick on the ground. "Do that. Let your ghosts be the infantry to face the charge of Kest's fighters. Then your riders will come in from both sides. They can use swords?"

"Some of them have fought in battles and come home again as victors. The others, no."

"Spears? Slings?"

"Those, yes."

"And fire," Oron said. "Can you send out a ghost that will catch fire?"

Edron smiled. "I will attempt to manage that."

Oron said, "Your land is parched. The grass, trees—all as dry as tinder. We will use that to our advantage, as well." He stretched his arms as though exercising his strength and preparing already to enter the field. He said, "Once we've advanced to the gate, we must break through it. Or scale a wall. How many more fighters does Kest have inside?"

"Perhaps fifteen or twenty," Irté told him. "Only enough to relieve fighters camped outside every few days."

"Then they must be killed, as well. I'll teach your fighters how to confront blades."

Edron told him, "Irté can use spells I will teach her to free the goddess from her prison. The gate will be opened. And by then, those inside, weak as they are, will attack the other fighters Kest has kept by him."

Oron asked him, "And will Kest be weakened by your spells, and Irté's, so that my sword can take him?"

"Yes," Edron said. "Kest has made it his life's work to make himself as strong as he is, but still…it is the work of sorcery and incantations, spells and fire, ghosts and gods and demons. The same will defeat him. If that were not so, why then should I attempt this? Sorcerers have fought each other since life first came up from the fires and out of the shadows."

"True," Oron said. "I have witnessed this."

"Kest will die, one way or another, and his spell over us be broken. This god will make it so." He gestured toward the cave. "And then I wish to be done with gods and demons and sleep again in my own bed."

## 4.

Yawning, Oron went to the horses. He and Irté had secured their reins to the branches of nearby trees, well enough away from the cave opening and any danger they might sense there. He saw that his stallion seemed to be keeping aware so that Irté's warmblood could rest in safety. Now he led them both to a creek to let them refresh themselves and enjoy the plants that were there.

He turned at the sound of Irté approaching.

"Did I startle you?"

"No."

She told him that she, too, wished to check on the horses and help calm them. From the purse at her waist, Irté removed crushed petals and buds. Oron immediately recognized the scent of lavandula. Irté spread the petals and buds on the ground.

"To help them remain calm," she told Oron.

"Those plants have that effect, I know. Even Nevgans are aware of that."

She let out a small laugh. Oron was surprised to hear it, Irté had been so somber all this time. She told him, "Come with me now, please."

They returned toward the campfire, which now was burning low. Irté led Oron, not toward the fire, but to a tent that sat some distance from both the fire and the cave opening, in the deep darkness within a crowd of larch trees.

"In here."

"I intend to sleep outside to confront whatever comes."

"Oron, we're prepared for that, as well. Please. With me."

He hesitated, then went in as she directed. The tent was not sufficiently tall for them to stand, so both crouched, then sat with their legs crossed on the mats and animal skins that were there.

Irté told Oron, "Edron made this tent so that he could sleep when he wished to away from the dreams and memories of that cave. He asks you and I to sleep here tonight."

"Why?"

"So that I can work a way by which the Goddess with help protect you."

She reached into her purse once more and removed a second square of metal on a chain. The sign on it was different from that on her own.

Irté said, "Edron made this to protect you. I have further enspelled it with words to Ethed. Please assure me that you'll wrap it around your sword to guard you as we confront Kest and his fighters."

Oron took it and did so right then, tying the square beneath the pommel of his weapon. Even as he did, he had a sensation from the thing. "It has power," he told Irté.

"You feel it so soon. Good," she said. "The marking on it has been passed down by women among themselves and to wisdom workers and magicians from the First Days. There is strength in the agedness of it, just as the earth is strong because it is old. Powers collect over time."

Now, as they sat facing each other, Irté moved further, coming closer to Oron and touching his face with her strong left hand.

"There is more," she told him, and removed her fine boots, soiled now with dead men's blood and the dirt of the earth, then began on her dress. "You as well, Oron."

He helped her removed her dress, one-handed as she was, then undid his cuirass, with Irté assisting in undoing the leather laces at the sides of it, then removed his own boots, his tunic, and his pants. Already he was erect.

"Lie back, Oron,"

He did so, watching her eyes.

She asked him, "Are you afraid? Don't be afraid."

"Not afraid," he told her. "Uncertain."

"Don't be. I wish only to summon further magic to protect both you and me. We must enter into this with such potency."

"I have heard of such magic."

"But you have experienced it before now?"

"No."

"You will find that it is gentle in its power. More subtle than not. It is woman's magic."

In the dimness, she moved herself atop him, and they settled together so that their breathing was the same, and their movements, which gradually hastened. As she moved, Irté murmured words unknown to Oron, although he understood her when she panted, "Let such be. *Let such be!*"

A wind came up outside and moved the walls of the tent. Oron felt himself building to his climax and felt that Irté was reaching her peak, as well. When they met each other in the same moment, hearts pounding, breathing in short gasps, holding onto one another, they were interrupted by the whinnying of the horses out by the stream and then by a scream.

A man's scream, and then other howls.

Oron said hoarsely, "Spies. From Kest."

"Yes." Irté, still panting, rose from him now. "Can you feel it?"

"Yes." It was a sensation new to him, not simply the afterglow of love-making but something else. It was deep in his gut.

He told Irté so.

"That is Ethed," she told him. "You will feel a warm center for some time. It is the strength she gives us."

They both rose to their feet and, not troubling to cover themselves, stepped outside into the warm night.

Edron was there, standing by what remained of the fire, and told them, "Kest's men have dared it once more."

He lifted a hand to his left and sent from it more of the green fire he had conjured earlier, a ball of it, which floated head-high to the perimeter of their camp. By the radiant green light, Oron and Irté saw three dead men resting in a pile.

"Will he continue to send spies to die this way?" Oron asked.

"No," Edron said. "This will be the last of them. Otherwise, they will turn against him. He knows that."

His sister told him, "Oron has accepted the sign, Edron."

"I have," the Nevgan said.

The sorcerer nodded. "Then we will be as protected as possible against what we face."

* * * *

Morning.

Irté awoke in the tent to find Oron still stretched out beside her and watching her, studying her.

She yawned and asked him, "Did you sleep well?"

He grunted. "Irté, what did he mean, the bandit I killed, when he called you a whore?"

"Not what you must think."

"I don't think anything yet."

She sat up. "It has to do with Kest."

"I have thought that."

"Then you do read people well, Nevgan."

She told him that when Kest arrived in Weslen, she felt as though some spell from him had fallen over her. He appeared to be so wise, and he had come to do good for her people. Inevitably, Irté, who had had few lovers in her life because of her elevated station and the remoteness of her village, gave herself wholly to Kest and contemplated a future with him. Only when he turned on her and her people, entrapping them, did she realize how damnably she had been tricked.

"It is my shame," she told Oron. "This is also why I pray to the Goddess, after all she has suffered. And because of me."

"Not you. Even She herself surely fell victim to the sorcerer's tricks, his and his demon-god's."

Irté admitted it. "But still, I am ashamed. How can I not be?"

He shrugged. "It has made you what you are."

She looked him in the eyes and told him, "Live long enough and you become a new person. Haven't we both learned this?"

"It is true."

"The old us strangers to ourselves. I understand now more than I ever did before that everything is change, then sameness. Cycles. Such is life. Change, then sameness, then change anew. Still, much remains, hidden as it is to the casual eye." She said sternly, "Kest has desecrated this natural order."

"He will suffer for it," Oron told her.

"And I wish to see him suffer," Irté told him. "I am not above that, Oron. I wish to witness his suffering."

* * * *

The encampment of the Wesleners was half the morning's ride from Edron's cave. He stayed behind to complete whatever rituals or prayers were necessary to his god. Irté showed Oron the way, and the sky darkened with heavy clouds. Irté regarded those clouds with an expression of disdain.

"Kest," she said.

"The clouds?" Oron asked her.

"The clouds are from my brother. He is disguising the air so that Kest with his traveling eyes will not be successful. He would like to follow us into our encampment, find a door. Then he could force some of us to dream in fear to disempower us. But our wall is strong, Edron's and mine."

Oron winced. "His eyes?"

"Those phantoms of his that you saw in the fire. They can lift into the air and travel like clouds themselves to watch below. But they are no match for the darkness Edron calls up."

"The darkness is a danger to him."

"He knows this, Oron, but of course, he dares it."

By midmorning the skies had cleared—further work of Edron's—as Oron and Irté came through heavy trees and up a slope to a flat area fronted by further outcroppings. On this grassy plain were the felt tents and animal-skin lean-to's of the Wesleners, their fire pits, and the weapons they were preparing, smooth stones for their slings, spears, and arrows they pointed with lengths of sharp flint inserted, sufficient to pierce the leather jerkins and woolen shirts Kest's fighters wore, and easily capable of rending naked flesh.

A wide area in the middle of the circled tents and fires was by now scraped clear of grass and roots down to the stony dirt, the place where they practiced their swordplay and spear work. Several of the men and three of the women were doing just that as Oron and Irté approached.

"Sister!" called one of the women to Irté, lifting her spear in a pose of strength.

Irté said to all of them as she dismounted, "The practice goes well?"

A middle-aged man, bellied but wide-shouldered and heavy-limbed, came forward carrying a sword sufficiently large to split a man. He bowed his head to her. "It goes well, lady." His eyes moved to Oron, who was now on his feet. The man said with a touch of wonder in his voice, "He has come."

The Wolf told him, "I am Oron."

"And welcome you are, sir." The heavyset man shifted his weapon to his left hand and extended his right.

Oron took it. "Some of you have seen war."

"I have," this one told him. "And seven of the others." He turned to take in the group behind him, all of whom were now coming forward.

"Then you I will need you as leaders," Oron said.

The man nodded. "Of course. My name is Kelder."

Now a second man came forward, eager to meet Oron. With his eyes on the Wolf, he neglected to greet Irté but immediately ducked his head toward Oron. "We are honored to have you here," he said, smiling broadly.

This one was lean and not imposing, a man of the indoors who caused Oron to feel uncertain.

Oron asked him, "How are you called?"

"Ulast. I am Ulast." He faced Irté. "Lady, we have been practicing hard. And, your honor—" to Oron "—let me share with you some plans I have devised on my own to assist in the attack. Will you listen to me?"

"I will, later," Oron said, and noticed the frown on Kelder's face as Ulast backed away, proud of himself and still smiling as he turned to move through the group.

Irté lent the reins of her horse to a young man who bowed to her and offered to lead her mount and Oron's both to where the other horses were resting in a stand of birches. The lady continued to greet some of the others as they welcomed her.

As the Wesleners returned to their chores and their practice, Oron said to Irté, "Kelder is a man to trust."

"With my life and yours," she said. "My father knew him and respected him. He has been to war, as well, and some of the others."

"But Ulast…I don't like him."

"He assisted Edron and me in our work for the village."

"Let me speak frankly."

"Do so, please."

"In such a situation as this, there is often one who is a traitor to the rest."

"Not Ulast."

"He has the look of a man who has been hungry for too long. This is not where he wishes to be. He is soft but proud."

"Oron, this is why you are needed, to train them."

"But this one is not at all a follower. We need natural leaders. Kelder is one. The rest must accept whatever is necessary for all of us to survive."

"You think Ulast will not do this?"

"Watch him, is what I'm saying. He is too eager to please you."

"He's given me no reason to doubt him. He wants to live, Oron, like the rest of us."

"You've just said it for me, Irté. What will he do to stay alive?"

"Betray us?"

Oron told her, "We must watch him or any of the others who stand too far apart from us. Some people are dogs. Some, eagles or hawks. And some are vipers. The vipers crawl low and then surprise us with their fangs."

* * * *

Oron began training the Wesleners that afternoon, after all had had their midday meal and rested. There was ample food—deer and elk brought down with arrow and spear, fish caught in nets, rabbit and squirrel taken in traps, as well as good berries and roots and nuts. There was no beer or wine; all made do with the fresh water from the streams thereabouts. One of the men had asked Edron about charming some of that water so that it might be transformed into beer, and he had attempted to do so, without luck. (He didn't care for beer, himself.) So water it was for all of them.

The Nevgan was surprised to see a variety of swords and knives available, nearly as many as there were Wesleners, and was told by a young woman that some of them there had been of nights surreptitiously entering the village by that tunnel beneath the goddess's temple so that friends could supply them with these tools.

Oron complimented the young woman and, smiling, asked her, "But no beer or wine?"

She frowned and explained that Kest's fighters had kept all of the beer and wine for themselves. "The Goddess take them!"

Oron was pleased to see how many of the men and women there were prepared already to confront an attack. He commended those who had brought down the wild game and told those men and women, young and old, that hunting and killing other fighters required the same skills. He asked, "Who has trained these people?"

Kelder stepped forward, and seven other men.

"You have all been to war," Oron said to the seven.

They spoke up, some saying where and when and against whom they had fought. All had left home—Weslen—when young to cast about in the world, had seen life for what it is, and so had returned to begin their families and settle into farming or village life.

"But now this sorcerer has destroyed our orchards and our fields. Killed our flocks to feed his killers. You see the situation," Kelder said to Oron.

"I knew a similar situation when I was younger," the Wolf told them. "I have seen this more than once. You eight, please stay by me. We will discuss tactics."

He asked the eight each to lead a small group of Wesleners and told them to choose their fighters now, so that the members of each group would be comfortable with the others around them. Oron then walked among the groups as they practiced under veteran leadership. The eight had taught the basic guards and attacks of swordplay already, and all the Wesleners were adept with the spear and the bow. Several of them Oron considered would even now be welcome in the ranks of any company of renegades or mercenaries. These had anger in them, the rage that comes from suffering injustice, seeing their families, their children, their neighbors sickened, hurt, tortured, murdered.

By evening, all relaxed with aching muscles and cuts and bruises, but proud of their wounds and their pain. Oron sat with Irté and the veterans around a large fire and ate well of the venison and fish they were served. They agreed that the day had gone well and discussed when they should attack the village.

"Let it be soon," Kelder said. "We have been training for nearly a moon, my lord. The reflexes are sharp and the muscles, ready. We are an arrow waiting to be loosed."

"I see that," Oron agreed, and asked Irté, "What have you and Edron settled in this regard?"

She told him and the leaders, "He asks only that he be allowed to let his training reach a degree equal to that of the spirit in these fighting people. He is nearly in that situation." To Kelder, she said: "Your patience will be rewarded, friend. How much longer can we subject our people to this suffering?"

The question answered itself.

Oron, Kelder, and the other leaders, with Irté, now discussed the Nevgan's plan of attack. Perhaps twenty Wesleners lingered behind them, listening, eager to learn the details of the coming fight. Oron provided his plan but kept silent on the degree to which Irté and Edron would assist. Kelder and another of the veterans made some suggestions, to which the Wolf agreed. Then he looked up at the men and women gathered around them.

All nodded except one.

Ulast said to Oron, "Your plan is good, hero, but I learned of a better one while studying in our library."

Oron looked across the fire to Irté and Kelder, both of whom frowned. Irté began to speak, but Oron held up his right hand, cautioning her.

He told Ulast, "You're a man of learning, I can see it. No doubt you have ideas that could assist even true fighters. Come closer and tell us your ideas."

Ulast smiled and moved in to sit on one of the warm rocks between two of the other leaders, who pushed aside to allow him room.

"Attack straight ahead," Ulast said. When Kelder scoffed, saying that they did not have the numbers for a direct attack, Ulast told them all, "But that is why this sorcerer and his killers will not expect it. They will be positioned to the sides of the city as we come at the gate."

One of the veterans asked him, "And how do you know this?"

"I overhead Kest describe this plan to his retainers while I hid in the library."

Oron grunted, indicating that he believed Ulast, and shared a further look with Kelder and Irté. He asked Ulast, "But you've heard how we wish to use our archers at the wings. What would you do?"

"Let the riders lead the way. You, of course, will be up front at the charge—"

"I will allow no one else," Oron interrupted him.

"—and then, behind, we riders and the archers, and then the remainder of us with swords and slings and spears. By then, Kest's fighters will be routed, and the day will be ours."

Oron considered the plan for a space, then agreed. "Ulast, you are as wise in strategy as you are in book learning."

"Thank you, my lord."

And to the doubters around the fire, he said, "Let's take our rest now. I am pleased with what I've heard. We can make our attack the day after tomorrow or the next day if Edron will permit it."

\* \* \* \*

Before settling in to take his rest, Oron spoke quietly with Irté and Kelder, the three of them alone by one of the tents.

Kelder whispered to Oron, "As you surmised, Wolf. Even now he is out there, staying just inside our camp, at the perimeter, telling what he knows to betray us to spies Kest has sent. He told Kest weeks ago where we are."

Oron said to Irté, "You see? A viper in the camp." And to Kelder: "We follow my original plan, but with a change. Whisper it to the other seven leaders and have them share it secretly with the fighters. Let Ulast learn how treachery is punished by those true to their honor."

Kelder smiled deeply, made a fist of his right hand, and placed it over his heart—the old sign of respect between fighting men.

## 5.

Throughout the following morning and afternoon, the practice continued under the guidance of Kelder and the other veterans, but it was plain to see that the fighters were eager to face foes other that the tree boles and rocks they had made into targets. Oron and Kelder spoke to Irté about this, for the more protracted the wait, the more likely the Wesleners would lose their fighting edge. They had not spent their lifetimes among the rigors known to slayers, for whom the sword and bow and spear were familiar friends; these were people who would kill as they must, survive if possible, mourn those of theirs who fell, and then move on with their quieter lives. It was not their instinct to seek the next red battle to which to sell their prowess. Irté, as the afternoon waned, told Oron and Kelder that her brother would arrive that night; he had sent her a vision telling her so.

"Then we attack in the morning," Oron said, before reminding Kelder to warn the other trainers to share this knowledge with all but Ulast. "Let him think that we intend to fight in the afternoon, after Kest's hires have eaten and have too much wine on their bellies."

Then the Wolf retired to a nearby outcropping and sat on a boulder among the trees as the late afternoon went, its shadows coming and the sky taking back the daylight. Here he brooded, letting the thoughts come—his life among his people far to the north, all of them dead now by the actions of an earth-empowered sorcerer, the first of their kind to work with spirits and elementals that the young fighter ever had confronted. More he had met as he followed his trail, and he knew what made them, their desires as ignoble and selfish as those who sought to enrich or empower themselves by means other than sorcery. Human nature is as unchanging as the clouds that live above us, that swell and storm and fill again, and the wolves that harbor their cubs into parentage and the fish that spawn, all as the gods have made them. Ever returning, as Irté had told him.

It was the strength he had earned as a warrior that Oron now considered, his strength to lead these people, as small a band as they were, against another outsized sorcerer turning Nature into a tool with his scrolls and spells and knowledge so ancient it were better left alone. Oron the Wolf had been raised by his father and kin to use the sword and the knife and the spear and the bow, and he had learned well, taking to these weapons as naturally as sorcerers did their own unnatural tools. The Nevgans were fighters; all in the valley of the Nevga River knew that and were wary of the dark-haired ones with their quick tempers. Left to themselves, Oron's people fished and hunted, grew crops of vegetables, looked after their sheep and goats, and were pleased with what was sufficient. When troubles came and disease took the sheep and goats or what they had planted, then they raided their neighbors to steal their stores, and they thought no less of themselves for doing so, feared as they were, for this was the law of life, the Iron Law, that the strong prey upon the weak. Thus Nature and the gods willed it: the lesser continue as permitted by the stronger, the cleverer, the more intelligent. This was as necessary to life as keeping one's sword edge sharp and clean. How many times had he had this same discussion with fighters who, like him, wondered sometimes about the way of things rather than accepting what is. Why did the gods make some of us so turned that discontent comes, that we wonder, we brood, we let our imaginations travel where others are content?

He turned at the sound of a footstep and drew his sword as he faced what was coming.

It was a youth, Handar, a young man of skills but who now held back, startled by how swiftly Oron had freed his blade and aimed it at his heart.

"What is it, Handar?"

"My lord…the sorcerer has returned. Edron, I mean."

Oron allowed himself a slight smile as he sheathed his blade. "I took you by surprise when you meant to surprise me."

"I did not, my lord."

"But you did not run away. You have your own sword with you. You might have met me if we were enemies."

"But not defeated you, Lord Oron."

"But you could have tried."

"Yes. I could have tried," the young man admitted.

"That," the Wolf told him, standing and walking with Handar back to the camp, "is all that is asked of you. You handle a blade well."

"Thank you, my lord."

"You will do well tomorrow."

"I hope so, Lord Oron."

"But you fear Kest."

"Yes."

"That's proper. Be aware of his skills and temper. But try to think like him, if you can, Handar. Sorcery he may have mastered, but he is a man like us, nevertheless. He does what he can to impose himself on other men, but he cannot upset Nature without the balance being righted somewhere on his path. I have lived this."

"Thank you, my lord."

"And the men he has hired—they, too, are only men. Perhaps they have practiced more than you have or killed, as is their way. But they will display their weaknesses to a quick eye and arm. And you are quick, Handar."

"Thank you, Lord Oron."

"There's Edron."

He was dressed as he had been, without armor or defense of any sort so far as Oron could see, although the armor of sorcerers was often invisible and charged with the power of the earth or sky. Edron was standing by his sister at one of the fires and speaking lowly with Kelder and a few other leaders.

As Oron arrived, Handar hung close by, and Edron bowed shortly from the waist to the Wolf and said, "I am prepared to confront him. And your force is ready, as well."

Kelder spoke, rather than Oron—"We are"—but then ducked his head to see whether he had annoyed the Wolf.

Oron waved away the imposition.

Now the others in camp came forward, encircling the four at the fire, to hear what their leaders had to say. The plan was the same as had been discussed, Oron told them: Ulast's plan for arranging their lines straight, and they would attack early in the afternoon against the besotted fighters below.

Ulast, who had moved as close to the Wolf and Kelder as the crowd permitted, thanked Oron again for the honor of devising the attack plan. Then, as prepared as they were, all retired to their tents to take their rest.

Only Oron, Kelder, the sorcerer, and his sister remained by the fire, and they watched as Ulast also seemed to go to his sleeping mat. But in the darkness, away from the fires, he crept as close as he could to the guarding perimeter that had posed no danger to Edron and met the men of Kest, with whom he shared the Wolf's plans.

"You know of this one?" Edron whispered to Oron.

"From the beginning," the Nevgan told him. "And we have our plan for him."

Kelder grunted and smiled cruelly, while Irté said simply, "We are prepared, brother."

* * * *

Ulast thought he dreamed when, in the darkness just before the first gray of dawn, he was rudely awakened, pulled up from his blankets beneath covering elm trees, and brought to Oron's tent. There, standing at the fire just outside, were the four of the previous night.

Ulast struggled against the two men who held his arms, but he did not have the strength to free himself.

Edron said to Ulast, there in the darkness, "You are a traitor."

"No, no!" Ulast fought, as useless as that was. "Who's told you this? Let me see him!"

Edron waved a hand before him, and Ulast saw, as on a screen or tapestry hung in a temple, images of himself in the night speaking with Kest's fighters.

"This is a trick, a sorcerer's trick!"

Kelder fisted hims across the jaw, bringing a complaint from Ulast but reducing him to bloody froth. "Damn, damn," he whispered to himself, spitting out red drool.

Oron meanwhile had knelt by the fire and was holding over it his side knife, warming the tip of it in the flames. He looked at Ulast.

The liar caught the Wolf's stare. "What are you doing? What? Lord Oron, *what are you doing*?"

Oron stood and approached, saying lightly, "Why, cutting out your tongue, liar."

Kelder reached over to pinch Ulast's jaws, forcing his mouth open.

Ulast fought all the harder, trying to shake his head loose, as Oron lifted the smoking knife.

"Wait," Edron said. "Oron, will he not bleed to death?"

"No. Cut the tongue and the blade singes the stump."

Ulast whined.

"I ask because I could silence him with a spell. Whatever you wish."

Oron looked at Kelder, who shrugged, then asked, "You are certain it will keep him quiet?"

Edron took a step forward, cupped his hand over the traitor's still stretched mouth, and pressed hard, saying a few words.

Ulast went silent. Kelder stood back, and Ulast looked in every direction, working his mouth, trying to speak, to utter any sound at all, but his efforts failed him.

Oron threw his knife blade-first into the ground to cool it, then began to undo his cuirass. Irté helped him, and as they did it, the Wolf told the men as he faced Ulast, "Put my armor on him. And hold his hands before him. We'll tie him to my horse's reins."

Ulast's expression was one of horror.

Kelder hit him one final time, pushing him against the side of the head, before walking away.

\* \* \* \*

Not yet dawn but gray, as though the air had color, with just the beginning of light in the eastern sky above the encircling trees.

They placed Ulast at the forefront and ten riders behind him wearing whatever armor those Wesleners had managed to salvage or create from leather, wool, pieces of metal—even devising makeshift wooden breastplates. The gray now began to part and lift; mists rose from the damp earth; and Edron stepped forward, gestured, spoke, so that the mists held, partially disguising Ulast and the ten.

Behind them were the eight groups Oron and Kelder had devised, each led by a fighter—man or woman—skilled in the bow or spear, the sling or the sword. These would form the wings, four groups each, guarded by the soft mist and by the ghosts Edron would call up. Before them was the infantry, only fifteen strong but capable and armed, too, with slings and then blades.

Oron, on his horse and in heavy leather, as was Kelder beside him, sat off to the right of the moaning Ulast. On another horse close by sat Irté, her plan to follow the attack and then use the Goddess's magic as her own against Kest, a second wave.

No horn was sounded; no shields were struck. Oron raised his right hand, sword in his grip, and everyone there watched as he sharply lowered the blade. The infantry moved ahead, running and skipping down the inclined earth toward the east gate of Weslen, where thirty men, armed but asleep, leaned against the walls or lay stretched out on the ground. The first stones sent out by the infantry struck three of them as they slept, digging into their faces and foreheads. Two died that way; a third sat up and was struck by further stones, missiles that sent him back down with deadly tears in his throat.

Now Oron kicked his horse ahead. The riders around him moved forward, at first slowly, allowing for the mist that was gathering to obscure them, then at a gallop. That sound, the thunder in the earth, awakened the other swords at the front gate. Now they stood, several taking spinning stones from the front runners, and moved to their horses some distance away, costing them time.

And lives, for in their excitement and anger, several of the slingers drew out their swords and jumped at the mercenaries as they sought to mount their horses. Three of those hired killers were killed themselves, taken down by the stabbings of farmers and sheepherders, although two Wesleners, not as adept at sword work as the quick men they confronted, lost their lives—one of them his head—someone's blue-eyed father—which stared into the mist as it lay on the bent grass.

The Wesleners were howling now, screaming their anger and to keep up their courage, as the mercenaries called out to one another above the noise of sword strokes and the grunts of fighters at their work. Oron heard a cry beside him, higher up than the surrounding trees, and saw Edron elevated there, arms out, feet behind him, flying slowly or floating. And in answer to his voice came stones that pulled up from the ground all around the riders, stones the moved quickly, spinning, then losing themselves and becoming tall lines of mist or whiteness—ghosts upon the earth. Not all of the stones succeeded so, but the numbers were sufficient for the strongest lines of light to burst into flame and drag themselves that way along the grassy earth, catching afire whatever was there.

Including fighting men when they reached them. Kest's hires rode to meet the lines of fire as they would running men, swords out, but as their metal touched the burning air, those men became covered in flames themselves, and their horses, which bolted into the burning field land all around, losing their riders. Ten of them were lost in that manner, reducing the number of fighters outside the walls to less than half what they had been only shortly before.

Kept in his seat by sorcery, either Edron's or Irté's, Ulast was now clearly in view of those fighters. Three of them howled and hurried ahead, on horseback with blades out, eager to the be the one to slay the mighty Wolf of the North. The first managed to slice Ulast across the chest and arms; the second made a cut through the neck, awkward but sufficient, taking some of the shoulder with it, so that the head lolled on one shoulder as the blood came from the severed neck. Only then, when the horse turned and loosened its rider, did the three realize that it was not their enemy that they had cut but their own fool of a spy.

Oron was there immediately, and Kelder and the other riders, moving quickly among the falling number of defenders—impossibly quickly, as one of them realized. He looked up to see Edron and Irté both in the air, as high as the treetops, close beside each other and looking down at them. The mist had lifted and all fires had burned out—it had all happened so very suddenly—and then that watcher was taken through the belly by Kelder, pushing in and coming out the side. The steamy bowels slid free over his horse as that fighter continued to stare up as though held by a spell, his last vision that of a man and woman hanging in the air, watching him die.

Came now the eight groups, small platoons, hurrying alongside the walls of Weslen north and south, bowstrings sounding out in the morning, for the sun had come up. The smell of blood was everywhere, the smell of death and even the crisp odor, strangely sensed, of sorcery, pungent, sharp, with an aroma of its own.

There were few atop the walls, as Irté had said, and not all of them had bows. Unable to use their swords, they threw bricks and pieces of timber at the fighters on the ground, but that did them no good. Arrows found them one after another; a few tumbled from the height and did not move when they struck the ground.

Oron, Kelder, and the remaining riders now confronted the last of the men outside the eastern gate. The toll of Wesleners was high, although the many killed had died bravely. It remained for those who had seen fighting beforetime to take down the last of Kest's hired killers, and they did so gladly, happily warding off steel blows and cutting like butchers, slicing red faces, stabbing chests and necks so that freed blood was everywhere in the air, the morning's reward, coloring the fighters and their horses.

Edron and Irté came down from their height and took a moment, each of them panting, to confront the closed eastern gate. One lone defender above them tipped out a large stone. His aim was not true; the stone landed beside Oron's horse; one of the archers nearby arrowed him in the chest and he dropped back, out of sight.

As the bloodied Oron, Kelder, and other surviving swords watched her, Irté walked toward the eastern gate, muttering a pray. The riders and the remaining infantry felt the earth tremble beneath them, as though a wave ran from somewhere behind them to the great doors of the gate, which then slid loose. Irté fell back and knelt on the bloody grass as first one door and then the other moved like a fist opening to reveal its empty palm.

Inside was silence. No fighters confronted them. Oron's horse neighed and lifted its forelegs to advance, but Irté held up a hand, cautioning the Wolf, and stood. Her brother walked to stand beside her.

Edron looked back at Oron and the others there. "Slowly," he said. "Trust him not."

### 6.

Now Oron dismounted, prepared to charge other fighters or Kest himself. Kelder and the other riders also came down from their horses. Their mounts remained where they were despite the disturbing blood and bodies around them, perhaps aided by some charge of the sorcerer or his sister that held them there, safe.

No fighters confronted them. Edron and Irté walked at the fore, moving slowly, sensing what had been their home but now so changed. Alongside the inner walls and the small buildings abutting them lay the dead mercenaries just slain by Oron's infantry. Farther on, the carcasses and bones of dead animals lay in piles in the streetways and paths between homes, detritus left by Kest's mercenaries after their feasts. Among one pile of debris stretched the naked body of a young woman, broken, too, and bloody, further detritus cast there after the fighters had finished with her.

Irté looked to her right as someone within their home very gradually opened the door of the hut, peering out to see who was walking the paths, and then sobbed, a grown man, aged and white-haired, as he saw who it was. He came out and dropped on his knees in the dirt, tears filling his face, his hands clasped, joyful yet overcome. Behind him stepped two middle-aged women, no doubt his daughters or certainly kin, who approached Edron and Irté while watching Oron carefully, frightening as he was, sword out, dressed in blood, like some envisioned fighting man stepped out of history.

"Is it you?" asked one of the women. "Is it you?"

Irté took her hands and looked her in the eyes. "Yes, yes, woman, do not fear. We are here by right of the Goddess and an ancient god, the Setet, who sent us this powerful *dessek*, first among fighters. See how he has trained us to take back what is ours."

Still, they watched Oron warily. The Wolf spoke, telling Kelder and some of the others to follow the paths in the village and be aware of any mercenaries hidden in homes or alleyways, and to kill them.

"You will find few, my lord," said the old man, rising with the assistance of one of the women. To Irté: "Lady, they have taken themselves to the temple and guard themselves there. They killed two of the young men who fought them. Kest has desecrated the All-Mother's place."

"This we know," Irté told him. "We are prepared to face them."

The old man and the women now took their time studying Edron. The old man said to him, "Surely you have been taken over by a power, Lord Edron. I sense it even now."

"It is why I left you," the sorcerer told him. "With the strength of the Setet, I will fight Kest."

"Slay him and those with him," said one of the women. "Please, please, so that he is no longer on the earth but dead forever."

She looked at Oron, who lent her a slight grin, wolfish, and nodded. "Slain he is already, woman. I have killed such beforetime."

She made a sign before her, something of the Goddess, and then helped the second woman lead the old man inside.

Oron told Irté and Edron, "Your people are strong."

"They are," Irté told him. "I am proud to be of them."

Halfway to the temple in the center of the village, they confronted one of the free swords, who came into the morning light from the shadows of an alley and took a fighting posture. Already there was blood on him—the work of some of Irté and Edron's strong people, no doubt.

He mumbled through bloody lips, "I will die for Lord Kest, who frees my soul."

Oron began to step ahead, but young Handar, stained too with blood from the fight outside the walls, said, "Lord, allow me to help that monster free his soul."

Oron nodded, and Handar stepped ahead.

He had learned well from the Wolf and Kelder and the other leaders. He toyed with this mercenary, a ruffian who should have shown no fear standing before an armed young farmer, but he hesitated, first with one stroke and then with another. Handar read his enemy, came in, moved aside, feinted with a low movement, then slid quickly around to strike the mercenary from behind, well away from the other's blade. His edge came down the back of the dog from neck to waist, opening him, so that the mercenary fell forward, losing all strength, dead before he was face-down in the dirt.

"A fine move," was Oron's compliment.

"Thank you, my lord."

They continued toward the temple, confronting no other dangers as they went, and were joined by Kelder and the others who had searched out the nearby paths. They reached the open patio of the temple decorated with damaged mosaics and then the wide stairs fronting the building—thirteen steps, the number holy to the Goddess. The patio and steps all had been desecrated with the corpses of devoured animals and the defecations of the mercenaries. At the height of the stairs was a wide, shady portico and then the shattered stone doors of the temple entrance, the carefully carved designs of the panels smashed and smeared with blood.

Irté, strong as she was, nonetheless let out a sound to see it.

From her height above them, Ethed, stern and watchful in her marble posture, looked down as her daughter and Edron led the others inside. There, in the grand hall that led to another statue of the Goddess at the far end of the temple, Oron and Kelder stepped ahead.

Four mercenaries, the last of them, stood behind the stone altar at that end of the chamber. The bodies of Wesleners lay about them and also variously on the temple floor, some obviously murdered by Kest's killers, the others victims by their own wills.

The last of these now faced Irté. The young woman was on her knees and half naked, her robe torn in her grief, and she held a dagger in her right hand. She laughed at those she faced.

"Fools," she said in a low voice. "He has escaped you. You will never capture him."

Advancing carefully, Irté said to her, "Woman, he betrayed us all. Rise. Let us help you."

"You led us to him."

"I did," Irté confessed. "I did, I did, and I have since begged Ethed to forgive me. Will you forgive me, sister?"

That laugh again. "He was bringing us a new world. That was his gift. But what now?" And she pushed the dagger into her heart alongside a scratched bare breast and fell forward onto the marble.

Silence held for a moment before Oron said to Irté, "This is how he captivated you."

"It is, *dessek*. To my shame."

Edron now walked halfway across the temple floor. "He is here. I sense it. He has *not* escaped us."

Then came three Wesleners from a door in the northern wall, a marble frieze that slid open, a secret way. They pushed ahead of them the sorcerer, Kest now reduced to bloody rags, his rings and the powerful necklaces and jewels he wore displaced and damaged.

"He tried to take the tunnel!" said the largest man behind the captive as he held onto him.

But now the four mercenaries confronted them, the foremost demanding, "Release him to us. He is ours. We are so sworn."

"Swear to die!" called out one of the Wesleners, coming around with his blade to face the mercenary.

They fought, blades sounding with echoes in that great hall, as the other three mercenaries advanced. Oron, Kelder, and the Wesleners with them hurried ahead. The three faced them across the width of the altar, reaching across with their steel, then moving into open space.

Oron howled as he took the first of them, getting past his blade and joyously stabbing him through the heart. Then Kelder came alongside him and killed the second with a clean cut across the throat, opening the veins there so that blood poured down in a sheet, a perfect kill.

The third mercenary faced two Wesleners, Handar and one other too eager in his excitement. He was wounded across the upper arm when the mercenary caught him there. But that move cost Kest's man a moment, so that Handar came in and stabbed him well in the side, under the arm pit, the steel going into the lungs.

As the dying man fell, Handar helped his friend away, so that they sat on the marble floor, young Handar already tearing free part of his shirt to wrap around the wounded man's arm.

The last of the mercenaries now stood above Kest, who sat with his back against the front of the altar, to all appearances a broken man with nothing left in him.

"A trick," Erdon said.

Oron walked toward the mercenary, who held out his sword, facing the Wolf, whose blade was likewise aimed at the other's heart.

"Give it up," Oron said. "There is no shame in being defeated by the better fighter."

"I gain my strength from him. I will defend him."

"He takes your strength. He is a liar. Throw down your steel and ride from here."

"I cannot."

Oron frowned but said nothing more. He came up with his sword to meet him, and the mercenary did what he could as his master watched, lying there on the marble, bleeding from a cut on the left side of his bruised face.

His defender went down, Oron able to cut into the shoulder of the sword arm so that the limb nearly came free. All of the blood came out and the fighter gasped, dropped his weapon, and turned to look at Kest as though for comfort or intelligence. Then he dropped to his knees and sat back that way, his blood pooling on the marble floor, some of it reaching the sorcerer's boots.

Edron and Irté walked close to Kest. As they did, the marble floor rocked with their power or the power of their deities, and thunder sounded outside the temple.

"Your strength is gone," Edron said to Kest.

The sorcerer lifted a hand and made a sign. Further thunder sounded from outside. "I yet have power."

"The souls you owned are all dead."

"Not all," said Kest, as he made a fist and pointed it at Irté.

She let out a sound of surprise and felt herself begin to sink. Oron put out his free left arm to hold her up, and as he did, he felt a disturbance emanating from her—Kest, trying to steal her life from her and so save himself.

Edron stepped in front of them both and waved his right hand before him, disallowing whatever force Kest was pushing toward him.

The sorcerer sank back and made a sound of disgust. "I will ride from here yet. Have I accomplished so much to have it undone by you few?" He looked at Oron, his demonic eyes yet bright. "And you, outlander. Why are you here? Was this truly your path?"

"I was on my path when I met men no better than you. They robbed me and took my horse."

"Yet your path still brought you here. Why are you with them?"

"Your sight does not tell you?"

"My sight is for greater things."

"I needed a horse. Irté bought me a horse."

"A horse!" Kest coughed but laughed brightly. "Such is the jest. So. Your horse will do me fine. I shall use it when I ride from here. Be aware, outlander—you have tread upon my ambition. This is how I read you. We are motherless children, you and I. We are alike—cast out by the world so that we are men of our own making."

"You speak to stay alive and try to weaken us. This man and woman are here to kill you."

"You are dying even now," Edron told him, raising his hands to take a posture of attack.

"You. You. All of you," the sorcerer breathed, motioning before himself, making ancient signs to keep his enemies where they were. "Can you comprehend what I have done?" Kest tilted back his head and closed his eyes, as though briefly entering a dream. "I have seen dragons give birth in bright mists atop the oldest mountains. I have read scrolls so ancient, they came alive and spoke their phrases to me as I listened. I have consorted with goddesses and laughing demons, drunk the nectar of blooms that open but once in a century in valleys lost to all but me. And I have uncovered truths, the darkest of truths left unguarded by the monsters that made this world and the brightest of truths that even those demons recognized, like jewels alight in shadows." He opened his eyes to look at Oron. "You and I both recognize the truth, outlander. Wisdom is earned at the cost of lives, is it not? I have lost count of those I have sacrificed. The weak live by consent of the strong. Is this not the Iron Law we live by?"

Oron stared at Kest, then regarded silently all that lay about them, the waste of it, no better than useless human sacrifices, and said to the sorcerer, "You forget. What are the strong without the weak?"

Kest grew angry. "Let no one speak of that!"

Irté now said to Kest, "Was I that weak to you? Answer me! I loved you!"

Kest smiled. "And I have passed on. You no longer intrigue me."

There came again that rocking of the marble floor as though the Goddess were trembling in rage.

Edron opened his arms wide, feeling the strength that surrounded them all in that enclosed space, like the effort come alive of men pushing against mountains, like waves rising to attack a rocky shoreline, the power gained from moving into worlds aside our own but invisible to us, and with their own laws. The young sorcerer said, "Time to die."

Kest sat up straight and made two fists, holding them before him. "I have killed better men than you."

"But I am the man standing before you now."

The air whined as Edron pushed out his right hand. Oron saw that on it, covering the palm, was cut that same sign made on the metal square Irté had shown him days before, no doubt some sigil holy to the Setet. Now, however, as Edron walked forward, hand out, arm strong, pushing against whatever force Kest was using against him, the young sorcerer's sign began to bleed, the blood dripping onto the floor from the effort he was making.

His head shook, shivering with the work he was at. Kest sneered but was affected by the younger man's strength, weak as he was with the loss of the lives he had fed on. Oron began to step ahead, ready to assist Edron and slay Kest despite whatever force he might walk into that could endanger him, but Irté put out an arm to prevent him. Oron felt that power again in her, this time her own as she whispered prayers to her Goddess, supporting her brother.

Kest, fists still raised, shivering, looked to the mercenary Oron had killed, the fighter with the deeply cut shoulder. "To me!" he howled. "To me!"

The corpse shook, then moved rigidly and impossibly. Oron swore to see it. More quickly than he or Irté could prevent it, the dead fighter leaned forward on his knees and with his uninjured left hand reached for his sword.

The movement distracted Edron, who looked at the fighter just as that one lifted the sword and brought it down swiftly, taking Edron through the neck.

Irté screamed as Kest laughed, shaking his head back and forth. Edron's body dropped to one side, as did the dead mercenary's. The young sorcerer's head lay face up in its blood, and the eyes opened, looked to one side and the other, then settled on Oron.

"My hand!" Edron said to him.

Oron moved, and as he did, he felt the strength of that square Irté had given him, the chained sigil wrapped beneath the pommel of his sword. Gods against gods, as he had said, and here it was happening now, in this space within a temple, the air around him pulsing with strength, the air whining, and the floor beneath him sliding in one direction, then another, as though it were leaving or arriving from some other world, uncertain of itself.

"Time to die!" the Wolf yelled, jumping ahead, sword out and down. He freed Edron's right hand in that moment, cutting through the forearm, then swiftly knelt, grabbed the dead arm, and moved through the space between himself and Kest as though he were pushing through the mists of a dream, unreal but real, and breathing air charged with sorcery. He saw dragons being born and the words on scrolls come to life, *felt* them, the original speech of them, and Tython, more formless than formed, a black cloud swirling with ghostly arms and faces and small, distant, echoing voices otherwise lost to Time, and then another ancient god in a cave, the Setet, a monster drawing its sigil in the air in blood that caught fire as it did it, and the face of a goddess as bright as marble shining in brilliant sunlight....

Kest cried out in surprise and fear as Oron pushed Edron's hand against him, directly into his chest. The hand opened; Oron felt the dead young man's muscles move within the forearm; and Edron's fingers closed upon Kest's torn robe, then dug into the flesh, the fingers clawing in to reach the sorcerer's heart.

Standing tall, still within that dizzying space that put him in a dream, Oron came around with his sword to take Kest through the neck. The head fell free even as Edron's powerful fingers locked around the sorcerer's heart, deep within his chest, and held there as the body slumped aside.

Oron felt the air change around him, lose its charge, as behind him in that temple, desecrated with the blood of its enemies and the corpses of its defenders, Irté emitted a powerful sob that echoed and continued to echo, crying out, "*I can still feel him!*"

Oron looked at her, then at Kest's head. The eyes stared at him as though still able to see him, but the demonic light was gone, and the space around the Wolf now felt free. No heavy dreaminess. No sorcerous odor. Only the dead everywhere, as though they were on a red field of battle far beyond holy temple walls, and a sobbing woman wailing for the lover who had damaged her soul.

* * * *

They burned the sorcerer's corpse in a field outside Weslen's walls, dropping it first into a deep grave and with his head face down on his torn chest, broken where Edron's magic had damaged it. Prayers were said to curse his soul, and then malignant oils and foul-smelling poisonous plants and berries placed over him and the body burnt. By evening, when the corpse was sufficiently ruined, Irté and Oron watched as the villagers took turns shoveling earth over it, burying it so that, in time, none should know where in that field an evil monster had been buried and left to his demons in the afterlife. Shortly some noticed that vegetation nearby was going bad—flowers wilting, grass withering—the last of Kest's disappearing strength from his violated corpse. Soon enough, however, the flowers returned and the grass grew green again.

Edron, too, they buried, but high on a hill and with all the honors and prayers Irté and her faithful could lift in praise of him. Irté knelt to touch tenderly the corpse of her brother before leaving him to the earth, where she whispered words Edron himself had said: "And so he is done with gods and demons." Then she placed there a stone with his name carved into it and that sacred sign that had saved her and her people, so that the memory of his sacrifice would remain forever current. Let no one forget, and let all dwell from time to time on the mystery that had engaged him, cost him so dearly, and saved their world. As she lay down that stone, the sky rumbled with distant thunder although the morning was bright. Irté looked up and whispered a prayer, and smiled.

* * * *

The Wolf assisted the people of Weslen with the other many burials, allowing even the mercenaries the dignity of such an end. It was within the Goddess's bounteousness to so treat even these, for were they not as much a part of the earth as all else that she encompassed? It was only those who reached beyond her generosity and wisdom, the Kests of the world who turned from her and the earth in their pride, who earned her enmity.

Men chosen by Irté left with money from the temple's treasures to visit other villages and purchase from them heads of cattle, goats, sheep, horses—the herds and flocks they would need to begin their lives again. And the people of Weslen did what they could to repair the damages done by the mercenaries, although not all could be easily dealt with. Those among them who worked with stone and metal would need the coming months to replace much of the city with new handiwork.

Only some turned away from Lady Irté. She had erred mightily but had done so thinking that she was serving her people; that she had also been selfish was as human a weakness as any daughter or son of Ethed was well familiar with. But there were those few who could not forgive her, seeing her relationship with Kest as a betrayal. These Irté cast out; it would not do to have these people in Weslen. And so they went, taking their belongings with them in their carts, onto roads that led to new lives.

It became time for Oron to ride on. He had fulfilled his promise to Irté and her people and, besides, wanderer that he was, he was eager to be gone. He returned the charged sigil on its chain to the woman; it, too, had served its purpose, and the Wolf was wary of all things so done, the products of sorcery and witchcraft and even honest work with the gods.

Irté accepted it from him on a morning of quiet breezes and bright flowers as they sat in a resurrected garden outside the temple of the Goddess, speaking as only those two could of what they had managed. Oron told Irté of what he had experienced with a serpent woman of ancient wisdom, how she had even returned him to life after he had died for a moment, and how his being in the most ancient tunnels and rooms under a serpent mound had brought to him awareness of worlds and lives just touching ours, within our grasp if one dared to reach for them.

"I saw his wizard's visions as I killed him," the Wolf told Irté, "and yours, and Edron's. These crafters of sorcery and those who live within such worlds, they're familiar with these ancient powers. I was not made to be close to them. I'd rather remain a man than a creature such as that. But they are aware of worlds other than ours, as you are. No doubt even a man of the sword is closer to those regions than he thinks."

"True, Oron," Irté told him. "Such splendor endures. There is great power and openness to the world if we demand them of ourselves."

"But danger resides there," he reminded her. "I spoke once to an old sage, an old man. He lived deep in the forest, and he learned wisdom there. He told me that such as Kest defy the danger in their pride and seek to unbalance order, all of Nature, so that they may sit atop the world—as though the world itself cares about any such."

"Your sage was correct. I could feel the world balancing itself once more within the temple."

"As did I."

"I am sorry to see you go, Nevgan, but you have my thanks, and Edron's, as well."

"You sense him?"

"Of course. And I will until I join him and the others who shared this with us, come a day. That is also in the balance of things. You will ride far from here, I divine."

"Yes. I make my way as a fighting man."

"Then you shall never want for employment in this world!"

They stood then but did not embrace. Irté and Oron walked from the garden onto a path of the village, where a woman waited by a well with a horse for the Wolf, water in a bladder and foodstuffs in a satchel, and coin he would need on the road.

Oron mounted the stallion and rubbed its neck, nodded again to Lady Irté, and smiled at her. "For a horse," he said.

She returned his smile. "For a horse."

And so he left Weslen. He rode the stallion to the height of the hill outside the village where Edron lay under his stone and paid his last respects to the young man. He was answered by distant thunder. Then in the bright morning under a cloudless blue sky, Oron rode east, where wars awaited him.

⚔

# TRYING TO FIND IT IN MY CITY
## Chad Hensley

*I see a shining metallic sea*
*of machines of all sizes, some taller than sky scrapers,*
*these misshapen and monstrous*
*moving slowly, back and forth, far and wide*
*across a hazy, endless, oil-soaked horizon.*

*Spinning wheels as big as second story buildings*
*spray gleaming bits of sand and pulverized bone*
*into the smoky ever-twilight as enormous lights*
*on the tips of sharp-edged objects*
*glint like stars as if from great depths*
*should total darkness descend for even a split second*

*upon the mobile city, some inhabitants still maybe human some—*
*street cleaners or birth apparatuses, those way less than*
*cyborgs (as if that was ever even a thing) still have original body*
     *parts.*
*Though rumor has it that a non-enhanced, all-original woman*
*is kept, naked and bound in a cage*
*somewhere within the labyrinthine memory banks of the capital*
     *building.*

*I shouldn't be too hypocritical—My spectral vision is boundless and*
*I can breathe as easily*
*deep underwater or engulfed in the pitched smoke of burning*
     *plastics.*

*But my soft white body begins to combust and spurt red blood*
*when exposed to the atmosphere.*
*The augmented body armor,*
*USB chord plugged into a slot beneath my genitals, really helps.*

*On occasion, the hunter automatons swarm me*
*With waving, robotic tentacle-like arms and oversized iron talons.*
*Retractable razor blades spring from my body armor,*
*slice metal and marrow—steaming green and purple fluids spurt*
*from thousands of flesh wounds that seem to smoke.*
*Man-shaped husks melt and burn into a chemical bonfire*
*That makes my single human eye weep puss.*

*Night or day (I can't tell the difference anyway), it matters not.*
*I'm not even sure how long ago it was*
*I actually saw a sun or moon, for that matter.*

*But I am alive (I think)*
*And I will keep searching in my city*
*Until I find it...*

—After Richard Gavin's "The Benighted Path"